SLADE

Slade is on a bad streak wi[...] both his saloon and his pride in one day. With nothing left to lose, he heads out for his friend Chet Crispin's spread to rest and recoup. But what he finds there is an old love, May Hogue, her drunken husband, and no Crispin. He also finds a tinderbox situation about to explode. The town banker, Abbott, is playing the ranchers back and forth, knowing the railroad is coming. The diminutive sheriff, Wilkinson, is just waiting for the day when May's husband takes a stray bullet, chafing in his impatience to make her his. And Big Thomas is trying to build the largest ranch in the valley—by whatever means possible. Somewhere in all this, Crispin just gets in the way. And now Slade is the only man left who stands between Thomas and the Hogues, between what's right...and what is.

THE MANHUNTER

Ben Ross rides into town with only one thing on his mind—to find the man who gunned down his father and bring him back to justice. The townspeople know Ross is a manhunter, and they fear and detest him. But Sheriff Big Max sees a different man, one who carries a gun, but doesn't want to use it; a man tormented by conflicting memories of finding his dead father, and trying to sort out what really happened to him. At first it seems obvious that Ed Stanton, co-owner with his brother of the Broken S ranch, is the man Ross is looking for. Big Max promptly locks him up. But there is more to this situation than meets the eye. Outside of town, a range war is looming between the Broken S and the Crescent C ranches, and Ross has just put himself right in the middle of it.

Slade

The Manhunter

Arnold Hano

Introduction by Paul Bishop

Stark House Press • Eureka California

SLADE / THE MANHUNTER

Published by Stark House Press
1315 H Street
Eureka, CA 95501, USA
griffinskye3@sbcglobal.net
www.starkhousepress.com

ISBN-13: 978-1-951473-33-4

Cover design by Jeff Vorzimmer, ¡caliente!design, Austin, Texas
Book design by Mark Shepard, shepgraphics.com
Proofreading by Bill Kelly
Cover art by Verne Tossey

First Stark House Press Edition: May 2021

Contents

Arnold Hano
Master of the Western Noir

Paul Bishop

I enjoy writing introductions, but first and foremost I'm a fan of reading introductions. A good introduction brings the reader a new perspective or understanding of what is to follow. A good introduction is a mixture of researched facts and analysis of how those facts reveal a subject or individual in a new light. When Stark House Press head honcho Greg Shepard asked me to write an introduction to this collection of two novels from the master of Western noir, Arnold Hano, I was excited. I was a huge fan of Hano's iconic Western *The Last Notch*—which Stark House has also reissued under their Black Gat imprint. Hano's Westerns are marked by his unpredictable approach to the genre. His prose twists its way down dark trails getting beneath the surface of sagebrush and six-gun tropes to reveal the damaged souls underneath.

I already knew some things about Hano—He had written five pseudonymous Westerns, each one more challenging and subversive; he was a long time editor at Bantam books working directly with Western icon, Luke Short and others. He was also the first editor in chief for Lion Books in the 1950s, where he edited and guided the careers of Jim Thompson, Robert Bloch, Richard Matheson, David Goodis and others. I also knew he was revered for his non-fiction baseball book *A Day In The Bleachers*, which originated the style of sports writing, more common today, which focuses on one specific sporting event.

In talking with Greg Shepard about the reprint collection of Hano's westerns *Manhunter* and *Slade*, he mentioned Hano was in his late nineties, but still alive and kicking. I suddenly developed goosebumps. I felt compelled, I really wanted to talk to the guy. I asked if there was someway I could get in contact with Hano and was provided with an email address and a wish for good luck that seemed to me to carry a portent of ominous overtones.

I quickly sent an email to Hano explaining who I was and requesting an interview. Surprisingly quickly, I received a positive reply. A self-proclaimed Luddite, Hano explained he could only do an interview over the phone, but agreed to let me record our conversation.

What follows are excerpts from the transcript of my conversation with Arnold Hano, who was a delight to speak with, sharp of tongue and memory, seemingly growing stronger the longer we talked...

PB—Hello, Arnold. It's an honor to be able to talk with you today.

AH—I'm just glad somebody, anybody wants to talk to me, cause I ain't going to be around that much longer. Anyway, you got me now. So use me as you can and I'll do my best, but I have to tell you, I'm not very good anymore, so I don't think I'm going to be very successful...let's just go.

PB—You're going to be fine. When did you first get the idea you wanted to write?

AH—Oh, seriously when I was eight years old. My brother and the neighbor boy, who were eleven and twelve, decided to put out a newspaper for the street we lived on, which was Montgomery Street in the Bronx, and they said I could be their reporter. That meant, I would to run down to the newsstand at the end of the block and read the whole news, and then copy off enough of the stuff that I could adapt to Montgomery Avenue. So that was eight years old.

PB—That's fantastic. Were you born in the Bronx?

AH—I was born in Manhattan. When I was four years old, we moved across the river from Manhattan to the Bronx.

PB—After being an eight year old reporter, what was your next step?

AH—My next step was after I copied off enough other stories and made them fit the Montgomery Street newspaper, I said to my brother, I don't like this. I don't like to copy other people's stories. I want to do my own story. He said write it. So, I started a serial novel with a police officer as a hero who would fall to his knees when he shot the bad guys. I called the whole thing Sitting Bull. I ended each episode with him facing imminent danger or death—like he'd be tied to the trolley tracks and the trolley cars were coming, or he'd be hanging down from the roof by his fingertips and the bad guys were stamping on his fingers, stuff like that. And I did that for about, I don't remember now, but I would say six episodes. Either I pooped out or the newspaper pooped out and that was the end of that.

PB—Being so young, where did you learn to do cliff hanger chapter endings?

AH—My mother's brother, Bertram, was a screenwriter when he was nineteen. He was writing sixteen episode serials for *The Perils of*

Pauline, and he would send copies to my folks. He'd been sent out to Hollywood and was living on some fancy-schmancy street, and we were very thrilled by all that. And I was thrilled to see how somebody wrote episodes that he would solve the next morning or the next day. So that was how I did it. I copied his format.

Also, I was reading when I was three years old. I read everything, absolutely everything—all the Baseball Joe books, and *Bomba The Jungle Boy*, and Tom Swift. And then I graduated to *Treasure Island* and other good stuff. I think from the beginning it was meant for me to end up writing. When I went to grade school, I was smarter than most of the other kids because I could read and write, so I skipped a lot of grades, including all the intermediary grades. I was not quite eighteen when I finished college.

Anyway, I thought I was going to become a doctor. So I was taking all these science courses and doing terribly. And then in my sophomore year, I walked past the college newspaper office and I could hear people inside were laughing, and I thought, *gee, I didn't know you were allowed to laugh*. So I opened the door and went in and I became a member of the newspaper staff and I changed my major from science to English and journalism. And that was my sophomore year. And my junior year, I was a sports editor of the paper. And my senior year, I became co-editor-in-chief of the newspaper.

PB—You're revered for your baseball reporting and your baseball books. How did your love of baseball start?

AH—Two reasons. My brother was three and a half years older than me and was the captain of a lot of baseball teams. He knew I could play the game and even though I was only fifteen, he would always include me with these other kids who were eighteen and nineteen. I held my own against them even when we began playing semi-pro games.

That was one thing. The other thing was when I was born, we lived across the street from the Polo Grounds. The Giants and the Yankees played there until 1923. And I went to the Polo Grounds to see some of Babe Ruth's early games and I was hooked. Back in those days, when a game was over you were allowed to run out on the field. My brother and I would run the bases. I would slide into second base then get up, run to third and then keep going and slide into home. Or I would stand on the mound and make believe I was striking out Lou Gehrig or Jimmy Foxx—those guys. It was the most exciting thing in my life going to ball games.

PB—That's fantastic. What a great memory of those days.

AH—It remains great memory. I still see myself maybe eight to ten years old, standing on the mound of the Polo Grounds. I had watched

Carl Hubbard throw screwballs, and I'd be thinking I was throwing screwballs past all the top American League hitters.

PB—How did your newspaper career continue after graduation?

AH—When I finished college, I answered an ad in the *Daily News* for a copy boy. I didn't know they advertised for those, but there was the ad. Anyway, I answered the ad and was selected over the six or seven others who applied, including a guy from Harvard. I once said to the city manager, *Gee, that was pretty nice selecting me over the Harvard guy*. He said, *we selected you because you were the youngest and therefore we thought you'd be the last one drafted*. So that's how I got my job as a copy boy at the *Daily News* earning sixteen dollars a week.

One day a week, the newspaper would let us be what they called junior reporters. I think other papers used the term cub reporters, but we were junior reporters. We sometimes wrote small stories of our own, or we would be sent out on a story and have to call it in to the rewrite desk— things like that. So, I was getting to writing some, and I wasn't very good at it, but I was learning. All of that was the good stuff.

In 1941, after December 7th, my brother and I were excited about joining the military and then killing Hitler and stuff like that. The two of us would be at the supper table arguing about which one of us was going to go where, and our folks would fall silent. People don't realize how cruel war is to parents. There we were, four people sitting in the kitchen chairs, and suddenly two of them were going to be empty. It's a terrible world.

I got into the army in the Seventh Infantry Division, and we did a lot of island hopping. I did a little bit of writing on my own when I could. Then, when I was on a troop transport, I saw the captain giving out paper, and I could see they had been mimeographed. I said you've got a mimeograph machine someplace. He said, *that's right*. I said, *if you lend it to me, I can get a newspaper going for the staff and for the thousand troops we have here*.

He said, *you really can?* I said, *I'll give it a shot*. So he agreed to let me use the mimeograph machine. I found a guy who could write some very funny poems, other guys who could write stuff, and I put out newspapers from San Francisco to the Island of Attu, which all the troops were reading.

PB—That's incredible. Writing was definitely in your makeup.

AH—It was, yes. Which is why it bothers me that I'm not writing a lot these days.

PB—Did you write short stories first or did you go straight to novels?

AH—I started writing short stories for the pulp magazines, especially *Street & Smith's Sports Stories* magazine. Some of my other stories appeared in *Ellery Queen Magazine* and *Esquire*. One lengthy novelette appeared in *Argosy*, which people tell me was very good. It was called *O'Rourke*, which was the name of the main character. It was about a nasty recruit who falls into the hands of a sadistic Sergeant who thinks he can turn him into a good soldier. It was about eighteen thousand or twenty thousand words and *Argosy* paid me $1,600. That was a lot of money back then. I was rich.

PB—*Argosy* was a top market.

AH—It was a top market. One of the editors there, who was rather young, said, *O'Rourke* was the best story *Argosy* had every published. He didn't realize Hemingway had written for *Argosy*, and other writers of that quality. So that was flattering, but pointless.

PB—You eventually made the move from short stories to novels?

AH—My first novel was a baseball story, *The Big Out*...You probably don't know it...

PB—I do know *The Big Out*, I have a copy on my bookshelves.

AH—How about that? Still, when it came out, it perished quietly. There were no reviews or anything. Then six months later a review turned up in the Sunday *New York Times*. The guy who wrote it said *The Big Out* was one of the most thrilling sports novels he ever read. That would have made for a nice ad when the book came out, but the book was already dead. That people still have it and like it today surprises me. Somebody wrote recently it was the best baseball novel ever written—and he said, that's including Bernard Malamud's *The Natural*. That was pretty heady for me because I think Malamud was a great writer. And so that was nice. I like compliments. I think it's a compliment you want to do this interview...[laughter]

PB—When did you first decide to take a shot at a Western?

AH—One Friday night, Bonnie and I were going to go out to somebody else's house for supper in Manhattan. She takes forever to get ready, so I sat down at the typewriter and I typed, *The year 1874 was a mean year, but I think well of it*. And I looked at it and I thought, what the hell does that mean? Why was it a mean year, and why would he think well of it? So I wrote a second sentence. By the time Bonnie was ready, I'd written six pages. I wrote forty pages on Saturday and forty more pages on Sunday. Then I wrote an hour every day during the week—because I was working nine to five—and then again on Saturday, and the novel was finished. It was a Western [*Valley of Angry Men* as Matthew Gant, Gold Medal Books, 1953]. It was about a Black cowboy and the publisher wanted me to change his race because, he said, there weren't any Black cowboys. I said, *there are now*.

PB—How did you come to edit Jim Thompson when you were with

Lion Books?

AH—My associate, Jim Brian, had read some of Jim's hardcover novels. So he got in touch with Thompson's agent and said to bring him to the office. Meanwhile, Jim and I were always writing synopses of novels we would like to see as part of our book list. So one day, Jim Thompson comes to the office and we showed him some of the synopses we had written. He read through them slowly, and then he went back and read them again. Eventually, he picked and said, *I'll do this one*, and it became *The Killer Inside Me*.

So that, that was my introduction to Jim Thompson. We became personal friends. Jim and his wife, Alberta, and Bonnie and I, would supper together. The trick was to keep Jim from drinking. The mistake Jim made was listening to whoever it was who said, *come out west and writes movies for me*. He went out there and wrote movies, but what he hadn't realized was you wrote them and then a whole gang of other people got involved and whatever it was you wrote gets lost in the process. It really was the end of Jim Thompson. He started to drink again and he couldn't work.

PB—When you started writing your own westerns, you seemed to give them a noir twist.

AH—People say that, but I never even used the word *noir*. I knew noir was a French word for black, that was my only knowledge of noir—I didn't know that I was writing it. That said, *The Last Notch* [as Matthew Gant, Pyramid Books, 1958—reissued as by Arnold Hano, Stark House, 2017] and *Flint* [as Gil Dodge, Signet Books, 1957—reissued as by Arnold Hano, Stark House, 2012] got pretty dark. Especially *Flint*, which is my favorite. It was a copy of Jim Thompson's *Savage Night*. I had asked Jim, *would you mind if I took your novel and set it back a hundred years?* He said, *be my guest*. I did. And he read it. And he said, *your version is better than mine*—which was very flattering.

PB—When you're writing, do you struggle or does it just come to you?

AH—Both, but I think more just comes to me. I believe strongly with what a book review editor once told a class I was teaching—he said, *let the writing write the writer*. I have found that at certain points with anything I write, if I relax the writing continues and I have practically no control over it, and it turns out just like I wanted. Almost everything I've ever written that's any good had that element of letting the writing write the writer in it. You've got to direct the plot and so on, but if I had a character who had a problem, and I didn't know how to solve it, I'd just relax and let the writing take over and proceed from there. The very best thing I ever wrote was a short story for *Ellery Queen Magazine* in 1954—*The Crate At Outpost 1* [as Matthew Gant]. I'm proud of that story. It's set far in the future and deals with book burning, and it just flowed out of me because I was letting the writing write the writer.

PB—Stark House Press is currently set to reprint two of your Westerns—*Manhunter* and *Slade*...

AH—Yes. I'm glad there are folks who still want to read those. I did *Slade* as Ad Gordon in 1956 for Lion Books, and *Manhunter* as Matthew Gant in 1957 for Signet. I don't remember too much about writing them except the characters had been sitting in my head for a while, so I just sat down and let them tell me their story. I didn't have any particular plot in mind, I just started writing. Part of the reason I hadn't read a lot of Westerns at the time is I didn't want to be influenced by what others had done before.

PB—After you were at Lion, you moved on to Bantam Books.

AH—When I got the job with Bantam books, I had written some Westerns, but as I said, I'd still only read a couple by Zane Grey. But by then I knew about what a Western had to be, and so Bantam made me their Western editor.

PB—Was Luke Short writing for Bantam at that time?

AH—He was writing for me. My favorite Western writer. Peter Dawson was also writing for me, they were two of Bantam's important authors. Luke Short was a wonderful storyteller, and Peter Dawson was a wonderful stylist. They worked together well, and I learned a lot from them, including that to be a Western, a novel has to have a Western theme—it has to be about rustling or branding or land control or water rights, things like that. You can write all kinds of different stories, but it still has to have a Western theme to be a Western.

PB—What was it like to work with Luke Short?

AH—I was so flattered that I could be his editor that I think I just gave him his head and let him do anything he wanted. But as an editor, I was a little different. I'm fast, and almost everything I did back then was fast. If you gave me a novel over the transom, I would take it home that night, read it that night, and get back to you the next morning. That helped me at Lion Books, in particular. I'd say to somebody, I like this, can you get me another 10,000 words by such and such a date, and I would immediately put the $2,000 for the writer into the commerce of the publishing house. Writers knew I was an editor who works quickly and pays his writers just as quickly.

I was reading *Publishers Weekly* every week, and one week there was a big one page ad for a novel called *The Golden Sleep* by Vivian Connell. At the top of the ad, it said, *by the author of the Chinese Room*. This was in 1947, I think. I'd never heard of *The Chinese Room* and figured it must've come out during the war, but it hadn't been published in paperback yet.

So I went down to O'Malley's Bookstore, which is an institution that has come and gone. It was a great institution. You could get any book published by anybody at any time for a couple of bucks. I asked if they had a copy *The Chinese Room* by Vivian Connell, and they said, *Oh yeah, sure it's up on the third shelf over here to the left.* The guy went up and got it, and for two and a half bucks, I had *The Chinese Room.* I read it that night. The next morning, I said to Ian Ballantine—who was the boss at Bantam Books, *I have your first million copy seller.* At that time, Bantam had never sold a million copies of any one title.

He looked at me askance, but he said, *I'm going to get a haircut today*, and he took the book with him to the barber. When he came back, he said, *you're right.* And eventually, we got around to publishing it, and when I saw the finished product with the cover and everything, I said, this will sell three million copies. It sold five million.

Editors were important back then. I don't know quite how it works anymore, but when I was an editor, publishing was pretty interesting. I thought it was exciting. I don't think that's true anymore, but I may be wrong.

PB—How long have you been Bonnie be married?

AH—It's coming up on seventy years in June.

PB—Where did you guys meet?

AH—We met at Bantam Books. She worked in the business office. One day, she and two or three other young women from the business office came prancing in to see the editors. I saw Bonnie and it was lust at first sight. It was pretty hot.

PB—Anyway, that's an amazing story, 70 years to be together and still in love. That's a wonderful thing.

AH—We said we take care of each other. She's finishing her second round of ovarian cancer, and I've just found out that I have cancer. So we'll continue to take care of each other as long as we can.

PB—I hope you continue to do so for a very long time.

AH—Thank you. I'll be ninety-nine on March 2nd. That's a goal. People say, *I suppose you're aiming at a hundred now.* I tell them I'm aiming at next Thursday.

PB—What was the last story you wrote?

AH—I'm working on a play. When the guy comes with a new reading machine, I do really get going on it. It's a good play, but it needs some work.

So, there you have it. Arnold Hano—a month away from ninety-nine years old, still writing and still making up stories. Talking with him has inspired in me the hope that when the same age approaches, I'll also still be doing those things—fingers crossed and with a following sea.

What you hold in your hands is not a book, but two dangerous and unpredictable adventures filled with powerful emotions as written by a master of the form. *Slade* takes one Texan and throws him to the wolves in a gunfighter's paradise. *Manhunter* is a revenge tale that will either end in vindication or damnation. Whatever you think you know about Westerns as you ride hell for leather into these strories will not be what you encounter. There is something different here—something exciting, challenging, and subversive. This is Arnold Hano, raw and at the top of his form.

—February 2021
North of Los Angeles

Novelist, screenwriter, and television personality, Paul Bishop is a nationally recognized behaviorist and expert in deception detection. He spent 35 years with the Los Angeles Police Department where he was twice honored as Detective of the Year. Co-host of the weekly *Six-Gun Justice Podcast* (www.sixgunjustice.com), he has written sixteen novels, numerous scripts for episodic television and feature films, and three non-fiction Western reference works: *52 Weeks—52 Western Novels, 52 Weeks—52 Western Movies,* and *52 Weeks—52 Western TV Shows.*

Slade

Arnold Hano

Writing as Ad Gordon

CHAPTER 1

He heard Lu's heels click-clack up the wooden stairs from the saloon below, and he heard the crowd shout for her to come back. They always did that. He didn't blame them. Then she came into the office and stopped in the doorway. He sure as hell didn't blame them. She sang pretty good, but not great, and she danced with her hips and nothing else. He eyed her with almost a detached stare, a bit regretfully. She had it, and he knew it. So did she. She let her hips roll at him and then stretched and yawned with deliberate movement, and he knew all he had to do was walk over to her, put those hips under his palms and make love to her.

He didn't feel like it. He felt like hell, gritty-tired and drained.

Worse than that, too. He felt scared. He was dead broke for the first time in over ten years, and he felt scared, uprooted, licked. He felt like the thin-money-belted drifters and bums he had seen for ten years, the desperation a yellow sheen in their eyes, their mouths slack and their hands quick and nervous. For ten years he'd seen them, from across the gambling tables, his side piled high with chips and silver coins, theirs even higher with fear.

He'd seen them come in, all right, the suckers and saddle tramps, sometimes the big eastern gamblers and the Mississippi riverboat cardsharps, the gold-strikers, the silver boomers, the daredevils, and the crooks—and he'd seen them go out, leaving their money belts behind them. For ten years he'd held the luck of the world in his great hammy hairy fists. He'd matched cards, played poker, flipped silver coins, rolled dice. He'd won. And won.

And won again.

His name was Slade and he ran a saloon in a town called Cutter in the hottest corner of sun-frizzled western Texas, where the cattle seemed to grow bonier and leaner every year and the most water a man ever saw was the sweat scalding his eyes.

The saloon wasn't the real trick. Oh, it was a good enough saloon, Slade guessed—he served a full measure and fairly decent whisky, and he had all the props a saloon ought to have: a broken-down piano and a broken-downer piano player who had consumption, and a girl named Lu who could sing pretty good and shake her fanny even better.

The piano player was saving his money so he could have his right lung collapsed, but when he started coughing and spitting, he had to have a drink or two or seven. Slade would have bet even money the piano player never died of consumption; alcohol would get him first. But Slade didn't care terribly; it wasn't his lung. He paid the piano player fifteen dollars a week and steered him a loose-ends prostitute every so often for him to pimp off. The piano player should have had his money saved six years ago. Slade doubted he had thirty-five dollars put away.

The girl who sang was a different proposition. Slade steered Lu to nobody but himself.

But even with the props he knew that the real thing, the kicker, the hole card, was himself. Slade was a gambler, and he was lucky.

Was.

Now he was through, dead broke, scared, looking into a pair of unwinking snake eyes. He was thirty-five years old, with a curious slouched-down body, as though some invisible hand lay heavy on his head and was constantly pushing downward. Slade was broad-browed, big-nosed, wide-mouthed, short-necked, and nearly as big through the shoulders as a heifer was long, almost as thick. He was not short, but he looked it, and he weighed two hundred and five pounds.

He leaned into the mirror that was nailed to the wall of his office over the saloon—no, he thought, not *his* office anymore—and he squinted at his face. Through the mirror he could see Lu buffing her nails.

He said mildly, "Beat it, kid, I'm closing shop."

She was red-haired and white-skinned, freckled the way redheads usually are, with a pair of legs that were astonishing, and the cleverest little trick of moaning when he made love to her. Slade knew she didn't mean it, but he liked it and he paid her twice as much as he had ever paid a whisky-throated singer before.

She stood up, and it made him suck in his breath. She did that to him, whenever she moved, and he thought he was going to miss her. She said with indifference, "All right, Slade. Be seeing you." She shimmied out with elaborate gestures and Slade knew damn well he was going to miss her. He also knew she was wrong: she wasn't going to be seeing him.

He went to his desk and opened the lower drawer. There was a big outsized sock in the back of the drawer, an old woolen sock stretched out of shape, and it was heavier than lead in his meaty hands.

He thumped it against the wooden desktop and he frowned. He was a liar, he knew. He wasn't really broke. He couldn't be, if he had the sock. It was his own hole card, just in case his luck ever ran out. Five hundred silver dollars—more than enough for a man to get a stake on, enough for a man to buy a piece of land or take a hand in a big poker game.

He could even have held out an hour longer with the little rancher who had walked into the saloon two days ago and started matching high-cards with the saloonkeeper. The rancher's name was Johnson and he had come into Cutter with his foreman, and twenty cows for sale. The foreman's name was Dilt and he was an immense man, a head taller than Slade and nearly as wide. His head was bald and knotty with bone, scarred in a dozen places from pick handles, knives and fists. Dilt was a brawling man with a wicked look in his eye whenever he passed another man in the dusty street of Cutter. Every man he saw, he measured.

But this time the little rancher named Johnson had sent Dilt out to sell the cows while he made his brief play at Slade's gaming tables. Dilt was to return to Slade's with the money from selling the beef and then the two planned to take whatever was left after Johnson's stint and shamble off to the local cathouse.

So for two days Johnson and Slade had sat there, matching cards, forty-eight hours without a moment off for sleep. For a couple of hours they seesawed, and then Johnson started pulling the aces and face cards while Slade kept catching the deuces and treys. Pretty soon there was a crowd watching them, at first with an indifferent enthusiasm, then with a growing wonder, and finally with a hoarse wild joy as the underdog kept on hitting.

Once Dilt had walked into the saloon with the money from the cows, but Johnson had just waved his hand at him and said, "Spend it. Get some sleep. I'll be here tomorrow morning."

The ranchers poured into Slade's when Dilt spread the word: Slade is being taken—and they milled about the table, their eyes brightly hot as the two-bit rancher kept eating away at Slade's resources.

Lu was there, too, Slade remembered, her white face glowing in the big room under the hanging oil lamps, and then she walked off with unconcern and Slade knew she was counting him out.

Three times he had sent to the office for fresh sealed decks of cards, tearing the old packs in his hands and scattering them on the floor. Once he heard a harsh whisper from the hovering black circle of onlookers, "Do you think them new cards are marked?" and Slade turned slowly in his seat until he had spotted the whisperer.

"You," Slade had said. "You. Knapp, come here."

Knapp stumbled forward. He was a puncher from a ranch on the other side of the bowl of hills, in the great dry valley where grass used to grow.

"Did you call me a crook?" Slade said.

Knapp licked his lips but no words came.

"Did you?" Slade said.

Knapp shook his head.

Slade held his stare and then he took a bill out of his pocket and poked it at Knapp. "Here," he said. "Go across the street to Leo's and ask Leo for five decks of cards. Sealed cards. Tell him they have to be dated cards. If he says he can't sell them, tell him Slade wants them and that he'll pay twice what they cost."

Knapp took the bill and ran out, glad he was let off so easy. He remembered the way Slade tore those cards with his bare hands.

Slade remembered, too. He remembered how he tore the cards and how he put on the act with Knapp, how he ordered drinks for the crowd and went to the john to relieve himself and had Lu bring him a steak sandwich and coffee and the same for Johnson. He remembered on that second day how Dilt came back to jeer, "Now you know how it feels, Slade, seeing the other guy win. I hope to Christ he takes you for all you're worth."

And Slade had ripped back an oath at the great scarred bald head that shone ugly and yellow over all the others in the room.

But it had all been an act, a reprieve, momentary, against that terrible weight that closed down on him. The weight was fear, and the knowledge that he was through. He stalled it off as well as he could, but he was licked.

That was why—he thought—he hadn't gone upstairs to the desk and got his sock. It was no good, the way his luck was running. Twenty times five hundred, yes, that might have made a difference, but the sock was only a stopper, an hour at best. Johnson was hot, the way he, Slade, had been hot for ten years.

Now he was down to his socks.

He walked to the door where his holster hung from a nail, the .44 smelling faintly of oil, and he strapped it on. He jammed the sock into his shirt. Then he turned and looked at the office.

He had said to Johnson when his money ran out—thirty thousand dollars in cash, notes, and bankbooks—"All right, the works."

Johnson had looked quizzical. "Everything? Saloon and all?"

Slade nodded. "Everything except my gun and my horse."

Dilt had said, "Make him put it in writing, boss," and Johnson snapped back, "Don't be a fool, Dilt, the man's honest. Go buy yourself another drink." Then he looked at Slade. "How much do you think it's worth—the saloon, the land it's on, everything?"

Slade looked into the crowd. "Boyle," he said, "step up here, will you?"

A tall, gray-haired man in a dark suit and shoestring tie pushed hesitantly to the table. "Yes, Slade?"

"Boyle," Slade said, "you worked on that last assessment of my property, didn't you?"

Boyle cleared his throat. "Well," he said, "I—the bank, that is—why, yes, I did."

"How much is the saloon worth, as she stands?"

"Well," Boyle said, clearing his throat again, "of course, I wouldn't want to—I'd say—you understand this is not an exact—I'd put it at, oh, twelve or thirteen thousand dollars. As she stands."

Slade looked at Johnson. "Good enough for you?"

Johnson nodded. The little rancher counted quickly. He threw twelve thousand five hundred dollars in the pot.

"High card?"

Johnson looked at the deck, grinned once, and reached.

He pulled a card out slowly and drew it toward him. He didn't look at it, but let it lie, face down, in front of him.

Slade reached for the deck and quickly picked his card, flipped it in the air and let it fall, face up. It was the king of clubs, the first face card he had seen in the last half hour. The crowd sighed.

Johnson turned his card over.

The ace of clubs.

Slade felt the wince form but he wouldn't let it break through, and then he shook Johnson's hand, and walked upstairs.

Now he looked at what used to be his, the big pine desk, two chairs, a sagging cot, and a heavy three-drawered commode which had all the clothes he owned except what was on him. He left the saloon's business books on the desk so Johnson could see how he ran the place, his outgo and income, his papers of ownership which he had signed over to the rancher. For two days he had sent messengers to the town bank, emptying his several accounts. Now nothing was left. Thirty thousand dollars, plus the saloon—all shot to hell.

Everything gone, except the sock jammed deep in his shirt. Johnson wouldn't mind his taking the sock. Slade never considered it part of anything. It was a separate thing, his charm, his amulet. Now it had become more than just a separate thing. It had become everything. He licked his fingers and pinched out the blue-yellow flame in the oil pot. He stalked out, leaving the door wide open.

He went down the stairs just as Lu finished her song. They were shouting again. He shouldered his way through the crowd, and somebody said, "Tough luck, Slade," but Slade could tell he didn't mean it. He hunched his shoulders and stiff-armed the swinging doors.

The night air hit him and he realized suddenly how tired he was. He hadn't slept for two full days and nights and now he felt it catch up. The stable was at the far end of the main drag—the north end of town—a half-mile trek he used to take at a half-lope. Now he plodded along, head down, shoulders tight and high, his eyeballs burning, and the cool night gripping his thighs. It was early May and though the sun was a red ball of fire at noon, when it sank over the Finlay mountains every evening, the air turned chill. He walked on, a man with bleak thoughts turned inward.

Still, he should have seen Dilt lounging in the shadows, should have sensed him out there, tall and rangy, an immense bald man with too many drinks in him and the nasty feeling of victory teasing his guts. But Slade wasn't thinking of any trouble—any more trouble. He felt he had all there was, all that any man could handle. He felt like a pendulum at its far zenith; now he would have to swing the other way.

So he felt raw shock hit him when Dilt said, "All right, Slade. End of the road." The foreman stepped out into the street, some far-off light meeting his bald head and sending out a pale dapple in all the darkness.

Slade said, "Get out of my way, Dilt."

Dilt stood there.

"I said get out of my way."

Slade could make out the man now; the moon was shoving its thick wax through a cloud. The street glowed weakly. Behind them was the town activity, muted. Otherwise they were alone. The stable was two hundred yards ahead, a lantern winking red.

Dilt said, "You've had this coming for ten years, Slade. You and your goddam taking ways."

Slade said, "If I ever took you, Dilt, I took you fair." He didn't like what he was saying; he didn't want to have to defend himself to this drunken angry man. But he was tired and he was trying to keep his rage down where he could control it.

Dilt shook his head slowly. "Fair or not, I don't know. But you took me. You've got a couple of hundred dollars of mine through the years and I want them back."

Slade said, "Ask Johnson for them." He started forward, but Dilt stood there, swaying a little. Slade could see the bloodshot smear in Dilt's eyes now and the wet shine of his mouth. The man was crazy-drunk and nursing a grudge. Slade wondered foolishly how many others he was leaving behind like this: hating his guts. It was a nice legacy.

Then Slade's foot hit something in the street and he stumbled forward, his shoulder driving into Dilt, and the bald man let out a great roar of animal joy. He grabbed Slade and tried to get his arms around his waist but Slade jabbed out his elbows and broke free. Dilt threw his right fist at Slade and suddenly Slade was licking dirt, his head a red ball of pain. He rolled over and he heard Dilt come down, knees first, where he had been lying. Now he got up and he clawed at his shirt to get the sock out of his way. It was heavy and he couldn't swing his arms the way he wanted to. His holster and gun were bogging him down, too, and Dilt was able to hammer him again with that right hand, driving Slade before him.

He grabbed Dilt's right arm when he saw it come roundhouse through the night and wrenched the man toward him, pinning the arm with his own left and reaching into his shirt with his other hand, while Dilt smashed him twice with his free fist, great clubbing blows to Slade's ribs that made him gasp open-mouthed for air.

Now he had the sock in his right hand. It was a weapon, he knew, and he could have killed Dilt with it, but somehow he felt himself tossing it to the side of the street, thinking: it's over there, about four feet from that little white rock. He had to remember where it was; it was everything.

Dilt never gave him much chance to slip off the holster and gun. The right fist swept by Slade's head and then came clubbing back, catching Slade on the side of the jaw. He whirled, tried to keep his balance, grabbed Dilt and then fell backward, dragging the foreman down on top of him.

He wrapped his legs around Dilt's middle and started to squeeze. He heard Dilt cry out and begin to writhe, and he smelled the man's foul whisky-breath all over him. Then Dilt pulled his head back and drove it forward into Slade's mouth like some great battering ram. Slade felt a tooth break off, and the blood ran warm over his tongue. He rolled over and lashed out with his fist and he felt it sink four inches into Dilt's belly, and then they were up, an arm's length apart, swaying and beaten, both of them.

Slade knew now was the time for him to do it, to reach Dilt and chop him down. The man was ready. The alcohol had burned out his wind and dulled his reflexes. The brief throttling he'd given Dilt with his legs and that last driving fist to the belly had sucked out the man's strength.

But while he stood there, measuring him, his right arm crawling to his hip ready to smash forward, he lost his man. Now the two full days of sleeplessness, now the whole knowledge of his defeat at the card table rushed over Slade. His arm made the arc, but Dilt was inside, grabbing him by the middle, lifting Slade's two hundred and five pounds and throwing him backward and dropping on him, knees driving into Slade's groin.

Somehow—he scarcely remembered it, except as a wild red nightmare in later years—Slade got up and was driven down again. He pulled himself to his knees and started to rise when Dilt smashed him back down again. This time he grabbed Dilt and clutched the man's legs, trying to pull himself up that way. Dilt drove both his fists to the back of Slade's neck and kicked himself loose. Yet somehow he got up again. Finally, the wild red washed through him and turned gray and the last thing he remembered was Dilt saying hoarsely, "Fall, you son of a bitch, fall."

When he came to, he was five yards from the stable door. He had walked that way, out on his feet, instinct telling him his escape was here. A faint mist was falling from the heavy skies, gray now with false dawn trying to break up the sullen night. Slade thought, *the rain will do the grass some good*, and he passed out again.

This time he recovered completely, sitting there on the ground, pressing the back of his hand to his mouth to staunch the flow of blood. He put his hands on the ground and pushed upward, against the ripping pain of his battered ribs, and stood there, trying to remember what it was he had to remember.

But he couldn't, and he didn't much care.

He staggered to the stable and said through broken lips, "Williams, I want my horse."

The stableman—a lean white-haired Negro who had lost his right arm fighting for the Union forces in The War Between the States—came out of the back, smelling of sweet straw.

"Well," he said, "somebody sure carved up on you, Slade." He pulled Slade inside and shoved him down on the cot. He took cotton from a pail and said, "Wait here a minute. I'll be right back."

Slade heard the splash of water from the well, and then the stableman was leaning over him again, touching him with water-soaked cotton, drawing out the sting and cleaning the dirt from the ugly open bruises. They were silent for five minutes, and then the stableman straightened and said, "You oughtn't ride tonight."

Slade said, "Get my horse, Williams," and the stableman went to the back.

Williams led the horse out through the rear of the stable and Slade followed, walking unsteadily, but better. He said to the stableman, "Is my account straight?"

Williams said, "As a string."

Slade nodded. "That's good." The stableman stood there, tightening the big saddle, and Slade guessed he had heard about the loss of the saloon. He got up on the horse and said, "Thank you, Williams," and the stableman shrugged his empty sleeve.

The horse headed west, toward the Rio Grande, into the driving mist that soon turned into steady rain, and they had gone from true dawn to morning when Slade remembered the sock. He stopped the horse and half-turned him, jolted, frightened, trying to recall the white rock off the edge of the main drag back in Cutter.

He shook his head and turned the horse west again. He wasn't going to crawl in the mud.

Then his thoughts mocked him: *don't be a goddam hero, Slade, you'd crawl if you thought the sock was still there.*

Dilt probably had picked it up, or one of the farmers riding through town early with his produce, or a cattleman with a load of yearlings going to meet the train that had finally thrust its rails as far as this hell they called West Texas.

Slade prodded his horse and the sun came out at noon, burning away the mist, turning the slick wet footing to heavy viscous mud and then in three hours' time baking it hot and hard again. Slade shook his head. It wasn't a place fit for a man. Then his mouth twisted in a white-lipped grin. He had a hell of a nerve. He'd liked it well enough for ten years; now he was getting a look at the other side of the coin.

That is, if he had a coin to look at.

He squinted into the shimmering heat that flowed off the ground and he looked at all the big empty country all around him. One man alone, he thought. He wondered what the odds were.

CHAPTER 2

Slade was not just drifting. He knew where he was headed. When The War Between the States had broken out in 1861, he was eighteen years old. He was tired of dragging plow for his father on their farm down in the southern edge of the state of Kansas, and his sympathies were not with the Union forces. So when Kansas had become a free state in 1861—old Bleeding Kansas, split in two camps, each side talking big and doing nothing—he chucked the farm and the war and went out farther west.

He was a strong kid then, tough and untouched. He worked the cow ranches for a month's stretch at a time, collected his pay, shoved it into a leather money belt that he never took off, and kept pushing until he hit Utah. In his nose was the smell of gold and he found the source of the smell one night in December in a little no-name creek in Utah outside the tiny town of Mammoth. He panned his gold and went into town where he met a boy named Chet Crispin who also had the gold itch. For no reason he ever quite figured out, Slade took Crispin to the half-frozen creek bed and they panned together.

On reflection, Slade concluded it must have been Crispin's older sister, a long-legged young woman who was visiting her brother. Slade wanted her and he thought Crispin's friendship might help. That it cost him approximately five hundred dollars—Crispin's share of the little strike—to watch May Crispin cast eyes at the older men of Mammoth while ignoring him didn't bother him at the time.

Even then he was a gambler, except later he learned greater respect for the odds. May Crispin had gone back east, leaving Slade with an ache inside him.

He had taken his money and back-tracked, ending up in Texas gambling towns until he had a good-sized stake and then his saloon.

Crispin had gone down to New Mexico where he bought a piece of land on the gentle slope that formed the north cup of the Sierra Verde valley, high up near the source of fine water, a little cattle ranch now.

The two men had corresponded infrequently through the years. Though Slade had not heard from Crispin in six months, he knew he always was welcome.

He had one hundred and fifty miles to go. His horse could make forty miles a day, with pushing. But Slade wasn't going to go four days without food, and he didn't have the first cent to buy any. The horse would have to go at the first trading post.

So the four days stretched to nearly ten times that.

Slade hit the Rio Grande forty miles below El Paso, across the river from the Mexican border town of Guadalupe. A trading post sat on the river edge, a sign reading: HORSES, ASSES WELCOMED.

He was sweat-caked and tired to the bone. He had napped once that day, but he still was way behind on sleep. A hole was forming in his belly and starting to ache.

He pulled up at the post at seven that night. A Mexican sat in front of the horse pen, picking his teeth with a piece of straw. Business was poor, Slade knew. The sporadic raids by Mexican and Texas bandits on the border towns of the Rio Grande had slackened. There was little market for new, unmarked horses, or at least horses with different brands from those ridden to the post by thieves. Horse stealing was a fading art; the cattle rustlers now held sway.

Slade said, "Howdy," and the Mexican tipped his hat. He remained on the ground, the piece of straw suspended in the air.

Slade said, "I want to buy a mule."

The trader scrambled to his feet. "Well," he said in a combination Midwest twang and southern drawl that was a perfect duplication of Slade's speech, "why didn't you say so? Thought you wanted to sell that old nag you were riding."

Slade laughed. "You've got me," he said. "That was my aim. I figured you'd be more interested if I said I was buying, not selling."

"You do want a mule, though?"

"Yes."

"I'll give you twenty dollars for that horse. My mules begin at five and run to ten."

Slade said, "I want forty dollars for my horse and I'll give you five of it back on the best mule in the pen."

The Mexican's hat tilted up. There was a mixture of surprise and pleasure on his face. Just as Slade was a gambler, it was obvious he was a trader.

"Your horse is nine years old," he said. "Maybe ten. His left hind leg is a quarter-inch shorter than his right. His shoes are shot. Twenty-two dollars."

They settled on twenty-five, and five for the mule. Slade left with twenty dollars in his pocket, his knees gripping the bulging sides of a flat-eared gray mule.

He took the twenty dollars into the first town on the river, had a meal, and then went to a saloon where the dice were loaded, so he didn't risk any of his tiny stake. He bedded down in the local stable for twenty-five cents and slept ten hours and the next morning bought five dollars' worth of canned tomatoes, jerked beef, and cigars. He kept pushing west, and then north.

The mule lasted three days and then went mad, trying to butt itself to death against a sunbaked canyon wall three miles inside the New Mexico border. Slade tried to give the mule some water but the animal bit him on the wrist. He had to shoot the mule and continue on foot to the next town.

It was a long month—possibly the longest month he had ever lived—before Slade rode his new horse, his canned goods and two dollars into Cowpoke.

He had never seen Cowpoke, but once he had, he knew it well. It was a cowman's town—like so many others he had gone through—dusty and dry and loosely thrown together as though the town fathers were in a hurry to get it put up so they could then leave and rush to the next platted community and whip up another town. It was as though the town, in fact, did not count—as, indeed, it didn't. What made Cowpoke important lay outside the town, on the other side of the hills that framed the Sierra Verde valley. Grass grew on that side, and water ran in clear gushes down the north and west slopes onto the ranchlands below. Cattle lowed calmly, their tails swishing at flies, and over their snouts and backs a fine faint cloud hung, that misty smell of animal and grass and water that gave the cow valleys their peculiar and rich trademark. In Cowpoke, the trademark was the mixture in the street of horse chips and dust.

Slade headed for the first saloon he saw. Not because he was thirsty. Nor hungry—though he knew from way back that a saloon was not where a man ate. The saloon was home base to the Slades of the West—the smell of it was tangy and familiar, beer and whisky and sweat and urine conjuring up a heavy perfume that tried so hard and so vainly to overcome the smell of cows and horses that came in with the cowmen and never left even when they did.

The look of it was familiar, too. The wooden plank of bar, the wooden tables and chairs, the sawdusted floors, the thick beer glasses and false-bottom shot glasses, and even now—at noon—the figure slumped face down on a table, his hat on the floor, a glass on its side at his elbow, and his breath joining all the other smells, good and bad, that made up the saloon.

It was where Slade belonged, and he knew it.

He said to the bartender, "Beer, please," and put a silver dollar, his next to last, on the bar.

The beer was cold and good, clearing his nostrils. He said, "Pretty quiet in here."

The bartender grunted and walked away.

Slade's eyes slitted. The bartender was busy on a glass, polishing it beyond the need of further polish, but still at it. Slade had an uneasiness steal over him. A silent bartender in an empty saloon, unless you counted the drunken puncher, on a hot dry noon didn't make full sense. Slade thought: to hell with this place; there must be another saloon in town. He picked up his change and started to turn.

The voice froze him halfway around. It was the deepest voice he ever heard, more a croak than a voice, full though and resonant as a bullfrog's in mating season.

"Come around slow, bucko," the voice said. "Hands out from your sides and real, *real* slow."

Slade pivoted and stepped away from the bar, his hands out, his right hand a full eighteen inches from the butt end of his .44.

The man with the voice wore a badge. The badge was nearly as big as his head. He didn't reach Slade's shoulder, and he couldn't have weighed ninety-eight pounds. He was tiny in every way, small white hands, delicate long fingers, peaked chest and shoulders, a waist the size of Slade's upper arm, dainty feet in clean, magnificent leather boots. The face was bland, unlined, ageless.

Slade started to grin.

The man's face changed then. It went hot with fury and hate, and Slade knew he shouldn't have laughed at this little man. The mouth twisted, razor-edged and cruel, the eyes blue one moment, ice-gray the next.

"What are you laughing at, bucko?" The voice was still full and deep, the voice of a man three times the size of this little sheriff who didn't wear a gun.

Slade said, "I guess that's my business."

The sheriff said, "What's your name?"

"Slade."

The slumped figure in the center of the room stirred a bit.

The sheriff said, "What are you doing in town?"

Slade said, "See here, get off your goddam high horse. What have I done—broken some local ordinance about drinking at noon?"

The sheriff said, "You're wearing a gun. That's enough for me."

Slade took a deep breath and gambled that the sheriff didn't have a hideout gun someplace on him, and if he did, he couldn't get to it before Slade had finished. Slade moved then, incredibly fast for a big man, fast for any man, his right hand dipping low, a blur in the big room, the only thing moving as the bartender froze and gasped and the sheriff stared popeyed, and then Slade had the gun clear and he was throwing it— gently—in a soft loop, straight to the sheriff.

"There," Slade said, "now *you've* got the gun. Does that make you a dirty word?"

The sheriff said, "I didn't call you any names." He was puzzled, staring first at the .44 in his hands and then at Slade. Slade watched the sheriff's fingers as they turned the weapon over. They were—for all their fragile whiteness—capable fingers. Slade felt the sweat break out all over him. He had taken a hell of a chance. The sheriff must have had a gun some place on him; he looked the type.

Slade said, "That's true. You didn't call me any names, but you sure as hell acted like I had blackleg."

"You wore a gun into my town. You're a stranger. That's two things we don't like."

"Mighty hospitable town," Slade said drily. "You must be aiming to grow into a real big cemetery."

The sheriff's face went mean and hot again. Slade saw he was going about it wrong. The sheriff had his tender spots and Slade was hitting them all. "All right," the sheriff snapped, "suppose you tell me what you're doing here."

Slade said mildly, "Suppose you tell me why you want to know."

The sheriff relaxed a bit. He walked to the bar and laid the gun on the wood between Slade and himself. Slade put his hand next to the gun butt but he didn't touch it. The sheriff flicked his fingers and the bartender ducked below the level of the bar and fished out a bottle of brandy. He poured the brandy two inches high into a water tumbler. The sheriff picked up the glass and drank it down in one swallow and turned to Slade.

"We're having some trouble in the valley," he said simply. "That's why I'm disturbed."

Slade said, "What kind of trouble?"

The sheriff shrugged. He spread his hands. "Just trouble. Pushing kind of trouble. People talking hard all of a sudden. Ever since the drought two years ago—you know about the drought of '76?—I've smelled it coming. The kind of trouble you feel before it really happens."

Slade felt a mild kinship with the sheriff. It was instinct, the sheriff was saying, that had warned him. If the sheriff were not such a touchy little devil, Slade might even have found himself liking him.

Slade stared into his beer and the sheriff flicked his fingers and a second brandy appeared. The bartender disappeared and silence flowed through the room.

Then everything shattered.

The man who was slumped over his table swayed to his feet, his elbow sending the glass crashing to the floor. He stood facing the bar, bleary-eyed and disheveled, as though this was the tag-end of an all-night drunk, his beard an ugly black shadow. He slushed his words but they still came out clear enough. "You're a goddam liar, Wilkinson," he shouted. "You know what all the trouble's about." He tried to raise his right arm and point it at the sheriff but it fell heavily to his side, his slack hand slapping his thigh. "Wilkinson," he said again thickly, "you're a goddam liar."

The sheriff turned to the man and Slade admired the way he carefully gritted his teeth to bunch up the jaw muscles and lend strength to his face. "Don't talk to me like that, Hogue. I'll clap you in jail so fast that thick head of yours will spin loose from your neck."

"Yeah," the man said, "try it, Wilkinson. Just try it."

The sheriff said to Slade, "Excuse me," and he walked to the man. When he was two full steps away he stopped and suddenly leaped forward, thrusting his legs out before him, high and kicking. His boots crunched against the drunken man's face and blood spouted and Hogue went down like a broken strawman. It was a shocking sight. The sheriff bent down and wiped his boots against Hogue's shirt and returned to his place at the bar.

Slade said in a tight voice, "That wasn't necessary, Wilkinson."

Wilkinson said, "Yes it was. It was very necessary. I'm the law in this town. We're going to have trouble. I know it. I feel it. But if there's the slightest chance in hell that I can stop it—if I can prove I'm wrong about the trouble —then I don't care if I kick in a dozen men's faces."

"Even a drunk like that?"

Wilkinson said, "You're soft, Slade. Most big men are soft. They ride along like kings, every one of them, taking everything for granted because they sit so high in their saddles. But just let something come along that throws them a bit, and they don't know a horse's end from his eyeballs."

Slade said, "I think you're a little son of a bitch, Wilkinson, and if you ever try to kick me in the face, I'll rip your leg off."

The sheriff looked at Slade strangely. There was no hate on his face now, just a trace of wan bitterness. "Sure," he said, "you're just like the rest of them. You can't even call me a son of a bitch without throwing in that word."

Slade frowned. "What word?"

The sheriff said, "Little."

A shiver ran through Slade. The sheriff was insane. He wondered how Wilkinson ever got his badge. True, for a long while the territory was owned by Mexico. Americans had been slow coming out, and when the United States took over the land in 1848 there was only a handful of American traders and miners living there. A man could become the law of a town—even of a county—just by writing a letter to Washington, D. C. That might have accounted for a Wilkinson. Still, Slade thought, that only explains the badge. It doesn't explain how he's been allowed to keep it.

Slade didn't like the setup. Trouble in the valley—where Crispin had his spread and where he, Slade, was heading. And a cruel little sheriff running the show.

"I'm sorry," Slade said, "I'll watch myself in the future. I still think you're a son of a bitch."

"That's your privilege," Wilkinson said. "Just ride out of town today and don't come back, and I won't hold it against you."

Slade said, "How far does your badge take you?"

Wilkinson said slowly, "County limits."

"Into the valley?"

Wilkinson nodded, his eyes searching Slade's face. "Why?"

"Because I'm going to be in the valley for a while."

The sheriff's lips tightened. "You working for Thomas?"

Slade shook his head. "Never heard of him."

"Who then?"

"I'm visiting a rancher. Man named Crispin."

Again the room swirled and clattered. The bartender stopped polishing. The glass slipped from his hand and banged and rolled on the floor behind the bar. Venom crawled over Wilkinson's face.

"Get out of here," the sheriff said. "Get out of town, out of the valley. I don't want you around. I swear, you stay around, see to it you never go anyplace again."

Slade reached out and grabbed Wilkinson by the shoulders. He shook the little man and the sheriff's head lolled on its thin neck. "Listen," Slade said. "I don't know what's biting you. I'm going to see Chet Crispin. He's a friend of mine. I'm going to visit with him as long as he wants me and as long as I can stay. Stop making threats to me. I haven't done a goddam thing in this town of yours and I don't intend to. But if you keep pushing me, I'll take that badge of yours and ram it. Understand, Shorty?"

Wilkinson pulled free and when he talked, his lips were slashing razor blades. "Bucko," he said, "nobody lays a hand on me twice. Remember that. I swear, if you give me half a chance, I'll have you taken apart." He turned and walked to the saloon door. Slade watched him as he tried to add inches by bouncing as he walked. When the sheriff reached the doors, he drew back his right fist and smashed it against one of the wooden swinging doors and swiftly followed it out. Slade heard a horse clopping on the wooden walk and then drumming its way down the dirt street.

Slade turned to the bartender. "All right," he said. "Give. What the hell was that all about?"

The bartender said, "If I were you, I'd take Wilkinson's advice and beat it the hell out of here."

"Why? He doesn't scare me."

The bartender snorted. "Him? Of course not. Not him. He kicks drunks in the face and slaps whores around, but that's all. Still, there's going to be trouble, just like he said. And if you knew Crispin and you intend to stay out there, you'll be right in the center of it."

Slade said slowly, "What do you mean—if I *knew* Crispin?"

The bartender flushed. "Nothing," he said. "Only—only that Crispin ain't been seen for a couple of days and people are saying—" His words trailed off and his eyes went past Slade. Slade turned. The figure on the sawdust floor had struggled to his feet again. Blood coated his cheek.

"Sure," the man said thickly. "Sure he's missing. They killed him, that's what." He staggered to the door and stumbled into the street.

Slade said to the bartender, "Missing?" He tried to keep the panic from showing. Christ, he thought, the long trek, his money gone, his saloon gone, the sock gone, and now Crispin. But this was worse, for it meant his involvement, he knew. Slade was a man who had his fears, like any sensible man, but he had his courages, too. He didn't want Crispin to be missing; he didn't want to have to side with him in a beef war or whatever it was that had stirred up the Sierra Verde. But he knew he would have to.

The bartender said, "Yeah, missing. Nobody seen hide nor hair for two days. Not even him." He jerked his thumb at the door through which the drunk had just stumbled.

"Who's he?"

"Hogue? He works for Crispin."

Slade said, "Thanks," and paid for his last beer. He walked out. They were lining up already, he thought, and he didn't like it. The sheriff of the county was on one side, a drunk on the other. And he—Slade—would have to side with the drunk and with a missing man against the law of the county. He thought: I'll get on my horse now and I'll push on. There's another town up the road, and another one and another one. My pile's lying in one of them, waiting for me to come along and pick it up. That's what I'll do.

His hand went to his money belt. He reached inside and felt the remaining silver dollar. He felt more than that. He felt fear, again. One dollar. It wasn't enough. It wasn't near enough a stake. A man couldn't wander into the middle of nowhere with just a dollar in his pocket. He had to have more. He just had to.

He looked up the street where a horse trailed off toward the valley. The man named Hogue sprawled against the horse's neck. Slade started after him.

CHAPTER 3

Wilkinson had ridden off in the other direction, a short clopping ride, on a tiny brown mare, the length of town to the clean white front of the Cowpoke Bank and Trust Company. He looped his rein to a post and walked through the front of the bank to the office in the rear, no longer bouncing. Fear was inside him now and he had no time for showing off.

He knocked on a door marked *Private* and a voice said, "Come in."

He walked in and threw his hat on the big desk and said, "Jesus Christ, I told you hell would pop."

The man behind the desk said, "Take it easy and don't talk so goddam loud. I know you've got a big voice. Turn it down a little."

The sheriff flushed. "Don't worry about my voice. You're going to have plenty of other things to worry about now. There's a friend of Crispin's nosing around this town."

The banker said, "So?"

Wilkinson said, "Look here, Abbott, maybe you and Big Thomas are looking for trouble, but I'm not."

Abbott said, "You know I'm not looking for trouble. I'm just interested in seeing good come to this town. For your sake as well as anybody else's."

Wilkinson said, "You call killing a man good?"

Abbott got up and walked around the desk. "You know, Wilkinson, I think you need a vacation."

The sheriff turned pale.

Abbott went on. "Killing Crispin lies as much on your shoulders as it does on mine and Big Thomas'. We all stand to profit from it. All we've got to do is get Hogue out of the way, and we're set. Big Thomas will get the land he wants. You'll get your chance at Mrs. Hogue. And I'll—I'll just know that good has come to Cowpoke, prosperity and law and order firmly established. That is what you want, isn't it, Wilkinson? Or do you think you want a vacation—such as the one some fools think Crispin is enjoying right now?"

The sheriff was silent.

Abbott said, "So we won't hear any more about killing Crispin, will we? That's settled, once and for all?"

Wilkinson licked his dry lips and nodded. "But I'm telling you it won't stay settled. There's a stranger in town asking about Crispin. He says he's a friend of Crispin's and expects to stay at the ranch a while."

Abbott made a tent of his fingers. "Well, that's not very serious. Once the stranger sees that his friend is—on a vacation—he'll leave. If we have to, we'll—encourage him to cut short his visit to our peaceful little community."

"He's already met Hogue. He saw me rough up Hogue a little."

Abbott said, "That's your problem. I told you to watch that temper of yours. You bantams are too tough for your own good. I swear, you're the nastiest little viper I've ever seen."

Wilkinson tried to keep from smiling. He liked it when Abbott called him names like that. Even with the word *little* tacked on.

He said, "When you got me my badge, I said I'd keep this place under control."

Abbott said drily, "I had the senator get you that badge because the place already *was* under control. If I ever thought we'd have trouble in Cowpoke, you'd have been the last person we'd make sheriff."

Wilkinson said in a strangled voice, "There isn't a better man in this town than me." His hands clawed at his side in twitching fury at this cool man before him.

Abbott said, "That's true. Not a better man in town than you. That is, pound for pound." He laughed heartily at his stupid little joke.

And Wilkinson knew—if he ever had the chance—he would kill Abbott. Just as he had sworn to kill Crispin, only Big Thomas and his men had got there first. He had hated Crispin almost from the first, the way the man rode and talked, the utter fearlessness of him, the way he fought back at Big Thomas when the rancher started pressing Crispin to sell his place. There was envy in Wilkinson, remembering how Crispin had retaliated when Big Thomas burned his alfalfa patch and ripped out a piece of fence. Crispin had ridden to Big Thomas' ranch house in the middle of night—the night after the fire and fence-ripping and emptied two guns through the windows. Then he was gone. Nobody was hurt and nobody knew for sure who had done it, but the next morning there were the tracks of one horse leading in and then going out, straight back to Crispin's place.

Wilkinson envied Crispin, and because he envied him he wished him dead. All this was four days ago. The next day somebody mentioned Crispin's name and Wilkinson said something—he didn't remember what, but it was obscene and heated—and Big Thomas had looked at Wilkinson curiously and said, "You sure don't like that man, do you?"

That night Big Thomas and Abbott came to Wilkinson's office and they had a few drinks and some words. The next night, Big Thomas and his men did in Crispin.

Now it was Abbott he hated, just the way he hated Crispin. They hadn't let him get Crispin himself; he'd try to make sure of Abbott.

He said, "What happens if this friend of Crispin's turns up the body?"

Abbott said, "He's not likely to."

"But if he does?"

Abbott sighed. "You're becoming a drag, Wilkinson. I don't know why we tolerate you, Big Thomas and I."

The sheriff said, "Goddammit, I don't want my neck stretched."

Abbott looked at him sympathetically. "Of course not. Neither do I. That's why we take precautions. He won't find Crispin. And if he does— why, he'll do the correct thing. He'll report the finding to the proper authority. You. And you'll tell me. And then Big Thomas and you and I will take cognizance of the new situation and remedy it as fast as we can. Just as we did when Crispin became ornery."

The sheriff grumbled a bit, but he knew Abbott was right. They were all in it, a tight-knit team, and he'd have to keep under control or he'd be hurting everybody, himself included. He didn't mind hurting the others, but he didn't like getting hurt himself. It always had been so easy to hurt him. The least little push or slap would knock him sprawling. Even worse, the wrong word would send the hot anger flooding through him until his very skin seemed alive with smoking bubbles.

He'd have to watch his step. He liked his badge. It made him feel so big.

He said crisply, "You're right. I'm sorry I blew off that way. I'll keep my eye on Crispin's friend and let you know if anything is brewing."

Abbott said, "That's the way to talk. You're an intelligent man, Wilkinson. There isn't a thing intelligent men can't do in this world."

Wilkinson nodded, but his mind was thinking, stubbornly, *Intelligence doesn't knock a man sprawling.* And he knew that the badge only made him feel big. He walked out, his legs trembling and he smelled his own fear like a cloud of sweat inside of him.

Abbott sat immobile after Wilkinson left. He was a thinking man, not a man of action, and he was genuinely sorry that some of the consequences of his thoughts lay in violent deeds. Still, it was all very refreshing, this unholy alliance he had formed: he and Big Thomas and Wilkinson.

Of course, the alliance had many different aims. Big Thomas wanted—needed—Crispin's ranch and its water, plus the two tiny spreads that bordered it. His own water, running from the west slope onto his graze would go to the railroad when it came through. Abbott had pulled strings, spent money and filled the ear of a senator—but, by God, he had pulled it off. The railroad was coming straight through the Sierra Verde valley.

The bank had been the first source of the news of the railroad's coming through. The news was still secret and had to remain so if Big Thomas was to be able to buy cheap—or reasonably cheap—the three spreads that owned the only other major source of water in the Sierra Verde.

Crispin was the key to this water. If he sold out to Big Thomas, the others would follow. That's why the pressure had been exerted first on him. Once he was out of the way, Big Thomas would wave his guns around—and some money—and the others would sell. Then Big Thomas would truly be the big man in the valley—with a graze-full of cows, and a railroad line within hollering distance. He could get his cattle to market quicker and cheaper than any ranch in this part of New Mexico. There was the dream of empire in Big Thomas now.

The alternative to Big Thomas was disaster. If the little ranches didn't sell, and the railroad took over his water, he'd be washed out of the valley. Big Thomas was heavily in debt to Abbott and the Cowpoke bank. The drought two years back had cost him heavily. Now he stood a chance to recoup everything—and then some. He was plunging, for the biggest stakes of his life.

Wilkinson's role in the triumvirate and his goal were far different, far simpler and more primitive. He wanted a woman, the first real woman of his life. He'd been to the cathouses, but that sickened him and he got more joy out of slapping the whores around. Now he wanted the wife of Crispin's foreman, Hogue, the woman who also happened to be Crispin's sister.

Abbott—he sat there and thought and frowned in the silence and comfort of his big office—he was not unlike Big Thomas. He, too, had the vision of empire before him. His empire, however, was not the domain of grass and cows. His lay in the realm of—power. Abbott owned the Cowpoke bank. The Cowpoke bank was one of a loosely held combination of banks in that part of the country which had heavily financed a railroad into New Mexico. Thus Abbott also owned a piece of the railroad. But when a man owns a piece of a combination of banks and a piece of a railroad, he is at once satisfied and discontent. He must have more.

He sat there a moment longer and then started shifting through some papers. Bank statements, mortgages, deeds—*ah*, he thought, *here we are*—applications for loans. The two tiny ranchers up on the north slope with Crispin, Ben Mudge and Wilbur Early constantly strapped for money, short of equipment, hit hard by that same drought that sapped Big Thomas—had applied for sizable loans, enough to see them through the year. Abbott smiled thinly. He would have to talk to Mudge and Early, a kindly talk, nothing specific, enough to make them wonder whether the bank would see fit to meet their requests. The problem was to keep them on the hook, fidgety, so they'd be ripe to sell when the time came. Not yet. Not until the Crispin affair was concluded. If it appeared that there was a concerted effort to buy up the whole north slope and all its water, people would become suspicious. Somebody might find out about the railroad coming through Big Thomas' land. Big Thomas would have a tough time then; the asking price would go sky-high, even for the ill-kept land that belonged to Mudge and Early.

Abbott let the thin smile play upon his mouth. Suppose, he thought, the word *did* get out too soon. Wouldn't that put Big Thomas in a vise? Abbott let his thoughts run unheeded.

When the time came to break up the triumvirate, Abbott knew that Big Thomas would have to go first. Once more, genuine regret entered the picture; violence was a necessary consequence of having to break with Big Thomas.

He would kill Big Thomas, Abbott thought, simply by breaking his empire dream, by wiping him out financially.

On the Crispin ranch, May Hogue—formerly May Crispin, the older sister of Chet Crispin and the woman Slade had vaguely yearned for years before in a Utah gold town—stood at the corral fence and stroked a horse that had nuzzled its head against her soft palm.

She was a tall woman, dark-haired and dark-eyed, with a tired line to her jaw and tiny wrinkles crowding the corners of her mouth. Still, she was an attractive woman, full-bodied and with a loose, animal gait and long legs that had ripened since Slade had first seen them, now voluptuous whereas they had then been slender and only faintly curved. She was a woman of nearly forty who had held out too long for the "right" man until no man in her circle back east thought she was the marrying kind. She had become desperate. Chet Crispin had told her of his new foreman, a solid respectable widower who wanted to buy into Crispin's ranch and who looked like a good potential husband to a decent woman.

May Crispin had come out to New Mexico a few months ago, and she had let Hogue make love to her the first night on the ranch. Hogue knew she wasn't a decent woman but he had to have her after that one night and she steadfastly refused until he agreed to marry her. Now she hated his guts. And the solid respectable Hogue, in turn, had started to drink heavily.

May Hogue stared at the pass across the valley and saw the two tiny specks that had to be horsemen coming down the far slope and treading slowly toward her.

She thought, *so now they've got to help him home, the drunken bastard.* Her next thought was, *maybe it's Chet!* But she didn't believe it.

She knew that Crispin wasn't simply missing for two days. He wasn't the type. Something had happened to him. Big Thomas was out to get Chet, ten men to one (*unless you threw in Hogue*, she thought with contempt, *then it's ten men to one and a half*). Big Thomas wanted Chet's spread—though only God knew why, with his own place a dozen times as big and rich, his water all his own, instead of split three ways by those two filthy scabby little ranches that festered next to Chet's.

She watched the two men—one she could now see was Hogue—creep nearer at a tired jog. The other man wasn't Chet. He loomed bulkier, thicker, but somehow she thought of Chet when she saw him coming on. Chet was tall and slender and blond, and this man, with his hat flapping on the side of his saddle, was heavy-set and dark. Yet she kept thinking of Chet. There was something about the man.

When they were two hundred yards away, she knew it was Slade. A tremor passed through her, delicious and painful, and she was suddenly, strangely, fiercely glad.

CHAPTER 4

They sat in the parlor, Hogue leaning back against a big soft sagging chair, rags soaked in icy well water against his swollen cheek where Wilkinson had kicked him.

May Hogue said in disbelief, "Little Wilkinson?" Slade watched her and he saw the contempt creep into her eyes. She still stirred him, he admitted, but he could see what she had become, a conniving woman today as against the flirt of yesterday.

Slade said, "Hogue didn't stand a chance. Wilkinson just kicked him without warning."

She said, "If he were sober, it wouldn't have happened." They spoke as though Hogue weren't there, which was the way May felt at the moment. Slade had changed, for the better. He was settled, no longer rash or impetuous. There was a studied calculating air about him, not sly actually, but careful. And yet she missed the other, the brash brazenness of the boy who had staked out his woman with the same eagerness he had staked out his gold claim. The woman was herself and he had struck nothing with her, of course. Now she vaguely regretted that she had not given herself to the boy Slade; she thought she'd have to make up for it as quickly as possible.

Hogue said to her through the muffling rags, "You'd be drinking, too, if you had the sense to be scared. They killed Chet and they're going to kill me and if you stick around, Slade, they'll kill you."

Slade forced himself to laugh. "Why would they want to kill me?" But his mind was racing. He had come away from Texas dead broke. Crispin was his destination then, his laying-up station where he might somehow recoup and then start off fresh again with a little stake and a place where he could hold chips and cards and stacks of money.

Instead, he was at a ranch in New Mexico run by a frightened drunk and his wife, where his friend was missing and maybe beat up someplace or even dead, and where his own presence seemed to constitute deadly peril to himself. And on top of it all, he smelled in May Hogue the hardness and evil and he was drawn to it, hating it and her and himself.

The thing to do, he told himself, was to find Crispin, make sure he was well, and get the hell away. He was an animal now, hunted and desperate, and he didn't like it.

He said to Hogue, "When did Crispin leave the ranch?"

"Two nights ago, after supper. He went out to look at the fence that Big Thomas knocked down. He figured nighttime was safer. Still, it had to be early enough so he could see what he was doing." Then he added bitterly, "Light enough for Big Thomas to see, too."

Slade said, "Why does everybody call him Big Thomas?"

May said, "His name is Bigelow. He's really not that big at all."

"No?" Hogue said. "He's the biggest man in the valley."

She said, "Chet didn't think so." Then she let her eyes play over Slade's frame. "I'm not sure I think so either."

Hogue laughed hard and short. "Yeah. And that's why Chet's dead."

Slade said, "How do you know?"

"Because I know Big Thomas. He wants this place. Christ, for all I care, he can have it. Just so he leaves me be."

Slade felt sorry for the man. Hogue wanted his spot in the sun and enough to lap out of his feed trough. Slade said, "Do you have a piece of this place?"

Hogue hesitated a moment and his face became crafty. "Yes," he said.

"Goddammit," May Hogue said, standing up, "answer the man. Tell him how you talked Chet into making you full partner for Christ knows how few dollars. What a fool he was."

Hogue turned to her. "I wish to hell he hadn't done it. Now when Big Thomas finds out, he'll mark me down. I go next."

She said, "Oh, don't be so melodramatic. He'll scare you off without laying a hand on you. He'll sick Wilkinson on you."

Hogue flushed. "Shut up," he said.

Slade stood up. "All right," he said. "That's enough. I'm going to ride out and look over the spread. Maybe I'll drop in and see this Thomas everybody's so scared of."

May Hogue sucked in her breath. She had to admire him. He didn't seem to want to do it, yet he was going to make a try. She'd like to see Big Thomas and Slade lock horns. It wasn't fair, of course; Slade was by himself—like Crispin—and Big Thomas had his men and the sheriff behind him. Still, she hoped Slade would start throwing his weight around.

She watched him walk to the corral and past his own horse, to saddle up a fresh horse he had never seen before. He got up and rode off, slouched deep down and hulking, an ugly graceless man who had a wild look in his eye as though he knew he was biting off more than he could swallow.

May Hogue was right. Slade rode the spread with a care that was dictated by fear. He wanted to bust out of sight, out of this valley that smelled so good and looked so green and lovely and held out the taste of death. But he was a man on the run and he knew he had to stop before he destroyed what little there was left to destroy.

Still, had he not fallen from the new horse, he would have finished his search in a half-day's time, lingered on a bit and then, when no new word was forthcoming on Crispin, taken off, looking for the easier road to the pot of gold he had to have.

The luck that had dogged Slade—at first good, and now recently bad— had determined his fate for twenty years. He had grown used to letting fortune take him.

Yet another man might have looked more closely and seen that Slade had used his talents and strengths so well and so forcefully that luck had naturally followed.

For instance, his choosing the horse from which he later fell. It was a horse he had never ridden. There were six others in the pen: his own, worn out from the trek up; Hogue's, a tired horse also; and four others, of clean lines and power. Still, unerringly, he had gone for this one, big and brown and knobby-boned. Slade didn't know it, but it had been Crispin's horse, the same horse he had ridden out two nights ago, and the horse which had returned empty-saddled that night.

Was it really luck that made Slade pick this horse? Or was it his innate knowledge, his eye for such things—the same knowledge that Crispin possessed when he chose that horse for his very own and favorite? Slade—like Crispin—had to arm himself with the very best that was available. This horse was the best on the ranch. He had taken it for the precise reasons Crispin had originally.

So Slade sat Crispin's horse, and the horse, given rein, started to lead Slade. And when they reached within sniffing distance of the torn-up fence toward which Crispin had ridden on his last day on earth, the horse started to nicker nervously.

Slade absently patted the horse's neck and urged it forward. The horse refused. Slade prodded it. The horse gave in reluctantly and then suddenly raised high in shrill terror, twisted in panic and threw its rider.

Slade landed hard, but on soft grass. He rolled away in case the horse was coming down. He didn't know whether the horse was mean, but when he saw it edge a few yards away and stand perfectly still, waiting for him to get up, Slade knew it was other than meanness.

The horse was afraid of going any further. Now: the lucky stupid man might then have remounted, turned back and swapped the horse for another one in the corral. Instead, Slade patted the animal and started on foot. A quarter of a mile away was the gap in the wire. He could see the charred rails lying on the grass in front of him. He had to skirt a little crevice that suddenly dropped below him, a narrow sliver in the ground where—countless centuries ago, maybe scores of millennia—the earth had boiled up and split open and then frozen over and left this tiny flaw in all its natural beauty. Slade walked around the crevice when his back started to crawl.

He looked down.

There was nothing to see, except black shadows in the narrow ledge-like draw that dropped some forty feet and was only three and a half feet across the mouth.

He started to walk on, and then with the same care that peril had created he shrugged his shoulders and dropped onto a ledge within the draw, squeezing his body through the opening and like a cat going down the crevice.

Call it luck, then—Big Thomas did, and later Wilkinson and Abbot did—and even Slade did, but it was more than that. It was the instinct of an animal and of a man who—now the quarry—understood the ways of the hunter. The fox hides in a bush after leaving his drippings a quarter of a mile away and leading in another direction, because he knows how the hounds will run. Slade, hunted now, sensed how the hunter would ride.

It was the flaw of Big Thomas that he had never been the quarry, the prey. It had softened his instinct and made him careless.

Slade stood at the bottom of the draw, looking up now to the sky, down now at—nothing. To one side stood a rounded boulder, five feet high, sunk in the earth since God only knew.

Slade's back prickled again.

It *wasn't* sunk in the earth long. Where he was standing—and where nothing else now stood—was where the boulder *had* been. Slade could see its outlines against the hardened shale at the bottom of the pit. It had been rolled from where it once was to where it now was. He moved to the side of the boulder. He had to sweat to squeeze himself between the boulder and the sheer wall of the draw, but he managed it. He worked his way to the top of the boulder and with his heels, braced all his strength against the rock, trying to teeter it forward.

It held.

He clawed the smooth wall, trying to get a grip with his hands, but he couldn't find purchase. He shifted on the boulder and he poured all his strength down through his bull-shoulders into his thighs and down to his heels. The rock teetered and came back. He tried again but succeeded only in moving it forward three inches before it rolled back, a half-ton rock pushing his heels with it.

But the three inches had been enough.

The crushed body of Chet Crispin came into terrifying focus and then was wiped out.

Slade would not try again; every time he moved the boulder, he disturbed the broken body of what once had been his friend.

Slowly, with growing awareness and a slowly simmering rage that was replacing his fears and his self-concern, he pulled himself up the crevice. He walked—slowly, his body shaking now with fury, a black and fevered fury—to the horse and he touched the horse's neck gently, whispering, "Easy, easy, boy, don't be frightened. Easy, easy, boy."

He mounted, and rode back, a man dedicated to a war that had not been his but which he would now claim. He wondered a bit as he rode. Crispin had not been that close a friend all these years. Yet Crispin's death had become his crusade, and then he thought he knew why. He hadn't allowed himself to crawl in the mud for his five hundred silver dollars or to beg of Dilt that he return the money—a month ago, a century it seemed—and if he wouldn't grovel for money, he'd be damned if he'd let killers and land-grabbers—for surely that was what they had to be—crawl all over him.

He wasn't Hogue, he thought, all craven, seeking courage in a bottle and finding—nothing. He wasn't Hogue, ready sell out and fly. He was Slade.

He hit the horse and his hand was heavy and hard, and the horse went into a careening gallop, chewing up the sod while the air whipped Slade, the air and the horse's mane, and the sound was the keening of the wind, urging them on.

... Meanwhile, Big Thomas had watched from his ranch house. He, too, declared war.

CHAPTER 5

When Big Thomas was twelve years old, he had the habit of running away from home. This meant leaving the tiny ranch on the west slope of the valley and its sweet chest-deep grass, climbing over the peak and heading toward the sinking sun. Usually about eight or nine, when the evening air took on a nip and the moon failed to make its appearance and rain hissed from the heavy skies, Big Thomas—he was Bigelow then—scurried back over the peak and into the family barn, to fall asleep in the hay.

One night around ten, after such a brief adventure, Bigelow skirted the outer edge of his family's tiny holdings, on his way back to the barn. He carried a long rifle, unloaded, and a loaf of bread, half-eaten. It was to sustain him to California territory. Now he was going home.

He smelled the smoke before he fully understood what had happened, and though he crept closer to the shelter of the trees, he thought little of the smell until he burst into view of what had been his home. In two hours' time it had been reduced to ashes. Bigelow stood there, looking at it, still not appreciative of the extent of the tragedy. Then he stepped to what had been the door and with the barrel of his rifle, poked at the ashes until he found his parents.

All that was twenty-eight years ago. For twenty-eight years, Big Thomas had remained on the spot where his parents had burned to death, swearing that no one would ever run him off his land. He had become a big rancher—big in terms of the valley, which was not very big—and he had expanded his family's original holdings until he owned the whole west slope and the great sprawling meadow lands in the center of the valley. He was a relatively comfortable man now, with ten hands to run his cows and fence in his graze, fight off grass fires and winter snows. He had a thousand head of cattle and everybody within forty miles of the valley knew the Big T.

But Thomas was not as comfortable as he would have liked to have been. The Homestead Act had sent Mudge and Early to the north slope, a pair of squatters who pulled the wool over the government agent's eyes and got away with doing nothing to their land. Finally they had a couple of dozen cows and were able to expand their graze until they owned four hundred acres between them, plus water from the slope that sloshed into the graze and made the land all the way down as rich as bottom soil any place in the country.

Then Crispin arrived with his own money, to buy land, not beg it, and Thomas saw that an interloper had come onto his grass. Thomas was not afraid of interlopers—he had long outgrown fear—but he did not want them around.

Still, he was an honest man, or reasonably so, and there was little he could do. Once he thought he might buy Crispin out, but in 1876 the drought came in summer and the blizzard in winter, and by the time he had finished his winter count of cows, he was a man very near bankruptcy.

He had gone to Abbott then, not understanding the ways of banks, and before he knew it, he had all the ready money or credit he needed, and Abbott owned a mortgage on everything Thomas had built. Then Abbott told him about the railroad coming through and Thomas knew he could climb back to where he was and then far past—if he drove Crispin and Mudge and Early from the valley.

His men had been surprised when he told them what he wanted done—and one of them had quit him flat the day before Crispin was killed. But he wouldn't talk, Thomas knew. He had trailed the man himself, over that same western peak, into the same sinking sun, and when the rain came out of the leaden sky, he found the man in a copse of trees, sleeping in his heavy sack. Thomas shot him five times through the sack and carried the man to a cliff on the edge of the slope and hurled the man to hell—or wherever he was headed anyway.

That made killing Crispin easier. Once in, Thomas found the water fine.

But killing Crispin and keeping him killed were two different things.

Big Thomas watched the horseman ride toward the fence, then fall from his horse. He breathed easier then, but it had been a brief respite. For the man kept coming, on foot, and when he dropped into the crevice, Thomas didn't waste time wondering whether the man would or would not find Crispin's body.

At first Thomas thought it was a range detective, a man from a Cattleman's Association, but he felt such a man would have contacted Wilkinson and Wilkinson would have warned Thomas.

Then he accepted what had to be true: the man was a friend of Crispin's or Hogue's, looking into the disappearance of the rancher.

He said, from the window, even as the man climbed out of the crevice and looked straight at Thomas' ranch house, "Morgan. Morgan, come here." Then he realized he was inside the heavy stone house and nobody could hear him (as his parents must have called out twenty-eight years ago, unless the Indians had ripped out their tongues, Thomas never could tell). He strode outside and walked to the bunkhouse, a bronze man with sleek black hair and a heavy underslung jaw with a tight-shaved blue beard. He flowed when he walked, the skin drawn tight over rippling muscles and fine strong bones. He was not very big, but he gave off an aura of confidence and strength. Once, in that bad winter nearly two years back, he had wandered onto a crippled mountain panther coming out of the hills, cold and starving. The panther had jumped him, but its crippled leg, from an old bullet wound undoubtedly, failed it and the leap landed a yard in front of Thomas. Thomas picked up the beast—which weighed one hundred and forty pounds—and strangled it.

Now he walked, slapping his hand against his thigh, feeling the reassuring weight of holster and gun, and he called, "Morgan, goddammit man, Morgan," until a man came out of the bunkhouse, rubbing his eyes.

Thomas stared at the sleepy man and thought: this is what I'm taking myself to war with. He didn't like it, but he had no choice.

"Morgan," he said, "get Connors and Tasker and bring them to the house."

Morgan said, "Connors is riding line." He stopped and looked at Thomas and then he said, "All right, I'll get him."

Thomas said, "Of course you will," and he walked back to the house. Morgan was a big man, not very bright but that was good for what Thomas wanted done just now. The man who had dropped into the crevice looked big and he had moved with a slow care that had an obstinate quality about it. Well, Thomas thought, Morgan ought to be able to test the man for him.

Thomas knew he could not kill the new man on Crispin's land with Hogue and his woman looking on, not unless he expected to kill those two at the same time. But Thomas was still drawing lines; he hadn't killed that much that he could cold-bloodedly shoot down an inoffensive drunk and his woman. Especially if he could run this new man off with a little show of guns and muscle. Things still looked pretty good, Thomas thought. Crispin was out of the way. Mudge and Early were no problem. The new man was the poser now, but Thomas would have that looked into before the day was out.

He walked back to the house, sunk in thought and hope.

An hour later Morgan, Connors and Tasker piled through the door into the big gloomy living room of the Thomas house.

Morgan said, "All here, boss."

Thomas said drily, "Thanks, I can count," and Morgan flushed.

Connors and Tasker wore their guns very low and were very swift with them. Neither was a killer, though both had killed in fair fights, Connors having shot down a money-snitching saddle tramp who had been hired one day and tried to sneak off the same night with three money belts. Connors had called the man, who went for his gun. Connors got to his first.

Tasker was once mistaken by a young deputy for an Oklahoma desperado, and the deputy fired five times at Tasker who was sitting against a fence rail, sunning himself. The deputy had trailed Tasker a hundred miles all because Tasker limped on his right leg and looked a bit like the killer. The killer had broken out of jail a hundred miles from the valley, a bullet in his right knee. But the five shots had all gone awry, and Tasker slowly got to his feet, a stunned look on his face. He had taken a herd of cattle a hundred miles east and had ridden hard to get back. He was a tired and surprised man when the bullets started coming at him. Then he quite slowly removed his own gun while the deputy frantically reloaded, his face gone yellow with fear. Tasker fired once and walked away, vomiting.

Tasker said, now, to Thomas, "What do you want, boss?" He had been in on the killing of Crispin and he hadn't got sick that time, but he hadn't relished it.

Big Thomas said, "A man went down that crevice on Crispin's land." He paused and Morgan grinned, his teeth showing yellow and snaggly. "I know, boss," Morgan said. "A man sure did. Name of Crispin." He laughed out loud and the room smelled bad.

Big Thomas slapped his hand against his thigh. The sound was like a rifle going off. "Shut up, you hyena," he said. "I'll do the talking." He turned to the other two who stared soberly at their boss. "A man went down there *an hour ago*," he said, and the three of them let their hands crawl to their hips (which made Thomas feel a bit better), "and then rode back to Crispin's ranch."

"Who was the man?" Tasker said slowly. The whole thing was playing wrong, he thought. Killing never was the answer, he knew. Still, he was getting his pay.

Big Thomas shrugged. "A man. Big sort of man. Thick through here," he said, his hand sweeping his own shoulders. "A new man in the valley, I think."

The three were silent.

"I want you to see him," Big Thomas said. "Persuade him he ought to leave the valley. Ought to keep his mouth shut about anything he might have seen. Don't—" he said with sudden haste, "don't talk too goddam much," and he looked at Morgan, "about Crispin and his body. If the new man found the body, he'll know sure as hell what we're getting at. If he didn't, he'll still know we want him out of here. But don't hang yourselves. And me."

The three nodded. Morgan said, "You want I should—" He held up his fists.

Thomas said, "If you think it's wise. Size him up. If he's the running type, words may do it. If he's not, beat the hell out of him. Let Connors and Tasker cover you, though. I can't afford to lose any men."

"A fair fight, though," Morgan said stubbornly. He was a proud man, and stupid.

Thomas said, "Goddammit, yes. A fair fight. I want this man tested. But I don't want one of you killed. If he goes for his gun, shoot him down. He won't though." Thomas wasn't sure of this, but the man had moved so deliberately that he appeared to think out each act. Such a man might risk a beating, but not a bellyful of lead.

The three of them surged out and two minutes later Thomas saw them getting their horses from the pen. Morgan was rubbing his right fist into his palm, staring straight ahead, at Crispin's little ranch house off to the north.

Big Thomas went to a dented tin box on a wooden table in the room and took out some papers. He studied them carefully, trying to absorb the fiscal knowledge therein. He owed Abbott ten thousand dollars. His cattle would net him nearly that if he got them all through the summer healthy and fine for the trail to the railhead. He had ten men to pay wages to. He had four miles of fence in sagging disrepair. He had an alfalfa patch burned up by heat lightning and another one just starting to come up.

Against this, he had Abbott's word that the railroad would be coming through before the summer was over. There would be no delay then; the railroad people would buy him out and pay a pretty price. Abbott would see to that. Abbott, was the man who would appraise his property and turn the assessment over to the railroad. Then Thomas would get the money, lots of it.

But he'd lose his land.

He didn't like that part of it. Ever since the Apaches had burned down his old home and murdered his folks, he'd hung to that land like a leech on the side of a fat beef. Even when he was a kid, with nothing but charred wood to stir with his rifle barrel, he managed to stick, living out the summer in a tent, then in a lean-to, and finally in a little shack that the neighbors threw together for him. But most of it was his own work, hiring himself out to prod cows when he was twelve years old, sweep out bunkhouses, run errands. But he had hung on.

Now he'd have to get out.

But not out of the valley. He'd have Crispin's place by then, and Mudge's and Early's, though the latter two spreads didn't interest him. The soil was good but untended and it wouldn't last. The houses, barns, fences and corrals were rotten beyond repair, a piece of land that existed only because of the water on it.

And for that water, Big Thomas would take over the three spreads. Water and a railhead. He'd be able to chop the price on his beef until nobody in the nearby Territory could beat him. He'd grow then. This valley and the one to the northwest and maybe the huge sprawling protected winter graze a hundred miles to the west. All his. Provided Crispin's ranch changed hands.

He put the papers back in the box and flipped shut the lid. He wondered vaguely why Abbott was doing this: letting him in on a great fat deal where the money would roll like cartwheels into Big Thomas' hands. Then he thought: to hell with it. Abbott owns the bank and a piece of the railroad. He's got plenty to worry about without denying a piece of fortune to Big Thomas.

He walked quickly from the big living room, steeped in shadow, to the kitchen in the rear of the house. A woman was working back there, preparing a meal for eleven men, Thomas and his help. She was a young woman, black-haired and sullenly attractive.

Thomas said, "Maria." His voice was low, with an urgency to it.

She turned and smiled. The smile was mechanical, though she didn't want it to be. She couldn't help it. She had worked in the cathouse in Cowpoke for six months, smiling at the drunken cowmen who used her body, and she had hated it, until one night Thomas had come in, undrunk and gentle. A week later he had returned with a proposition. She would work for his ranch, cooking for the men and doing odd jobs. He would pay her, not as well as she was being paid in the cathouse, but as well as he could. He thought later he would be able to pay her quite well indeed. He would expect her—well, she understood, didn't she?

Maria might not have taken up with Thomas had she not just finished a trick with the sheriff, Wilkinson. Wilkinson was a little tomcat, fierce and ugly in bed, and more fierce afterwards. She held her hand to her cheek where the outline of Wilkinson's open palm still showed, and she said to Thomas, "Why not? I go with you."

That had been six months ago.

Thomas now looked at her, his mouth hungry, and he was angry with himself. He had a disciplined body, not given to sudden thrusts of lust such as this. He thought he knew why he had to have Maria just now. He would be lying in her arms at just about the time Morgan was testing the new man. He didn't want to think about it.

He said again, "Maria," more urgently, and his mind was saying damn that railroad, damn Abbott, damn the whole valley and Crispin's bold ways. And especially damn Crispin's body, under that rock.

Maria wiped her hands on her apron, removed the apron with a delicate demureness and walked to Thomas, her head cast down. She had long since removed the mechanical smile and a smaller, more real tremor played at her lips.

"Damn you too," Thomas muttered, and he swept her to his hungry angry arms.

CHAPTER 6

Hogue said, "You're not going to leave his body there, are you?"

Slade spread his hands. The hot fury had passed and left his body trembling and weak. "Why not?" he said. "He's on his own land, where he'd want to be. All we'd do would be to hurt his body."

May Hogue sat in the large easy chair, her face white and her lips thin. She looked older, her full near-forty years, yet Slade thought she was more attractive, far more attractive right this minute than he had ever seen her before. She had cried out once when Slade told them about Chet and the boulder and two or three minutes later she had said, "Oh, no," to the room, and started weeping softly. Now she was dry-eyed, pale and lovely, her beauty a ghostly glow in the room.

Hogue said, "It seems pretty cruel, letting him lie behind that rock."

"Oh, don't be a fool," May Hogue said. "You heard Slade. You can't move that rock without—without disturbing him."

Hogue was silent for a moment, looking through a window out toward the crevice, the burned fence, and Thomas' land. Then he said to Slade, "I suppose you'll be going now."

Slade shook his head. He still didn't know why he was staying on. It wasn't his fight, except somehow it was. "No," he said. "I think I'll stick around awhile."

"Where?" Hogue asked. His voice was sharper, and there was a glint in his eyes. "In this house?"

May Hogue said, "Oh, for God's sake, don't worry."

Slade felt the heat crawl to his cheeks. "You've got a filthy mind, Hogue."

He snickered. "Seems you both understood me pretty damn quick. I still want to know where you intend to stay."

"Well," Slade said, "if Chet's room is all right with you, I'll take that."

Hogue said, "Why wouldn't it be all right with me?"

Slade said, "Isn't it the best room in the place?"

May Hogue laughed then, a thin hollow laugh. "Chet gave us his room when we got married. Chet had been using Hogue's old room. It's no bargain." She got up. "I'll clean it up for you."

Hogue looked at her queerly. "That's right neighborly of you," he said. "I don't recall your cleaning my room when you came out."

She looked at him levelly and Slade thought: she actually hates the man. Then she walked out.

Slade said, "It's not my place to advise you, but I think you handle her wrong."

Hogue snarled then, his eyes black and little. "You do, huh? Just don't decide to give me any demonstrations."

Slade said, "You're a jealous fool. I don't take another man's woman. In case you're interested, I don't steal another man's horse, either, or his money. Also, I don't kick lame children."

Hogue said mildly, "I think you mean what you're saying, but I'll stick to what I said. Don't take a notion to May. And don't think it's going to be easy not to. If you think it is, you're the fool."

Slade said, "I think we'll all have plenty to do, keeping alive." He wanted to get away from this topic; it was bothering him more than he wanted to admit, and some of the annoyance stemmed from the way he felt about May Hogue. She was a lovely woman, sick of her husband, and she still was interested in Slade. That much he could see.

Hogue said, "There's no problem keeping alive if you just ride out of here. I'll sell this ranch in five minutes to Thomas."

Anger flared in Slade. "That's just it," he said. "Chet wouldn't have sold. You know it." Hogue was silent, staring through the window again. "You let Thomas kill him and you want to sell the ranch to the man who killed him."

"We don't know that," Hogue said. "We don't know Big Thomas did it."

"No," Slade said, "we don't. That's why I'm staying. I want to know. I want to know why Thomas wants this spread so bad that he might have killed for it."

Hogue said, "What do you propose to do?"

Slade felt a little better then. He didn't know that Hogue still wouldn't sell the ranch. He could if he wanted to, unless he didn't want to face May's scorn. But it looked now as if Hogue was going to let Slade do the leading.

He said, "Sit tight a bit. Let Thomas make his move. Hold out as long as we can."

Hogue said, "Go to it." He was staring through the window once more, his head craned forward. "You're going to get your chance. Right now." He got up and walked to a closet in the corner of the room. He opened the closet and pulled down a bottle of whisky. He opened the bottle and poured two inches into a water tumbler. He waved his hand to the window and said, "There it is, just as you asked for it. Big Thomas."

Slade walked to the window. Three horsemen were on the land, riding to the house. His hand went to his holster and the gun butt tingled against the heel of his palm. Then he took his hand away.

One of the men was big, husky—big and riding with a swagger that made him look even bigger. The other two men, flanking him to the rear, were smaller, neat-looking men, compact and quick, their heads moving in darting sweeps from side to side, casing the land in front of them.

Slade said, his face close to the window, "Is the first man Thomas?"

Hogue snorted. "Hell, no, Big Thomas doesn't ride for little game like us. That's Morgan. The other two—I don't know their names. But they're not Big Thomas. He's back in the ranch, laughing like hell."

"Bigelow, Bigelow, where are you, boy?"
He tried to answer but he couldn't. A mountain of ashes lay on him and he tried to push it away. He wanted to get to the woman's voice, but he couldn't. He pushed hard, hard as he could, and suddenly the ashes moved, and he was through, to the blinding, dizzying, trembling light.
"Now," he said. His eyes were wet with tears.

Slade stood outside the house. The men were fifty yards away now, silhouetted in the red ball of sun that fell behind Thomas' spread. He could see Morgan, the big one, hatless and huge, his lips pulled away from a sharp-toothed grin, one hand on the horse's neck, the other hanging lumpily at his side, the fingers opening and closing. The other two men were more difficult to make out, their low-crowned hats shading their faces, men of businesslike manner. One of them had a short right stirrup.

They pulled up then, and stared down at Slade. Morgan raised his right hand and rubbed the edge of his jaw with it. The other two were motionless in their saddles.

Slade decided to wait them out. It looked like trouble but he didn't know how much. He thought he would be safer, letting them play their cards to him. He hoped they weren't reading his hole card; he doubted it was bigger than a two or a trey.

Morgan said, then, "Who the hell are you?"

Slade felt like laughing. They had come to look him over almost as though they were scared of him.

"General Grant," Slade said. "Who are you?"

One of the men in the back said, "Funny boy. That's what you are. Funny boy." His mouth was hard and his hand close to his gun.

The other one, the one with the short stirrup, said, "Take it easy, Connors. Morgan will handle him."

Morgan said, "Yeah. I'll handle him all right." He got down from his horse and the other two fanned right and left, about twenty yards apart. Morgan took two steps toward Slade.

Slade said, "Why don't you two boys come on down and join him? I think he's going to need you." He was starting to enjoy himself. It had been a long time coming, he knew. The gambling loss to Johnson, the beating by Dilt, the killing of Crispin—all, in a way, aimed at him, aimed at pinching him in, aimed at throwing the fear of God in him until more than one time he had felt like pitching everything and running like hell.

Now matters were righting themselves. Somebody didn't want him around. Well, he'd sure make it tough as blazes before he'd be run out.

Morgan stopped and squinted at him. "You really think I need them two?" He jerked his hand behind him.

Slade said, "Wouldn't be a bit surprised," and he walked forward until he was an arm's length from Morgan. Then he hitched his right shoulder, as though he were readying a punch, and as Morgan bent away, Slade swung his left arm, hand open. The slap was a shocking sound, Morgan's head bobbing violently with the blow, his right cheek dead white for a long second, and then crimson and streaked.

Slade slipped his hands to his pistol belt and quickly unhitched the buckle and let the holster and .44 fall to the ground. He wasn't going to make the mistake he had made with Dilt; he wasn't going to fight all bogged down around the middle.

Morgan looked puzzled, his dull mind trying to read what had happened and make sense of it. The man had slapped him, once, an awful flaming shot, but that was all. He stood there, the new man did, hands at his sides, eyeing Morgan, and Morgan started to wonder.

Then he got the full message and he cried out, "By God, I'll—" leaping forward, cutting off his own words as he smashed out with his right fist at the new man's jaw.

But Slade wasn't there. He stepped back from the roundhouse blow and then threw himself forward, shoulder-first, crashing into Morgan's off-balance body, and the man went down.

Still Slade stood there. He was trying to humiliate the man, find out what he wanted, and whip him at the same time.

Morgan rolled on the ground, his hands covering his head, protection against the other man's boots. But nothing happened. He got up slowly, and half-turned to the men behind him.

"That's right," Slade said, "you need them, don't you. Bring them down. That ought to even the odds."

Morgan opened his mouth to bellow once more, and Slade drove his right fist straight at those snaggle teeth, horsey and yellow. He felt the skin of his knuckles rip but the impact was good, riding right to his shoulder and into his neck muscles. Morgan staggered back, his mouth broken and blood spilling from the corner of his lip. He was hurt now, and uncertain, but he was not a coward. He came at Slade, his mouth shut, throwing his right fist, but Slade was inside the blow, driving both hands to Morgan's middle. Morgan bent forward and Slade stepped away and to the side and aimed at the juncture of jaw and lower ear. He drilled the man with his right fist while Morgan hung bent in two, and then the big man pitched forward, his face all twisted, while queer noises sounded in his throat. Then he hit the ground, his buttocks sticking up in the air, and he lay that way, on face and knees.

Slade thought: that was too easy. I'm right where I was a minute ago.

He walked forward then, angry clear through, and he reached up at the man called Connors, the one who had called him funny boy. He grabbed the man's leg and started to jerk him from his horse. Then he stopped. Connors held a gun six inches from the top of Slade's head.

Slade said, "Put it away and I'll take you both at once."

The gun was firm.

Slade said, "All right, keep it. But let me get my own and we'll see. You two and me." He was white hot and not sure of what he was saying, but he didn't care. They weren't going to use their guns, he thought, and he knew he could push them more than this. "I'll even turn my back on you," he said, "the way you like."

The other man said, "Easy, Connors, don't mind him. He's blowing hard, but that's all. The boss won't like it if anything happens."

Slade stepped away then. He looked at the two men, now crowding close together, and he said, "All right, get the hell off this land."

The one whose name he didn't know said, "Who the hell are you to order us off?"

He was the shrewd one, Slade knew. "My name is Slade," he said. "Go back and tell Thomas my name is Slade. I'm a nobody here, but I'm staying a while. Now get the hell off."

Connors said, "You know what, Tasker? I think maybe the boss wouldn't mind if I put a round in him."

Tasker swore once and said, "You heard him." Then he turned to Slade. "I still want to know how come you're giving the orders. Where's Crispin? He owns this ranch, don't he?"

Slade grinned. "Sure he does. Tell that to Thomas, too. Tell him that Crispin still owns this ranch. Nobody else."

The two men looked at each other. They were hitting a blank wall. The one named Tasker took a deep breath and said, "I'm going to give you some advice, Slade. Pack your bedroll and get on your horse tonight. You'll live longer."

"No," Slade said, "I'm not getting on my horse tonight or any night. I'm staying."

Tasker said, "Suit yourself, Slade. Remember that I warned you." He patted his gun with his right hand, almost lovingly, but his face was drawn.

Slade said, "You know, I think you're going to get sick, friend. I don't want you to get sick on this land. You take that green face of yours out of here now or in a minute you'll be taking a little rest like horsey, here." He pointed to Morgan, stirring now, his aims pushing against the ground to raise his body.

Connors said, "Morgan, get the hell up."

Morgan climbed to his feet, swayed once, and then lunged at Slade.

Slade caught him in his arms and said, almost softly, to Connors, "Help him on his horse. If he starts in with me again, I swear I'll kill him."

Tasker said, getting from his horse and putting an arm under Morgan, "If you do, it will be the last man you ever do kill."

Then Slade said, "And who was the last man you ever killed, Tasker? Tell me."

Tasker was white now, limping on his bad leg, fighting the dizziness and nausea and he thought: I'll get Morgan on his horse. That's what I'll do. I won't listen or think. I'll just get Morgan on his horse.

Connors was down and helping and finally Slade pushed them off and picked up Morgan and threw him in the saddle.

"There," he said. "Now ride. And tell Thomas I'm still here. Send three other men next time. Or else tell him to come himself. I'm dying to meet him. Don't forget—the name is Slade."

The three men got on their horses.

Slade watched them ride off, watched them skirt the crevice and he thought Tasker looked down once, but he couldn't be sure. He couldn't be sure of anything, but he thought he was right. Thomas had killed Crispin, all right, Thomas or his men. Maybe he'd never really know, but that was the way it added. He'd have laid ten to one on it.

Thomas and his men, nobody else. But the big question still remained: why? Why had they been riding Crispin? Why had Thomas tried to shove Crispin out of the valley?

Slade shook his head. He doubted that he'd ever know. It was going to be war soon, and when it got to be war, questions like those remained unanswered. People just got too busy killing each other.

He turned around and walked back into the house.

And there was May Hogue, at a window, a rifle sticking through the opening, trained on the land in front of the house.

"What the hell," he breathed.

She stayed at the window a long moment and then withdrew the rifle. "I wasn't taking any chances," she said simply. "The first time I thought

Connors might use his gun, I'd have let him have it."

He strode forward and took the rifle from her hands. "Don't do anything like that again," he said. "I know what I'm doing."

"Do you?" she said. She was looking at him out of tired eyes, but Slade thought he saw something else riding in her glance.

"Yes," he said. And then, for no reason he knew just then, he said, "Where's Hogue?"

The something in her eyes got hot and she let a smile break through her white face. "In his room, getting drunk. It's habit now. First sign of trouble, off he goes, bottle in his hand."

Slade was silent. Hogue was getting drunk. May was standing here, offering herself. Sure as hell, that was what she was doing.

She said, "You didn't thank me."

"For what?"

She pointed to the window and looked down at the rifle, in Slade's hands. "For covering you."

His voice was harsh. "I told you it wasn't necessary. I know what I'm doing."

She leaned forward. "So do I," she said. She let her lips part and she looked up at him. She whispered, "Put the rifle away, Slade, you don't need it with me."

He thought: a month traveling, a month away from Lu. A month without a woman. He turned and walked the rifle to the far wall where two nails stuck out. He hung the rifle and sat down in a chair across the room from May Hogue.

He said, "Listen to me. I came up here because I was scared, a man on the run. I was dead broke, still am. I came here to lay up a while, get a little stake, maybe, and then take off. That's all I came for. Now all that is out. I've still got no money, and I won't have any, up here. I'm going to stick around a short time and then pull out, and try my luck elsewhere. That's all, though. Nothing else. Maybe I'll find out about Crispin, who did it and why. Maybe not. But when I'm ready to go, I'm going. Nothing's going to stop me."

She stood twenty feet away, pale and lovely, and she said, "Why don't you go right now?"

He said, "I told you why. I want to find out what happened to Chet. No other reason."

"Slade," she said. "I'm a woman. I don't think the way men do, the way you do. So maybe I'm all wet. But I think you're staying for another reason, and I'm going to give it a try, all the way. You understand what I mean?"

He nodded. "You're wrong, though," he said.

"I'm glad you said that," May said. "I want to be wrong. I want to keep your hands off me. I want to keep mine off you. I'm not going to be able to do it, though. And I don't think you are either." She held her gaze on him and then she lifted her head and walked to the door. She stopped and turned back. "I'll take you to your room," she said. Her voice was flat, colorless.

He got up and followed her, through a short dark corridor and to a closed door. She swung it open and stopped in the doorway.

"Chet's," she said.

He walked past, scarcely breathing when he went by. She had shaken him. He knew she was wrong, but she had shaken him. He was sticking because he saw a chance to do something decent, to get out of the way of the hounds for a while, to stop running. So far, he was holding up, and he was glad. He could have left earlier, in the bar, when he knew Crispin was missing. He should have left—the old Slade would have—when he found Chet's body.

He hadn't.

But now he wondered which was the greater pull, the desire to fight a decent fight, or the simple fact of May Hogue. Or the fact he had only one dollar in his belt—maybe that was it.

He looked at the room and May came in to stand by him. He said, "All right, May, I know where it is now. Thanks. I'll see you at supper—that is, if you're eating."

"Hell, yes," she said. She shuddered. "Imagine spending the rest of the day in there, with him."

Slade said, "Why did you marry him?"

"Why do you have to have money?" she asked.

He frowned. "To feel comfortable," he said.

"That's how a woman feels about marriage." She turned and walked out.

CHAPTER 7

Slade rode the knobby-boned brown stallion across the face of Crispin's land—Crispin's, he thought stubbornly, not Hogue's—his eyes sweeping the deep healthy vigor of the soil, the curious twisting water that rolled in a fork across the range. He edged the horse to the extreme eastern boundary of the land, where the fence announced the end of Crispin's domain.

The rest of the land on the north slope belonged to the former nesters, Mudge and Early, Ohio farmers who had come out with the Homestead

Act. Hogue had spoken of them with disdain and Slade knew that a man below Hogue's contempt was not much of a man at all.

He eyed the land across the fence, grubby land, despite the same water that twisted through it. A handful of cows slouched under a shade tree, munching thin brown grass. Then Slade saw the two men.

They rode like farmers, bouncing in their saddles, headed for the pass across the valley, leading to Cowpoke. Slade said, from across the fence, "Howdy," his eyes thin and curious.

They looked up in surprise, men so alike they might have been twins. "Howdy," one of them said, the taller one, Slade thought, and maybe a bit leaner, a bit more watery-eyed.

"My name is Slade," he said. "I'm a friend of Crispin's."

The watery-eyed one said, "I'm Bed Mudge. This here is Wilbur Early. We're neighbors of Crispin's. We own these spreads."

Slade nodded solemnly, still across the fence. They were dressed up a bit, he thought, their clothes sprucier than themselves. But their eyes shifted and their mouths were slack, and Slade knew they were beaten men. He had seen men like that in Cutter, across the gambling tables, weasel-men. It had almost been too easy, taking their money.

"Nice land," he said, in deference.

The shorter man smiled weakly. "Sure is," Early said. "Why, with new equipment and seed and alfalfa, we'll have two of the nicest spreads in the valley. That's why we're going in to see Abbott—"

"Shut up, Wilbur," Mudge said. "You talk too much."

Early flushed.

"Who's Abbott?" Slade asked.

"Town banker," Mudge said. "Come on, Wilbur." His mouth had firmed up a bit, and Slade knew he was the better man—or maybe just the less beggarly.

The two men trailed off, Slade's eyes following them. He rode, then, across the rest of Crispin's land, thinking: two ranchers, dressed like dudes, going in to see the town banker, a man named Abbott. They were going in for money, sure as shooting. They had the look of men who wanted—needed—money.

He reached his own hand to his money belt and slapped the pocket, waiting for the jingle to answer him. But there was no jingle, and he remembered. He had had two dollars when he hit Cowpoke. A few drinks in the saloon—where Wilkinson had kicked in Hogue's face—and he was down to one dollar. One dollar, all that was left. He thought of the man named Abbott. The town banker.

Slade rode through the dusty street until he came to the Cowpoke Bank and Trust Company. It was a strange experience, coming begging for money. He shrugged his shoulders and got down from his horse, looped the line to a post and went on in.

A nervous-fingered young man said, "Can I help you?" He wore a cotton jacket. On one lapel had been stitched the name *Loomis*. On the other, the word *Clerk*.

Slade said, "I want to see a man named Abbott."

The clerk's fingers went to his black string tie, playing with it uneasily. He said, "Well, can I help you? Mr. Abbott is quite busy. Is it a new account? I can take you to our teller—"

Slade grinned. That was good. He still looked like money. They thought he wanted to deposit some money. Fine, he thought. "No," he said. "I've got some private business with Mr. Abbott." He winked at Loomis as though to convey the import of the private business. The clerk nodded quickly and walked to the rear office, marked *Private*.

The silver-haired banker looked up with a tired curiosity at the new man. And suddenly he knew who he was: *Crispin's friend*. He was big and moving with a slow deliberateness, yet moving, and moving forward. A tiny chill went up Abbott's back, and then he quickly dispelled it. He said, distantly, "Sit down, friend. My name is Abbott."

Slade sat. "Slade," he said. He waited.

So did Abbott. This was more like it, he thought. The man had stopped moving. He seemed less formidable, sitting down. Abbott thought that Wilkinson was a fool, worrying about such a man. Slade could be handled.

Slade finally said, "I'm here to try to arrange for a loan." The words came out thin, slowly.

Abbott let a tiny smile play across his mouth. "Ah," he said. "A business loan?"

Slade flushed. "No," he said, "a personal loan."

Abbott let his head move from side to side, his mouth pursed. "You've got some security, of course? A piece of property? New machinery? Mortgages, deeds?"

Slade said, "No, I haven't. I haven't a blessed thing in the world." He said it fast this time, with a note of challenge to the words.

Abbott frowned. "I don't quite see how we can arrange a loan if you've got nothing to back it up. We're not in the habit of advancing money to strangers without some strong collateral."

Slade said, "I'm a friend of Chet Crispin's. He'll vouch for me."

Abbott's fingers clawed at his desk for a fleeting moment and then relaxed. But when he looked at Slade, Slade's eyes were riveted on those fingers. *Damn*, he thought, *now I'm letting Crispin bother me.*

"Well," he said, "that's better, of course. Send Crispin in any time and I'm sure we can arrange the papers."

Slade felt like exploding. The banker irritated him. He was so sure, so smoothly confident—yet he had jumped when Crispin's name came up. There was something funny here, Slade felt. "Crispin's away just now," he said easily. "I'll send Hogue in. He's Crispin's partner, you know."

"Hogue'll vouch for you?" Abbott said, his head cocked.

And Slade wondered. Would he? He doubted it. He said, "Why, yes, I think so."

"You're not sure?"

"I haven't asked him, that's all."

Abbott smiled his thin smile. "I'll tell you what, Mr. Slade. You go on back to Hogue's ranch—Hogue's and Crispin's, I mean—and ask him about it. If he'll back you up, have him run on down. Then we'll see."

"What do you mean: we'll see? If Hogue says yes, what's there to see? What's the kicker?"

Abbott said, "My dear man, bankers just don't operate like that. We don't rush our money out of here at the first little whim. You'll have to be investigated. So will Hogue. I don't even know how much you want— how much do you, by the way?"

Slade said, "Five hundred dollars."

Abbott shook his head again. It was all so easy he felt like laughing in the big man's face. He'd keep him guessing, the way he'd been keeping Mudge and Early guessing. But this man was even easier. He had nothing. He'd soon pack up and go. Poor Wilkinson, worried about such a man.

He said, "Well, that's a lot of money, you know."

Slade exploded. His hand crashed down on the table and the thunder rolled across the floor and shook the pictures on the far wall. "A lot of money," he said, his mouth curling and his eyes hot. "Five hundred dollars, a lot of money. Why, man, I'd bet that five hundred on the turn of a card." And instantly he knew he had defeated himself.

"You're a gambler, Mr. Slade?" Abbott said.

"I've gambled," he said.

Abbott shook his head, more crisply this time. "I'm afraid the Cowpoke Bank and Trust Company frowns on lending money to gamblers. Not the sort of risk we enjoy taking."

Slade leaned forward. "Do you carry an umbrella on sunny days, Mr. Abbott?"

Abbott frowned. "Why, no, I don't."

Now Slade shook his head. He clucked. "So you gamble too."

"How so?"

"You're betting it won't rain."

Abbott said, "That's just a touch of faith, Mr. Slade. I have some pretty strong faith in my judgment. And just now my judgment leans to not advancing you any money. Of course, if Hogue or Crispin comes around, I'll be delighted to make a second judgment."

Slade knew he had played it badly, and yet he felt it wouldn't have mattered. Abbott wasn't going to advance him any money no matter how well he had gone about asking. Slade got on his horse and plodded up the street, toward the other end of Cowpoke.

Ahead of him were two figures, jerking in their saddles. Mudge and Early, Slade knew. He spurred his horse to catch the men. Misery loves company, he thought. At least he'd have somebody to ride through the valley with.

He said, "Hey, Mudge, Early."

They whirled around and Slade was shocked at their faces. If they had looked like defeated men before, now they looked half-dead. Despair lay over them like a cloak. They waited for Slade to catch up, eyes blank and mouths loose, shoulders slumping forward like men about to pitch off a gallows.

Slade said, "Heat's pretty bad today."

Mudge said, "Hadn't noticed."

Early said, "Nothing's bad, except not having money."

Slade said casually, "Been in to see Abbott, too?"

Mudge nodded, eyes careful. "What do you mean too?"

"Abbott just turned me down on a loan."

Early cursed bitterly. "That makes three of us."

Slade said, "Ask too much security?"

"Hell, no," Mudge said. "That's just it. We've got land. Maybe it's not up to Big Thomas' spread, but it'll get by. We offered a big piece of it as security. Abbott didn't seem interested. Said he'd have to think it over. Told us to come back in a week or so."

Early said, spitting his words, "He's been telling us that all month now. Come back in a week. Come back in a week. And when we do, still no answer. Just—come back in a week. The man's playing with us, that's what I think."

Slade said, "Why would he do that? Bank stands to make money, making loans to sustaining spreads."

Mudge spread his hands. "That's what gets me. There's something else behind it. He just doesn't want to lend us money."

Slade said idly, "What will happen if he doesn't lend you? Can you get the money elsewhere?"

"We've tried," Mudge said bitterly. "Seems the whole valley knows Abbott won't approve us. Nobody will now."

Slade persisted. "And if you don't get some cash?"

Early turned to Slade. His face was narrow and mean. "What do you think, friend? It will drive us under."

Slade rode in silence then. But a thought was worrying his head, teasing at him. First, Thomas had tried to buy out Crispin. Now, Abbott wouldn't let Mudge and Early get a toehold. They'd have to go, if they didn't get some money. The whole north slope—Crispin, Mudge and Early—would be wiped out of the Sierra Verde. Only the Big T would remain in the valley. Big Thomas wanted Crispin out. Abbott apparently wanted Mudge and Early out. Thomas and Abbott. And a little sheriff playing ball with them.

The thought twisted to the same dead end: *why?* He shook his head and rolled on, toward Crispin's.

When the three men reached Early's spread, Slade stopped. He said, "Has Big Thomas ever tried to buy you out?"

Early laughed harshly. "What for? He's got more land than he can use. Why would he want mine?"

Slade said, "I don't know. Why would he want to buy Crispin's?"

Mudge said, "Crispin's land borders on Thomas'."

"So does yours."

Mudge shook his head. "Well, not as big a front as Crispin's. Besides, Crispin has a better piece of graze than we have."

"But," Slade said, "if Early's right—if Thomas has all the land he can use—why would he want more?"

Mudge said bleakly, "Some men just want more. That's all."

"I don't know," Early said, eyes searching the valley. "Big Thomas never seemed so anxious before. Always struck me as content to develop his own spread. Of course, ever since the drought—"

Slade said, "What about the drought?"

Mudge said, "We all took a terrible beating during the drought—and the blizzard that followed—two years back. Even Thomas."

"What's that got to do with his wanting Crispin's land?"

Mudge said, "Dunno, actually. It just seems to me—to Wilbur, too—that Thomas started looking over Crispin's land not much after the drought. Maybe he figured Crispin would sell cheap—maybe Crispin needed money after the drought." He shook his head. "I just don't know."

Early got down from his horse and bent to a thin sliver of running creek. He sluiced cold water over his face.

Slade stared at the water. "That's real good water you've got, isn't it?"

Early said, a touch of pride in his voice. "As good as any you'll find in the whole territory. Of course," he added, "that's not saying too much. New Mexico ain't exactly famous for the amount of its water. That's why it's taking so damn long to build this place up, you know. Not enough water power for industry, for railroads, for anything. Except right here." He let his hand trail in the crystal-clear water. He acted as though it were gold, panning through his hand.

Slade said, "If a man needed a watered graze, he wouldn't have to look much farther than this slope, would he?"

Mudge looked up at him curiously.

Slade looked back. "It seems to me that the one thing your three ranches have that's of prime value is your water."

"So?"

Slade didn't know. Thomas had water, too. Just as much, and all his. He shrugged again and said, "Nothing, I guess. Just trying to figure why people are so damned hot to knock you fellows off the north slope."

Early said, "Hell, all they have to do is offer me money for my spread, and I'll be off the slope with a day's notice."

"You would?" Slade said sharply.

Mudge said, "Me too. Why not? We break our backs on this land—and what for? For some smart-aleck banker to turn us down just when we're about to see pay dirt. Sure I'll move if somebody wants to buy me out. But I don't hear anybody asking."

Slade said, "I've got a hunch you will. Pretty damn soon."

Mudge said, "Sure. Somebody's going to come running up this hill with green bills choking his pockets. Just for us." He laughed loud and short, like a dog barking.

Slade said, "Do me a favor, will you? Just in case I'm not crazy, when he does come running up the hill, will you let me know before you say yes?"

Mudge eyed Slade closely. "All right," he said finally. "I figure if it happens, I'll owe you something for that crystal ball of yours."

"Thanks," Slade said. He turned off then and rode away from the two men. Then he wondered bitterly how Mudge would be able to let him know about any future offer. With a dollar in his pocket, Slade didn't see how he could stick it at Crispin's more than another day or two.

CHAPTER 8

Abbott was thinking more or less the same thing. But Abbott was not a man to let circumstances take their course. Slade probably would move on soon, he reflected. Probably. Not positively. Abbott wanted to be positive.

He got up slowly at the end of the bank's day and walked to Wilkinson's office. The sheriff was not in. Abbott let himself into the big easy chair and opened the lower drawer of Wilkinson's huge mahogany desk. Abbott grinned at the desk. Everything Wilkinson had was huge. His badge was outsize, battered into shape by the town blacksmith. It had cost Wilkinson ten dollars. The official star lay in some forgotten corner of the office, gathering dust. Abbott smiled again. The desk in front of him was bigger than his own, back at the bank.

Abbott pulled a bottle of brandy from the drawer and poured a drink into a glass tumbler on Wilkinson's desk. Then he started to think of how best to drive Slade from the valley. The best way, to Abbott, meant the smoothest way, the way of the least repercussions.

He thought he had it figured when a horse clopped to a halt in front of the office. Big Thomas walked in. His mouth was thin and though color dotted his bronze cheeks, Abbott thought the man looked drawn. Good, he thought. The more worried Thomas was, the easier it would be to break him.

Thomas grunted as he sat in a large leather chair. "Well," he said, "two-thirds of us ought to be a quorum. I want some action, Abbott."

Abbott said, "Action on what?"

"On this man Slade."

Abbott felt the little chill run up his back again. Slade. Slade was getting to be like Crispin. Everyone was interested in Slade. "What's he done?"

"Beat the hell out of Morgan. Scared the wits out of Connors and Tasker. That's what he's done."

Abbott said, "Took on the three of them?" He sat upright and sipped quickly from the brandy.

Thomas nodded, grim-faced. "The man knows Crispin's dead and he thinks I—or my men—did it." He swore once, foully. "The lucky bastard stumbled over the crevice we tossed Crispin into."

"Saw the body?"

Thomas shrugged. "Who knows? I'm not going to ask him."

"But you think so?"

"Hell, yes, I think so."

Abbott felt the first alarm race through him. He had expected Slade to report finding Crispin's body to the law. Now he felt certain Slade hadn't done so. He was guessing wrong on Slade.

"I think," Abbott said, "we'll have to do something about Slade. He's starting to bother me."

From the office entrance, a deep voice boomed. "Good," Wilkinson said. "I told you so. The man's dangerous."

Abbott said mildly, "Shut up, Wilkinson. Come on in and shut up. I swear, one day I'll cut out your vocal cords."

Wilkinson said, "Sure. Just because I was right and you were wrong."

Abbott said, "I don't pretend to be infallible, you know."

Big Thomas stared at the banker. "You don't? That's funny. I always thought you did."

Abbott said, "Nonsense. But, being fallible, we all have to exert ourselves more. We all have to be extra careful. Not that there's anything really to worry about. We have our man—Slade—right here. We want him out of here. We have many choices. We either persuade him to leave or force him to leave—or ..."

"Or kill him," Wilkinson said eagerly. He was glad Abbott was talking this way now. Things would move smoothly.

"Or kill him," Abbott agreed. "But remember: our main problem is to get Crispin's ranch. Then Mudge's and Early's. I spoke to Mudge and Early today. They're so shaky they'll sell at the first opportunity."

Big Thomas said, "All right. Let's give them the opportunity. Let's get Crispin's ranch."

Abbott said, "Agreed. Now we're all thinking alike. We're a team again."

Wilkinson said, "Why don't we just buy out Hogue?"

Abbott said, "You do want Mrs. Hogue, don't you, sheriff? Suppose Hogue has a wad of money. Do you think his wife will leave him then?"

Wilkinson shivered. "No," he said softly. He had to have May Hogue. Nothing must jeopardize that.

Big Thomas said, "But that's the whole crux. Eventually we'll have to buy out Hogue."

"Ah," Abbott said, "eventually. But not until Slade is gone. With Slade around, I have a feeling Hogue will develop a little courage. With Slade suddenly gone, Hogue will sell out—and sell out cheap. Too cheap—" Abbott said, turning to Wilkinson—"to keep a woman like May Hogue very content."

Big Thomas frowned. There was something too deliberate, too careful about the plot. He, Big Thomas, was the one most likely to suffer if time droned on. The railroad would soon come on through. The cat would be out of the bag. Nobody—not even Hogue—would sell cheap then.

He said, "But, man, we can't wait too long."

"Precisely," Abbott said. "So we move on Slade. Pronto."

Big Thomas said, "How?"

Abbott leaned back and propped his chin with long carefully manicured fingers. "Slade was in to see me today," he said. "He wants money. The man's dead broke. I turned him down. It strikes me that a man like that has to have money. He used to be a gambler, you know."

Wilkinson said, "No, I didn't know."

Abbott nodded. "More or less told me."

Big Thomas didn't like it. He was a betting man himself. This whole play for the north slope was a huge gamble. Gamblers did not act according to a narrow prescribed rule of behavior. Gamblers sometimes flung their naked weight on you, without warning, without reason.

Abbott continued, "So if he's dead broke—as I'm sure he is—there are laws to deal with him. And right here, we've got the dandiest little law-dealer west of the Big Muddy. Eh, sheriff?"

Wilkinson licked his dry lips. "Laws?" He did not like the thought of tangling again with Slade. He still recalled the way Slade had lolled his head on his shoulders, shaking the sheriff's body under huge hands.

Abbott said drily, "Yes, Wilkinson, laws. The things you're supposed to be enforcing. Well, now you've got one to enforce. Vagrancy. A man will not be tolerated in this territory with no money on his person."

Thomas laughed hollowly. "Hell, that's rich. Half the 'punchers in New Mexico would be run out under that law."

Abbott shrugged. "We're not interested in half the 'punchers. We're interested in one man. Slade." He leaned forward. "Write out a warrant, sheriff. Ask Slade to prove he's a man of means. If he can't, slap the warrant on him and chuck him in jail—or on the first stage out of Cowpoke tonight. And tell him if he comes back, there'll be a nice long rest for him—in the Cowpoke pokey."

Wilkinson shivered. In his mind's eye he was starting to warm to the issue. He pictured himself facing Slade, staring the man down, ordering him to a coach, even picking up the big man and flipping him onto the stage, and then lashing the sweating horses, driving them down the road and into an empty blackness.

"Yes," he said. "I'll do it. By God, I'll do it." He licked his lips again.

Big Thomas cracked the dream into a million bitter pieces. He said, "And if he opens his money belt and shows Wilkinson a wad big enough to choke a horse? What then, Abbott?"

Abbott sighed. "He won't. And if he does, we'll face up to it. We'll have to throw some more weight at him. Not just that bag of manure, Morgan, but somebody more skilled at these sort of things. Slade absolutely must go."

Thomas nodded. "Damn right, he must."

Wilkinson from the fringe of the group nodded also. "Damn right," he whispered. He was trying to piece together his fantasy. "Damn right," he whispered again. "I'll drive him out, that's for shooting sure."

Abbott said, "You're not just trying to blow some courage into yourself, are you, Wilkinson?"

The sheriff raged inside. Once more, the red thought leaped to his brain: he'd kill Abbott someday. Fury dulled his mind and clogged his tongue.

"Because," Abbott went on, "if you really need courage, if you need good reason to chase Slade out of this county, think of this: he's a big man, Wilkinson, big and strong and with a certain animal attractiveness. May Hogue is a woman hungering for a man, not a piddling creature like her husband. Slade and May Hogue are going to be bumping into each other in that ranch house, and I swear when they do, you'll hear lightning and thunder."

Wilkinson stared at Abbott. The man was a mesmerist. Wilkinson pictured May Hogue, long-legged and deep-chested, walking a dark corridor at the Crispin ranch house, her husband asleep in his bed, and Slade prowling the area like some soft-padded beast. He saw them clashing, their bodies bruising each other.

Wilkinson's hand opened and shut spasmodically. He groped for a blank warrant sheet. With shaking fingers wrapped around a slender bending pen, he wrote rapidly, furiously, stabbing the paper as silent oaths tore him apart.

With the warrant in his pocket and evening falling darkly over Cowpoke, Wilkinson took his taut body to the saloon where a respectful place was made for him at the bar. When he had drunk seven shots of brandy, he lurched from the saloon onto the black street. Five minutes later he stood before a clapboard building a quarter of a mile from the main drag, a modest little house with a pale yellow light in the window.

He pounded on the door and a slender gray-haired woman in simple rough cotton led Wilkinson into a dim foyer. The muted sounds of laughter and liquor being sloshed into glasses wafted through to Wilkinson.

"Well, sheriff," the madam asked.

"I want Maria," Wilkinson said thickly.

The woman frowned. "Come now, sheriff. Maria hasn't been with us for months. You know that. She's up at Big Thomas'."

Wilkinson remembered vaguely. He liked Maria. He liked her dark hair and pale skin and the way she cringed when he hit her. He said, "Who then?"

The woman shook her head. "Nobody tonight, sheriff. Why don't you go on home and when you're feeling a bit better, then come on over for a pleasant evening? But not tonight, sheriff."

He shoved her aside and walked into the big sitting room. Two 'punchers were sitting on a sofa, heavy-set girls on their laps. Drinks were on a table in front of them. Wilkinson sneered. He said, "What'll it be, boys? Five days in the pokey or a nice quiet polite little goodnight to the ladies here?" His voice, though laced through with brandy, was deep and booming, and the 'punchers stared with foolish eyes at the little man who represented the law.

One of the 'punchers said, "What's the matter, Wilkinson, we stealing your special little playmate?"

Wilkinson let his eyes narrow. "How'd you like a gun barrel down your throat, McCoy?"

The cowpuncher flushed. "You talk damn tough, sheriff. Take off that badge and you wouldn't walk so loud."

Wilkinson smiled thinly. He walked over to McCoy. He took his badge between his fingers and swiftly unpinned it. "There," he said, "it's off. Now get up."

The 'puncher, bewildered by the sheriff, got up slowly. He was halfway to his feet when Wilkinson leaped forward, the two-inch pin of the badge driving into McCoy's groin.

McCoy screamed and collapsed on the sofa, his body writhing in agony.

Wilkinson said clearly, the alcohol suddenly drained from his brain, "All right, Weltzen, get your friend out of here." He smiled then at the girl who had been sitting in McCoy's lap, a fading blonde with baby-bright blue eyes. "You won't miss him, honey," he said. "I don't think he'll be much good with the ladies for a while."

The two cowmen stumbled out. Wilkinson led the blonde to an upstairs room, and even when he shut the door he could still hear McCoy's jumbled moanings, trailing off down the road. The sound was pleasant in Wilkinson's ears and he started to walk toward the blonde, a soft smile on his mouth, his hands closing into tiny hard fists....

Meanwhile, Big Thomas, riding slowly, was reaching his land. He and Abbott had talked long and in the fretful circles people talk while time is being marked. Yet Thomas realized, with mild irritation, Abbott did not seem to mind the way complications were attaching themselves like bloodflies to a branded calf.

Thomas laughed bitterly into the night. Why should Abbott mind? What did he have to lose? A bit of decorum, perhaps, a disturbance to his personal ease. But not a damn other thing.

Thomas pushed wearily into his darkened house. He wondered how he would handle Slade if Wilkinson didn't run the big man off Crispin's land. He had confidence in his own strength, in his neat disciplined body. Yet Slade was raw power, clumsy perhaps, a bit uncertain the way strangers have to be uncertain when they're on somebody else's land, every hole and draw and crevice a hostile place, but still a man crudely strong.

Thomas thought it would come down to a simple test: himself or Slade. If Morgan had been unable to do it, the others wouldn't, either. He and Slade, that was the way it would finally play. He *or* Slade, his dogged mind insisted.

He went to bed and dreamed—again—of a house in charred ruin, and a twelve-year-old boy searching out whitened bones in all the tiny mountain of ashes.

Abbott walked crisply to his hotel suite, nodding an affable good-night to the sleepy clerk on duty. He had some ledgers in his sitting room to work over, and while he worked, a recess of his mind allowed itself to fill with the wandering thought of power. He would soon own the west slope. Thomas was starting to fray at the edges. A little more time and Abbott would be able to let out the news of the railroad coming through. He thought of Thomas driven wild by the news. Big Thomas, shrinking to the size of bankruptcy. He worked on, a tiny smile at the corners of his thin hard mouth....

May Hogue lay next to her husband, trying to shut out the rhythmic noise of his clogged nostrils. A faint smell of whisky hung over the wide high bed. Twice she started to get out of bed, to go to the kitchen. Each time she had decided against it. She must not appear too eager. She had told Slade her intention; now she would let her words play on his nerves. He wanted her. She knew it. She put the back of her hand to her mouth. Dear Jesus, she thought, he *had* to want her. He just had to. She wanted to get out of bed and look down at his body. That was all. Just look down at it.

Instead she turned away from her husband and closed her eyes. She tried to sleep....

Slade lay on his back, eyes unseeing, wide open. Water, he thought. The only thing those three ranches have in common is water. Somebody wants that water. But why, *why?* The question remained unanswered, no matter how often he asked it, and he asked it again and again, till the minutes ticked by, and then the hours, and dawn started to break up the silent sky.

Water. Water. *Why?*

He had to know soon. He had to. One single dollar lay in his money belt, strapped to his sweaty waist. Enough to buy him a chip in a gambling house in some town a few miles outside the valley. One chip. That was all he needed. He had the feeling, returning to him like his own blood pouring back into his heart: his luck was changing again.

But he didn't want to go. Not until he knew.

Why?

In the valley, cattle lowed into the coming light. They nuzzled each other and bent their great heads and huge white eyes to the good green grass that lay before their chomping mouths. No thought worried them. A new day was breaking before them. A day of fine sun and water and clean blades of sweet juice between their jaws.

Their lowing was a peaceful murmur all across the Sierra Verde valley.

To them, the valley was a good place.

CHAPTER 9

At breakfast, Hogue said to Slade, "You wore a gun into here. How come you're not wearing it anymore?"

Slade said, "What for? I don't need it."

Hogue breathed, "Well, what a brave fellow you are. Or maybe a damn fool."

Slade said, "What's eating you, Hogue?"

"Nothing," Hogue grunted. He returned to his plate. May Hogue watched the two men in silence.

Slade said, "I'm not a miracle-maker, Hogue. I can't just strap on my gun and frighten Big Thomas out of existing."

Hogue forced out a laugh. "And you wouldn't try, even If you thought you might."

Slade felt anger roll inside. Hogue was baiting him. Trying to force him into a showdown. It didn't make sense. Hogue must have known Slade couldn't take on the whole valley. Certainly not yet. Not the way everything was stacked.

He said, "Crispin's dead already. Why do you want me dead, too?"

Hogue put his hands in his lap. Slade could hear them rubbing together, the dry skin faintly brushing. "I don't want you dead," Hogue said shortly. "I just want—I want something to happen, goddammit. This place is getting me down."

May Hogue said, "Nobody likes the situation. It's tough on all of us. But until we know the way they intend to move, there's nothing we can do."

Slade stared at her. She was like a man in moments as these. He wondered whether she wasn't getting some enjoyment, some strange thrill out of the simmering violence that encased them. He drank his coffee in silence. He hoped Hogue and May didn't know how worried he was. The place was getting him down, too. It wasn't fair that some men could make war and others had to receive it.

He put down his cup. "Why do you think Mudge and Early can't get a loan out of Abbott?"

Hogue said, "Couple of tramp farmers, that's why."

Slade said, "The government thinks they're more than that."

May Hogue snorted. "The government! Why, that pack of lazy critters never even sent a man down to investigate the land. Just took Mudge's and Early's word for it."

Slade said, "Still, with a little help, they'd have a couple of fairly nice spreads up here. And Abbott wouldn't have anything to lose. Mudge and Early say they offered a big hunk of their land as security. If they failed to meet their loan, Abbott would have lien to the spreads."

May Hogue was silent, her eyes thoughtful. Finally she said, "You think there's some connection between Thomas trying to buy out Chet—and then killing him—and Abbott not lending money to Mudge and Early?"

"I think so, yes."

"But what sort of connection?"

Slade said tentatively, "I don't know. Something to do with Thomas' land not being as good as we all think it is. Maybe something to do with his water. Water's the only thing common up here. Maybe Thomas wants—needs—the north slope water."

May Hogue said, "Abbott and Big Thomas are together a lot, you know. They meet in Wilkinson's office in the evenings. I've seen them down there a half-dozen times."

Slade said slowly, feeling his way, "Suppose they wanted to drive everybody off the north slope so that they could take it over. Would that make sense?"

Hogue said, "Only if you're right about Thomas' land not being as good as we think. If there's something wrong with his spread, then he might want this north slope."

Slade felt a tremor in his belly. "Suppose—suppose Thomas' water had been tampered with, suppose it was bad, diseased somehow. He'd have to have these three places, wouldn't he? Or else quit the valley?"

Hogue laughed harshly, "Forget it. His water's as good, if not better, than anybody's up here."

Slade persisted. "You sure? How do you know?"

"I don't see his cows dying off on him. Nor his men either. That's their only water, that river up there. They drink out of it every day."

"Well," Slade said, still fighting his way through a maze of uncertainty, "maybe the source is endangered somehow."

May Hogue said gently, "Forget it, Slade. You're wasting time, guessing this way. Let's face facts. They want these places. We don't want to give in. Maybe we'll have to fight them for it. Isn't that enough to worry about without wandering off in another direction, down some blind curve in the trail?"

Hogue said, "As a matter of fact, here comes little worry-boy himself."

Slade looked out through the kitchen window. Wilkinson was riding slowly, his shoulders swaying in the slightest swagger, toward the ranch house.

Slade patted his waist. Hogue looked at him curiously. "How about it, Slade," he said, "let's get that gun strapped on?"

Slade shrugged. He removed the money belt and laid it on the kitchen table. He walked to his room and put on his holster, his right hand easing the barrel of the .44 back and forth in its leather sheath. Then he walked out of the house.

Wilkinson stared from his horse at the big man. May Hogue walked outside and stood near the doorway, watching. Wilkinson could feel her eyes on him. His mind cooled. A granite-hardness touched his eyes, turning them gray once more.

He said, "Slade, I told you once before to get out of the valley. You didn't listen to me. Now I'm telling you again. Get on your horse and ride on out of here."

Slade said softly, "Go to hell, sheriff."

Wilkinson dropped lightly to the ground. He reached into his back pocket and Slade's hand strayed to his gun butt. Wilkinson laughed nastily, his eyes bright. "Don't be a fool, Slade. When I want to kill you, I'll let you know. Right now I just want you to see something." He pulled out the warrant and handed it to Slade.

Slade read it swiftly, anger boiling inside him. He said carefully, "How do you interpret vagrancy, sheriff?"

Wilkinson chuckled. "I knew you'd ask that. I spent an hour this morning reading the law. It's a simple little law we've got in the territory. A man has to have fifty dollars on his person or on his personal belongings, or else can prove he's been gainfully employed in the territory for at least the past thirty days." He waited, the chuckle frozen in his throat.

Slade thought: what an odd way to end it all. Run out of town because he didn't have fifty dollars. He said, "My belongings are worth easily double that. Saddle, gun, holster, clothes."

Wilkinson shook his head. "That won't do, Slade. The law says money, not barter. Let's see your money belt."

May Hogue said, "I'll get it for you, sheriff." She slipped into the house, a strange expression lurking in her eyes and teasing her mouth.

In a few seconds she was back. "Here," she said, handing the money belt to Slade. For a wild moment he thought: she's put some money in. His fingers trembled as he opened the clasp. Then he reached in and pulled out—the same single dollar.

Wilkinson said, "One dollar. Is that all?"

Slade nodded mutely.

"Just a cheap tramp."

Slade said, "Your insults don't come with that warrant."

Wilkinson flushed. "Get on your horse, Slade."

Slade said mildly, "Suppose I don't want to?"

Wilkinson went hot. The picture flashed before him—throwing the big man onto the stage like so much baled hay. His lips thinned and turned white. "I said get on your horse, Slade."

Slade weighed his chances. He could drag the sheriff into range of his right fist, smash him to the ground. But where would he be?

Then May Hogue said from behind him, "Just a minute, Slade."

He turned around.

She said, "Here." She reached a hand into the bodice of her dress and removed some bills. She stood there, waiting for Slade to come to her for the money. The same bright look, hard and dazzlingly clear, lurked in her eyes.

Slade knew what it meant. She was buying him, or trying to. He looked at Hogue, standing in the shadow of the house. The man's face was worried, gray.

Wilkinson said, "Hold on. I won't stand for it." He couldn't bear looking at May Hogue, the way her eyes had lit up, the wet smear to her mouth as Slade walked slowly, step by step, toward the hand still close to her bosom, a bosom that rose and fell, gently, rhythmically. He said again, "I won't stand for it, I say." His voice bellowed out, but Slade kept right on walking, and Wilkinson knew Abbott had been right. May Hogue and Slade. The sheriff felt a wall growing around him, a wall of human beings, big men, all of them. Abbott, he had to be cut down. Slade, he had to be cut down. Hogue, too, no doubt. Wilkinson felt himself stifling, behind the wall.

Slade took the bills from May Hogue's fingers, his eyes six inches from hers. He saw the yellow flecks rimming the black pupils and he smelled the fine warm smell easing out of her body, reaching to him, urging him. He said, "Thank you, May. I'll try to pay you back as soon as I can."

Wilkinson said hoarsely, "I'll get you yet, Slade. Don't worry about that. You won't get away with this." His horse was rolling under him now, worried by the fierce tension that cut through the air.

Slade said, "I'll be here, waiting for you, Wilkinson."

Hogue said sullenly, trying to rebuild his own role on his own land, "Get off my spread, sheriff. You've completed your business."

Slade said, "No, wait a minute, sheriff. I want to ask you a question."

Wilkinson's eyes raced from Hogue to Slade. Suddenly he was a man under fire, and fear clamped its old hold on him. The picture of himself tossing Slade onto the stagecoach dissolved; now it was a little boy backed into a corner by the two school bullies, and their fists lashed him while he cried.

He said, "What do you want, Slade?"

Slade said casually, "Why does Big Thomas want this land?"

Wilkinson looked from Slade to May Hogue. He said with scorn, "Some people just want things, that's all. They can't help themselves."

Slade shook his head. "No, that won't do. He's never been terribly interested before." Then he plunged. "What's wrong with Thomas' land, Wilkinson? What's happening to it?"

The sheriff's eyes bulged. His mouth twitched and then steadied, but the color had washed dead away. He said, "Nothing—nothing's wrong. What—why do you think anything's wrong?"

Slade waved a hand. "No reason. Forget it." He had his answer in Wilkinson's startlement. Something *was* wrong.

Now Hogue spoke up again. "Come on, Wilkinson. Get the hell off my land."

The sheriff whirled the little brown mare angrily and slashed its rump with a short crop. The horse bolted once, then steadied down and flattened out, racing for the distant pass back to Cowpoke.

That evening Hogue said, "You're still wearing your gun, Slade."

Slade touched his middle. "So I am," he said.

"You think there's going to be trouble?"

He grunted a short laugh. "Hell, yes. Don't you?"

"I mean—soon?"

He shrugged. "Who knows?"

May Hogue said, "Thomas knows."

Slade felt the bitterness in his throat. The Thomases always knew where and when the trouble would break out.

She went on, "It seems to me, though, Thomas must not be so sure of himself."

Slade said, "Why so?"

"He'd have done his job by now. He's got the men, the guns. There must be something holding him back. I wouldn't be surprised if he wouldn't take a couple of lickings, delaying things the way he is."

Slade eyed her closely. He felt the weight of his holster and the bogged-down end where the gun hung. Now he knew why he hadn't taken off the gun. He didn't think Thomas was going to erupt on this day. But ever since they had thwarted Wilkinson, and the sheriff had revealed himself over Thomas' land, Slade had felt for the first time that they—he and May and Hogue—were on the offensive. Maybe he ought to keep it that way for as long as he could. He said, "May, get me an empty canteen and cover from the kitchen, will you?"

She looked dubious. "All right," she said. She walked slowly inside.

Hogue said, "What the hell do you want an extra canteen for?" Irritation rode his voice.

Slade snapped, "I'm a thirsty man. That's why. I feel like drinking two canteens-full. Christ, man, stop asking so damn many questions. I know what I'm doing."

"Do you?" Hogue said mildly.

Slade hunched his shoulders and let them drop. He grinned, angry at his little outburst. "I don't really know. This is just a whim, I guess. I'm thinking of taking a little ride tonight."

Hogue's eyes lit up. "Where to?"

Slade waved his hand toward Thomas' holdings. "Haven't had much chance to look the place over."

From inside May called out. "Slade, come in here. Pick out the canteen you want. Some of them are pretty rusted around the mouth."

He went inside the house.

May Hogue said in a fierce whisper, "Don't be a damn fool. He's been baiting you all day to get hurt."

He was silent. It was true. Hogue had practically challenged Slade into wearing the gun. Now Hogue's eagerness was obvious once Slade had announced his intention of riding over Thomas' graze.

But so had May been pushing him. They each had their own reason, Slade thought. Hogue wouldn't have minded Slade dead, and the ranch sold. May thought Slade might be able to swing the war their way, to fight off Thomas and help them keep the land. And maybe she had another reason, Slade thought. Maybe she just wanted him riding and smashing; she seemed a woman stirred by the primitive. Such women disgusted Slade; they also excited him.

He said, "It's my own idea. I'm still curious about what's wrong with Thomas' land. I'm going to look at his water."

She said bitterly, "Don't get drowned over it."

He took the canteen and went outside. Hogue watched him sullenly until Slade had walked to the corral and saddled up the knobby-boned brown stallion. Then Slade said, "In case I don't come back, Hogue, try to hold off selling. For Chet's sake." He heard Hogue snarl a response, but Slade didn't push it. The man hung to the ranch by a thread. Heat could burn him loose. Slade whirled the horse and loped off, his fingers straying to the butt end of his .44.

He waited at the west edge of the ranch until darkness closed down. Meanwhile, he had eyed the flow of water as it spilled through the twilight, its phosphorescence revealing its source. The water came from two flattened hills to the west, big-bellied creeks running down to join in a wide rushing river that coursed through the highlands of the west slope and then dropped in a dozen directions through the center meadowlands.

Slade's target was the wide juncture of the two creeks. All he wanted to do was scoop out a canteen-full of water, high up near the source. He was sure there was something wrong with it.

His eyes had slowly searched out the whole distance, from the fork of water to the fence between Thomas' and Chet's spreads. It would be tough, edging across the valley and up the slope without being seen or heard. But he had to chance it.

He gently prodded the horse with his heels. They came flush to the fence before Slade stopped the horse. Then he got down, removed a pair of wire cutters from his saddlebag, wrapped rags around the section of wire he had to cut and around the cutters, and quickly and silently ripped away enough fence to push on through. He put the cutters back in the bag, made sure the canteen was in the bag, and started pushing across Thomas' Big T.

Tasker reached down and rubbed his right thigh. The leg throbbed at night and he resented riding guard at the upper end of the valley. Still, Thomas didn't make him ride up there too often. Tonight was one of the few nights.

He rambled his horse toward the dark reaches of the western hills that looked down on the valley. Farther west was a big black peak, with the best view of what was going on below. Tasker knew he should have ridden to the peak and up, but the pain in his leg was jolting him now. Going up that peak and then jouncing down would start the aching something awful. He stayed at the flattened hills, near the creeks. The sound of rushing water filled his ears. It was a good sound, a friendly sound. Later, when his leg would really begin to ache, he'd get down and sit next to the water. Maybe have a drink. He carried a canteen in his saddlebag, but it wasn't cold or fresh like the rushing water above and to the west of him.

There was another reason, vague, unformed, why Tasker resented riding guard and particularly why he didn't want to venture to the black peak up ahead. Ever since he and Connors and Morgan had ridden over to Crispin's ranch and met Slade, he'd had a nagging inside that things weren't going to work out right. This business of range war was not for him. Tasker didn't like killing. He especially didn't like the idea that maybe he'd be one of those killed. Slade had planted the idea.

He pushed closer to the water. His leg was reaching that point where the throb became a pain. He let his hand stray from his gun butt to his thigh and back again to his gun. Pain and killing, they were associated in Tasker's mind, ever since that Oklahoma deputy had fired five shots at him while he sat against the fence, easing the ache in his leg. Then he had killed the deputy.

He got down from his horse and emptied his canteen in the water. Then he bent to the ground and drank the clean sweet ice-cold water. His teeth ached but it was a good pain. He filled his belly and lay there a long moment. Then he pushed his canteen into the stream and listened until the air bubbles stopped sounding. He recapped it and got back on his horse.

Then he heard the alien sound.

He was too close to the water to identify the sound precisely, and he was suddenly too frightened to move away from the water so that he could make it out more clearly. And so he froze while the sound came closer, and Tasker's hand edged to the gun butt and gripped it with chilled stiff fingers.

Slade had seen the rider, off and on, for the past thirty minutes, edging his way along the skyline, his horse's hooves striking rock and sending blue-white sparks into the night. But the noise and sight had trailed off and Slade had to assume the guard had ridden farther off, toward the peak at the end of the valley. Slade could see nothing now, except the twin pale glimmers of the water, coming down the hill and joining. Where the streams met, he could hear the strong rushing sound. The fork of water was a hundred yards up the slope.

Slade got down from his horse and quietly led it to a piñon. He tied the horse lightly below the scent of pine needles and patted its nose sharply, hoping the horse would know to keep quiet. The horse edged into black shadow and stood patiently while Slade walked up the hill, canteen in one hand, his .44 in the other.

Tasker kept thinking: I'll wait until he's close enough to identify before I let him know I'm watching him. That's what I'll do. And another thought kept urging him: it's somebody the boss sent over with a message. It's nothing important. It's Connors or Morgan or maybe even Thomas himself, worried about the bad leg, wondering whether a new guard ought to be posted.

But Tasker felt his stomach roll, and jelly formed in his knees. He gritted his teeth and his eyes strained into the blackness, burning holes in the night. And even as he thought: I'll wait until he's ten yards away and then I'll recognize him—even as he thought, his strangled words leaped from his frozen throat, "Hey, who's there!"

Instantly, an oath from down the hill. Then black silence.

And Tasker felt the dread creep up his body. He knew who it was down the hill. It was Death down there, not the boss. And he was carrying a message, all right.

He cried out again, "Who's there, dammit?"

Slade lay still, belly and face hugging the soil. He had heard the uncertainty, the fear in the man's voice—a voice he thought he recognized as that of one of the men who had come over to Crispin's the other day—*was it only yesterday?*—and Slade knew all he had to do was lie still and wait.

Slade had worked his way across the graze and up the slope. He had taken three hours to get here. He hadn't seen another Thomas rider all the way across. The man up here could scream his head off; nobody would hear him. Gunshot, yes, but voices, no. Slade hoped the man would be wise enough not to reveal his position by firing his gun. Slade would find him, he thought grimly, even in all that blackness.

He heard the man's foot slip on wet rock and a shrill "*Damn!*" hurtled down at Slade. Then the man scrambled back to his feet, and while he scrambled, Slade moved swiftly, running low and to his left and up the slope. Then he dropped again, face digging grass. He had cut the distance in half.

The man said, from quite close, his words angling off toward the spot where Slade had been, "You come any closer and I'll shoot!" But fear was riding his words, and Slade felt the exultancy of victory tearing at his guts. He got to his feet slowly, silently, a small rock in his gun hand. He silently laid the canteen on the ground, put his .44 in his left hand and looped the rock in the direction and past the figure who stood cloaked in darkness, approximately twenty yards away. Then he bent, picked up the canteen, shoved it quickly into his shirt and raced forward.

The rock clattered; the man whirled and screamed; and Slade was on him, one hand reaching for his chin, jerking his head back and up and the other crashing down with the gun, butt-end first.

The gun battered through the felt Stetson and against the man's skull. He fell, with a whimper, surprisingly clear and childlike. It sounded to Slade like, "Oh, no." Then the body of the man hit the ground and lay still.

Now Slade was uncertain. He stood over the man. Then he turned him over, reached for his gun, searched him for any other hideout guns, and stuck the one .44 into his belt. He found the man's horse and slapped it on the side. The horse kicked back at Slade and then started to run. Slade didn't want the injured Thomas man to find his horse too easily when he came to. The longer it took him to get back to the bunkhouse, the longer it would be before anybody started trailing Slade.

Then he filled the canteen and carried the sloshing water to his horse, tied to the piñon. He put the capped canteen into the saddlebag and got on his horse. A minute later he was single-footing his way down the slope, toward the far-off cut in the fence. He let the horse have its head; the horse searched out its own smell and followed its own trail up all the way back.

Morning had cracked the sky when Slade and the stallion wedged through the fence and entered Crispin's land again.

CHAPTER 10

Abbott said, "Dammit, Thomas, I can't let you turn my bank into a crying towel."

Thomas felt a nerve twitch along his jaw. He rubbed the spot, fighting for control. He said, "I'm not crying, Abbott. I'm just laying some cold facts in front of you. You've been so damned officious up to now, I thought maybe you'd like to take charge of some more knowledge."

Abbott said, "So one of your men had his skull creased. I can't see how it affects me. Or us. Tell him to wrap it in cold rags. Or—dammit—tell him to cut it off at the neck. The pain won't bother him at all then."

Thomas said, "Abbott, suppose somebody took ten percent of this bank's holdings and put it in a hole in the ground someplace. How'd you like that?"

"What's that got to do with Tasker's head?"

"Tasker represents ten percent of my working force, that's what. And he's just as good as buried in the hills somewhere, for all the value he'll be the next week or so."

Abbott bit his lip. Thomas was right. Tasker meant something to them both, and not just because his head had to be tended. The man was a casualty of range war. And range war was the only thing Abbott could not tolerate just yet. If the railroad ever heard that the Sierra Verde was an unhealthy spot, it would look elsewhere for its rail bed, no matter how much stock Abbott owned in the line. Nobody was going to ask men to lay rails between bullets. Violence against the Taskers—or against anybody in the valley—had to stop.

And yet that was the dilemma. To stop the violence meant more violence. Swift, terrible violence. The complete eradication of the opposition. The end of Slade and Hogue and Crispin's ranch. The wiping out of Mudge and Early—but that, at least, could be accomplished with one upraised fist.

Abbott sighed. He didn't like it. The consequences were beginning to become giants of their own, bigger than the major issues that spawned them. He had to put a stop to it—soon—before the violence mushroomed and uprooted everything that had been planted.

"All right," Abbott said finally. "We'll move on Slade." Then he thought for a moment. "No," he said decisively, "we'll make him move on us."

"And bust another man's head?" Thomas asked.

"Maybe. That's the price we have to pay."

Thomas cursed. It wasn't the price Abbott had to pay. It was the price he, Big Thomas, had to pay—and one of his men—or maybe even more. Slade had already ruined Morgan. Now Tasker. Who next? Still, Thomas knew no other way, either, of getting rid of Slade. He had to be killed. "What do you mean," he said, "make him move on us?"

Abbott leaned forward. His mind was already a step past this little plot. Getting rid of Slade was as good as done. Now he was preparing to sell out Thomas. He said, "Listen, it's very simple."

His words set up a low murmur in the room, like summer flies droning in the hot afternoon. He talked on and Thomas listened, while in Abbott's mind his own voice was talking to himself, and in Thomas' mind a worried thought kept plaguing him: *why is Abbott doing it? What as there in it for him?*

But when Abbott had finished, Big Thomas nodded his head and stroked his clean heavy jaw. Thomas held a strong hand over his emotions; now that Abbott had laid out the next steps, he forgot all other problems. Slade was the immediate worry, not some vague presentiment about Abbott and his role. So Slade filled Thomas' mind, Slade storming into Thomas' land, Slade being forced to race into Thomas' guns, Slade going to his death. Step by step he thought it through, as Abbott had dictated it. And he nodded again and walked out of the bank.

Abbott waited fully ten minutes before he decided on his next step. Then he called, "Loomis. Loomis, will you come into my office, please."

In thirty seconds, the pale, nervous, hand-washing banker's clerk entered Abbott's office, head bowing and teeth showing as he edged slowly toward the big desk.

"Yes, Mr. Abbott?" he said, holding the smile.

"Loomis, bring me the current assessment papers on Big Thomas. The ones we made up six months ago."

Loomis bowed and scraped his way to the door and silently through it. In a minute's time he was breathlessly back, a thin sheaf of papers in his hand.

Abbott took the papers. Without looking up, he said, "Sit down, Loomis."

The surprised clerk sat.

Abbott said, "First, Loomis, how much money are you earning?"

The clerk said, weak-voiced, "Twenty dollars a week, Mr. Abbott."

Abbott said, "How'd you like that raised to twenty-five?"

Loomis gulped. "That—that would be fine, sir."

"Think you deserve it?"

Loomis turned pale. "Why—yes, I mean no, sir. That is, whatever you think I'm worth is all right with me, sir."

"Dammit," Abbott said, "answer my question. Is there any reason on God's green earth that I'd be giving you a raise at this time? And a big fat five-dollar raise, at that?"

The clerk said helplessly, "No, sir. Nothing."

"That's right," Abbott snapped. "So I want you to earn your money. Do you think you can?"

"Well, sir, if it's a task you wish of me, just try me."

Abbott grunted. *The little man*, he thought. "All right," he said. "I shall. All I want is your confidence."

"My confidence, sir?"

Abbott groaned. "Yes, confidence. Simply that, nothing else. I want you to respect my actions, to have confidence in what I propose to do. What is going to go on here in the next few minutes will be between you and me, nobody else. Is that understood?" He paused, holding Loomis in his stare. "Your raise in wages will be determined by this."

"Oh, yes," Loomis breathed. "I understand perfectly."

The hell you do, Abbott thought. "All right, then. We're going to destroy our copy of the Thomas assessment papers." The clerk gasped. Abbott narrowed his eyes. "What's the matter, Loomis? You don't think it's ethical?"

The clerk paled.

Abbott said, "You're damn right it's not ethical." Then his voice rose, steel-edged. "But it's perfectly legal, isn't it? Isn't it, Loomis?"

"Yes, sir," the clerk whispered.

"A bank can change its assessment of property anytime something drastic happens to the current set of values, can't it? And the railroad coming through is a pretty drastic occurrence in this area. Right, Loomis?"

The clerk's face brightened. "Oh, yes, sir. You mean we're going to reevaluate Mr. Thomas' land at a higher figure than six months ago?"

Abbott paused. His eyes once more seemed to reach out for the pale face in front of him. He kept his gaze directly on Loomis' eyes for a full minute. Then he slowly shook his head. "No," he said, "we're going to cut the value down. Way down."

The clerk seemed to fall back in his chair. "But—how can we, Mr. Abbott?"

Abbott smiled. "Because nobody else can. It's our job, nobody else's. And anyway, Loomis, what exactly is the worth of Mr. Thomas' holdings? No," he said, waving a hand, "I don't mean on paper. Don't look there. Just think it over. A nice piece of land. *Which the bank practically owns.* Cattle, ready for slaughter. *Most of which the bank practically owns.* A ranch house, bunkhouse, corrals. *All of which the bank owns.* It seems to me—just commonsense-me, not banker-me—that Thomas is a man facing bankruptcy."

Loomis said, "But the railroad will pull him out. It needs Mr. Thomas' land. It needs his water. And it will pay handsomely."

Abbott frowned, his head shaking back and forth. "Ah, Loomis, it's you who are not quite ethical. You're asking the bank to practice nepotism, of course."

"Nepotism, sir?"

"Naturally. If the bank owns most of Thomas' land—and if the bank makes the assessment by which the railroad will pay Thomas for his land—that means the bank will be doing most of the collecting. I don't think it's quite fair for a bank to establish with one of its partners—the railroad—how much money it should be paid. I'm all for conducting this business in such a way that nobody—ever—will be able to say that the Cowpoke Bank and Trust was taking money out of its left-hand pocket and putting it, with interest, into its right-hand pocket."

Loomis licked his lips. The whole affair had gone beyond him. All he wanted was for Abbott to end this discussion, to send him out of the office and back to his work.

Abbott said, "So it turns out, you see, that not only is this legal, but it's perfectly ethical, too. Right, Loomis?"

"Right, sir," the clerk whispered.

"And we'll write up a new assessment that will cut the value of Thomas' land to—oh, let's say—one-third its current price? We'll do that, Loomis? Right now?"

"Right, sir," the clerk whispered.

Abbott slapped his hands together. "Fine," he said. "And that raise will come through this week, Loomis. You're a fine worker. And a man who respects confidences. You have confidence in what I'm doing. And I have confidence in your keeping this whole matter strictly between the two of us. Right?"

"Right, sir," Loomis whispered again. "Oh, yes, sir."

Abbott's mouth tightened. "Get out, Loomis, and get that assessment written up. I want it in my hands by the end of the day."

Loomis fled.

Abbott leaned back, gazing down at his empty desk. He was a satisfied man. He had just cut Thomas adrift. No matter what happened, the rancher no longer had his last bulwark to fall back upon. His own holdings had just depleted in value to practically the vanishing point. Thomas would never be able to get a stake going out of what the railroad would pay him for the honor of cutting his land to ribbons.

Abbott idly wondered what Thomas would do when he found his dream of empire had been just a wild nightmare. What would a man do—Abbott mused—who planned on owning a valley and who suddenly found he was lucky to claim his horse and a pair of guns out of the whole mess? Would he turn one of those guns to his temple? Would he race his horse to some precipitous gorge, and then on over into space? Or would he just disappear, into the maw of trail towns that twisted in every direction, a man on the bum, drifting, begging for twenty dollars a month and found?

Abbott enjoyed such thoughts. He was a logical man and he enjoyed presenting all the possible alternatives. He could not imagine Thomas— or anybody—doing anything other than the alternatives he had just conjured. Unless, of course, Thomas went raving mad, his mind snapped. Abbott giggled at the thought. It seemed almost obscene to imagine a healthy, nearly prosperous man like Bigelow Thomas suddenly broken, like—that!

Abbott looked down. In his hands were the two halves of a pencil. He frowned. He did not recall even picking up the pencil, much less snapping it.

He got up from his desk, mildly irritated and not knowing why. He walked from his office to the door. Before he opened it, he said to Loomis, working at a tiny desk in a dim corner of the bank, "Never mind that assessment for today. Just make sure it's ready by tomorrow noon. I won't be back the rest of the day."

Loomis nodded wordlessly and continued to work. The door slammed behind Abbott.

The banker walked into Wilkinson's small office. The sheriff was drinking brandy, staring at a handful of wanted posters.

"Ah," Abbott said, "the lawman, on his job. Hot on the trail of a couple of deadly killers?"

Wilkinson tossed the placards on his desk. "Postal robbery, business fraud, attempted robbery," he said in disgust. "Not an honest-to-God desperado among them."

"You'd have made a good one, Wilkinson."

The sheriff smiled. "You think so?"

Abbott nodded. "Yes, I do. A real killer, if I ever saw one. Grim, tough, courageous, uncompromising, and—necessarily—nearly as stupid as a Texas Ranger."

Wilkinson flushed. He said, "Abbott, one day I'll surprise you."

Abbott stared at the little sheriff. He saw the white pinpoints in Wilkinson's eyes and he knew he had better stop needling the man. He said softly. "You probably will, Wilkinson. Most people do. Sometimes I surprise myself." And when he sighed, he knew he had spoken the truth.

Wilkinson said, "Slade surprised you, that's for sure."

Abbott frowned. "Now what has the man done?"

"You've heard about Tasker?"

"Oh," Abbott said, relieved, "that. Yes, I've heard."

"And about the way he beat our vagrancy rap?"

Abbott nodded. "That's not so serious. The man still is short of funds."

Wilkinson smiled wickedly. "But maybe he won't be after tonight."

Abbott started. Wilkinson couldn't know what was going to happen tonight. Only he and Thomas knew, and maybe a handful of Thomas' men. Thomas had sworn his men would be tight-mouthed about what would go on tonight. He said, "What about tonight?"

"You haven't heard about the card game Slade has arranged?"

Abbott shook his head.

"At the big saloon? You're the one who said he was a gambler. Well, tonight he intends to prove it. He's asked the bartender to arrange a little game of poker, four or five men at the 'tender's discretion. Small stakes. I tell you, Abbott, the man plans to get himself a fat roll to see him through this—this trouble."

Abbott felt a laugh form inside. It was so perfect. Slade could not have played more neatly into their hands. He said, "You don't intend to break up the game, do you?"

"Why, yes, I do," the sheriff said.

"You thought we'd like it if you threw some anti-gambling ordinance at Slade, eh? Keep him from getting his money?"

The sheriff nodded.

"I wouldn't, if I were you, sheriff. The vagrancy law was perfectly proper. There is such a law on the books. This would be so transparent that somebody might be upset. Somebody other than Slade. The word might leak out. We can't afford that. We want to keep our little problem tight to the valley here. I say—let the man play. Can't do much harm."

"No? Suppose he picks up a few hundred dollars, or maybe a couple of thousand? And starts hiring hands? *Then* you'll have yourself a nice little range war. And it'll be one sweet chore, trying to keep it quiet *then*."

Abbott chewed his lip. Christ, he thought, every little step unfolds into three big ones. He said, "Don't worry, sheriff. He won't have time. Slade will be dead by tomorrow morning."

The sheriff looked up, his glass of brandy fixed an inch from his lips. "Dead?"

Abbott nodded.

Wilkinson drained his glass. "Good," he said huskily, "good, good, *good*." And then Hogue, he thought, and then Abbott.

And he and May Hogue, making love.

With shaking fingers he poured himself another drink.

Abbott went back to the bank and to the vaults. He withdrew an envelope marked, "Private Funds," and dropped a penciled note in its place. Then he walked to the stable for his horse.

Abbott did not like to ride long distances. But this time he had to see Thomas, and see him quickly. The sun had not dipped below the western hills when he reached the ranch house. Five minutes later, he was back on his horse, riding to the draw leading to town. He and Thomas had made the few minor changes that were necessitated by Slade's latest move. Thomas had the money, for the game that night with Slade.

Damn the man, Abbott thought. Slade, always Slade. And then he smiled. By tomorrow morning—maybe even by midnight tonight—the man would be damned, all right. For all eternity.

CHAPTER 11

Hogue said, "You intend to gamble that fifty dollars?"

Slade nodded.

"What if you lose?"

"I won't."

They sat on the porch, May Hogue inside, making noises in the kitchen.

Hogue bit his lip. "You sure?"

Slade said, "See here, Hogue. You want me to lose the money May loaned me?"

"Loaned you! Ha, that's a good one. Gave you, you mean."

Slade said, "I told you once before—I'm not a thief. I'll pay the money back."

"Sure," Hogue said bitterly. "Sure you will."

"Shut up," Slade said mildly.

Hogue swore once and got down from the porch seat. "You really intend to play that poker game tonight?"

Slade nodded.

Hogue walked from the porch and went to the corral. May called from inside, "Where you going?"

Hogue waved his hand in irritation and got up on a horse. He rode into the gloom.

May came out to join Slade. "Good riddance."

Slade still could not join her in such thoughts. The man was her husband, for good or bad. He said, "He's got me worried."

She snorted. "Him? He wouldn't hurt a fly."

"No-o," he agreed. "He wouldn't. Not exactly, anyway. But he doesn't want me around. And if I'm lucky tonight, I aim to be around to see this thing through."

"What can he do?" May said.

Slade shook his head. "Nothing, that I know of." Then he grinned. "Forget it. I'm seeing hobgoblins tonight."

She frowned. "That's bad, isn't it? If you intend to risk all the money you own, you ought to have your mind free of—of hobgoblins, oughtn't you?"

"Easier said than done," he said.

She stood over him. "I could take your mind off hobgoblins, Slade. Off

Hogue, too. Off the whole valley. All you have to do is say the word."

He got up, laughing. "May," he said, "I admire you. You've got the patience of a—of a I-don't-know-what."

"Of an impatient woman," she said. "Of a woman who knows what she wants and wants it bad. Just say the word, Slade."

"Nonsense," he said. "That's the word. Nonsense." He walked to the door, patting his money belt and his holster.

She said, "Slade, you don't have to worry about that game tonight. If you lose, you know where to come for more money."

He turned, his face shocked. "Don't," he said tightly, his voice straining in his throat. "Don't buy me, May. You disgust me when you do that."

She laughed, deep and free. "I told you, Slade. I wouldn't stop trying. You might as well give in now."

He walked swiftly to the corral. The brown stallion moved when he came close and Slade thought: a man, a horse, a gun. And a deck of cards. That was all he wanted.

He rode toward Cowpoke, knowing he was a liar.

Hogue was frightened. He didn't like what he was doing, yet he had to do it. May didn't understand. He loved her. Maybe it wasn't the way she wanted to be loved, carried away by a big man on a horse, a man like Slade. But it was the best he could do.

He loved her, and by God, he was going to keep her.

Slade.

That was the rub. Slade. Get Slade out of the way, and he'd have May all to himself. May *and* money. With Slade out of the way, he'd sell out to Thomas. Not just for peanuts, either. Thomas wanted the ranch, wanted it so bad he could nearly taste it. That was apparent. Why, maybe there was gold on the land. Maybe that was it.

He laughed. Not water. Not water, like Slade had thought. Wasn't that a laugh! Taking a jar of water into town and having it tested by the assayer. And what did it turn out to be? Water. Just plain good old drinking water, fresh from a river, full of honest-to-God minerals and nothing else. Wasn't Slade the fool, though?

And yet Slade had risked his life for that jar of water.

Damn Slade.

Hogue prodded his horse. He entered Thomas' land at the new break in the wire and worked his way across open graze straight to the ranch house. He didn't want anybody to think he was skulking. He didn't want to risk a shot flung out at him because they thought he was a troublemaker. He rode out in the open, a cringing man, terribly sober now because he was afraid not to be, with Slade around the house. He stopped at the ranch house and then swiftly pounded on the front door.

The girl Maria let him in. He kept his eyes down, not daring to offend this girl who he knew used to be a whore and now was Thomas' mistress. He didn't want to risk any conflict with Thomas. Why, he thought, Thomas had killed Crispin. A man had to be awfully brave—and awfully careful—to do what Hogue was doing: openly seeing Thomas on Thomas' own land.

A few minutes later Big Thomas walked into the sitting room, a smooth-faced man, trim and panther-quick, a gun belt strapped to his waist. He grunted when he saw Hogue. "Well," he said sharply, "what the devil do you want?"

And Hogue said it, much sooner than he intended to, ruining whatever chance he had of getting the price he wanted. Yet he didn't care. As soon as he said it, his role in the fight was finished. He had made his peace. He felt relieved.

He said, "I want to sell my ranch."

Thomas gave a little start, his heart thundering in his throat. "When?"

Craft flitted across Hogue's face. "As soon as Slade is—gone."

"Why do you have to wait on Slade?"

Hogue frowned. He didn't want this to be an inquisition. He just wanted to sign some papers and get out. But no questions. He doubted he could stand it. "Because," he said helplessly, "I have to."

"He's got you bulldozed, Hogue."

Hogue flared weakly. "No, he's not. It's just—just—" His words trailed off and the two men stared at each other.

"All right," Thomas said briskly, "we'll arrange the necessary papers once Slade leaves."

Hogue cracked his knuckles. Did Thomas really expect Slade to leave? Didn't the man know what was going on? That Slade stood in the valley, big as a mountain, and until they chipped him down, there'd be no peace?

He said, "I—don't think Slade—is going to leave."

A cold smile played at Big Thomas' mouth. "I do," he said flatly.

Relief washed through Hogue. "Soon?" he said, his voice a low whisper in the room.

"Very soon," Thomas said.

"Then we'll sign the papers?"

Thomas nodded. He did not like this man in front of him. He was a foul creature, a vulture. He said to Hogue, "Tell me something, how come you're arranging the sale of the ranch? I thought the ranch belonged to Chet Crispin." The smile stayed, at the surface, while the rest of the face was glacial-edged.

And Hogue understood the question. Thomas was testing him. If Hogue said the ranch was his to sell, it meant he knew Crispin was dead. And knowing Crispin was dead was tantamount to calling Big Thomas a killer.

His eyes swelled. He felt sweat coursing over his face. Salt dripped to his lips. He said, "Chet—and I are partners. Whatever either of us does is all right with the other. When Chet—gets back to the ranch, he'll approve anything I've done."

Thomas nodded blandly. "Of course," he said. "I just wanted to clear that up." But the icy look never left. And Hogue started to crack. He wondered if he ever could sell the ranch. Maybe—maybe he'd be admitting Crispin's death no matter when he sold. And how could he face up to Thomas, the both of them knowing that Crispin lay in that crevice below that crushing rock, a Thomas bullet someplace in his body?

He thought wildly: to hell with the ranch. The truth burst over Hogue, scalding hot. To hell with the ranch *and* to hell with May. All he wanted was his own skin, whole. He started to edge to the door, his voice a thin scream now. "Why don't you kill Slade?" He said it again, the words babbling out of his mouth across the room to the man of ice whose hand stayed two inches from his gun butt. "Why don't you kill Slade and get it over with? I swear, I'll just run away. I'll disappear. Just kill the man and leave me alone. That's all I want."

He felt himself turning then and running from the house, tears racing down his face. He got on his horse and fled back to the ranch he owned—YES, DAMMIT, *HE* OWNED. NOBODY ELSE. UNDERSTAND?

He clapped his hand to his mouth in horror. He had been screaming aloud.

CHAPTER 12

Slade did not like the way the poker game was going. It was too easy. When he bluffed, they let him get away with it. When he held the cards, they called him. He had begun with fifty dollars—and that single silver dollar still in the money belt—and now he had six hundred. He looked up from his cards at the three faces rimming the table.

One of them was a cowhand from the other side of the valley, a good-natured man named Brink who had announced he had a hundred and fifty dollars his aunt had just left him and which he intended to throw away or make a fortune with. He was not making his fortune.

Still, he was playing normal poker, winning maybe one pot out of five, which wasn't quite good enough in a fourhanded game.

Slade looked at the muscle-heavy man next to Brink, across the table from him. He was a Thomas man. His name was Voss, and he was Thomas' top hand, now that Morgan was still scarcely able to waggle his jaw. Voss was a careless man with his cards, which disturbed Slade. Careless men just didn't get to be foremen of big ranches. Voss seemed to be playing—just to pass time.

Slade glanced to his right, at Connors, another Thomas man. Connors was one of the men who had visited Crispin's ranch that first day with Tasker and Morgan. Connors had called him, "Funny boy." Connors hated his guts, Slade could see, yet Connors was the big loser, practically throwing his money at Slade.

And that was another funny thing. Connors and Voss had too much money for cowhands, even frugal ones. Slade had been cashing in his chips every twenty minutes or so, stashing his money into the belt. Every time he had done so, Connors and Voss bought more chips. They had nearly two thousand dollars in front of them.

Slade said, "And I'll raise that ten." He stared down at his hand, two pair, eights and nines, staring back. Brink squinted at his cards and then folded. Voss tossed a blue chip—a ten dollar one—into the pot. Slade waited for Connors to call. Connors had held three cards going in. So far as Slade could tell, Connors had never held a kicker all night. When he held three, he had three of a kind. Still, Slade felt it was worth ten dollars to establish that fact.

And Connors tossed his hand face down on the table. "Can't call you, funny boy," he said.

Slade frowned. He watched the five cards Connors had tossed into the dead pile. Slade was to deal the next hand. He said to Voss, his eyes still riveted on the five cards Connors had discarded, "Two pair. Nines over eights." He hoped Voss had him licked. He didn't want to sweep in the chips while he was trying to get a look at Connors' cards. Once he would have thought such a trick was worth a bullet in the hand. Now he didn't care. These men were not gamblers and the rules of gambling were overboard. There was something fishy about the game.

Voss said, "You've got me," throwing his cards away. Slade reached out with his left hand for the chips, his right flipping his cards face up so the others could see his openers. Only the outside 'puncher, Brink, bothered to look. Then with the same right hand he started to gather the cards. His left hand kept playing with the chips. He said, "Damn," as a chip rolled away. He reached out for it hurriedly with his right hand and the deck of cards flipped over. Connors' five cards had been on the bottom—now they stared at Slade. Slade tried to scoop up the elusive chip and the cards with both hands, and somehow he fanned the five cards Connors had thrown away.

He said, "Sorry I'm so clumsy tonight. Haven't played in quite some time." The five cards were three fours and a queen and jack. Connors had thrown away the winning hand for ten dollars. It didn't make sense.

Quickly he drew the cards together, riffled them and dealt. The game went on, unchangingly, except that Connors and Voss managed to throw a couple of pots to Brink, keeping him in the game, and once in a while took one themselves. Slade continued to win. He had taken a thousand dollars out of the game when somebody beyond the table said, "Well, it's midnight. Time I rode on home. The old lady will have the lantern swinging." And the saloon started—slowly—to empty out. Voss and Connors looked up at Slade swiftly and Connors said, "Not thinking of running off with all our money, are you, Slade?"

Slade said, "Not while you still want to give it to me. Never did see such stupid poker players." Voss flushed but remained silent. Connors said, with a forced chuckle, "Funny boy's being modest. He's just too good for us, that's all."

Slade said, "Horse chips. Deal."

At one o'clock, Brink took his last two blue chips and tossed them in the middle of the table. "Let's double it up," he said, "and get me home." The others shrugged. Voss dealt the cards. Brink looked at his hand in disgust and stood up. "Good night, gents," he said. He walked out, into the black night.

Slade said, "I'm not much of a one for three-hand poker. How about cutting it short?"

Connors snarled. "I knew it. Wants to run off with the winnings."

Slade said evenly, "I'll play all night and day, if you insist. But it hasn't been a good game up till now, and it's going to get worse."

Voss said, "What's the matter, Slade, aren't we fast enough a crowd for you?" There was a nasty look around the big man's mouth and Slade thought: he's got fight in him.

Slade said, "Forget it. Just bet your hand, Connors." The two Thomas men grunted and looked at each other. Malicious smiles lit up their eyes. Slade wondered what made them so happy. They had lost nearly fifteen hundred dollars between them, counting the money in his belt and the chips in front of him.

And then the little saloon—occupied by the bartender, the three players, and two stuporish onlookers—was shattered by the swinging door smashing in, and a hoarse cry, "Fire! Fire in the valley!"

Slade started to swing out of his chair. Voss suddenly leaned back and kicked his legs against the rim of the table. It skeetered forward and pinned Slade, halfway up, to his chair. The chair skidded back a foot and wedged against the wall. Slade pulled his arms free just as Connors hit him with a left hand, turning Slade's head.

And before Voss was able to reach across the table with his long heavy right arm to grab Slade and hold him for Connors to hit him again, Slade realized what was happening. They were just keeping him in the saloon. That was the reason for their poker tactics. It didn't matter how much he won—Thomas and Abbott could afford fifteen hundred dollars, Slade thought thickly, the blood in his mouth—just so long as Slade was kept out of the valley long enough.

And the word *"Fire!"* burned across his foggy brain.

He knew what it meant: the ranch—Chet Crispin's ranch—was on fire.

He twisted his head and Connors' fist grazed his jaw. He kicked up with his knee against the table, tilting it forward and though pain streaked to his hip, he got the room he needed. Now he pushed the table into Voss and he grunted with satisfaction when the man moved back. Connors was leaping on him, grabbing his head between his arms, trying to throttle Slade, but Slade knew Voss was the man to fear.

He shook his body and Connors started to slip. Then Slade ripped his shoulder up and caught Connors under the chin. The man yelped and started to slide away. Slade feinted his right fist at Voss and saw the man hesitate for an instant; then Slade turned to Connors, smashing the man in the ribs with his left hand.

Connors gulped and fell to the sawdust floor, his legs floundering like a fish out of water, his hands beating weakly against the floor.

Slade stepped out from his corner and advanced to the middle of the room. "Now," he panted. "Now, Voss. Come on, man. Let's find out."

And Voss came on, as big as Slade, a thick-lipped man, carrying out his orders: keep Slade busy as long as you can. He winced as Slade hit him three times around the side of the jaw with heavy right hands, but he got to his man and pumped his fists into Slade's body. Then they stood in an awkward embrace, Voss gripping Slade about the waist and trying to lift the man and throw him back into the table, and Slade pressing his hands into Voss' upper arms, his fingers cutting into the man's muscles. For a full minute they stood there, red-smeared eyes two inches apart, breathing into each other's sweaty faces, and then Voss cried out and fell back, his arms twitching at his sides.

And Slade hit him, the long hours of hate piling into his fists, the deceit of the other man making Slade a wild man, a man who would have killed if Voss hadn't finally caved under the thirty-fifth punch that thudded into his broken face.

Slade turned then, looking down at Connors, still sitting on the floor, a foolish look on his face, wondering why he couldn't get up and why his lungs felt as though somebody had stabbed them with a hot knife.

Slade reached over the bar and grabbed his holster and strapped it on. He moved through the door, into the street, a staggering, bone-tired hurting man, but mostly a wild man still. He was on his horse, sweat-blinded and angry, and his fist dug the horse's side until the big brown had flattened lower than he'd ever been, and his legs moved like they'd never moved before.

Thomas heard the wild drumming hoof-beats from the pass five miles off, and he shouted hoarsely, "All right, that's enough. Drop your brands and beat it the hell back." And the four Thomas riders touched their flames to the grass until the fire licked its way forward, and then they took off, fleeing for the graze of the Big T.

They had ridden out at midnight, chopping and burning the entire periphery of Crispin fence before May Hogue had wakened. Then while she screamed and fired a rifle at them, they broke up into two pairs, plus Thomas by himself, and scorched the alfalfa. Thomas had wanted to ride to the house itself, but the fierce rifle fire kept him off. Still, he knew it wouldn't have been smart. Abbott had warned him how to play it, and Abbott had been right. A good-sized range fire, enough to hurt them, but nobody killed. The bank and the railroad, Abbott had warned, wouldn't stand for too much bloodshed.

And so Thomas and his men had waited until everyone was asleep, until the valley itself seemed to be slumbering before starting out. His men would keep Slade busy back in Cowpoke. (And Abbott had warned of that, too: not to kill Slade in Cowpoke, if anybody was watching. A town killing would not go unheeded. Just keep him busy, that's all.)

Now that Slade was here—Connors and Voss hadn't succeeded completely, Thomas knew, and the knowledge sent tiny messages of peril to his brain—now that Slade was riding in, he and his men would go back, and wait.

Abbott had said Slade would ride into Thomas' land like a madman, the way Crispin had done. But this time Thomas would be waiting for him. And on land where he didn't belong, Slade would be chopped down. His body would disappear, like Crispin's, except more surely this time. And the violence, bitter but brief, would be ended.

He had Hogue's word. The man would sell. And the business with Mudge and Early would take but the time for money to pass into their hands.

Thomas passed through the charred fence and onto his own land. Quickly he set up guards at the fence, working their way back to the ranch house. In case Slade got all the way through, he, Big Thomas, would be waiting for him in ambush. The man didn't stand a chance.

When Slade reached the Crispin house, he yelled, "May. Hogue. Are you in there?"

And a woman's sob, dotted with weariness and hope, answered him. The two of them came out, then, and with Slade they started to attack the fire.

They dug firebreaks, he and Hogue, Hogue following Slade sullenly, a tired beaten man, dully doing what he was told, doing it well because once—long ago, years ago it seemed—he had been a good worker. And so they ripped up the sod and left the grass fire with nothing to do except burn itself out, curling back on itself and dying.

And May Hogue was all over, a heavy blanket in her hands, flailing like a woman obsessed. Her hands were raw-hot and her feet blistered, but she beat at the fire with all the fury of her body.

Mudge and Early, skulking in fear until they saw Slade and the Hogues battling the flames, came from their land, and the five of them beat the fire—three hours after it had been started. Fifteen acres of land lay in black ruins. Crop and feed were ashes. And a hundred terror-struck cows huddled against themselves, pawing and bellowing, too frightened even to stampede.

But with all the ruin, the ranch still stood. And Slade looked at the black smoke climbing to the sky and he knew what he had to do: he had to ride Thomas down and kill the man. It was either that, or quit. He had come too far to quit.

The black edge of night began to fade. May Hogue lay on a patch of grass near the house, tired, crying softly. Hogue lay a few yards off, also tired, his mind refusing to believe what was happening, all but a little piece of it that kept saying: the ranch is saved; maybe the price will be decent.

Mudge and Early beat down little spitting ashes that still threatened to erupt into flame, and then when the last had sputtered out, they looked around and crawled away. Shame touched them briefly; then a bit of pride replaced it. They should have come out sooner to fight the fire; that they had come out at all was a shining revelation. They looked at each other oddly as they rode off to their own grubby, still untouched land, and they sensed that the battle, now joined, was theirs also.

Slade stared to the distant Thomas fields and he wondered how the man had managed to get away with it. The townspeople of Cowpoke had known about the fire from that first hoarse scream in the saloon nearly four hours back. But they had stayed away. And Slade knew why. They all had decided that a war was going on; the Crispin graze was no-man's land. Only a fool—or a combatant—wandered onto such perilous grass. They had screamed out the warning—not to Slade or Hogue or Mudge or Early—but to themselves. *Fire*—and watch out, you may be burned!

Slade could not blame them. For ten years he had lived his own life, behind a table piled high with chips. The chips had kept others off, and himself away from others. But Johnson, back in Cutter, had swept away the chips, and now he saw the bleak world of losers, not winners.

Then he gave a little start. He felt his money belt. All night long he had been cashing in his chips, packing the green bills into his belt. The brawl back in the saloon had kept him from realizing the full extent of his winnings, but he still had crammed in more than a thousand dollars. Now he no longer sat with the losers. He had his stake, more than he had figured on. He could ride out, or even back to Cutter—no, not there, he murmured, the thought black in his mouth—but any place else. He could buy a little piece of land or a deserted store or shop and turn it into a saloon. He could crawl back to the night-world of bettors and brawlers, winners and losers. No, not of losers. Of winners alone. The others would do the losing. His luck had turned again, as he had known it would.

He felt the warm thickness of the belt and all that it meant to him. Wasn't that why he had come to Crispin's place? To recoup his strength and his winnings? Was there any further need to hang and rattle around Crispin's place?

And the answer stabbed him, every time he thought the words: *Crispin's place*. Crispin's place had become a grave under rock on land charred black by men who plundered when they rode, and rode when they wanted to.

Crispin's place. It had become more than a place for Slade to lie back and feed his vigor until power returned to his body and confidence to his spirit. True, it had given him his chance to ante up again at any table in the territory. But it had given him more.

He was grudgingly changing his attitude toward losers. The scrabblers and beggars, the hopeless and helpless and ever fearful—he was finding out why they were like that.

There was a Big Thomas in their life or an Abbott or a weasel sheriff or a mortgage or rusted machinery or grubby land that wouldn't sprout no matter how much sweat watered it. The losers, he thought. There was something grand about them. Lucky men won, gritty men lost.

He turned and looked down on Hogue and his wife. Slade said, "Here, hold this for me." He took off his money belt—that symbol of his old life, the stake he had fought back for, his freedom—and he put it on the ground between Hogue and May.

Hogue said, eyes glinting in the early light, "What's that?" His voice was tired.

Slade said, "That's my winnings."

May rolled over. "How much did you win?"

"Over a thousand dollars."

Hogue sucked in his breath. Greed tried to battle with his need for sleep. He tried to think of the money, how Slade was sure to ride off for Thomas' land and get killed, and how the money would be lying there, waiting for Slade to come back, but Slade wouldn't. But Hogue couldn't carry the thought any farther. Slade would go off and the money would stay. He wanted to picture himself strapping on Slade's great money belt, but he couldn't go that far. The fire had sapped him, and maybe done a bit more than that. Maybe it had touched the old Hogue and tapped it, and decency was in the man.

Hogue didn't know. He was too tired to know. He grunted and rolled back over and while Slade watched, the man went back to sleep.

May whispered, "Where are you going?"

Slade waved his hand toward Thomas'. "Over there."

"Why?" she breathed fiercely. "Why, fool?"

Why? he thought. Because that's where it would end, he answered. He and Thomas, locked together, one of them dying. "Because I've got to see Thomas," he said.

"See Thomas!" she jeered. "Get killed by Thomas' men, you mean."

He shrugged. One or the other, he or Thomas. That was the way it was playing.

"You can't," she said.

"Why?"

She waved a hand weakly over the rangeland. "This," she said. "After you go, then what? Then they burn some more and scare some more, and finally Hogue sells, and Mudge and Early. And what have you accomplished?"

He didn't know. She was probably right. Winning wasn't everything, he answered to himself. So he might not win that one. Still, he'd be the better man for it.

And his own selfishness stung him. *So he'd be the better man!* His thoughts raged inside, sneering at his vainglory, at his mock heroics. So he'd face up to Thomas and get riddled by ten men's bullets. And they'd say that Slade was a brave man. He lost magnificently the battle and won his own personal war.

His war.

She was right. He was still fighting *his* war. Not Chet Crispin's. And if he didn't fight Chet Crispin's, nobody would. Chet wouldn't, that was sure.

Slade licked his lips. He knew what he ought to do. He ought to stay and nurse his wounds, and May's and Hogue's and the ranch's, and when they all were strong, in a week or two or three, then they'd have to figure how to face up to Thomas' next threat, his next move. Maybe if they held firm just a little longer, Thomas would get panicky. Maybe Thomas' next move, dictated by desperation, would play all wrong, and the man would hang himself.

Then Slade snorted. Maybe.

Maybe not.

And to hell—he thought—with all this theory, all this high-toned strategy. He said to May, "You're right, but it doesn't matter. I'm going to try to see Thomas. Now." And he walked off, his ears trying not to hear her sobs and then not hearing them, and he knew she had cried herself back to exhausted sleep, on the black smoky ground that she was trying to guard.

The brown horse bobbed his head to clear the poisonous smell from his wet nostrils. But it wouldn't clear. Edgily, nervously, the horse began to move under Slade, a tired man now, drained of much of the fury, a cold man trying to fight two battles, his own and the ranch's, and not knowing whether he could win even one of them that way.

They drifted in a wide arc, Slade urging the horse far off to the timber line that skirted the hills, three-fourths the way up, over at the extreme west rim of Crispin's land. He was a stubborn man, Slade, doing what reason said he oughtn't do. But he was at times a cautious man, and in this brash act, caution held the reins. And so they drifted, away from the straight line that led to Thomas' ranch house and a final settling of all the past pains. Slade wasn't thinking much. He was just moving. And he moved wide, in a great circling sweep, under cover of Crispin's own land until he reached the hills. Then he'd have the hills and the timber for cover. It would be broad daylight then, and Thomas would start to relax his guard, knowing that Slade wouldn't be riding up anymore, thinking maybe that Slade had decided the best course was flight from the valley, with his new fat stake.

That was how Thomas would figure, Slade thought, because Thomas still ran with the hounds. Soon, Slade thought, that would change. And he wanted to see Thomas' face when Thomas knew he had become the prey, not the hunter.

CHAPTER 13

Wilkinson sat in his office all that night, the brandy filling him but doing him no good. Abbott had warned him to stay out of sight. There was no use rubbing it in, Abbott had said. Men would ride and maybe die; better that the law be invisible rather than standing on the side of the riders and killers.

Abbott remained a wise man, Wilkinson thought bitterly—a banker and a railroad man to the last. Violence, he had said, was unfortunately necessary, but it must be kept to a minimum. Otherwise—long finger shaking in Wilkinson's face, and in Big Thomas' too—otherwise, the railroad might change its mind about the Sierra Verde valley. Nobody liked to build a railroad under the fire of grass war.

And if word leaked out that the sheriff of the county was siding the war makers, new law would be hustled in, and the whole affair would go up in smoke. Thomas didn't want that; he wanted a cow empire. Wilkinson didn't want that; he wanted May Hogue.

So while Thomas' men kept Slade busy in the saloon, on Abbott's money—reports filtered down to Wilkinson all that evening and night— other Thomas men had fired Crispin's ranch.

And all the time Wilkinson kept to his office, a sulking man, a little man feeling useless and impotent in a moment of great smouldering action. Others rode and burned and smashed. He sat and drank.

The whisky, untouching him all night, finally started to work when the stars started to slip away to their daylight roosts and the black sky began to turn gray.

Wilkinson lurched to his feet then, to stand at the door of his little office—little, he thought bitterly, every goddam thing in his life little— and he looked up and down Cowpoke's street. It was deserted. The early morning traffic of produce people had not started. The rest were asleep. Only he was awake.

Surprisingly, the thought made him feel better. While battle had exhausted all the others and sent them to their slumber, he— Wilkinson—had ridden out the storm and was still awake and eager to get into the fray.

It wouldn't matter now, he knew. It was his duty. He had to ride out to the valley and see the extent of the damage, to assess the casualties and make his reports which he stuck into a desk drawer and promptly forgot. And it must not be said that the law had died in the Sierra Verde. His role demanded his presence on that grass. Self-importance filled him. He strode from the office, a cocky man now and before he got on his horse, he took the bit and twisted it cruelly in the little mare's mouth. The horse screamed in the night-morning, a trumpet of sound that shattered Cowpoke's street and Wilkinson looked around. He wanted somebody to see him, to see his strength and red furies.

But everybody slept or cowered behind drawn blinds.

Wilkinson shrugged, a lopsided grin on his face. Afraid, he thought. They all were afraid. He rode down the middle of the street and clattered through the early dust toward the bowl of hills and the distant pass.

Wilkinson was wrong. They all weren't asleep. Abbott wasn't. He was awake, and had been so all that night, awake and waiting, just like the sheriff. Abbott had tried to remain imperturbable during all the planning, all the hours when he knew Thomas was raiding Crispin's ranch. But it hadn't worked. Now he sat in his hotel room, waiting for word. Thomas had promised to send a man over when the fire had ended and the damage was known, and when Slade had walked into Thomas' trap.

But the night was lifting, and no Thomas had appeared. When a horse screamed outside, Abbott had leaped to his feet, but the hoof beats had gone toward the valley, not coming in from it. He had sat again.

The second sound of hoof beats was less noisy, more the sound Abbott was listening for. Still, they did not seem to come from the valley. Yet they were coming to a stop in front of the hotel. Abbott unhooked his screen window and looked down into the dim morning.

The man slowly getting down from his horse was the biggest man Abbott had ever seen. He thought: that's a new man. Thomas has hired a new man. Abbott shook his head in admiration. He didn't know how Thomas found them, but he sure knew a fighting man when he saw one. At least this one was a fighter.

He seemed to stand six and a half feet tall, a rangy man with broad sloping shoulders and a thick chest. And the pale oil lamp outside the hotel lit the man's great bald head, a head that was crisscrossed with the blackened scars of what seemed to Abbott to have been a dozen battles. Abbott leaned from the window. He said quietly, "You down there. Are you from Big Thomas?"

The man looked up in surprise. His eyes were sunk deep in his face, broad blades of cheekbone protecting them so that the eyes seemed— in the dim morning light—black gashes in a face of chinked marble.

The man said, in Texas drawl, "No, I'm not."

Abbott continued to look down, deep in thought. The man was a drifter. He had come up from Texas. He was looking for work. That was how it figured.

He said, "You looking for a job?"

The man cocked his head. "Right now," he said, "I'm looking for a bed."

Abbott said impatiently, "There's a law against vagrants in this town. You looking for a job?"

The man's eyes seemed to slit even more, until just a black edge faced Abbott. The banker shivered. The man said, "You the law in town?"

Abbott said, "No." He did not see fit to add that he was the man who made the law.

The man said, "Then go to hell, Mister."

Now the silver-haired man frowned. He said to the big stranger, still standing, holding the loop of rope in his hand, his horse silent at the post, "I know where there's work for you."

The big man said, "What kind of work?"

Abbott said, "Look here, come on up to my room. We can talk better there. Room twenty-two." He pulled his head in and sat down. He didn't know whether the man would come up, but he sensed he would. The man had a hungry look about him. Abbott smiled thinly. He knew the look. He had seen it on the posters in Wilkinson's office. Abbott thought contemptuously how he had credited Thomas with hiring such a man. Why, this man was twice a man like Morgan. He was more a man like Slade, maybe even better.

The door to Abbott's room trembled under a sudden knock. It was the new man.

He came in.

He said his name was Dilt.

The two men talked briefly and with mute understanding. And Abbott saw the wild light gleam in Dilt's eye when he told him of the trouble in the valley. It was enough. The man was a fighting man. Abbott spoke carefully, however. Dilt was a new man. He didn't know how much a man like that could be trusted. And Dilt would not be working for him. He'd be working for Thomas. So Abbott did not mention too many names. Dilt would find out for himself. A man like that ought to be tested. There was no way of knowing how reliable he was. Too many men liked to fight for the sheer thrill of it—and then when the fight was over, had to go on fighting. Dilt was a man like that, Abbott thought. He'd have to be careful with him. Give him a job to do—like putting Slade under the ground with Crispin, in case Thomas failed again—and that was all.

Violence would win the war for Abbott. It could also lose it, he knew.

The third sound of hoof beats interrupted the talk. This time they came from the valley and again they stopped at the hotel. Abbott knew it was a Thomas man, with the word.

When the door opened, Tasker came in, a dirty bandage around his head. Until he recovered from Slade's blow, Thomas used him as a messenger and guard.

Abbott said, "Tasker. Sit down."

Tasker looked uncertainly at Dilt. Abbott nodded his head. "You can talk," he said.

Tasker said slowly, "We fired the place. Burned it up pretty bad. Then Slade came—"

A hoarse exclamation rose from Dilt. "Slade?" he roared. "Slade, you say?"

Abbott said softly, curiously, "You know Slade?"

Dilt laughed, his voice filling the room. "I know a man named Slade. Damn right, I do. Big man. A gambler."

Abbott nodded. "That's the man."

Dilt rubbed the closed fingers of one hand into the palm of the other. His eyes were lit up. "Man, man, man," he murmured. "I'll work around here for nothing. Just to see my old friend Slade."

Abbott said, "You don't like Slade? He once whipped you, is that it?"

Dilt roared again. "I drove Slade out of town. I beat the man half-dead and drove him out of town." Dilt reached into his shirt and felt the sock, still filled, with lead though, not silver. He patted it gently.

Abbott said drily, "He's not half dead anymore."

Dilt said, "That's good. I'll bring him back there and then some."

Abbott looked at Tasker. He said, "Will it be necessary? Or have you people taken care of it already?"

Tasker shook his head and swore once. His head throbbed. "No," he said. "Slade never showed up. You were wrong about that."

Abbott felt the tiny peril again. He had been wrong about Slade a half-dozen times. The man didn't respond as Abbott had expected. But the peril disappeared. Now they had a trump card. A man named Dilt, just longing to get on Slade's back. Abbott smiled. "It won't matter. Now."

Wilkinson reached Crispin's land by seven that morning. The early sun informed the sheriff of the damage. He scarcely noticed it. The alcohol had been burned out during the hard ride through the valley floor. He suddenly realized why he had come out here. Not to see how much of Crispin's place had been destroyed.

He had come to see what had happened to May Hogue.

Fear nagged him. For all he knew, May Hogue was part of those ruins. Big Thomas was not a man to worry about useless bloodshed, despite all of Abbott's precautions, and May Hogue's death would not even have been useless. It was she, together with Slade, who held Hogue to the ranch. It had been her brother's ranch. She would not let go so easily. Thomas would know all that.

So Thomas could have easily—and with no qualms—shot May down and left her among the ashes.

Wilkinson spurred his horse. Sweat—even on this cool early morning—began to work into his eyes. If May were dead, the whole thing would be so futile. He cursed Abbott aloud for leading him into the plot.

Then he saw her. And at first his fears were confirmed. She lay so still, he was sure she was dead. Then he bent closer, still on his horse, looking down at her body, and he saw the slow even swell to her breasts, the slow even fall. He watched her that way, breathing, and he sighed his relief. His eyes leaped to Hogue, lying nearby, and the proximity was a slap in Wilkinson's face.

The two were man and wife. May belonged to Hogue, he to her. It was wrong. Hogue did not deserve her. No man did. Only he, Wilkinson. The crafty madness stole over the sheriff's face as he watched the two people, begrimed and sprawled in obvious exhaustion, sleeping on the ground.

Between them was a money belt. Wilkinson's eyes narrowed, and the acid began to eat away his soul. It was Slade's money belt. In it was the money May Hogue had given Slade to keep him on the ranch. Wilkinson had almost whipped Slade that day. He had almost driven him off the land. But May Hogue had given the man fifty dollars.

Slade and Hogue. The two of them were keeping Wilkinson away from May. He wanted to bend down and whisper in May's ear that it wouldn't be that way much longer. Wilkinson would take care of that. Instead, he sat his horse and his mouth pursed the words, silently.

"May Hogue," Wilkinson said, silently, "What I'm going to do now will release you from this man. You mustn't mind, you mustn't fight, you mustn't care. It will be to your benefit, because I only do things for your benefit." His hands had clenched into fists, but Wilkinson scarcely noticed. It was habit with him. Love and lust and his little body, leaping forward, lashing out with fists and oaths and hot passion.

He continued, getting down from his horse, silently, so that neither would wake, "After Hogue, I'll take you away from Slade. Then you'll be where you belong, where you have to go." He bowed his head slightly then and with a quick, catlike move picked up the money belt. It was far heavier than he had expected, and the crafty look deepened on Wilkinson's face. The belt was of heavy leather, studded with silver. It was long and supple, oil-sheened and hand-rubbed. It seemed to Wilkinson that such a belt was strong enough to, say, support a man's dead weight.

He said, silently, to May Hogue, "Your husband is going to leave you now. It's God's will." He frowned at that thought. It was God's will, all right, but he was the agent. No one else ought to get the credit. Only he, Wilkinson. "Someday you'll thank me for this."

He stepped over toward Hogue, sleeping on his face and belly, his arms along his sides, the back of his head about four feet from the sheriff.

He eyed the man, measured him and let the ghost of a smile play on his lips. He breathed softly and thought how lucky Hogue was. He had had May, and now, in his sleep, he would leave her. No pain.

(and while Wilkinson measured the distance, his right leg drawing back, the immaculately-leathered toe pointing toward the back of Hogue's head, the sleeping man had one last thought. He thought, in his sweet sleep, that Slade was gone and with Slade gone, the ranch could be sold. May would be glad. They would get so much mon—)

The foot thudded home.

Quickly Wilkinson looked at May. She breathed deeply, once, let her breath out noisily and her legs stirred, sluggishly. Then she rolled away from the tiny disturbance beside her, and continued sleeping.

Wilkinson looped the heavy money belt about the throat of the unconscious Hogue. Then he tied a rope about Hogue's middle, the other end around the saddle horn, and softly urged the horse forward. Hogue's body scraped loudly along the ground, but May slept.

At the foot of a piñon, the sheriff stopped the horse and untied the rope from the horn. Then he looped it about a low branch of the tree, slip-hitched the rope and pulled it tight. He tested the strength of the branch, pulling himself up the rope so that his feet dangled from the ground. The branch bowed slightly but sprang back into place when Wilkinson dropped to the ground. It would hold, he knew. Now he cinched the short dangling end of rope to the money belt, tightened it until the edge of the leather cut under Hogue's chin, pulling his head up. The man's face began to purple.

The sheriff made sure he had plenty of rope. He spotted another tree nearby and swiftly measured the distance between the trees. The rope would reach. He slapped the rump of the animal and slowly the mare responded. Hogue lifted clear of the ground. The horse walked to the nearby tree as Wilkinson grudgingly let out rope. Then the sheriff led the horse several times around the second tree, the rope circling the trunk of the tree. Wilkinson unhitched the end from the saddle horn and tied it to the tree.

Hogue hung, legs swaying softly in the morning breeze. May Hogue whimpered once but continued sleeping. Wilkinson looked down at his lady love, tenderness on his face. Then he got back on his horse, and quickly rode from the valley.

May woke an hour later, suddenly frightened. She rolled over swiftly, her arm reaching out, and then she remembered the fire. She lay for a moment, staring up into the vast blue sky, before she looked to her side where Hogue had been.

She screamed.

…When she found his body, she thought at first he had killed himself. Then she realized dully that he couldn't have managed it. With shaking fingers and a kitchen knife, she cut down the body and not knowing why she was doing it, covered it with a tarpaulin.

Then she fled back into the house and crawled to her bedroom and, dry-eyed, sat at the window, a rifle in her hands. "Let them come," she whispered fiercely, "let them come, whoever it was. Let them come now." She was ready for them.

CHAPTER 14

Slade stood in the noon shade of timber along the northwest corner of the valley. He had crossed onto Thomas land a half-mile back. Now his horse was watering.

Slade looked along the curling piece of land below him. Tiny dots shifted before him with swift darting movements. They were men on horses, Slade knew. Thomas men. He counted five of them, stretched out in intervals from the charred fence between Crispin's ranch and the front of Thomas' ranch house, deep inside the Big T.

That meant up to five others were elsewhere. Maybe one or two in town. Maybe one or two sleeping—those who had been on the fire raid last night. One or two behind the ranch house or in with Thomas.

Slade knew he couldn't get to his man. There was no way to do it. Certainly there was no way to get away, once he had done it. He grinned, tight-mouthed. *Once he had done what?* he thought. Killed Thomas? Shot him in the back from a window? He laughed harshly. Nonsense. He couldn't shoot a man from ambush. That was for killers … or cowards.

Still, he wanted to get closer, just to see what he could see. Maybe it would matter, someday.

He continued to sweep wide, but this time he was driving for Thomas' house.

In an hour's time he had worked his horse to the direct rear of the ranch house. He sat his horse in a clump of trees on a tiny rise. Two men were standing together in the hollow rear of the house, between the house and the barn, off to one side. They had pistols strapped to their sides. One of them had a rifle across his back. They stood two hundred yards from Slade.

Slade frowned. It was a damn fool trick he was doing. Two hundred yards away lay death, and ten miles back was a moderate safety. He got down from his horse and took a handful of matches from his pocket. He tied the horse to a tree, deep in the clump, and bounced his finger against the horse's nose. He didn't worry much; the big brown was a good waiter. He'd be quiet.

Then Slade walked forward, toward the barn. The men were a hundred and fifty yards away, their backs to him. Slade pulled his hat deep over his eyes and continued walking at a normal pace. Once, one of the men started to turn and then swung back. Ice crawled up Slade's spine.

He reached the barn on watery legs. He looked inside and smiled. There was nobody, nothing alive in there. He scooped up a bale of hay and shoved it against the wooden wall of the barn. The hay crackled in his arms. It was dry as sand. Slade's smile deepened. It had been a crazy damn fool trick all along, but now it was starting to pay off.

He took a match, scratched it with the horny edge of his thumb nail and tossed it onto the hay. Then he swiftly bent down and picked up a heavy roll of wire and walked out of the barn. Nobody would bother him—he hoped—lugging wire. He was just another Thomas man. There was a piece of fence needed tightening. He was going to do the fixing. He walked along, wrestling his wire, his nose sniffing the air for the first smell of smoke.

Then he was in the clump of wood, the wire at his feet. He leaped onto the stallion, whispering, "Go on, boy, go on." The horse plunged through the woods until they hit the high trail that curved away from the ranch. They had gone fifty yards when Slade heard the first thin cry, "Fire! The barn's on fire!"

He grinned and then let his face form into a taut thin line. It hadn't been much, but at least it was the way Chet Crispin would have played it. He kept driving the horse until they reached the northwest corner from which he had viewed the ranch an hour or so before.

The tiny figures were moving more swiftly, all of them going toward the barn. Two new figures hove into view, from across the far valley floor, coming up from the pass. One of them Slade thought he recognized. It was a man with a bandage around his head. Tasker, no doubt.

The other man was a big man, hatless, and the afternoon sun was striking his bald head. Slade frowned and then continued to push the horse back toward Crispin's.

But a line of dust rode in Slade's throat and for some unknown reason, he was shaken.

He noticed the tarpaulin under the piñon and then went past, leading the frothing horse to the water trough and then to the corral.

There wasn't a sound to be heard at the ranch other than the horse's lapping of water and then its hooves crossing into the corral. Slade frowned. May and Hogue were no longer sleeping outside. There was so much to do that he doubted they had gone back to sleep inside the house.

He called out, "Hello, house."

Her voice reached him, strangled in her throat. She said, "Slade," from the window, a thin piteous wreck of a word, wrung from a tortured mouth.

He bounded to the house and through the door, alarm racing with him.

She turned from the window to meet him and she opened her arms to grab him while the sobs wracked her body.

They stayed close together that way for a full two minutes, while May Hogue cried, and then she leaned back and pushed Slade off. And she told him.

...Slade said finally, "Who could have done it?"

She shook her head. "What difference does it make?" she said, her words toneless.

Stubbornly his mind stayed there. "Not Thomas," he said. "It doesn't sound like his work."

She shrugged. She didn't care who it had been. It was the horror of it that still held her.

Slade thought of the new man he had seen with Tasker, the big bald man, and he wondered whether it had been he. The new man had Slade worried.

He said, "I'll bury the poor man."

She shook her head. "No, not yet. Tonight. When it's dark."

He said, "Why then?"

"Because I couldn't look at him now, in the light."

"I'll do it myself," Slade said.

She said softly, "He was my husband. At least I ought to be there when he's buried. I wasn't much good to him other times."

Slade was silent. He was glad for her softness. She was more womanly at this moment than she had ever been before, to Slade.

"What will you do now?" she said.

"Do?" he frowned.

"You can't stay here, you know," she said. "Now that—that Hogue is dead, you can't stay on."

"Of course," he said. "I—hadn't thought."

She bit her lip. "You never do. You never think of me that way, do you?"

He was embarrassed. "Let's not talk about it now," he said.

"Why not?" she said softly. "I can't pretend that I loved Hogue. He died a horrible death, and I'm saddened by it, but it doesn't change things much. I've wanted you ever since you rode in with him. The day he was dead drunk. But you never really wanted me."

"I did, once," Slade said.

"Sure," she said. "When I was a little chippy in that Utah gold camp. But not since then."

He didn't want to tell her how she stirred him, and how often. And yet she wanted to hear it. "Other times, too," he said.

She smiled. "That's nice. Even if you said that out of pity, that's nice."

He said, "I'll get my stuff ready. I'll pull out of here tonight—after the burial."

She nodded. Then her face clouded. "I'll sell the ranch, you know."

He wanted to cry out, "No, you can't," but he knew he had no right. It was her ranch, just as it had been her brother's—and now her husband, killed. Nobody could take more than that. He wondered if he could, himself.

He said, half-pleading, "Can you hold off a couple of days? Two or three?"

She said, "Why not? We've held off this long. Two or three days won't make any difference."

It might, he thought. In two or three days, he might have it whipped.

He said, "Stay here, in this room. Don't go outside."

She shivered and eyed him blankly. "Outside? Why would I go outside?"

He looked at her. She hovered near a state of shock. "Wait here," he said, stepping from the room. He went to the kitchen, to a lower pantry where Hogue kept his whisky. He pulled out a bottle and rushed back to the bedroom. She hadn't moved, her face waxen.

"Here," he said, jabbing the bottle at her.

She stared, unseeing.

"Here," he said harshly, putting the mouth of the bottle to her lips. He tilted it and the burning liquor forced its way down. Suddenly May pulled away, coughing, eyes running water.

"Good," he said grimly. "Now, are you all right?"

"Sure," she said, "I'm great. I never felt better in my life." The tears remained at her eyes.

He turned then and walked out of the house. She would be all right.

He got another horse from the corral, May's horse, a slender mare with white knees. The horse was graceful and Slade wondered how it would respond to so much more weight than it was accustomed to. He got on and the horse turned her head to stare white-eyed at her new rider. Then she accepted Slade and started to prance off.

Slade turned her to the piñon under which Hogue's body lay. The horse shied and then gave ground stubbornly. Slade hit her and cursed her and she moved, slowly. That was all right, Slade thought. He was going to trail another horse's marks, and you can't trail fast.

He prodded the horse to the tarp and then got down and removed the canvas. He looked at Hogue's body, and his eyes narrowed when he saw the deeper-dark imprint and the matted blood on Hogue's skull. It appeared as though the man had been struck in the head first, before he had been strung up. Slade forced the frightened horse to sniff all around the body, and then he got back on the mare.

Slade saw May's footprints among the black ashes under the tree, the heavy dragging marks of the tarp. Then he found the other marks. They led from the tree to another tree, thirty yards away. He saw where the rope had burned into the trunk of the tree, before May had cut it free. The marks below the tree—horse's hoof prints—turned and started back across the valley. Whoever it was had not gone on to Thomas', but out of the valley via the pass at the far end. That made it tougher, Slade knew, yet it made more sense, too. It had not looked like a Thomas job.

He followed the horse's tracks, losing them often in the dry unburned grass and picking them up in the ashes. Sometimes he came across the same steps, slightly shorter as though the horse and rider were in less of a hurry coming into the valley. That, too, made sense, Slade thought grimly.

He knew for sure, then, that the man on horse who had hanged Hogue had come from the valley pass and had gone out that way.

He let the mare smell the tracks again and again. Then he gave her her head. She followed, eyeing the invisible trail, heading straight for the pass.

Slade kept thinking: two or three days. With a break now, it might be less.

The mare led Slade through the valley and into the hills and down again, toward Cowpoke. In the dusty street, mixed with the marks of a hundred other marks, the mare lost the trail once and stood in bewilderment, nostrils quivering. Then she plodded forward.

When she stopped, two hours after Slade had picked up the trail at the base of the piñon, they were outside a hitching post attached to the sagging white-fronted office of Wilkinson, the sheriff. A brown mare leaned against the post, white-muzzled, panting.

And Slade knew.

The sheriff was the only man capable of such an act. And the sheriff was the kind of man who'd lead his horse back to his hitching post without watering him. He was the kind of man who'd not bother to cover up his tracks. Inside, Wilkinson must have felt he was too big to have to stoop to caution.

Slade looked into the office. Nobody was there.

He tied his horse to the same post after watering her across the street in a tin trough, and then Slade started walking the main drag of Cowpoke.

At the saloon, he stopped. Then he walked in.

Wilkinson was at the bar, drinking his brandy.

Slade stepped to the bar. He said to the bartender, "A beer, please." He had peeled some bills from his money belt before he threw it on the ground earlier that morning; he knew he'd have to have some to see him by.

Wilkinson looked up. "Well," he said, "the big do-gooder. Everybody's little helper."

Slade said, "And the little sheriff who kicks drunks in the head."

Wilkinson's face went white and he drew back. "What do you mean?" he said quietly. His hand played with a button on his shirt, up around the chest.

Slade watched the sheriff. Wilkinson had a gun hidden in a shoulder holster, he guessed. He said, "Oh, you know. That day in the bar, kicking poor Hogue in the head."

Wilkinson kept his thin-eyed stare on Slade. "That's—that's what you're talking about?"

"Why," Slade asked, "have you kicked anybody else lately?"

The sheriff snarled and drained his glass. He started to turn and walk away.

Slade said, "Not so fast, sheriff. I just want to let you know I'm aware of your savage little ways. And I don't intend to keep it all to myself."

The sheriff said, "What are you talking about, Slade?"

Slade said, "You know damn well what I'm talking about. Tell Thomas and Abbott that Slade doesn't intend to let this little war remain so secret. Tell them Slade knows what they're up to—and what you're up to, too, you little bastard."

Wilkinson's hand started to rip at the button. Slade grabbed his shirt front and wrist in his left hand and twisted. The shirt clutched at Wilkinson's throat. "How does it feel, Wilkinson?" Slade said, his face close to the sheriff's bugging eyes. "How do you like it? The pressure on your throat until you can't breathe?"

The bartender looked at the two men. He said uneasily, "Here, now, no fooling around." He didn't want to lose his license. The sheriff was just that sort he'd take it out on some innocent spectator.

Slade said, "Mind your business, 'tender. He won't bother you. Wouldn't be a bit surprised if he never bothered anybody again."

Wilkinson's face was crimson, his forehead beaded with sweat. He struggled against the hand at his shirt, twisting the material until a knot like a small rock started clamping down on his air pipe. Something seemed to pull in his throat and then the pulling increased until it felt like a muscle tearing in there. He tried to cry out, but no sound came from his throat.

Then Slade swiftly ripped open the shirt and reached in with his left hand. He came out with a single-shot derringer, a dainty weapon, the kind women like to play with. He hefted the little gun and pressed the stubby barrel to Wilkinson's head. "Just tell Thomas," Slade said, "that I'm waiting for him at the ranch. Tell Abbott, too." Then he shoved the sheriff from his stool, the little man clattering to the floor, lying on his back, his hand at his throat. He was too frightened to move.

Slade walked out, the derringer in his pocket. He went back to the ranch, to help bury Hogue.

CHAPTER 15

Abbott said, "All right, Wilkinson, stop squealing." Another killing. Good God, how could he stop the damn thing before it burned him?

Wilkinson shook his head. The pain in his throat was still dagger-sharp. All night he had lain in bed, cold rags around his throat. But the pain eased only a trifle. And when he talked now, it—it was just dreadful. "No," he said, a thin piping sound coming from that broken throat, "no, I won't stop. You've got to do something. I'm in this because you wanted the protection of the law. Now I need some protection. If you don't get that man out of the valley, I swear I'll go to Santa Fe and spread the whole thing before the Governor." He clutched his throat. The pain was unbelievable.

Abbott smiled. "And face a charge for killing Hogue? And complicity in Crispin's death, too? No, you won't do that, sheriff. You couldn't stand up to that. Besides, they'll never believe it's you, with that new soprano you've suddenly developed."

Wilkinson said, "All right, test me." He got up and walked to the door. He was bluffing and Abbott knew he was bluffing, but Wilkinson was sure Abbott couldn't afford to take the chance that he wasn't bluffing.

Abbott stared at him. Then he sighed. He said, "Sit down, Wilkinson. You win. Soprano or not, you're the toughest man I know. Sit down, we'll try to figure things out. Once and for all, this time."

Wilkinson returned to his chair, lips trembling. He said, through the pain, "There's nothing to figure out. Send Thomas over there with a few men and kill the man. Shoot him down. It doesn't matter anymore how you do it. Just have it done. Cold blood, ambush, murdered in his bed. What difference does it make? Just so long as we're rid of the man."

Abbott acknowledged the truth of it. They had let it slide too long, trying to play it quietly and in little acts. But the result had been all wrong. The little acts added up, and the whole stage was aflame.

He thought of Dilt.

"All right, sheriff," he said. "I'll see Thomas. It will be done."

Wilkinson whispered, "It better be done. I'm sick of that man, grabbing me." The shame flooded him, hotter than the pain. Twice now Slade had laid his big hands on him. The second time should have been the last. He should have killed Slade, on the spot. But—and he sobbed inside—Slade hadn't let him. It was so unfair.

Abbott said, "What are you waiting for? I told you it would be done. Clear out of here, I've got work to do."

Wilkinson got to his feet. Now Abbott was ordering him around. His hand went to his shirt. His fingers played with the frayed thread of a missing button. His hideout gun was gone. Wilkinson thought: Abbott is a lucky man. If the gun were in there, Abbott would be staring into it, right now.

He walked from the bank office.

Abbott got on his horse and headed for the valley. He would see Thomas, later. First he had some place else to go. He pointed his horse for the north slope, a tired man, still trying to hold the broken strings in his hand, trying to tie them together before they flew away.

Now was the time to deal from both ends of the deck. Slade and Thomas. Then it would be over. Abbott couldn't afford to wait any longer.

He headed his horse for Ben Mudge's spread.

Mudge said, "How come you've changed your mind, Abbott?"

They sat in Mudge's kitchen, drinking cold milk. Abbott said, "I've not changed my mind, Mudge. I've finally come to my decision. We can see clear to make that loan. That's all. You people just don't know how banks operate. We can't hand out money until we're sure it's going to be put into productive use."

Mudge said, "And now you reckon this spread'll put your money into productive use?" He waved his hand and Abbott followed with his eyes. The rundown land, the untended fences, the sunburned crops.

He said, "Look here, man, can't you be thankful for what the bank is doing? Stop looking a gift horse in the mouth, Mudge."

The little rancher said, "Oh, I'm thankful, all right. Don't misunderstand me. The money's right welcome. But I can't swallow your explanations. I never figured you for a big-hearted man, Abbott."

The banker forced a grin. "I can't afford to be, in my business. Still, sometimes we find ourselves with lots of unfrozen funds and we decide to invest them. Every investment is a gamble. We're gambling on you, Mudge." He broadened his smile. "And I'm betting we both win."

Mudge sighed. He was a stubborn man, and right now he smelled dirt. He said, "How about Early? You betting on him, too?"

Abbott drummed the kitchen table with his fingers. He stared at the rancher. The time had come. He said, "Yes, as a matter of fact, I am."

Mudge shook his head. "His land's in worse shape than mine. I'm thinking you're a damn fool, as bankers go, Abbott."

Abbott said, "Mudge, I suppose I'll have to tell you." He paused to lend weight to what was to follow. The rancher sat stock still, staring at him. "You people here on the north slope are coming into a landfall."

Mudge said, mouth unmoving, "How so?"

"Southwestern Lines is building through the Sierra Verde valley."

The other man let his breath out softly. "The railroad?"

Abbott nodded.

"Coming through here?"

Again Abbott nodded.

Mudge got up and started to walk the kitchen floor. "Up the north slope?"

Abbott shook his head. "Don't be a damn fool. Why would anybody build on the slope when they can build on the valley floor?"

Mudge spun around, his eyes popping. "They're going to lay rail across Big Thomas' spread, is that it?"

Abbott said, "Yes, that's it. But not yet. Not for another month or so. And they'll not do it if the word gets bruited about. The railroad will pay fair money for the land it buys, but it doesn't want to be suckered."

"But Thomas knows about it," Mudge exploded. "Don't try to tell me he doesn't. No wonder he's been trying to buy out Crispin."

Abbott said, "Thomas knows, but he doesn't know how soon. And take my word for it, no railroad is going to come on through here if there's any more trouble in the valley."

Mudge said, "Damn right they won't. I know that." His eyes still shone. "The railroad, eh? Buying up Thomas land. That will make me and Wilbur and Crispin's place kingpins in the valley. We'll hustle our steer to the cattle cars cheaper than anyone in the whole damn territory."

Abbott laughed. "Maybe not the whole territory."

Mudge waved his hand. "No matter. So it won't be the whole territory. We'll still pay less to get our cows freighted than anybody within forty miles of the Sierra Verde."

"Until the railroad builds a little further."

Mudge nodded. "Naturally. I'm no hog, Abbott. I don't expect a monopoly on luck. Just a little bit now will be enough."

Abbott said, "It shouldn't be a little bit. So far as I know—and I'm in a pretty good position to know—there are no immediate plans to extend the rail line much farther up the territory. Not yet, anyway."

Mudge pounded his fist against the table. "God," he said, "we'll clean up, Wilbur and me. After all those lean years. God!"

Abbott said, "But don't spread the word. Understand? I'll tell Early myself."

Mudge said, "Don't worry. I'm not slitting my throat. Just so long as that wolf Thomas keeps away for a while."

Abbott smiled thinly. "I think Big Thomas will have enough to worry about for a while." He got up from the table and extended his hand. "Good luck to you, Mudge. Your money and credit are waiting for you down at the bank. Come on down any time—tomorrow morning, in fact—and we'll pass it along."

Mudge took Abbott's hand. And even in that heady moment, the little rancher felt doubt ride in the handclasp. He said, "What if—what if Big Thomas *does* try to take over this place? I don't mean try to *buy* it, I mean *take* it." He licked his lips. "Then what? What do I keep him off with?"

Abbott said smoothly, "That's easy enough, Mudge. Just tell him that in case of your death—and Early's—the land will revert to the mortgage holder." He tapped his own chest. "The Cowpoke Bank and Trust Company. Thomas might run you off, but it's not going to do him a bit of good."

Mudge said, wonder breaking through his voice. "You're a helluva gambler, Abbott. Now I see why you're writing out that loan. The value of this land is going to double, maybe treble—and you'll own it, in case we go under."

Abbott shrugged. "That's the way banks operate."

Mudge said, "I'm not so sure I'm going to come on down for that loan and credit, Abbott. Maybe we'll squeeze by until then on what we've got. At least we still own most of our land."

Abbott opened the door and stood there, the valley lying before him. "Suit yourself, Mudge. Don't take the loan. Keep the land mortgage-free. But you'll never be able to expand your holdings, build up your graze and your cattle. And if Thomas runs you out, the bank won't protect you. Take the loan, and the bank becomes your partner. Thomas is not going to crowd you off land that he wouldn't be able to claim even then. That's just common sense." Abbott turned and walked swiftly to his horse.

Mudge called, "It ain't common sense to kill a man or burn someone else's land, is it? I'm not so sure Thomas thinks the way you do."

Abbott got on his horse. There was no need to answer such a man. If he didn't see that it *was* common sense to kill a man for his land or burn it down to scare another man off, why, then, Mudge wouldn't listen to any explanation. Of course it was common sense.

Abbott rode to Early's spread, adjoining Mudge's. He was thinking it would soon be over, nice and neat. It was a lucky thing, Abbott thought, that this was 1878. Ten years ago, there were no railroads, no banks out here. Ten years from now, there'd be too many, and too much law. There would have been no reason to pull this off ten years ago. Ten years from now, there would be no opportunity.

A man was lucky to be alive in this day and age, Abbott thought.

A half-hour later he blew the dank smell of Wilbur Early's property out of his thin nose and turned the horse across the valley, to the west. Early was not a man to turn down money. He'd be at the bank the next day. So would Mudge, Abbott thought. Once the news sank in, he'd come around, all suckered-up, looking for his pot of gold. The rainbow had sunk its end into the north slope of the Sierra Verde.

The other end, Abbott mused, lay in the cool vaults of the Cowpoke bank.

Abbott glanced to his right, where Crispin's range began. He saw the black rails of fence, strewn on the equally black ground. He wondered what Slade was doing, just now.

The thought jolted Abbott. No longer did he feel confident about the other man's actions. He had been wrong too often. Now he had to wait on Slade's next move before he knew what it was. Was he skulking about the emptiness of Crispin's? No, Abbott thought, he couldn't do that, not with Hogue dead. Abbott was amused. The proprieties held steadfast even in the face of war. Slade wouldn't be at the ranch. Where then?

In town? In a room at the hotel? Abbott nodded. That would make sense. There would be less likelihood of a Thomas man lying in ambush in the crowded street of Cowpoke. And violence in town might not go unheeded. Yes, Slade might be at the hotel.

Abbott frowned, working his horse closer to Thomas' ranch house. Or he might not. Slade was not running, the way other hares had run, frightened and hellbent for a safe dark hole in the ground.

Well, it didn't matter. Thomas and Dilt would flush him out, wherever Slade was.

Abbott tied his horse near the winding creek and walked the remaining quarter-mile to the house. He felt better, walking. It was more civilized. He was feeling quite exhilarated when he knocked firmly at the ranch house door and Maria let him in.

Slade watched Abbot enter Thomas' house. He and the big brown stallion had worked their way swiftly to the rise behind the house, in the clump of trees. There were no men on guard behind the house. The barn, half in ruins, stood neglected. A rear door—undoubtedly into the kitchen—was unprotected. Sometimes the woman he heard called Maria came through with trash for burning. Otherwise, the door was vulnerable.

Abbott said, "I'm sorry, Thomas, but the railroad can't wait any longer. The first rails will push through in ten days' time."

Thomas, his face flushed, a vein pounding and bulging in the center of his forehead, stood in the middle of the room, his grace impeded by his fury, muscles bunched in knots. He said, "But it has to wait!"

Abbott said, "You don't understand, man, there's more to this rail laying than one man's fortune. You can't stop progress. The rails are coming through and that's that."

Thomas' hand crashed down against a dark mahogany highboy. "No, dammit. That's *not* that. I've got my whole life staked out on this one bit of business. A hunk of rail isn't going to snuff it out. I won't allow it."

Abbott raised an eyebrow. "You won't, eh? What do you propose to do about it?"

Thomas' face burned black beneath his smooth olive skin. His hands groped at his sides. He said, voice low and hissing, "It's got to be stopped and it's going to be stopped. And I don't care if ten banks and a dozen railroads don't like it. I'm not going to allow myself to be stampeded out of this one chance to see myself clear the rest of my life. There's empire out there, and I'm going to have it." He walked over to Abbott on springy legs, his words forcing optimism into his body. "You'll slow down that railroad. I'll move fast in the valley. We'll have it licked. But I won't have a ten-day deadline staring me in the face."

Abbott cracked his knuckles. He had told Mudge and Early that the rails would take another month. Now he had said ten days to Thomas. He could give in a little to the rancher and still be safe. He didn't want to tell Mudge and Early that the rails would be in sooner—because if they weren't, the men would start to crack. He wanted them to stand firm. A month was not too much to ask.

Yet if he compromised now with Thomas, the man would regain his composure. Abbott continued to stare down at his hands, deep in thought.

Thomas leaned over. "Well?" he said. "Do I get the time?"

Abbott said, "Thomas, do you know when the payment on your mortgage is due?"

Thomas frowned. "Now what the hell," he breathed. "What's that got to do with it?"

Abbott sighed. "The bank can't carry you any longer, Thomas. That date is already due. In fact, it was due two weeks ago. I haven't bothered you because—because there's been enough around here to keep your mind off money details. But I can't let it ride any longer. In ten days the railroad men will come through—sooner, possibly—to start proceedings to buy you out. Unless—" Abbott bent his head forward and with silent satisfaction he watched Thomas pull back— "unless you meet that mortgage payment, there won't be any need to deal with you at all. You won't even own the Big T." He kept his eyes on Thomas.

And the man broke.

"You damned money-eating bastard!" he roared. "What the hell are you trying to do?"

"Nothing," Abbott said softly, "nothing at all, except run my business along business lines. I've helped you right up to this point. If you can't follow the rest of it through—if you can't conclude your dealings with Mudge and Early and Crispin's, then I'd be a damn fool to finance you any further. You're becoming a bad risk, Thomas, did you know that?"

Thomas reached forward to the other man's shoulders. He dragged Abbott out of his chair—like a man pulling a scarecrow from a pole—and he said, "All right, Abbott. You're a double-crossing son of a bitch, but you've got me in a hole. I'll conclude my dealings, all right. Beginning with you." He pulled back his right fist.

Abbott smiled at the man. He said quickly, "Careful, Thomas. I don't even have to give you ten days."

Thomas swore once and hurled Abbott back into the chair. Then he turned and walked swiftly to the door. He jerked it open. "Get out of here," he panted. "Get the hell out of here before I—before I—"

Abbott said, "Before you lose those ten days." He walked past Thomas, barely brushing the man and he could feel the electricity bristling.

Thomas stood in the doorway, watching the banker walk to his horse, mount and ride toward the valley pass. Thick anger lay like a boulder on his chest. A red smear passed across his vision and he had to wipe the sweat from his eyes. There in front of him was his land, good fertile land, sweet deep grass, big-chested cows. It had always been good land. It was never better than just now.

And it was slipping away. Wearily, he tried to remember how it had started. With Crispin, he thought. No, not with Crispin. Crispin had been there for years, and he had never minded him. It had begun with Abbott. With Abbott's news about the railroad coming through. Abbott had boasted slyly how he had pulled wires until the rails were headed straight for the Sierra Verde. Abbott had got the railroad to decide to come through.

Thomas swore. If Abbott could pull that off, he sure as hell could get the railroad to wait another two or three weeks. Ten days would probably be enough time, Thomas thought, but it might not be. Abbott could have given him those two or three weeks. He had chosen not to.

Thomas watched the man ride away, neat and clean in his saddle, a man who didn't belong on a horse but who rode with businesslike crispness when he got up.

Abbott.

Abbott could tell the railroad that Thomas had to use his valley floor for a couple of extra weeks. That he was trekking some cows across to get them out of the valley. That he was removing rock from the floor to make it easier for the road gang to lay its rails. Anything at all. Abbott could slow them down.

But he didn't want to.

And Thomas could see why. The man stood to take over Thomas' land. Yet that didn't even make sense. Abbott was a wealthy man already. Thomas' land didn't mean that much.

He called thickly, "Maria. Come here, Maria."

The woman's feet pattered swiftly. "Yes?" she said, at his side.

"Send Morgan in to me."

She said, "Yes," and waited a fleeting second. But he said nothing else and did not even look at her. She went.

Two minutes later, Morgan bulked in the room. His face was still blotchy from the beating he had taken, but he walked like a bear. He was not a man to remember a beating. He said, "Boss? You want me?"

Thomas said, "I want you to lay off five men."

Morgan said, "Lay off five men?"

Thomas swore. "That's right, dammit. Shall I spell it?"

Morgan shook his head. "I think it's a bad time to lay off men."

Thomas whirled. "Stop thinking, then. Just do it."

"There's a roundup coming up," Morgan said stubbornly.

Thomas advanced on him, his hands hard as rocks. He said, "How would you like to have your face smashed in again?"

Morgan said levelly, "Boss, I'll do what you say. But I don't like it."

"Don't like it. I don't give a damn. Just do it, I say." Five men wasn't much. But it would mean that much more money saved. He had to meet that mortgage payment. Two thousand dollars. He couldn't sell any cows in time—unless he brought them in for butchering in town, and that wouldn't mean much money, nor could the meat shops handle too much gross. Still, that would be something. But where would the rest come from? He rubbed his brow.

Morgan said, "Which five men?"

Thomas said, "Any five, dammit. The last five hired. No, not the new man. Keep Dilt."

Morgan's eyes narrowed. "Why Dilt?"

"Because I said so," Thomas said. "Stop asking so many damn questions. In a minute, you'll go too."

Morgan said, "You don't need Dilt to take care of Slade. I can do it."

Thomas said, "Yeah. Like you did the last time. Go on, Morgan. Get the damn thing over with. Five men. Make sure Tasker, Connors and Voss are among them. They're no good anymore." Once Slade had licked a man, he didn't seem much use to Thomas. Morgan was different, though, Thomas thought. He was too damn dumb and too proud to know he had been licked.

Morgan said, "Anything else?"

"Yes," Thomas said. "Send Dilt in here."

Morgan whirled without a word. He slammed the door and Thomas could hear his heavy boots along the gravel walk.

Thomas felt better. At least he was doing something. The five men and the butchered cows would bring him, or save him, three or four hundred dollars. He'd have to figure how to get the rest.

Meanwhile, he had two other moves to make. One was on Mudge and Early. That oughtn't be too hard. The other was Slade.

Dilt came in, hatless, the great bald head sweaty and lumpy.

Thomas looked at the new man. He was another thing Abbott had inflicted on him. The man was no cattleman, even though he had top-handed some Texas ranch, so he had said. He was a brawler and nothing else. Well, that was what Thomas needed. A brawler. He said to Dilt, "About ready for some work?"

Dilt shrugged indifferently. "Whatever you say. Not that I relish wrestling these damn cows."

"Rather wrestle your man Slade?"

The man's eyes glowed. "Say the word, I'll wrestle him right now."

Thomas said drily, "Fine. Go right ahead."

Dilt hesitated. "I mean, show him to me, and I'll wrestle him. I'll break his thick neck."

Thomas said, thinking aloud, "That's the problem, isn't it? Finding the man. For too damn long, we couldn't move without seeing him. Now we don't even know where he is."

"Maybe he's run out?"

"Maybe," Thomas said. "But why now?"

Dilt's chest swelled. "Maybe he saw me. Maybe he knows I'm around."

Thomas looked at Dilt closely. "You've got a hell of a big faith in yourself. Anybody ever lick you in a fair fight?"

Dilt said, "Not yet. They say there's always somebody who can take you, but I've never met the man. Slade sure as hell isn't the one. I practically broke him in two that night we tangled."

"What'd you scrap over?" Thomas said. The big bald man intrigued him somehow; fighting had become a way of life. Thomas wondered whether he wasn't on the same trail himself. There had been a time when brawling and gunplay were things that happened on other ranches, in other valleys. Now they swamped Thomas' life.

Dilt shook his head. "I don't recall, rightly. Over some money he owed me, I think."

"Slade doesn't strike me as the kind of man to back down on a debt."

Dilt said loudly, "I said I don't rightly recall. Maybe it wasn't a debt. Maybe I just wanted to tangle with him."

"You like fighting?"

Dilt leaned close. "Like it?" he said, low-voiced, intense. "Like it? Why, there's nothing in the world approaches it. You and him, see? You and him and nothing else, just the two of you trying to find out who's the better man. You stand there and try to beat him down, and he tries to beat you down. And when it's over, only one of you walks away. That's the right of it. One of you wins the right to walk away while the other one has to lie there, beaten. And when it's you who walks away, the blood sings in your ears and you're big as the sky and strong as a mountain. That's the way it is. There's nothing like it in the whole world."

Thomas said, "And when it's the other guy who walks away and you lie there, swallowing your blood?"

Dilt said, his lip curling, "I wouldn't know. It's never happened."

Thomas said, "But when it does, if it ever does? Then how will you feel?"

Dilt said, "I don't know. But that's the chance of it. That's what makes it so great. You never really know—no, not even me. It's a fierce game, I tell you."

Thomas said, "You make me sick, Dilt."

Dilt said, "Every man to his poison. You make me sick, thinking of ways to steal a man's land or kill a man."

Thomas looked at the bald man sharply. He said, "Go into town and look for Slade there. Ask around if anybody's seen him. Stay overnight if you have to. Then check back in here."

Dilt said, "Right. And if I find him?"

"Find out again who's the better man." Thomas leaned forward. "But if you do tangle with him, you've got to handle it this way—" He spoke quietly and swiftly, and Dilt nodded, his left hand wide open while his right fist burrowed into it. Once he stopped and said, "No, that's not fair," but Thomas said, "You'll do it my way, or not at all. Do you understand?" Dilt nodded again, finally, and then he turned and left the ranch house.

Slade had felt the breath whoosh out of his body when Dilt walked from the bunkhouse to the ranch house. Then he remembered the big bald man coming in with Tasker the other day, and he remembered, too, his own sense of uneasiness. Somehow he must have known the man was Dilt. The wild red nightmare of a man knocking him to the ground, time after time, and saying hoarsely in his ear, "Fall, you son of a bitch, fall," swept back over Slade.

Well, he thought, it had come down to this. He had no time to waste. If it meant tangling with Dilt to bring Thomas down on him, he'd have to tangle with Dilt. Slade had only a day or two to finish it up. Then May Hogue would sell her ranch and get out. And whoever bought it would undoubtedly knuckle under when Big Thomas came around, guns waving, and asking for the land. Mudge and Early would fold, too, Slade thought.

He worked the big brown horse back to the timber and then back to the south, toward the pass. It was unfamiliar ground and they moved slowly, Dill's big rangy frame fading from view. But Slade did not worry. He knew Dilt was going to town. The big man would be in Cowpoke, in one of the saloons, probably the big one. Slade would find him. He wondered whether any other Thomas men would be with Dill. He had to be careful; they could work him into a corner and make him reach for his .44. Then they'd gun him down, and the war would be over.

He'd have to hurry. Dilt was alone thus far. Maybe Slade could keep it that way. He hurried the horse, not knowing that every time he spurred the animal, he was Playing Thomas' game, not knowing that Thomas was trying to flush him out just as fast as Slade was trying to flush Thomas out.

The late afternoon sun flooded Cowpoke, dust and heat wrapping their dry tentacles about the little cattle town, Slade moved his horse behind the main drag on a fluted road of rock and dust. He kept looking across to the main street, but Dilt was not there. The man had holed up someplace, probably in one of the saloons. Dilt was a drinking man, Slade knew.

Once Slade had seen five Thomas men, small packs on their backs and their saddlebags loaded, riding through the town. He had pulled his horse into an alley and watched, but they had their eyes straight ahead, hats drawn down and bandannas across their throats. They looked like men headed for a long drive. Slade watched. They went straight through town, watered at the last trough and kept right on going. Slade wondered where Thomas was sending five men—half his force. The confidence of Thomas, the cool contempt of the man shook Slade. Thomas was acting like a man who didn't have a care, cutting his guns in half just when Slade was trying to work the war to its final shootout.

Then Slade thought: they'll be back. Thomas wasn't a damn fool. And he kept looking for Dilt.

Finally, when evening started to crowd the sun to the center of the street and shadows crawled along the wooden walks, Slade worked his way to the main drag and to the saloons.

He was dry and tired, saddle-aching and dulled by the grinding days and nights of fire and clash. He had slept the last night on the ground— after he and May had buried Hogue—in the timber at the northwest corner of Thomas' ranch, his hand on his .44. But at least he had slept. The night before had been the poker game and the grass fire and the long ride to Thomas'.

Now another night faced him, bitter and full of more grinding hours of movement. And after that, maybe another. Then—no more. May Hogue would sell her ranch and Thomas would swarm in. Slade drew breath into his lungs and walked through the swinging doors of the big saloon.

He walked on through and drank a beer at an empty bar, the cold amber brew washing the dust through him, clearing his head. Then he turned and stared at the room of half-filled tables, the evening drinkers beginning slowly in the twilight heat, the night still not full on them.

And at a table in a dark corner, Slade saw Dilt. The big man was alone—though Slade did not know for sure which man was a Thomas man and which was not in that dim room of slowly rising clamor. Dilt raised his shot glass to his mouth, looked across it to the bar and the two men locked eyes. Dilt reached into his shirt and took out the sock, hefted it three times while Slade stared at it. Then Dilt laid it on the table and slowly got up, a huge man, filling the room. He took off his holster—and Slade breathed easier—and laid it next to the sock, and then he stepped into the middle of the room, arms out at his sides, curling forward like baling hooks.

Slade's hands moved to his holster and unsnapped it. The money belt was underneath, weighing him down, but he wasn't taking it off. Once before he had tossed his stake to Dilt.

The holster lay on the bar and the bartender snatched it up and hooked it below the bar, out of sight. Then Slade stepped swiftly to the open area of the room, tables scraping next to him while space cleared. Two or three men moved quickly to the door and through, and Slade thought: those are the wise ones.

But the rest leaned back, out of the arena, yet close enough to smell the sweat and see the blood. Saliva gushed through their mouths and their chests contracted and then swelled. The fight was theirs, too.

Dilt said, "Come on, man, let's get it over."

And Slade came on. He, too, wanted to get it over. After Dilt, there surely would be a Thomas man going back to his boss: come on out, Slade's still standing.

The only problem, Slade thought as he walked into range of those hairy bailing hooks that dangled from Dilt's shoulders, was to keep standing.

Dilt lashed out with his right fist, swinging it in a wide arc and Slade turned his left arm and ducked it, the blow bouncing off the meaty part of his shoulder. Still, pain jolted to Slade's skull. He kept his shoulder high and bent his body low, below the taller man who squinted at him and then raised both hands and brought them down, fingers clasped into a two-fisted hammer head.

But Slade moved inside and the blow swept off his back. Slade pumped out his right hand into Dilt's body and the rangy man backed off. Slade swung his left in a short half-circle, the fist smacking against Dilt's cheek as the man pulled away. Dilt lurched back and someone in the crowd yelled, "Look out, he's going down!" But Slade knew the man's own backward movement had sapped the punch of its power. Dilt hit a table and righted himself and rushed Slade.

This time Slade got inside the right fist, but Dilt had his left held low and ready, and he clubbed it into Slade's side and then brought it up savagely and Slade staggered away, the blood washed from his brain and his body suddenly fairy light and trembly. Dilt was on him then, grabbing him with his left hand about Slade's upper arm and swinging the right to Slade's heart. Slade ducked and swayed and through hazy eyes saw Dilt measuring him for another downward punch to Slade's aching ribs.

And Slade said, "You're through, Dilt, you don't know how to hurt a man anymore."

Dilt stopped and swore. "I'll hurt you, Slade," he said, "I'll kill you," he panted. And he swung the crushing right again.

But Slade shoved his left elbow down and Dilt winced as his fist cracked against the lump of callus and bone on Slade's arm. Then the two men stood apart and Slade leaned forward and smashed his right hand into Dilt's open mouth. Dilt cried out, blood at his lips, and a half-tooth followed the cry.

"Come on, man," Slade said, balancing himself, and as Dilt roared and lunged forward, he drove home the right hand again, into the mouth once more and the blood rolled down the side of Dilt's chin.

Now Slade moved into his man, the left fist pounding the body until Dilt started to bend at the waist, and the right crashing against the side of Dilt's face. Slade felt Dilt's cheekbone splinter and the man's face suddenly turned lopsided.

Dilt pulled back, his hand to his face and the tiny yellow lights in his eyes began to fade. Then he stepped back farther, toward the dim corner from which he had first padded forth, Slade on top of him, his arms lashing the bald man until it seemed he had to fall.

But Slade knew Dilt wouldn't go down until his backward march had stopped. Dilt was riding the storm and Slade's arms were heavy as oaks. But once Dilt reached the edge of the table from which he had risen, he'd have no place to go, except into Slade's fists.

Dilt backed up a step at a time, his eyes glazing and his mouth foolish, but his legs held firm. Someone cried out from across the room, "Wait till the big guy hits that table. He'll go over like a tenpin."

And Dilt hit the table. The foolish look disappeared and a crafty look replaced it. Dilt reached back behind him, and for an instant Slade froze, thinking: he's going for his gun.

Desperately Slade leaned into the man, smashing one last right hand at Dilt, seeing the man bend with the blow and nearly topple over the table. But he righted himself again, and in his hand when he faced Slade was the sock.

Slade stared down at the heavy sock, and he knew he should have used it on Dilt in the street of Cutter that night long, long ago because, sure as hell, Dilt was going to use it on him. Slade leaped forward, both hands grappling for the sock, but Dilt pulled it away, dangling it and then swiftly it raised and whirled and came down, the night air whistling and then singing and turning bright yellow and red, while Slade's skull seemed to crack open. Then the night air whistled softly and the colors were all gray and black and whirling far, far away. Slade thought: face down into the sawdust, *it's all over, it's all over*. In a way, he was glad.

He didn't hear Dilt mumble thickly, "All right, leave him be. Just a friendly brawl. I'll take him up to my hotel room, and he'll be all right. Just leave him be."

Nor did Slade feel himself clumsily lifted by the still pain-sick Dilt and another man who had come out of the shadows, and carried into the cool night air and up a wooden flight of stairs.

The other man, a Thomas man, said to Dilt, in the hotel room, "Now what?"

Dilt said, "Now we let the boss know, Haydn." Haydn moved to the door.

Dilt said, "Wait. The boss said bring back Slade's money belt and a key to the room. Take the belt off the man."

Haydn removed the belt from the slowly squirming Slade. The weight of it surprised him. He licked his lips.

Dilt said, "We'll count it together, Haydn. Then if you don't show up with all of it, I'll know."

The man stopped licking his lips. Quickly they counted out the money—the near one thousand dollars of it and the one silver dollar—and then they tied Slade securely and tossed him on the bed. Haydn left with the money belt and the key, and Dilt could hear the horse's feet beating toward the valley pass.

Dilt turned from the window and pulled up a chair. He sat down next to the bed and he murmured to the unconscious man, "You're a hell of a man, Slade." He felt his own fractured cheekbone, the broken bone under a half-inch lump that sent black-yellow streaks up to the eye and down to his jaw line.

Dilt felt a mild disappointment with this brawl. He didn't like to brawl under orders of another man. It had been Thomas' idea to use the sock if he had to. Dilt shook his head. He didn't know for sure, now, whether he could have taken Slade. It had ended all wrong. Maybe the man on the floor, beaten unconscious, had been the better man, and the man who had stood up had been the loser. Dilt didn't know, and it was important to Dilt that he know. Back in Cutter, he had thought he was the better man. But tonight had been different. Slade had fooled him.

He looked at the unconscious man again, and he said, "Boy, sometime you and I are going to tangle with nobody around and nobody to make rules except the two of us. Then we'll find out."

The words hung in the room and then Slade stirred and opened his eyes. He let his gaze move about the room, until he had gained an idea of where he was. He looked down at himself, at the rope binding his ankles and his wrists. He said to Dilt, "Untie my hands and feet, and I'll beat your guts in. You dirty coward."

Thomas stared into the black maw of the valley, night coming in thick and wet. A summer mist blotted out the stars and put a wet haze on the moon, and a man breathed water, not air. He flung the door of the ranch house open and sucked great gulps of the humid air into his lungs. He felt that he was drowning.

Then he heard the far-off hooves. Thomas turned for a brief second, into the sanctuary of his own house. Halfway around he stopped dead, frowning. He had never been much to frighten any. Now he was starting at the sound of horse's hooves. Thomas forced himself to walk into the night, standing a dozen yards from the ranch house, waiting for the rider to swing toward or away from him.

The rider came on.

Now the only problem was whether the man was one of his own, or Slade.

He didn't expect it to be Slade, and yet Thomas didn't feel like a man running with the tides, lately. If it was a man on his payroll, it probably was Haydn, the man he had sent in after Dilt, to report back in case anything happened. It didn't seem likely anything would have happened, so soon. It wasn't midnight as yet. Dilt was in town less than half a day, and Slade had been hiding out.

Still, the man came on recklessly, as though he knew he was on friendly land, and soon the sound was familiar. Thomas knew how his men rode. It was Haydn.

The man burst into dim view twenty yards short of Thomas. Then he reined sharply and the horse began a neigh that Haydn broke with a heavy hand on the side of the neck. He was down a second later, stepping quickly to Thomas.

"In here," Thomas said quietly. "In here, man. Quick."

They strode into the house and Haydn grabbed his breath and stood while Thomas looked at him and at the money belt in the man's hands.

He said, "Slade's?"

The man said, "Yes."

Thomas stared at it, mesmerized. It sagged in Haydn's hands. Thomas knew it was full, but he was afraid to find out. It might be the answer or at least half the answer—if it held as much as Slade had won two nights before at the poker table.

He took the belt and the weight sent the sweat pouring down his chest. He ripped it open and started to count.

Haydn said, "Pretty near a thousand dollars. Me and Dilt counted it."

Thomas looked up. "Pretty near? How near?"

Haydn frowned. "Nine hundred eighty-something, as I recollect. Dilt knows for sure." He grinned. "Seems he didn't trust me to ride it all in."

Thomas snorted. "You'd have been dead tomorrow if you hadn't."

The man paled. "I ain't a crook," he said.

Thomas said, "That's good. Where's Dilt?"

"In the hotel room." He handed the key to Thomas.

And then Thomas asked the question that meant everything. He thought he knew the answer already, but he wasn't sure. Maybe they had somehow stolen the money belt from Slade, but they didn't have Slade himself. Thomas said, "And where's Slade?"

The man snickered. "In the same room. Out cold."

Thomas said, for no reason he could think of at the time, "Dilt did it with his fists?"

Haydn said, "No-o, not quite. Had to use that sock full of lead he carries with him. Neatest job of cold-cocking a man I ever saw. Swish, thud, *out*." The man grinned.

Thomas said, "Had to use the sock, eh?"

"Damn right," Haydn said. 'That Slade is one tough sweetheart. Almost had Dilt. Then—the sock."

Thomas nodded. "Tied up nice and tight?"

"Tight as a twelve-year-old," Haydn said, still grinning.

Thomas said, "Shut up. You annoy me."

The man said sullenly, "All right, boss."

"As a matter of fact," Thomas said, "get the hell out of my sight."

The man turned, puzzled. He went to the bunkhouse.

Thomas was angry with himself. Now he had Slade, now came the worst part of it. He had to use Slade, then kill him. This was cold-blood, cold-head sort of killing, the kind Abbott might do, but not the kind Thomas could stomach. They had lured Crispin out and made him reach for his gun. Then Thomas had been able to kill him, the anger coursing like blood through his chest.

Still, this had to be done.

He strapped the money belt to his waist and went outside. He saddled up his huge white horse and rode, across the valley, to the north.

May Hogue never knew before how lonely a lonely person could be. She prowled the emptiness of the ranch house, and as she walked, she stirred the echoes of Chet Crispin and Hogue and, most lately, of Slade. They were the three men of her life, her brother, her husband, and the man she wanted more than either—and now she would have none of them, ever. Two of them dead, and the other ready to fade into the night—a night or two hence—and remain, just an echo. She felt age creep toward her on molding, dusty, tottering legs.

She shook herself. Nonsense, she thought sharply. She'd be out of the ranch soon, in a day or two, and she'd bury her past. She'd go somewhere, maybe back east, a respectable widow with a tinge of glamor about her, and she'd find someone else who'd want her—and, maybe with luck and God willing, whom she'd want in return. The way it hadn't really ever been before.

In her hand was the curling-edged deed to the land and the houses on the land. She would take them into town the next day and arrange with the land office for the sale of the place. It was good land. Someone would want it.

Thomas would, for sure.

She shook her head. She didn't want to sell it to Thomas. Crispin wouldn't have wanted her to; neither did Slade. Hogue—he wouldn't have cared. But she had little choice. She didn't want the place and she'd need the money. In time, the bitterness of selling to Thomas would fade, she knew, just as everything else faded. Once more, age came on and she shivered.

Then she heard the horse, at a steady trot, a neat short-paced trot. She wanted it to be Slade, but Slade rode hell for leather and gone again, and this man was a man of tight restraint. Her fingers clawed and she realized she still held the deed. What she wanted, however, was the rifle.

She moved quickly to the far wall from which it hung by two nails, a black thinly-oiled Spencer, its long bore dulled down by charcoal, yet still grasping the gas lamp and holding it, a tiny spasm of light on the dark wall.

May held the rifle across her body, standing at the open doorway. The rider came on, slowly, and she called out, "Who's out there? I swear, I'll shoot."

The rider stopped and May sensed his puzzlement, sitting out in the black night.

Then Big Thomas said, "Don't be a fool, May Hogue. You're silhouetted in that doorway and I'm in pitch blackness. I could kill you this instant."

She sucked in her breath. "What do you want, Thomas?"

"Just to talk, May Hogue. A minute or two. That's all. I have a business deal."

"Can't it wait until morning?" she said sharply.

He said easily, "Of course it can. I just thought you'd want to conclude it now. Especially when you've heard it through."

Damn the man, she thought. He wasn't rattled. He wasn't even trying to force her. He sounded as though he knew the business was already concluded. He sounded like a man who knew something of immense value to him, and to her.

She said quietly, "Come in, then. Straight to the door and stand there." She stepped back swiftly when she heard his first footsteps and now she knew she had the advantage of position. She had vanished into the room and he was coming toward it, toward the thin light emanating into the night. Now she could see him, his trim body flowing, pistols tied down low. He didn't pause at the doorway, but came on through, and the bow he gave her just inside the room held no trace of the mockery she knew had to be there.

He barely glanced at the rifle and she knew it was a useless weapon in whatever ensued. She walked it to the wall and hung it by the nails.

Thomas said, "I'm here to buy your place, May Hogue."

"Not mine," she said wearily. "Chet Crispin's."

Once, Thomas would have been careful. Now, there seemed neither need nor time. He waved his hand. "Please. We both know of Chet Crispin's unfortunate death. One of my men came across the body in that crevice. A terrible thing."

Hate flamed inside her. She said, "Yes, one of your men. You. You shot him and put him there. Filthy killer."

He said, "We'll not get anyplace that way, May. I suppose you think I did in your husband, also."

A tiny smile, gray and ghostlike, crossed May's face. She said, "And how do you know of Hogue's death?"

Thomas flushed.

May went on. "Nobody knows about Hogue's death, except me and Slade and the man who killed Hogue. Unless he did some talking. And I can't imagine a killer talking about what he'd done, other than to one of his killer friends. Which are you, Thomas, the killer or his sidekick?"

Thomas said smoothly, past the initial sense of blundering, "Neither. Your man Slade told me."

May laughed harshly. "Slade. That's a fat chance! He wouldn't talk unless you threatened to rip out his tongue. Slade. Ha!"

Thomas said, "Which is exactly how it happened."

She stared at the rancher. "What do you mean?"

"We asked Slade where Hogue had gone to, and the man talked. He had no choice." Thomas patted the money belt, strapped outside his trousers.

May stared at it, blanching, horror dawning on her. Thomas had Slade somewhere. The man was his captive.

She said, "What have you done with Slade?"

Thomas said, "Nothing. Yet." He paused to let it sink in.

She said, "What do you plan to do?"

He waved his hand deprecatingly. "Nothing, actually. You're going to save us any bother about Slade."

"I?" she said thickly.

He nodded in quick jerks. "All I want is this land, May. I'm prepared to make a down payment right now. In return, I'll let your man Slade go."

She said, anger rising, "Stop saying *your man*. How do I know you've got Slade and that you'll let him go?"

"Simple," he said. "Just come along with me. I'll take you to him. You can see for yourself."

She thought: dear Lord, what does one do? A few minutes earlier she'd have sold her land to anyone, to Thomas, to the devil himself. That was before she knew about Slade. Now that Slade was involved, she didn't want to sell out. The man was her courage. But she knew the other course that Thomas would take. He'd kill Slade, if he had to. For all she knew, he'd kill him anyway. But she couldn't take the chance. She had to try to buy his freedom. It was the least she could do for Slade.

And yet the thought nagged her: he wouldn't have wanted her to buy his freedom with Chet Crispin's land.

She said, wary and past fear, "Take me in to him. I'll sell you the land."

A smile broke Thomas' face. Inside, he felt his heart lift and threaten to burst in his mouth. All the riding and killing and even Abbott's double-crossing—now they were ended. He said, "Do you have a deed you can just turn over to me?"

Without a word she walked to the tiny table where the paper lay. She nodded, holding it in lifeless fingers. Thomas stepped forward but May shook her head. "No," she said, "not until you come through with your bargain."

He shrugged. There was no need to press it. It was all settled.

She said, "Is Slade—far from here?"

"He's in town," Thomas said easily. "He's resting comfortably. We'll ride to him now, if you wish."

She nodded helplessly. They walked to the dark corral.

Slade stood in the hotel room on bloodless legs. He rubbed his wrists. His head throbbed and lolled on his neck. He was too weak, too splitting with pain to stand. Yet he stood.

Dilt said, from across the tiny room, "You ready yet? Say the word. I can't wait on you all morning."

Outside, the first streaks of dawn tinted the sky.

Slade thought: I'm insane. I've talked him into untying me just so he can club me down again. What for? He said, "A minute more. Christ, man, what do you want to do? Lick a man who can't stand?"

Dilt said, "It was your idea. I'd have let you lie there, but you wouldn't stop." Slade's words still rang in his ears. No man could say things like that to Dilt and expect him to take them. No one who lived could call Dilt a coward. Nothing else mattered except that word. And Slade must have said it fifty times. The word lay in the room, a yellow brand. Dilt had to wipe it out.

"Are you ready, I say? Dammit man, you've rubbed those arms and legs for a full ten minutes."

Slade said, "Sure, and I lay trussed up like a calf for—how many hours was it, Dilt?"

Dilt shook his head. He didn't want to keep talking. Slade was forever getting him off on these side talks. Didn't the man want to fight? "Come on," he said, "I won't wait any longer." He started across the room.

Slade said, "All right, don't give a man a chance. That's the coward's way. I'm surprised you don't go for your guns, Dilt."

The big man's head jerked to the side. It was as if he had been slapped. He roared, "Come on! Stop the damn talk and put up your hands."

Slade said, "I can't. Why don't you hit me with my hands down here?" The seconds crept by, and he could feel the blood in his legs. Now, he thought, if his arms would turn strong again. Dilt couldn't be in much better shape, he knew. He had taken a licking himself, and then while Slade rumbled on, unconscious, Dilt had sat there, stiff as a stick, waiting for Slade to come to. The chances were, Slade thought bitterly, that he'd only been out a short while. Still, it had worn on Dilt. It had to, he thought bleakly, wildly.

Slade raised his arms over his head and let them fall sharply to his sides, the palms slapping his upper thighs. He felt the needle-like tingle in his fingers. He closed his fists and opened them, surprised at the feeling surging through them. He knew it wasn't much, and he knew it wouldn't last long—through two or three of Dilt's punches, at best— but there was strength in his hands now, and strength everywhere in his tired body. He took a deep breath and said, holding the air in his lungs, "All right, coward. Come on. I'm ready, coward."

Dilt roared and plunged at Slade, arms wide apart.

And Slade nearly laughed with the joy of it. The man was such a fool, and so easily reached. It had worked, after all. All Slade had wanted was one good crack at the man, at that broken left side of his face, where the jaw met the ear, just an inch and a half away from that splintered cheekbone.

Slade rocked back and then swayed forward, his right arm lunging out in a straight line, all the power and fury of a lifetime in the punch. He smashed the fist against Dilt's jaw and the man made a queer gagging noise in his throat and then his eyes popped, sticking out of their sockets, huge and pure white like a slaughtered cow's, and then he started to tremble.

Slade stepped away, wondering, his right arm back at his hip and starting to crawl forward again. Then the tremble suddenly increased and the whole floor started to shake.

And Dilt came down.

He went to his knees and stayed there a long second, swaying like a man at fervent prayer, except it wasn't prayer in Dilt's head, it was choked-in anger and astonishment and, as his body toppled forward, stiff as falling timber, he howled, "You can't call me that!"

Then his body unhinged, lying there on the floor, a tiny pool of blood spilling from the left side of Dilt's face. Dilt lay still.

Slade stepped over the man into the room. He took Dilt's guns and holster and strapped them on. His hands wandered to his own waist where the money belt used to be, and he thought: once again, dead broke. But this time there was no fear.

He picked up the sock, emptied out the lead, and shoved the sock into his pocket. Then he stepped over Dilt's body and walked from the room. He hoped his horse was still outside the saloon. He had to get to Thomas' and finish it off. Time was the only enemy. He couldn't even afford to wait here in this hotel room—though Thomas had to be coming this way soon—because Dilt would come to, and there'd be another brawl and Slade doubted he could handle Dilt and Thomas, both. So he had to find the man if he could, before Thomas found him.

And Slade knew he had to ride to the valley for another reason. He had to see May Hogue, to make sure they hadn't hurt her as yet.

He stumbled down the flight of stairs and through the dank hallway and into the street. Then he went to the saloon and searched for his horse. But all he found was the length of hitching post, bare.

Slade turned and strode on unsteady legs to the end of town, away from the valley. There was a stable down there, and he hoped someone had had the decency to bed down his horse. He lurched away, toward the stable.

Big Thomas and May Hogue came single-stepping through the dawn street of Cowpoke, Thomas' right hand gripping May's arm to keep her quiet and—just in case—to keep her close by. Not that Thomas thought May would try to break away. She had too much at stake. May Hogue was not the woman to scream her way to freedom—and thereby send a man to his death. She rode alongside Thomas, neither acknowledging the pressure on her arm, nor trying to pull away from it.

Ahead of them, Thomas could see the dim outline of a man, drunk probably, staggering down the street on watery legs. The man weaved and almost went down and Thomas grinned in the shifting gray light. As least somebody had had a good time that past night. Now he was on his way home, to sleep it off. Thomas felt a vicarious pleasure. It had been a long time since he had had the right to enjoy himself. He envied the man, disappearing now in the gloom at the far end of Cowpoke.

"Here," he whispered. "Here's the hotel."

May Hogue obediently stopped her horse. They got down and Thomas looped the lines together and tied the single rein to the post. He reached out again and took her arm.

"Up here," he said, pulling her.

Now she felt the pressure, and resisted it. Fear clawed at her. For all she knew, they had murdered Slade for his money belt and all this was just a trick to get her away from the ranch. Still, her mind stubbornly fought such a thought. It didn't make sense. What was to keep her from screaming in case Thomas tried to coerce her to sign that paper? And she answered—only Slade's body, still alive. That would be the only barter.

And so she walked past Thomas, brushing off his hand on her arm, and slowly she mounted the stairs, the rancher right behind, gloating and half-drunk with joy. Just a handful of steps away was Slade, and right here was May Hogue, with the deed to the land. He started thinking how he'd have her write on the back side of the deed: "For the price of one dollar, I hereby sell the deed to the property and to all the material goods on the property, to Bigelow Thomas. I do this of my own free will."

Then they'd get Dilt to witness it, and maybe Slade, too, if he was in shape to write his name. The laughter started to rumble in Thomas' chest as they came to the head of the stairs and walked the corridor to the room.

The laughter was rising higher and higher as Thomas reached into his pocket and found the key Haydn had given him, and his words were bubbling when he turned the lock and pushed the door open and said, "Here she is, Slade, coming to claim the body."

The laughter went on and on, then, when Thomas saw Dilt lying on the floor, laughter and hysteria, laced with sobbing words that became unintelligible and jumbled. May Hogue backed off, staring at Thomas, and then she turned and fled, down the stairs and into the street and onto her horse.

And Thomas shrieked hysterically, the tears blinding him.

Finally, the disciplined years took sway. The sounds subsided, and Thomas' mind allowed the truth to shove in its ugly shape: Slade had beaten him again.

The rancher slowly backed from the room, and a last hope flitted before his mind's eye.

He was losing his own land, to Abbott and the bank. He hadn't been able to get Crispin's land, and he doubted now that he ever would. But Mudge and Early, they still held their spreads, high up on the north slope, two frightened dirt farmers who had turned to ranching because the valley despised farmers and Mudge and Early didn't want to be despised.

Thomas felt the money belt still tight around his waist. Mudge and Early were always strapped for funds. Abbott had turned them down on their loans, Thomas knew—hadn't Abbott said so a few days ago? A vague disquiet tried to pierce this new line of action, but Thomas refused it entry. He had had enough to cope with this long night. Fear was not to be allowed any further place. The hysteria was finished, beaten.

Thomas rode off, noting that his horse was alone. May Hogue had got away. He shrugged. It didn't matter. He'd have Mudge's and Early's spreads. Then he'd start the pressure again on Crispin's land. He'd learned a lot this past month about trying to scare men off. He'd do it right, one huge play, with everything he had. He'd drive off whoever was on that land—May Hogue or Slade or anybody.

Morning was climbing Thomas' back as he rode into the valley. Another day, he thought dully. Abbott's days were running past him, like stampeding cattle.

CHAPTER 16

May Hogue said, "What do we do now?" They had come in together to the ranch, May overtaking Slade halfway to the pass.

Slade rubbed his gritty eyes. All he wanted to do was sleep. "Sit tight, I guess," he said.

She shook her head. "No. He'll be back. He'll raid the place. He'll get hold of that deed and forge it. He'll kill us both and just take the place."

Slade didn't think so. He thought Thomas had blown himself at them and had failed to budge them, and now he'd move elsewhere. He said, "Just take that deed and scrawl something on the back, to the effect that this is the only true deed to this land and that under no circumstances are you turning it over to anybody. And sign it. Then mail it to the land office."

She looked at Slade. "Why didn't you think of that before? Or any of us?"

Slade shook his great heavy head. "Because we've all been playing this from behind our own sights. Nobody's really been thinking that what Thomas is doing is not our affair at all."

She said, "Now what does that mean? He's killed Chet and Hogue, and it's not my affair?"

"Well, what I mean is, when a man breaks the law, it becomes everybody's affair. That's what the law's supposed to be, isn't it? The protecting arm that hangs over everybody?"

"You mean you'd run to the nearest sheriff and yell for help, next time something like this happened?"

He grinned. The nearest sheriff was Wilkinson. "Probably not. But that's what a man should do."

She was silent. The thought jarred her. She never pictured Slade begging for help. Yet the man wasn't a coward. He must have thought a long time to come to such a decision. The law! Nobody ran to the law. It just wasn't done out here. "And when a man does," May Hogue said, "and the law turns out to be someone crooked as a sheriff usually is, what then?"

Slade shrugged helplessly. He knew he was right. Yet he didn't know how it would work. "Keep trying, I guess. There's someone, sitting in a judge's chair or law office, who's not an outlaw himself. And if he is, you have to keep making a big stink until somebody smells it and comes running."

"You've had your chance," May said.

"I know," Slade said, "and I've botched it. I've played it lone hand the whole way, nearly got killed, nearly got you to lose your ranch."

"That wasn't your fault; that was Thomas'."

"Oh, it was Thomas' fault, all right, starting all the trouble. But maybe we could have ended it cleaner and sooner if we'd run like hell, straight to the Territory capital."

"Yeah," she said, "and they'd have shuffled some papers and promised to look into things and politely showed you the door."

Slade didn't answer. There was no answer, that he knew of. She was right, yet she wasn't. Meanwhile, they'd have to play it this way. They had no time to go running off for help now. They'd run, and Thomas would swarm over the land and maybe track them down in the hills someplace. Maybe that's what those five Thomas men were doing, riding through Cowpoke yesterday. Combing the hills, looking for Slade or else waiting out there, in case he tried to break free. No, it would be settled here, by themselves. They had made their own world, and it was a small one, all right, bounded by the bare hills that looked down on the valley.

"It doesn't matter, I guess. We can't do it that way. We'll have to keep our eyes open in case Thomas moves against us."

She had walked to the window. Now she walked back and stopped, an arm's length away from Slade. "Us?" she asked. "You're talking about 'us'?"

He flushed. "Well, we're both here just now. That's what I mean."

She shook her head. "You mean we're both here because that's the way it had to be. At least for a while."

She stood close, breathing with opened lips, and in the harsh true morning light, Slade could see the bitter lines at the corners of her mouth and the black oily shadows below her eyes. He knew that his own face was grimy with sweat and dirt, and that he hadn't shaved for two days. He knew he was too tired to be standing next to this woman whose husband was dead not even two days, and that he couldn't be wanting any woman, the way he felt, his body still wracked by pain from Dill's fists and the everlasting churning jouncing ride through this valley of hell.

Yet he couldn't have stopped himself if he tried. He sure as hell didn't try.

He reached out and closed that arm's length, pulling May toward him, dragging her across that empty space of floor, not caring whether he was hurting her or not, certainly not loving her, maybe even hating her a bit, but terribly, terribly wanting her.

"Us," he said. "You're damn right it's us. Us against them." He rubbed his rough cheek against her smooth one. "May, May, why does it have to be this way?" He didn't know what he meant but she did.

She said, "I don't care how it is. Just so long as it is. I told you once, Slade, I'd have you. And I will. It doesn't matter that they're not playing violins out there." She pulled her face away from his and leaned back so that her whole body lay like dead weight in his arms. The man was so huge in front of her, the man she had wanted so long now, not knowing how much she had even wanted him when he was a boy, years back, but making up for it now, wanting him the way her body wanted breath, her veins blood.

She let her eyes close and she half-lay in his arms. Then he drew her face to his face, their open mouths clashing and roaming.

CHAPTER 17

Mudge listened quietly. He was frightened because he knew he wouldn't sell to Thomas, and he didn't know how Thomas would take it. There was in the rancher's neat, smooth face a dulled-out look to his eyes, a desperate unrest lurking beneath the taut bronze skin and flowing grace.

Thomas said, "And so you'll have a decent down payment—more probably than the land is worth—and in a few months' time, you'll get the balance. It won't make you a rich man, Mudge, but you'll have more comfort than you've ever seen before. Now—how's that sound?"

Mudge said carefully, "It sounds right good, Thomas. But I don't think I'll sell."

Thomas said smoothly, "The five hundred dollars isn't a big enough down payment, is that it? You want more now?"

Mudge sat silent.

"A thousand, then? How's a thousand dollars now and the remaining two thousand in sixty days? That's more than fair. It's practically a gift."

Mudge started to pace the living room floor. He wished he had two guns on his hips, the way Thomas had. Then he knew that was silly. What good would they do? He'd never shot at a man in his life. He wasn't very good picking off jack rabbits. He said, "I'd like to think it over."

A thin line of perspiration appeared on Thomas' brow. He removed his hat and wiped his forehead and ran his hand through his crisp black hair. He said briskly, playing his chips, "I'm sorry, Mudge. My offer won't wait. It's now or never. If you don't like my terms, I'll withdraw them. *Then* see what kind of price you'll get for this piece of crud you call your land."

Mudge flared. He was sick of people picking on his land. It was the best he could do. The land was all right, anyway, and certainly the water was fine. And with the loan he was getting from Abbott, and the money he'd soon be getting from the sale of his cattle to a nearby railroad—his land would prosper. Then nobody could ever pick on it again.

He said, "Maybe you call it a piece of crud. Some people don't."

Thomas frowned. "You mean some people like Wilbur Early? Of course he doesn't criticize your spread. He doesn't dare. Not with the land *he* owns."

Mudge leaned forward, breathing heavily. "And some people," he said, "don't criticize Wilbur Early's land, either."

Thomas said quietly, "What do you mean?"

Mudge said, "Mr. Abbott, for instance, he doesn't think too little of Wilbur Early's land. Nor mine, either."

Thomas said, "But he won't grant you that loan you've been begging for."

"Ha!" Mudge said, "the hell he won't. What with the railroad coming through, you're damn right he'll lend us money!"

The red roaring beat in Thomas' ear. He thought, Mudge found out somehow. He guessed it. Or he knows somebody who slipped the word into the valley.

Thomas kept avoiding the truth because he knew it was the truth and he knew its consequences. He said, "What railroad? What sort of pipe dream are you talking about, Mudge?"

"Pipe dream, hell!" Mudge shouted. He stepped back to a desk in the far corner of the room and he opened a drawer. He took out some papers and waved them in front of Thomas. "Call these papers a pipe dream, eh? Application for bank loan, here. Approved, here. Letters of credit, here." He slapped the papers against his hand, the sound like gunshot in the small room. And every time the noise cracked out, Thomas felt the tiny wince at his mouth. It wasn't so much the sight of Mudge and his bank loan papers. It was the knowledge of how he himself had been duped, right from the start.

The rancher saw it all, now. How Abbott had used him to build himself up. Abbott owned Thomas' land. He had loans on Mudge's—and Early's too, no doubt. Mudge and Early wouldn't sell now. They had no reason to. Hell, they'd be damn fools to sell. May Hogue wouldn't sell, either, because he'd been unable to cope with Slade.

And so Thomas knew the final truth: he was washed up in the valley. He was a man who once dreamed of empire, and who had only the waking truth now.

Big Thomas turned slowly from the room. He thought he would ride on to Wilbur Early's spread, just to make sure. Then he knew how futile that was. He'd just be wasting his time. There was only one place he had to go, only one thing he had to do. It wasn't much, and it wouldn't pay it all back, but he had to do it. There was just so much a man could take without striking back. The fury faded in Big Thomas' head, the red roaring subsided. He was cool now, with the cold might of a chained iceberg. But he could feel the waters about him cracking.

... Mudge watched Thomas ride off, toward the valley pass. He smirked, in self-satisfaction. It hadn't been so hard. He had faced Thomas down. Thomas had made his offer, and he had told him No.

Then Mudge frowned. Slade had once asked Mudge to tell him in case anybody came running up the slope with money in his hand to buy the land. Mudge had agreed.

Mudge looked at the papers in his hand and he remembered Abbott's words: *don't let anybody know. The railroad doesn't want it bruited about.*

Mudge thought angrily: Slade hadn't done anything for him. Why should he do anything for Slade? He nodded his head vigorously.

In the bank, Abbott said to the clerk Loomis, "I want you to write that letter today. To McAlester in El Paso. Tell him the rails can come through now. Everything is set."

Loomis said, "But you haven't concluded the purchase of Mr. Thomas' land."

Abbott said, "There won't be any need to purchase Thomas' land. The bank owns it. I gave the man notice several days ago, in person. He hasn't bothered to meet his deadline. As a matter of fact, it's an extended deadline. We should have had the installment two weeks ago."

Loomis fidgeted nervously. He said, "But—sir—don't we usually give thirty days' notice when a due-date passes? I mean, isn't that the way—" He stopped, staring at Abbott.

The banker said, "I guess we don't understand each other, Loomis. I thought we had covered all this the other day. When I ask for a man's confidence, and he promises it, I have to assume his word to be good. My actions concerning Thomas' land demand your confidence. You're not giving it to me." He paused, looking at the stricken clerk. "You're not, you know. When I sense your implied criticism, I feel that you have no faith in me. And when a man feels that his trusted underling no longer has confidence in him, he wonders whether to step down himself—or look for another underling."

Loomis' face washed to a gray-white. A tiny tic attacked his left eyebrow. He stammered, "Sir, I have the—fullest confidence in you. I—

just didn't understand."

Abbott smiled. "Ah," he said, "and now that you understand, you approve? You fully approve of what I am doing—and will never question it again, *nor ever breathe a word of it to an outsider*. Is that right?"

The man quivered. "I approve fully, sir. Believe me, I know that whatever you're doing is—is in the best interests of the bank."

Abbott shook his head. "No," he said, "that's not good enough. You forgot to add that you're positive that whatever I'm doing is perfectly ethical and aboveboard."

Loomis breathed heavily. "Sir, the question of ethics never entered my head. Anything you do, sir, would have to be of the highest ethics."

Abbott laughed, a full, easy laugh. "That's good, Loomis. That's very good. I knew I had misunderstood you. You're a fine man, Loomis. You're a diligent worker, too, and I want you to know that I appreciate it. Go on out there now, and snap the whip on those damn lazy critters we call tellers."

"I?" Loomis said. "I should give orders to the tellers?"

Abbott nodded, still smiling. "Why not? You're a vice-president of the bank, as of this minute. If you perform in your new functions as I'm sure you will, a new salary commensurate with your new duties and responsibilities will shortly be forthcoming. Now, get out and set a fire under my help."

Loomis turned and went, an automaton, his joy so complete he could not fully accept it. Abbott's smile stayed in Loomis' head, a warm smile. Loomis felt he would go through hell for Mr. Abbott.

And almost immediately, he saw the opportunity to fulfill Mr. Abbott's huge trust.

Big Thomas walked into the bank.

Loomis approached the man. Then his eyes strayed to the money belt, sagging full, wrapped around Thomas' waist. He beamed at the rancher. Mr. Abbott would be glad, he knew. Thomas was here with the installment on the mortgage. Mr. Abbott and Big Thomas were old friends. Mr. Abbott had been correct in demanding the payment from Big Thomas on time. You cannot allow friendship to intervene in bank affairs. You must—Loomis nodded—you must, in fact, lean over backwards, just as Mr. Abbott had done. No one would ever say Mr. Abbott had tried to do a favor for Big Thomas, just because they were old friends.

He said, beaming, "You just walk right on through, Mr. Thomas. Mr. Abbott will be delighted to see you."

Thomas turned and stared at the little man. He said, "You sure about that?"

Loomis nodded. Oh, it was so exciting, being in on all the inside affairs of the bank. Here was a big rancher racing his deadline, trying to get his money up in time to save his property. And there was Mr. Abbott, the banker, ever just, yet ever firm—it was firmness, Loomis thought, it just had to be, it couldn't be anything else—Mr. Abbott, ready to go so far in his fairness as to deprive a friend of his land because the friend had not fulfilled all the obligations. And outside the bank, the railroad was rushing its rails into the valley, bringing prosperity to the whole region.

"Oh, yes," Loomis said. "I'm sure. He's waiting for you." Now *that*— Loomis thought—was sheer improvisation. Still, in a way, Big Thomas had been the last piece of business Loomis and Mr. Abbott had discussed. Certainly it still was on Mr. Abbott's mind. And Mr. Abbott would only be delighted to have Big Thomas make his payment and save his land. It would be the proper end to the whole little drama.

Thomas grunted and walked past. He pushed open the door of Abbott's office and quietly shut it. Then he walked to the edge of Abbott's desk and looked at the banker.

Abbott said, "Oh, so you know."

Thomas nodded.

The banker sighed. "Well, it would have to get out eventually."

Thomas frowned. "Is that your only reaction to my finding out? You're not—you're not—"

"Bothered? Oh, of course I am. I hate to see these things come to such a sordid end, a man losing his land to a bulky piece of machinery. But—" Abbott smiled—"that's progress."

Thomas stood over the desk, puzzled. He knew what was going to happen, but apparently Abbott didn't. He looked into Abbott's eyes. What did the man expect?

Abbott returned Thomas' stare. He was waiting to see how Thomas would react. Half the fun of it all—half the game of winning the power empire—was in seeing how the other man reacted. What were the alternatives he had imagined—Thomas' putting his gun to his temple, or Thomas' driving his horse over a cliff? Thomas fleeing, disappearing into the no-name cattle towns that twisted a thousand miles into the wilderness? Or Thomas going mad? Yes, they were the alternatives. Now, which would it be?

His eyes strayed to Thomas' gun belt. He was surprised to see that the rancher carried two guns. Then Abbott nodded. Yes, that made sense. A man in desperation must add to his arsenal, puny as it may be.

Thomas said, "Abbott, what are you getting out of it?" It was the question he had fretted over, almost from the beginning.

The banker smiled and shrugged his narrow shoulders. "Do you play chess, Thomas?"

"No."

"Then you probably won't understand. It's the feeling you get in shoving the pieces about the board. Except my chess board—in this game we've been playing—is bigger than usual. And so are the pieces. You, me, Wilkinson, Mudge, Early—they're the pieces."

"Just a game?"

Abbott nodded. "Just a game."

"I hope you've enjoyed the game, Abbott."

"Oh," Abbott said, "I have, I have."

Thomas grunted. "That's good," he said. His hands went to his holster and then spread to the butt-ends of the guns.

Abbott eyed the rancher. The touch of melodrama added spice to the affair. The beaten rancher, his well-oiled brace of .44s, the tantalizing dilemma of how to face up to a situation that had already ended. Which alternative, Abbott thought, which one? Undoubtedly the last. Thomas, his mind snapping, Thomas, going mad.

The rancher drew the guns from their holsters. He hefted them and then turned the two bores at Abbott. The banker's face started to change. Puzzlement, astonishment, then chalk-white fear—and finally, the words tumbling out, "But that's not one of the alterna—"

The words were scream-high when they broke. Ten bullets broke them.

Thomas grunted again and replaced the smoking guns in his belt. He looked once at Abbott, leaning back in the chair. Abbott had no face.

Thomas walked from the office, past the petrified Loomis, past two customers, open-mouthed, past the two tellers' cages, and into the street. He breathed the thick dust and cattle smell. It was good, out in the open. That's where he had to be, out in the open. He got back on his horse and rode toward the ranch he used to own.

CHAPTER 18

When the shocking news reached Wilkinson, he was first angered that someone had killed Abbott before he had the chance. It always was like that, he thought. Crispin, now Abbott. Then he remembered Hogue, and the anger disappeared.

He walked jauntily into the bank and with Loomis went into Abbott's office. The sight of the man sitting back in his chair, a red-black smear where his face ought to have been, sickened Wilkinson and he wanted to lurch away from the scene. Instead, he found himself saying in a hoarse whisper, "You identify the man, Loomis? You're sure it's Abbott?"

Loomis gulped and nodded, his face green.

"All right, Loomis," the sheriff whispered, "that's all."

The little clerk—who'd ever know, he thought, that Abbott had made him a vice-president; who'd ever believe?—the little clerk stammered, "But—but aren't you—going to go after Mr. Thomas?"

Wilkinson said, his voice thin and tiny, "Sure I am." His hands went to his gun, a new .44 that he wore outside ever since Slade took away his single-shot derringer. "Sure I'm going after Thomas." He looked around the room and walked out. He kept telling himself that he had a job to do; a man had been killed and he, Wilkinson, was the county sheriff. He had a job to do.

Wilkinson mounted his horse and rode swiftly through Cowpoke, raising dust and muttered oaths from the narrow sidewalks. He didn't care. He had a job to do. If only—he thought—he had his voice again. Then he'd really be big.

Wilkinson was halfway across the valley floor, headed for the ranch house on the softly rising west slope, when he saw the thin spiral of dust coming toward him. He gasped and started to whirl his horse, to get away from the riders. Then he straightened the horse and stuck his head forward, his hand at his gun butt. He wasn't going to be scared off.

There were five of them, in a sullen silent file, all Thomas men, all with haversacks on their backs and their saddlebags stuffed so full the straps didn't close. The big man, Dilt, led the way, broken-faced and sagging in the saddle. He came straight toward Wilkinson, unseeing, his horse riding free.

The sheriff looked at the big bald man, fifteen yards away now. He said to Dilt, "Get the hell out of my way."

Obediently, Dilt moved his horse to the side and kept going, past Wilkinson. The sheriff felt his chest bloat. Dilt was afraid of him. Christ, they all were afraid of him. He patted his .44. If he only had his voice!

The next three men filed by. The last man was Morgan. Wilkinson said, "Where are you men going?"

Morgan spat into the dust. "Going? Hell, who knows? Thomas gave us notice and a helluva big pay. We're just going. That's all."

Wilkinson was relieved. There'd be nobody at Thomas' place. The other five Thomas men had been released earlier, he had heard. Now these five. Thomas would be alone.

The sheriff whispered, "All right, then. Get going."

Morgan stared at the little man. "Don't get tough with me, sheriff," he said softly. "I've taken enough these past few days."

Wilkinson squealed, "And you'll take more if you don't do as I say."

Morgan looked at Wilkinson, the foreman's face unchanging. Then he swung his arm, the back of his hand striking Wilkinson under the chin, against his bony Adam's apple. Wilkinson's head popped back and he toppled from his saddle with a scream. He rolled on the ground and came up, clawing at his holster. But Morgan's own .44 was steady as a rock, the open mouth three feet from Wilkinson's head.

"Now you get going," Morgan said softly, the gun firm. "On your horse."

Wilkinson sobbed and took his hand from his gun butt. He mounted in scrambling movements and spurred his horse viciously. He rode on toward Thomas' house. Once he looked back. The first four Thomas men had ridden out of sight. Morgan still sat his horse, his gun in his hand.

The anger was scalding Wilkinson when he dismounted. He left his horse unhitched and raced for the door. Big men, he thought, all of them. Big men. Cocksure and arrogant and so goddam tall their heads scraped the skies. Big men, he thought, the fury bubbling over until hot tears ran down his cheeks. He'd show them. He swore he'd show them.

He crashed his fist into the wooden door, heedless of the pain, of the thin line of blood that crept from his knuckles. There was no sound inside. Still sobbing loudly, he crashed his hand against the door again and then fell against it, trying to shake it down. Big men, big and wide as doors, a wall of them around him, trying to choke him. Well, he'd show them. He pounded both fists against the door and he screamed, "Open up, you son of a bitch, open up." He stared in amazement then, his jaw hanging. The noise of his voice still boomed in his ears. He was talking big as ever. A crazy grin started growing on his mouth, twisted and huge. Morgan had done it, with that swipe against his throat. He had knocked back in place whatever Slade had jarred out. Wilkinson shook his head, grinning. He never felt better in his life. His fingers clawed at his sides. He couldn't wait until he got Thomas in front of him.

Then he heard the swift frail patter of feet. A frown furrowed his brow, the grin fading. He straightened up and stepped back, puzzled. It wasn't Big Thomas.

The door opened. It was the girl Maria.

Wilkinson said, "Is—Thomas in?" He had to be. He was the last big man around, other than Slade. He couldn't handle Slade; Slade never gave him an honest chance. But Thomas was different. He'd prove how big he was—on Thomas.

Maria's face was wide-eyed, her mouth trembling. She said, small-voiced, "No—he's gone." A tear touched one cheek.

Wilkinson said, "Gone? What do you mean?" He was the sheriff, and she had to tell him.

She said, "He went away. Sent away his men—and went away."

"For good?"

She nodded and turned from the door. Wilkinson followed her in.

"What are you still doing here?" he asked.

She sobbed. "Cleaning up," she said. "It should be neat and clean, the house. For whoever it is that comes next." She walked away from him and moved toward the large sitting room. Wooden crates were half-filled with books, papers, bric-a-brac, a man's possessions, not even filling the crates.

He said, "What are you doing with those?"

She smiled wanly. "Maybe Mr. Thomas will tell me where he is, and I'll send these to him—or maybe even bring them." The smile brightened at this last.

Wilkinson sneered. The woman was just a whore. Who was she to think Big Thomas would want her? She was good for just one thing. Didn't she know that?

His eyes narrowed. "What are you going to do?" he asked. He felt himself licking his lips with a dry tongue.

She pulled back, but the light of a low-hanging oil flame illumined her face. She said, "For a while, I will wait."

He said, "And then?" He leered at her. "And then back to the house?"

She shivered. "No," she said evenly. "Not that. Never again."

"What's the matter?" he said. "Too good for that now?"

She put her hands to her throat. "No," she said. "I just—could not do that again."

"Why not?" he said, moving a step closer. And the thought of Maria and Big Thomas started the anger roiling again. He had come in to do in this big man, Thomas. But Thomas had fled. But his woman was still there. He'd get to Thomas that way. Through his woman. He'd show him. He was as good a man as any of them. Better.

She said, "I think you'd better go. Mr. Thomas isn't here, and you have no business here."

He reached out his hand and placed it on her bare arm. It amused him to see the flesh crawl below his fingers.

"No," he said solemnly, "no business at all. Just pleasure." He started to pull her toward him.

She screamed and pulled back. He felt his mouth twisting into a curse and the words boomed out, but he was too busy with this writhing creature to worry about what he said. Christ, he thought, she was so strong. His fist smashed into her face and she staggered away. Then he saw her—through swiftly reddening vision, through a curtain that always closed down on him—he saw her pick up something and hurl it. He laughed as it sailed by and he vaguely heard glass crash behind him and his vision cleared for a moment as a yellow flame seemed to light up behind him.

Then he laughed again and closed in on the girl, her hand no longer trying to push him off or grab things to throw. Her hand was at her bodice, reaching inside, and this time he was terribly surprised and disappointed when she drew out a needle-sharp knife. That wasn't fair, he thought. It meant she didn't want him to do what he wanted to do, and that wasn't fair.

He said, "Put that knife away, Maria." His voice was deep and he marveled afresh at the authority he could convey with such a voice.

She paused for a second, the knife held high and he said again, his voice a rich rumble in that room that suddenly had become difficult to breathe in and that suddenly had filled with long waving shadows and long reaching hot red-yellow fingers, "Put that knife away!"

She looked over his shoulder and screamed. Then the knife plunged into his narrow chest and he felt the air puff out like a punctured balloon. He gathered his breath for a terrible scream, but all that came out was a little "Oh," and he sat down, holding his chest with tiny hands that still ached from pounding the big wooden door.

He thought of the big wooden door and of how tall and strong it was and how unfair it was to expect him to shake it down. Then he heard the woman scream and race past him and he was glad. He was alone. Nobody would be bothering him. He coughed once and lay down and went to sleep.

The flames from the spilled oil lamp ate at the wooden crates and leaped across to the walls, crackling, hungry, consuming. The woman Maria came back to the room, a foolish brave woman with a glass of water in her hands. She threw it on the flames and then backed off, the smoke blinding her. She turned and walked into a wall and clawed her way toward the door. But she missed it and terror caught her in a steel grip. She whirled about in the center of the room, flame all about her and smoke choking her, and she cried out, "Mary, mother of Jesus, forgive me, forgive me!" Then a wooden beam fell heavily from the ceiling. She moaned once and dropped, beside the dead sheriff.

CHAPTER 19

When they wakened, Slade said, "This is foolish, May."

She put her hand to his mouth. "Hush," she said. "Foolish or not, I'm glad, Slade."

"So am I," he said, "but Thomas could ride us down like a pair of crippled pigeons." He got to his feet and dressed swiftly. Now that May Hogue would not sell the ranch, there still remained the problem of Thomas. Slade did not expect Thomas to hunt for him. But he might. And the chance could not go by unchecked. He said, "We're doing this wrong, I think."

"What do you mean?"

"You ought not to be here," he said.

"Where else should I be?" she said. She stood in the bright midday light, and his breath caught. She was a lovely woman. Yet he knew he did not love her. What they had done had sprung from intense need, on each one's part. Now they were placated. It was not love. Still, she excited him. He knew she always would.

"Not here," he said. "Just in case."

"You didn't think he'd raid the place before."

"I still don't. But we can't take chances." Somehow she had become more precious to him in those passionate minutes and sleeping hours. He felt protective of her. It was the closest he'd ever felt to a woman.

"All right," she said. "But you'll come with me."

He shook his head. Already he was strapping on his gun. "No. You go into town. Take this." He handed her the single-shot derringer. "I've got to stay here in the valley. I doubt that Thomas will come here, but I know he's not finished. Thomas won't quit trying until—" He let the words hang in the air, ominous, frightening. May Hogue shivered.

He went on. "So I want to be around. It has to be faced, you know. A man as hungry as Thomas doesn't get satisfied just because he's been thwarted once or twice."

She said, her voice flat, "He'll kill you."

"No," he said. "He won't. Not the way my luck is running." He looked at her and the emotion moved sluggishly inside.

"You'll be careful?"

He nodded.

"You'll come to me when it's over? To—to let me know?"

He nodded again. Yet he wondered whether he was lying. Would he come to her? Why would he come to her? She'd find out how it ended.

He wouldn't have to let her know.

She turned then and swiftly prepared to leave. He heard her in the inside rooms, puttering about the grey empty house that sat on the tortured land, like some great ghost trying to live on in a doomed body.

And when she left, Slade had his answer. He knew he'd not come to her when it was over. She was leaving, and she knew she was leaving. Maybe she'd come back to the house, but he wouldn't be here.

She rode away swiftly, headed for Cowpoke, and Slade waited only until he could see her horse no longer. Then he got out of the house and mounted his own horse, the one he had driven into the valley a week ago, the one that had taken him to see Chet Crispin, and instead led him into a bloody war.

He started off on the trail that was now so well worn. His horse didn't know it, but Slade did. He had ridden the big brown stallion along it so many times. He pushed to the west in a wide arc, well inside Thomas' territory, but far from the ranch house. He worked his way through timber and over narrow trails which crept along the upper lip of the valley, threatening to spill him and the horse into the rock-littered canyon below.

Then he climbed swiftly to the peak at the end of the northwest bowl. From here he could see down to Thomas' ranch, the whole valley floor below him like a soft green carpet, swaying gently beneath the wind that had sprung up from behind the hills. A black shadow raced across the valley floor, and Slade frowned. He looked up at the sun, obscured behind thick dark clouds. A summer squall was kicking up. Slade hoped it would pass.

He returned his gaze to the valley. He kept looking for the little dot on the white horse that would be Thomas. Thomas was the only man on the ranch—in the valley, in fact, who rode a white horse. But he saw no white horse. Only five men, drifting about the bunkhouses and corrals, in apathetic movement, the way men appear when their job at hand is done and there is nothing else to do, or when men are without orders, men without a leader.

And Slade ripped a curse from his lips. Thomas wasn't there, because Thomas wasn't around. Thomas was gone. The man had run off somewhere. Slade knew it. He felt it in his bones.

Slade studied the ground below him. His eyes searched the logical trail from Thomas' ranch house to the end of the valley and out to the other side, to the next valley below. He doubted that Thomas had gone back into Cowpoke, not after he had found Dilt. Even if he had, he wouldn't have stayed there, that was sure. He'd have gone back to the ranch and left his men with word to keep their eye on the place. Then—if Slade was right—Thomas would have taken off, to figure his next move, to lie low, to get away from the valley for a respite until he had recovered his strength and his courage—no, not his courage, Thomas always had that, Slade felt—and then to return for the big final move.

Slade bent closer to the ground. There was only one normal trail, leading from Thomas' ranch to this end of the valley. It was the trail Slade had ridden several times, ending up behind Thomas' house, near the barn, and going off in the other direction just past this peak on which Slade now sat his horse.

Thunder rumbled in the distance and the sun sank again behind black clouds. Slade searched the ground swiftly, frantically. Then he found the marks. They were heavy shoe marks, as if made by a big horse. Slade moved his own horse next to the prints and walked the horse, urging him the way a man on the run might urge his horse. Slade grinned, tightly. Thomas was learning, he felt. At last he was finding out how it felt to be on the run, instead of leading the chase.

Slade compared the two sets of prints, his own and the other. The other prints—made by a horse Slade was certain was the big white—were heavier prints than Slade's And they were more widely spaced, the prints of a big, long-legged horse, the biggest horse in the valley. It had to be Thomas' horse.

Slade started off in the direction of the prints. Then he looked back once, and he could see the five tiny specks who had to be Thomas' men, riding away from the ranch. Coming into the valley was a tinier speck, farther away, a jerking speck that was horse and man, so small that Slade could not make it out. But it was not a white horse. It was not Thomas. Slade wanted to wait and see who the newcomer was, entering the valley, headed for Thomas', but when he saw the new man stop and stand his horse next to one of the five Thomas men, Slade knew it was a man known to Thomas, and therefore not a friend of Slade's.

More important, Slade knew he'd lose Thomas unless he trailed him right away. The clouds were gathering over his head, swift and black, and the afternoon was turning dim. He cursed again, turning his back on the valley and on the five Thomas men leaving and the one little man entering. Thomas lay ahead. The prints were already faded and he knew Thomas had an hour or two start.

He pushed his horse over the peak and out of the Sierra Verde valley. Slade did not know why he was trailing Thomas, except that he felt sooner or later they would meet and it would be over. Slade preferred it be sooner than later.

He moved away from the valley and into fresh strange land, and when thunder boomed again and the sky grew dark, he wondered whether this was not a fool's chase. Lightning reached out and touched the far-off peaks that Slade knew were the foothills of the Sangre de Cristo mountains.

An hour later, rain fell, and in the swiftly sloshing ground, Slade lost Thomas' trail. He turned his horse in wide circles, searching for high somewhat dry ground—and the print of the big white horse—but he found nothing but slippery underfooting. Another hour went by. Finally Slade drove his horse into the protection of a canyon overhang. He thought they would stay dry until the late afternoon squall ended, and then he would push on. Once he thought he heard the sound of a rider, far off but coming closer. He strained his ears for the sound, but it was a half-mile away, headed back for the Sierra Verde valley. Slade ignored the sound. Thomas would not be coming back so soon.

When the rains fell, Thomas gave a sudden start. He was chilly and for no reason he could account, frightened. He was reminded of another day, another time he had left the valley and another time it had rained.

He dragged on the reins and the big white horse raised its head in surprise. "Turn around," Thomas snarled. "Turn around, you stupid brute." He whipped the horse around and started back for the valley.

Once he thought he heard the soft nicker of another horse, but he circled wide away from the sound. He didn't know why he was in this strange valley on the other side of the Sierra Verde, but he knew it was wrong. He ought to go back. They'd be expecting him, back at the house. Besides, it was wet and cold, suddenly. He started to shiver and he thought he'd have to control himself, or else he'd be crying. A boy doesn't cry, he thought, not a big boy like Bigelow Thomas. And running away—he thought—that was such a silly trick. Why, if he didn't hurry back, they'd really worry. He spurred his horse and drove him up the peak toward the northwest bowl, over the Sierra Verde.

A weight had lifted from his shoulders, as soon as he turned back. He started to whistle, through the rain and chill wind. He would go to California territory some other time. There was lots of time for a twelve-year-old boy.

The rain hissed down and the man-who-thought-he-was-a-boy named Bigelow Thomas drove hard for home. There was only one thing wrong with him. Abbott had been right, after all. The last alternative—the man's mind snapping under the strain—had occurred. It was, however, a bit late to help Abbott.

When the rain would not relent, Slade gave it up. He pushed through the darkness, back toward the valley. It had been a wild goose chase, after all. He had lost Thomas' prints in the river of water that suddenly sprinted down the sides of the canyon. Now he had wasted another half day. He was tired again. He wondered whether he'd ever not be tired again.

At the peak where he had first seen Thomas' prints, Slade smelled the charred smoke, and he thought wildly, *they've burned down Crispin's place.* He splashed through the narrow trail, his horse floundering and once going to his belly, but they kept going, and it was when they were within a half mile of Thomas' that Slade knew where the fire had been. The smell of wet smoke came from the Big T.

He stopped his horse, wondering, his hand at his gun butt. His other hand mopped his face with a bandanna. Then he knew that was foolish. It had stopped raining. He took his hat and shook it. Water sloshed to the ground. But no more rain was falling. And nearly as swiftly as the rain had come—a summer thunderhead sucking up the valley dampness and then bursting open and letting it flow back to the valley—just so swiftly the night cleared. Clouds retreated across the suddenly high New Mexico sky. Stars popped out and the air was cool.

Slade strained his eyes. He could barely make out the huddled pile that had been Thomas' ranch house. It was shapeless now. He slowly walked the edgy horse toward the pile.

Fifty yards from the house, Slade stopped. There was a curious brushing sound coming from directly ahead. Slade got down from his horse and walked forward, hoping the sucking sound of his shoes in the mud wouldn't warn whoever it was making that brushing sound.

Then a great cloud rushed from the sky, and the moon broke free, sailing like a lopsided silver dollar over the land. And Slade saw Thomas, standing in front of him, his back to Slade. The rancher was gently stirring the ashes of the ranch house with a long stick, listlessly poking he ruins as if he were half-afraid he would find something here he did not want to see.

Slade turned then. He did not understand what was happening, but he knew he ought not to watch. It seemed indecent. As though Thomas had suddenly revealed himself, all the neat trim disciplined ways rubbed off, and the wild frightened man beneath now all naked. Slade didn't want to watch, and he didn't want to listen. A stream of filthy curse words came from Thomas' mouth. They all seemed directed at himself.

Slade crept away, sick and ashamed. He had come into this valley and with him, violence had issued forth, violence and murder and—now—insanity. He crept away, toward his horse, hoping to get back to the valley floor and to the pass and into Cowpoke, and away. Away from it all.

Then his foot slipped in the mud and he fell heavily to the ground. He smothered a cry and scrambled to his feet.

But it was too late. Thomas had heard him. The rancher stepped swiftly from the charred ruins. He saw this new man—this dimly familiar man—standing on his land, and all the obscenity he had turned on himself suddenly veered toward this interloper.

He said, "What the hell are you doing here?"

Slade's hand tightened on his gun butt. He said, "Nothing. I smelled the fire, Thomas, and came over." He saw the money belt at Thomas' waist, and his anger returned.

And Thomas said, "Oh, it's you, Slade." Thomas felt a tremendous relief. This was Slade, and he was Big Thomas, and they stood on his, Thomas', land.

His land.

The land they had tried to take away from him. Crispin and Hogue and mostly Abbott. Now Slade.

But they wouldn't get away with it.

He said, "I'm going to kill you, Slade."

Slade said, eyes burning through the moonlight, "No, you're not. You're through killing, Thomas."

Then he saw Thomas move. The man hunched his left shoulder and dropped his right, his right hand snaking to his belt, and flame was an exploding red blossom in the night, the two shots sounding nearly like one.

But Slade knew he had beaten the man. He knew it when he saw Thomas move, because the rancher's move had been so swift and graceful, so smooth and perfect, that Slade would have had to be dead, unless he had beaten Thomas to the draw. He didn't know how he did it, except maybe it was the tiredness and the aching he still felt from the time he had tangled with Dilt or the time he had fought with Morgan or Voss or Connors. Or maybe it was the sudden knowledge that now—*now, dammit, now*—he stood a chance of stopping them from pushing him around. That he could stop running and riding and fighting—if he stopped this man in front of him.

That the whole war was over, now, if he put a hole in Thomas and sent him into the raw hell the man had made. That Crispin could sleep easy in his grave at the bottom of the crevice, below that half-ton boulder that crushed his bones to paste. That poor Hogue could sleep easy, his shadow no longer swaying in agony under that tree, his tongue twisted and purple.

Slade's right hand was at his hip and he knew he had squeezed off a shot because his hand ached where the .44 kicked and his finger remained taut as a stick on the trigger.

Then he saw Thomas start to fade. The man curled away from Slade, staggering to the side three heavy steps, and then throwing his arms up into the sky like a man screaming for help. Except no sound came from Thomas. He stood like that, swaying, a man with a third eye in his forehead, and Slade stepped forward involuntarily—to catch him, he thought. Then a cloud blotted the moon, blessedly, and Slade heard Thomas fall lightly.

Slade walked up to the man and removed the money belt. He opened the pocket and felt the lining. There was nothing in there. He didn't care. It didn't matter anymore. Then, in a far corner, folded under the lining, he found the single silver dollar.

Slade rode toward Cowpoke.

CHAPTER 20

Mudge and Early sat in the big outer office of the bank. Loomis spoke to them swiftly and in a low voice. He had not recovered from the shock.

He said, "The loans will be made, just as Mr. Abbott had approved. The Cowpoke Bank and Trust will not go back on its word."

The two little ranchers nodded. Their eyes glinted in the big cool room. The money would make improvements in the land. They would get their places fixed up. May Hogue had said she wouldn't put the fence back up between her spread and theirs. The graze would be common graze, for all three of them. Mudge and Early would profit by such an arrangement. Their cows would be better for it.

Early said, "There's no chance, I suppose, that the railroad will change its mind?"

Loomis shook his head firmly. "Not a chance in the world. Mr. McAlester—he's the railroad man we deal with—says it will be a long time before the Sierra Verde valley sees rails laid across its floor."

Mudge flared. "That's not fair, you know. It's not our fault. We didn't start the trouble."

Loomis shrugged. "The railroad doesn't care. It can't afford to run into any gun wars or the like."

Mudge said, "But that's over. There won't be any more."

Loomis sighed. He didn't like this any more than they did. "There probably won't. But there's been so much, the railroad has been scared off."

The ranchers got up. There was a bitter taste in their mouths. They had dreamed of riches. Now they had—a piece of common graze. They walked out.

On their way through town, they passed Slade. They waved at him, and he waved back. He yelled, "Good luck," and they smiled ruefully and went on. Luck, they thought. There just was no such thing. Least not, good luck.

Slade rode on through Cowpoke, and out of the town, the way he had come in. His hand strayed to his money belt. Empty. He grinned. His hand went to his pocket and he pulled out a heavy piece of wool.

It was his sock. He dangled it, still grinning. The single silver dollar bounced in the heel of the sock.

He didn't know how he'd get there, or how long it would take. But it didn't matter. He knew he'd get there. He wanted to ride through Cutter again. He wanted to see Lu, his old fanny-shaking singer. He wanted to see Johnson, in his old saloon. He wanted to match the man high cards.

Slade began to whistle. Later that day, out in the middle of nowhere, between towns, under a great blazing sun, a strange thought bounced along with Slade: *I'm home, I'm home.*

THE END

The Manhunter

Arnold Hano

Writing as Matthew Gant

CHAPTER ONE

The words rolled through the town like the whisper of wind across the Colorado plains, and maybe that's all it was. But each man who heard the words, or thought he heard them, gave a substance to them, and pretty soon the words had a lift and a life of their own, even when the Colorado wind sighed later that day, and died.

A farmer riding his wagon across the dry ruts that marked the beginning of the town—Oxnard, the town was called—thought he saw a man in the hills, and then he heard the words and shivered and tried to forget them. But they stayed in his head like the memory of drought and they sloshed around like last year's flood, and they made him cringe like the look on his wife's face had made him cringe, just before she spat her last mouthful of phthisic blood and died one day this past spring.

So the farmer shrugged his head into his shoulders and slashed the rump of his dray horse to get him into town so he could get rid of the load of sugar beets and potatoes, and back out again. He hurried the wagon, and the noise in the wheel ruts made a loud clamor in the chill October morning, but not loud enough. The words spun in his head, like the spokes on the wheels of his wagon, insistent, unrelenting.

And maybe it was the farmer who carried the words into Oxnard.

A drunken, drifting cowhand, lying in the ruts, heard them in his fogged-up head and he tried to laugh, but he couldn't, and pretty soon he got up and found his horse shivering in the cold gray morning light, spikes of sun across the valley to the west, but doing no good here in Oxnard yet, and then the drunken drifting cowhand was swiftly sober, riding hell for breakfast out of the town, trying to get away from the words on the wind.

Even the girl with red hair and hard painted mouth who had come into Oxnard off the three-thirty Concord from North Platte six months ago and who made a living singing and dancing in the saloon, and reading cards when she wasn't entertaining stirred in her sleep that morning and moaned once. Then she woke and rolled to the edge of her lumpy hotel bed where she crouched, eyes wide open in the gray darkness, listening.

And the sheriff, lurching out of his house onto his fat dun mare, holding the bridle reins down low so the horse wouldn't decide to take her head and go off for a morning run, even the sheriff heard the words; though he was hardly awake, his belt open and his .44 hanging from his right hip like an extra atrophied leg and just about as useless.

He stopped the horse and looked around, and his own dun-gray face thinned out a bit and his nostrils pinched as he smelled the east wind and tried to make out what it was he was hearing. He said to no one in particular, not even to the dun mare who wondered why she couldn't stretch and canter some of that fat off her flanks, "Now, what the devil? To Oxnard? What for?" He lowered the reins until they were well below the eye-level of the mare, and he made her single-step to his office, where the sheriff went to his desk and turned the apprehend notices over, one by one, filing the names and the blurry photographs in his memory.

By this time Oxnard was waking up, the frame houses stirring and emptying out: blacksmith and stable hand, banker and school teacher, grocer and bartender. One or two of them found themselves standing in the shadows of wooden doorways, looking around as though somebody might be watching. Nobody was, but they still shivered, standing there, because by now the words were as clear as the ugly scrub pine that jutted against the skyline in the hills above Oxnard.

By ten that morning, the town had girded itself and was waiting. And finally at noon, a puncher drummed the dry street and reined to a stop at the saloon, roped his horse to the tie rail, leaped to the plankwalk and strode through the swinging mahogany batwing half-doors.

His name was Ives, and be wore a branded broken S on an empty holster; his horse wore the same mark on its rump. Ives marched into the saloon and said, "Where's Tromper?" A man rose up from behind the bar, his apron laundered a neat blue white.

The cowpoke said, "Tromper, he's come," and the bartender said, "Who?" of course though he knew.

"The manhunter," Ives said impatiently, scratching the rowel of his right spur against his left trouser leg. "The manhunter's here. In Oxnard."

Then Ives went out, his job done. The town would know for sure, because the bartender now knew.

A manhunter had ridden into Oxnard. Nobody knew why, though the redheaded girl figured it had to do with her; and the drunken drifting cowhand had figured it had to do with him, so he rode on out; and even the sheriff wondered if maybe there was something wrong with the way he tried to run things in the county, sticking so close to the law nobody would have anything to do with him. Just about everybody, in fact, searched around inside and found good reason to be afraid.

None of them was as frightened as the manhunter.

His name was Ben Ross. He was a broad-shouldered, big-fisted lean young man, with a long, thin, feral face and long, thin lips and long, thin lines that crawled from the far corners of his eyes straight across

Indian-high cheekbones. His eyes were pale blue, and when he took off his hat to wipe his brow—though he wasn't warm; he was, in fact, quite cold—his hair proved to be lank and sandy. He rode his horse, a big, bony, hammer-headed sorrel, up a brown-gashed rocky hill, and when he saw the town of Oxnard in front of him at dawn that day, he gasped once, and for a moment he wanted to duck back down.

Instead, he lifted his heels from rough-thonged stirrups and jabbed the sorrel and at the same time raised the reins high. The horse crossed the crest quickly, and then the rider came down with the checkreins until the bit dug in, and the horse stopped. They stood that way just below the crest to the southeast of the town, so the sun, when it rose finally, would be in anybody's eyes in case anybody would be looking for him. They stood in shadow, the early morning light filtered and vague, but the man didn't take heart. He knew it didn't matter. It never did. Every town he had ridden into had stiff-backed him and watched him from around corners. They knew who he was. They could smell him, the way men smell blood, or bad luck at the poker table.

So he stood there, in the shadows, not so much to remain hidden, but more just to remain. He didn't want to leave that spot, though the Colorado hills had holes in them where winds seemed to be born and grew up and ran loose. Most of them—Ben Ross thought—must have been born right here, and they were all running at him. He was cold.

As the morning light grew, or the darkness faded, and the sun began to suck the last wisps of fog out of the draw bottoms, the man stirred in his saddle. He had another way to go, of course, and that was back. But he couldn't do that. His hand went to his pocket, and he fingered the curl-edged piece of paper, the deputization he carried up from Knox County, Texas, and then he released the paper. His fingers crept out of the pocket and went to his right hip where his Colt Walker .44 hung.

The fingers stayed there, just above and slightly behind the butt of the six-shooter. Then in a jerky, nearly spasmodic movement, they gripped the heavy butt and slid the big, nine-inch barreled revolver out of its leather sheath and back in again, just to make sure it moved easily.

Suddenly—though nothing before him had changed, neither the sound of a broken twig nor the sight of another man nor the sense of danger, none of these occurred—Ben Ross ducked his head behind his hunched-up left shoulder, and his right hand streaked to his hip once more, not jerky now, nothing spasmodic about the move, but a flowing move, smooth as glass, graceful and direct as a hawk in diving flight, and the heavy revolver was sitting in Ross's huge hand, its barrel un-wavering, pointed directly ahead.

It was the grim-visaged portrait of a man determined to kill another man.

Ross cracked the portrait with a short nervous laugh. He thought: That was good. The best yet, with the new gun. He wondered whether it would be good enough. Then he shook his head, in annoyance. That wasn't what worried him. He knew it was a fast move. It didn't seem possible anybody could move much faster. What worried him was whether he could possibly do the same thing with a man in front of him, *the* man. That was the kicker.

Ben Ross had never fired the gun to kill, not even at a brush hare or at yawking jays that winged at him and rushed away, laughing like crazy. He had certainly never fired it—or any gun—at a human being. But some day he would, and he was frightened by that knowledge.

That was why he had bought himself a new Colt and made the gunsmith back in Texas swear it was the best firearm he had in stock for the job Ross had to do. Hunt down another man, and fire it, once.

The smith had shown him a few Colt Pattersons, in .34 and .36 calibers, but Ross had brushed them aside. He wanted something heavier. The smith showed him a single-action .45, but Ross distrusted single-action revolvers. No, he didn't want another Colt Frontier .44— sure it was a good enough gun, but that was what he always had, what everybody had. He wanted a better gun, a special gun. Finally the gunsmith took a look at Ross's hands, went up to the attic, and came down with the Walker. It was the biggest revolver Ross had ever hefted.

"What does this thing weigh?" he had asked.

The smithy shrugged. "Four pounds and then some," he said. "Cap'n Walker dreamed her up for shooting holes in Mexicans. He shipped her off to Colt. Colt wasn't making guns anymore, of course, but Walker must of known Colt would fall in love with the design. Colt sent the monster on to Eli Whitney. Whitney made them in his plant, back East. I managed to git ahold of this one." He licked his lips. "She's the only one in stock. Maybe the only one in the whole Southwest, still unsold."

"What's wrong with it?" Ross said.

"Nothing. She's just too much gun for the average man. But you said you wanted a revolver for hitting a man and quieting him some. This here revolver will knock down any man she hits within fifty yards no matter where she hits him, and some men she misses."

Ben Ross, who had just been deputized to bring back or kill another man, bought the Colt Walker. He paid twenty-two dollars silver for it, which was about five times as much as he expected to pay for a gun. But he was satisfied....

Now he tugged the gun out of its sheath again, and he stared at it. This close to his prey, the gun disgusted him, and so did his little bravado act of drawing and sighting. All the way up to Oxnard he had practiced his draw, at first clumsily; the heavy revolver not lifting clear or else riding up so high the barrel rubbed the sides of his upper ribs in coming to the aiming position. But lately, the last two days or so, the draw was smooth and swift.

Ross shoved the gun back in its holster. He led the horse down the hill toward Oxnard, annoyance riding with him. It was a job to do that had to be done, Ross told himself. Like laying rails, he said to himself, or bulldogging steer or dipping diseased stock. It was all work, and some of it was harder and messier than other, and some paid better.

He had to say all these things, because when Ross thought of the real reason he was doing what he was doing, flame burst hot and white inside him, and he wanted to hurtle his sorrel at the man he hunted and trample him to a paste of white bone.

He took the curl-edged paper out of his pocket while he pushed the horse toward Oxnard. The warrant said that a man named Ben Ross was hereby and at such-and-such a time deputized by the county of Knox in the State of Texas to apprehend an unknown man for the purpose of making him stand trial in Texas, for murder. If the man wouldn't come, Ben Ross was authorized among other things to shoot the man down.

Ross cursed once, and the wind behind him snapped against his rough wool shirt that once was red but was now a faded, speckled brown, and his Levis ballooned at his thighs and then tightened. He pushed the horse harder, his eyes flattening, the long creases cutting across his sun-dotted cheekbones. Oxnard grew before him. Ross had followed the Red River and crossed it into the Panhandle; then he had snipped off a piece of Oklahoma and a piece of New Mexico Territory and climbed through Las Animas County up the eastern edge of Colorado Territory, the Raton pass through the Rockies to his left, the unending Great Plains to his right.

It had been nearly four hundred miles of drudgery and the acrid smell of damp sage, to look for a man who some said maybe was a killer and then again maybe wasn't, a man who could be found in Oxnard, and then again maybe not.

... Nearly four hundred miles earlier, Ross had been poking cows in Texas, in the rolling blackland prairie county of Knox where he had been born and raised. He came in one dawn after checking fences to find a note on the pillow of his bed in the bunkhouse. His bed had a cardboard sign hanging from the foot of it, reading, "Ross," so it was easy to find, even when you came in at dawn, with a small red oil lantern throwing a gloomy light over the inside of the long, log bunkhouse. Ross knew his bed even without the sign or the lantern, but once in a while the big rancher himself came in to check bunks or to find a man he wouldn't otherwise have known, except by the sign.

The note on Ross's pillow said: *Theres a man you might be looking for in Oxnard up in Colorado Terr. If you want to know more about him, bring five hundred dollars to Grants saloon tomorrow night. Ask for Gill.*

Nobody in the bunkhouse had noticed the man. He must have come in after midnight, and the one or two punchers who were still awake probably thought he had been just one of themselves coming or going on outhouse call. So he had gone unchallenged in the pale red gloom to Ross's bunk and pinned his note and went on out again.

Ross brought two hundred dollars, which was all he had, and three hundred in promissory notes, to Grant's saloon the next night, but Gill never showed. Ross came back every night for a week, but he never found Gill. Ross thought: the man's a liar or else he's crazy. Or else he wasn't, and he just got scared and decided he had talked too much already, and had run off. Ross figured the last was the least likely, but he wasn't missing any chances. He strapped his father's old single-shot Sharps carbine to a saddle pack and bought a new revolver and said so long to the punchers he worked with and the townspeople he had grown up with. Then he started off for Oxnard....

The town was right there, waiting for him, and maybe a man he'd never seen but once and that eleven years ago when Ross was just thirteen years old and wet-nosed.

It was noon or a few minutes after when he and the sorrel saw the brown grass turn to gravel under their feet, and they entered the pebbly dirt road that was the main drag of Oxnard.

Ross pushed the horse slowly, his eyes drifting right and left. A woman with a parasol walked the wooden planks and went into a dry goods store. Two punchers in wide-brimmed hats and crescent moons branded onto their horses came toward Ross and then swerved to the side. One of them spat in the street, near the sorrel's feet. The blacksmith's shop was open and a cowhand lounged in the doorway while his pony was shod. The cowhand wore a broken S on his holster, but the holster was empty. Ross wondered at that. Another cowman with a crescent moon branded on his horse passed the blacksmith shop and, when he saw the cowman with the broken S, he snarled at him, and the broken S puncher snarled back.

Then Ross saw the saloon on his left, twenty yards ahead. At first he thought he'd drift past and see the rest of the town before coming back, but he knew he was just trying to stall it off, this business of asking about a man named Gill and whether anybody from Oxnard had been down in Knox County, in the town of Gore, Texas, eleven years ago. He grinned at that, a thin bitter smile that moved his mouth but didn't change his eyes, cold and humorless. It was a long-odds chase, Ross knew, looking for the killer. The man Ross was looking for was a tall man, he thought, but Ross used to think his own father was very tall until somebody told him that Old Man Ross never stood over five feet nine inches. Heavy-set, too, Ross thought, yes, the man was heavy-set, but Ross was a skinny boy of thirteen then, and nearly every adult was a thick-chested giant. So maybe the man wasn't so tall, and he wasn't so husky. Dark hair. Black? Well, black or so dark brown it had looked black. But in eleven years black hair could change to iron gray or gray or no hair at all.

That was the phantom he was chasing, with a warrant in his pocket inviting the phantom to come down to Knox County, Texas, and stand trial, or else resist the deputy and take his chances. Ross felt the grin fade and his lower jaw jut out. He stopped his horse and tied him loosely, patted his rump, and walked toward the saloon.

A cowhand lounged outside, hat pulled low over his forehead (*but Ross could see the puncher was blond so he couldn't be the man he wanted*), and eyed Ross. He said, as Ross came within five steps of the saloon doors, "Stranger, you better put that gun away."

Ross said savagely, "You the law in town?"

The man flushed. "No," he said, "I ain't. But I know the law in town. I'm telling you, we don't want guns showing in Oxnard."

Ross looked down and saw the man also wore a holster without a gun. There was a bulge inside his shirt at the waist. Ross said, "People who wear a hideout gun shoot other men in the back. I'm showing mine. Get out of my way." He kept walking and the man moved away. Ross pushed inside.

Three men stood at the bar, their backs to Ross. There were tables on either side of the door, stretching from the back to just past halfway to the bar. Where the tables ended, there was a wide aisle of empty floor space, and a natural-wood piano along the wall. It was the only portion of the floor that looked as though it was kept up. The rest was trampled sawdust and spilled drinks and cigarette butts. Ross figured the empty floor space and piano were for a night show of some sort, dancing or singing women with frozen smiles and fat thighs. Good, he thought, if drink didn't loosen their tongues, then maybe the women would make them forget themselves and they'd talk a bit more.

He started for the bar when a voice said, "Read the cards, stranger?"

Ross turned. At the first table on his right, in the shadows of the doorway, was a young woman with red hair and a too bright mechanical smile. She wore a long dress, cut low, with a slit along the right side, through which her calf winked at Ross. It wasn't a fat calf, and he doubted it led to a fat thigh. But the smile was frozen fast. Ross let his eyes roam over her and she kept the smile and let him have his look. Then she said, "All finished?"

He grinned and said, "From this angle, yes."

"Would you like a closer view?" she said.

He said, "Now what does that mean?"

She touched the empty chair next to her. "Let me read your cards. Sit down and find out what your luck's going to be."

"For how much?"

She broadened the smile and licked her lips so the overhanging lantern bounced a yellow glow off the bright rouge. "Two bits, four bits, or a whole dollar."

"Do I get a better piece of luck for a dollar than for twenty-five cents?"

She snapped her mouth shut. "Stranger, I read the cards as they fall. Today's fortune for twenty-five cents. Today's and tomorrow's for fifty cents. The rest of your life thrown in, for a dollar."

He reached into his pocket and plunked down a dollar. He thought, she'll tell me I'm going to meet a man, the man I'm looking for, and conclude my business with him to my satisfaction. And I'll ride off with the golden-haired fairy princess.

He sat down and said, "Is this all you do?"

She shook her head, shuffling the cards with the expert indifference of an old monte dealer. "I sing and dance," she said. Ross thought she said it like a man saying he poked cows or assayed ore. Neither pride nor shame was in her voice. It was just a job to her, like his job was to him. Something that had to be done. She turned over the queen of clubs and frowned. She pushed it away and turned over the four of spades. She said, "Two black cards in a row."

He said, "What's that mean?"

She smiled brightly. "Nothing. Aren't you going to buy me a drink?"

"Sure," he said, getting up. "I'm going to buy you a whole gallon, you cheap gold digger."

She said, "Wait a minute. I'm not done. So don't buy me a drink. I thought maybe you wanted to be sociable. Forget the drink. I still read your cards."

He said, "Don't bother." He walked to the bar and said to the bartender. "Sour mash with two fingers of water."

The bartender splashed water into the bourbon and pushed the glass to Ross. Ross said, "And do you read cards, too?"

The bartender grinned uncomfortably. He kept shooting glances at

Ross's revolver. He said, "It's against the law to wear your gun on the outside here in Oxnard."

Ross bit off an oath and said, "I never met such a busybody town in my life. The next man who tells me I ought not to be carrying a gun will have to try and take it off himself."

One of the three men at the bar turned and looked at Ross. He was a big man, with dark hair streaked with gray. He said, "Stranger you're a pugnacious young pup. I'm telling you to take off your gun. Take it off, pronto."

He pushed away from the bar and stepped into the empty aisle between the counter and first row of tables. He was a graceless man, twenty pounds heavier than Ross and just as tall, but Ross was turning sore inside, trying to twist the fury that lay mute in his belly toward something tangible. Right now, the big man with the dark graying hair was tangible.

Ross said, "And if I don't? You'll take it off for me?"

The big man said, a grin breaking broad over his face, "Sonny, I'll take it off and ram it down your gullet."

Ross moved from the bar and walked within three steps of the big man. One of the other two men said, "Wait a minute, Max. He might use that gun."

Ross said, "I'm not going to need it."

The other man who had been drinking with Max said, "I don't know, Max. He's a foxy son of a bitch. Look at him."

Ross said, "Are you going to take it off me or not, Max?"

Max said, "Sure I am," and he raised his arms and moved toward Ross.

Ross clubbed at the big man with his left fist but Max lowered his head into the protective shell and the punch thudded against a heavy shoulder. It was a solid punch, Ross knew, and it should have budged the man but it hadn't. Ross figured the revolver at his hip was bogging him down and pulling him off balance but there was nothing he could do about it now. He circled to his right and swung a roundhouse to the big man's ribs. The big man let his arms come down and Ross pumped his left fist against the man's temple. Max lurched away and hit a table with his back. Ross waited for the man to slide to the floor. Instead he straightened up and rushed Ross, and Ross knew sickly he was going to be licked.

Ross managed to hit him twice, a left hand against the top of Max's head that sent pain spiraling to Ross's shoulder and made him wince, and a right that curled under the upraised arms and lifted Max's head. Ross heard the big man's teeth click and he saw the blood start to spill down the corner of Max's mouth to the dark close-shaven blue-gray jaw.

Then Max was inside Ross's fists. He thudded his own right fist against Ross's chest, and Ross thought somebody had dropped a horse on him. He tried to push Max off, but the big man stayed close, his left hand grabbing Ross by the right arm and holding it out, while the right hand suddenly crossed for Ross's hip and snaked the gun from the holster. He stepped away from Ross and said, "Catch," tossing the gun behind him. One of the two others caught the gun and laid it on the bar.

"All right, Max," the man said, "your beer's getting flat," and the other man said, "Finish it off, Max. I've got work to do."

Ross felt the rage swell inside and he threw himself against Max, trying to claw him down. But Max shoved him aside and hammered the side of his jaw with his right fist. Ross's head spun like a swinging door and then spun back just as a heavy fist came looping through the air in a neat, short arc, catching Ross's jaw with the meaty crunch of an ax striking a tree. Ross heard somebody groan and then he started to laugh because he felt so fine, so light and free. He didn't even feel the floor when it rushed up and hit him.

The hands on his brow were pleasant and cool, and he thought they smelled like flowers. That was it, he thought, somebody's putting flowers all over me. He thought that was very nice, and then the pain in his head made him open his eyes.

He sat up and the girl with the red hair and the perfume that smelled like flowers said, "Well, you're alive, after all."

Ross lurched to his feet and said to the bartender, "S'mash fingers water," and he knew the words were all fumbled, but the drink appeared. He drank it slowly. Then he saw his gun on the counter and he looked down the bar. The three men had gone.

The bartender said, "Max sure admired your gun. Said he'd give you fifty dollars for it."

Ross picked it up and started to slide it into his holster. Then he changed his mind and dropped it into his shirt, reached to his belt and pulled the barrel along his belly so it was held by his belt. It was heavy in there, but at least he wasn't apt to get cold-cocked for it.

He said to the bartender, "Who was that, Davy Crockett?"

The bartender laughed. "No, only Big Max. Nobody's ever licked him, they say. Not many try anymore."

Ross said, "He ought to wear a sign. Humans and small bears, stay away." Ross shook his head and the pain started to fade from behind his eyes. But his jaw felt like it was cracked loose from his ears.

He said, "What do I owe you?"

The bartender said, "Half a dollar." Ross paid and started out. Then he saw the redheaded girl, and he stopped at her table. He said, "All right, that's today's fortune. You owe me for tomorrow's and the rest of my life."

She searched his face, the smile gone. "You're—you're not hurt much?"

"What's the difference?" he said.

Her mouth tightened. It was a nasty mouth, the upper lip long and thin. Ross had an impulse to reach across the table and drag the girl toward him and kiss those hard, nasty, bright lips. He wondered how they would feel and whether he could make them soften any. He doubted he could. She said, "No difference at all. Sit down. We'll finish you off." He stared at the girl, thinking that his legs were still wobbly from the beating he had taken, and he ought to sit down and rest, but knowing that if he did, it was only because he was still stalling, still putting off the real meaning of his presence in Oxnard. He sat.

She started to turn the cards over and he said, "What's your name, Red?"

She said, "Laura."

He said, "That's wrong. Redheads are Belles or Stellas. Laura's a blonde."

She said, "My father was color blind. Shut up, I'm trying to figure you out."

He said, "Who's Gill?"

He had waited this long because he had had no choice. But if he had known he was going to get the reaction he got, he'd have done it exactly the same way. The girl's hand suddenly jerked like a rattlesnake striking, and the cards spilled onto the table, reds and blacks all mixed together. She looked at Ross, the color drained from her face.

She said, "Gill? What about Gill?"

Ross said, "I want to know who he is. Where I can find him."

She said, "I'm sorry. I don't know Gill. I wouldn't know where to find him, if I did. Why don't you get out of Oxnard, you bounty hound."

"Read the cards," Ross said hotly. "Tell me if I should. Tell me whether I'll find Gill."

She got up. "Read them yourself. How much are you getting paid to find Gill? What do men like you get out of life? Hunting down other men! You filthy bloodsucker!" She reached down and gathered up the cards and turned suddenly and ran through the saloon to the rear, into a room marked, LADIES.

Ross grunted, his eyes narrowed, watching her, his blood racing. He thought: *She knows where Gill is. I'll dig him out of her even if it kills her. She'll tell me. She's scared, white-faced scared, and maybe she paints her lips hard and bright, but underneath she's just a scared punk kid.* Ross nodded, the excitement—and maybe the bourbon, too—washing the pain from behind his jaw, flowing into his blood.

He said to the bartender, "Bring me another sour mash." His fingers drummed the wooden table. Gill wasn't a liar. He wasn't crazy either. Gill knew something. For the first time since Ross had left Knox County, he felt he had a chance. He didn't know he could pull it off, but he didn't know he couldn't, either. It didn't have to work out all wrong. There was a man in Oxnard who had been in the town of Gore, in the county of Knox, Texas, eleven years ago, and Ross balled up his fists and swore he'd find the man and drag him to the waiting noose, or else he'd raise that heavy Colt Walker and pour daylight into the man, a big piece of daylight, gaping like the holes in hell. He said to the bartender who stood over him with a drink, "What did Gill look like?" and the bartender squinted and clamped his mouth shut. He started to walk away and then he came back to Ross's table. He set the drink down and he said, "You wouldn't take my advice about not wearing a gun, and it nearly cost you a busted jaw. Now I'm advising you again. This is a quiet little town. A man comes in looking for trouble, he's apt to find it. Forget about Gill. Forget about Oxnard. Take your gun and ride out of here. Tell them you couldn't find the man you wanted. Tell them the information was wrong, the man wasn't in Oxnard and never was. Tell them to keep their goddam blood money to themselves. We don't carry our guns where they show in Oxnard, but we still carry them. A manhunter comes into this town, he's apt to leave it horizontal."

Ross didn't even look up. He said, "You believe in your justice?"

The barkeep leaned back. Ross sensed the man's hesitation, his confusion. Then he said, "Sure I believe in justice. But not your kind. Not bloodhound justice. That's not justice."

"What's your name, barkeep?"

"Tromper."

"Tromper," Ross said, "what would you do if a man insulted your wife?"

"I'd knock him bowlegged."

Ross grinned and looked up finally. "You see?" he said. "You do believe in my kind of justice."

"The hell I do," Tromper said softly, pride refusing to link him with this newcomer, this manhunter.

Ross's fingers kept drumming the table. It was getting easier and easier. They'd all talk. There was a keg of dynamite here, and he was sitting on it, but it didn't matter because that was the only way he knew. He'd make it explode, and when it did, he'd dig Gill out of the smoking ruins, and Gill would dig out the other man and then the other man, too, and it would be over.

He'd go back and tell them, all right. He'd ride back to Gore, and they'd see by his face, by his jaw, set hard and thin and murderous, that he'd done the job, and that he'd wear the badge of having done it the rest of his life. Good or bad, right or wrong, decent or evil, he would have killed a man and, though it would be tough living with himself for putting a hole in another human being, it wouldn't be half as tough as the other way, coming back slumped and slack and saying with a weak wave of the hand, "It's hopeless, boys. It can't be done."

But now—*now*—it didn't have to go that way. It could go the way he wanted it to go, with Gill summoned forth, and the other men.

He paid for his drink and got up, strangely elated. He had just had his head handed to him by a big man with dark graying hair (*who might just have been one of the men down in Knox,* Ross thought suddenly), but more than that, he had found out that Gill wasn't a liar and he wasn't crazy. The man he was looking for *was* in Oxnard. Ross's hands slapped his thighs and his fingers clawed. He'd dig him out. He got on the sorrel's back and whispered into the big horse's ear, "This county's got a sheriff. He ought to be in this town. He'll talk, won't he, boy?" And then from nowhere he started to sing softly:

> *Eyes like the morning star,*
> *Cheeks like a rose,*
> *Laura is a pretty gal,*
> *God A-mighty knows.*

There was an office a hundred yards from the saloon with a sign outside, reading: BIG MAX, SHERIFF, OXNARD COUNTY.

Ross stopped singing. The glow inside him faded. He should have made the redhead read the rest of the cards. They were starting to turn up black again.

CHAPTER TWO

The sheriff grinned through a split, swollen lip. There was a bruise the size of a robin's egg on his forehead. He extended his right hand, and Ross winced at the sight of it. Then he took it and the sheriff's shake was little short of a bear hug.

Big Max said, "You hit like a mule. I wish I had your hands."

Ross pictured the sheriff coming at him with four fists. It was an awesome sight.

He said, "All you had to say was that you were the law in town."

"It's seldom I get a chance to prove it," the sheriff said. "You were just the perfect opportunity to drum some sense into the fools who ride around here, itching to take matters in their own hands. I didn't really enjoy belting you, 'cept that it would get around—the bartender likes to talk—and maybe it'll quiet things off a bit."

Ross said drily, "It'll quiet *me* off, I'll tell the world."

The sheriff chuckled. "That's good, then. I'm supposed to be the law here in the county, but every time I say so, there's apt to be an argument. Colorado isn't a state, you know. We have half a dozen courts trying the same cases, one lawman arresting a man and another letting him go. Sit down, maybe we can share our miseries. You're a bounty hunter?"

Ross said heavily, "No, I'm not." He sat down and stared at the sheriff.

"Everybody says you are."

"Well," Ross said, "they're wrong. I'm no bounty dog."

"You're looking for somebody?"

Ross hesitated. After he told the sheriff, the story would be out. But then, the story was out anyway. Everybody knew what he was in Oxnard for. Maybe they thought he did it for money. That part didn't matter. He said, "I'm looking for three somebodies."

"Wanted men? I'd have apprehend cards on them?"

Ross shook his head. "I doubt it. Certainly not on one of them. I doubt he's wanted for anything, though I don't know for sure. One of the others is a killer, but it happened eleven years ago. Are your files that deep?"

The sheriff squinted behind shaggy eyebrows. "No," he said, "they're not. Eleven years ago they were just carving Colorado out of Kansas Territory. A killer, eh. Here in Oxnard?"

Ross shrugged. "I think so. Do you know a man named Gill?"

Big Max leaned forward. "Of course. Is he your killer? If he is, you're in the wrong—"

Ross waved his hand. "Gill is not my killer. But I want to see him, if I can. He knows where the killer is, and—I'm sure—who the killer is."

"Tell me about it."

Ross said, "And after I tell you, who do you tell?"

Big Max said, "I thought we had settled something. Or do you want me to beat hell out of you again? I don't think I'm going to like you, Ross. I don't like the way you go about things. I'm the law here. You've got a matter dealing with the law. You're under moral—and legal—obligation to tell me about it, if it falls under my jurisdiction. And it looks like it does, from what you've said so far."

Ross flushed. "All right," he said, "I'll tell you. And if this thing blows up in my face because you spilled, I hope somebody comes up here looking for you. Listen...."

They talked for ten minutes, Ross doing most of the talking and the sheriff listening. When they had finished, the sheriff knew as much about the killing in the town of Gore, in Knox County, as did most anybody back there, which still wasn't much.

... It had been a Saturday, Ross recalled, but even that wasn't too clear anymore. He remembered the year. It was 1862, and people most every place else were talking about Shiloh, and what Stonewall Jackson's foot soldiers were doing in the Shenandoah, and how come Farragut whipped the Confederate Navy down in New Orleans.

But that wasn't Knox County, Texas, in the prairie land where the only war going on was between the farmer and the sun or the farmer and the floods. And 1862 was a nice year all around. Lots of sun, lots of rain. Not too much of either. So when this herd of Longhorns came up from the Stockton Plateau, nobody cared much that three of the punchers got roaring drunk.

Nobody but the sheriff of Knox County. He was an upright man, a man who walked on one side of the law and swore everlasting war on those who walked the other side. He raised his son strict and whipped him when he disobeyed. Sometimes he smacked his wife—who was a sickly woman—when she wasn't fast enough in getting the boy to toe the line. Still, three drunken punchers wouldn't have bothered the sheriff too much, except to make him keep his eye on them. So the sheriff was nearby when one of them slapped a local woman in the street for what reason nobody ever did find out. The sheriff hauled the three of them into his office—yes, it was a Saturday evening, Ross remembered for sure—and he lectured the boys. He gave them an awful dressing down and then he slapped their faces and kicked them into the street. Literally. They were drunk and maybe the sheriff should have found out whether the woman wasn't a tart or somebody who had gone out of her way to taunt the drunken cowpokes, hot and tired and thirsty after the long trail, but he didn't find out and he did slap them, and kick them in the slats.

Two hours later—around ten or so—one of them, a big man, Ross recalled, with dark hair, walked into the sheriff's office. A shot was fired. The sheriff died at his desk, a hole in his right eye and the back of his head, blood spilling all over the wanted circulars he studied whenever he had a free moment.

The sheriff, you see, was a dedicated man. He turned his office into his home, and he lived there, with his wife and with his thirteen-year-old son. The son had heard the shot, of course, and for a brief while— seconds, probably, maybe half a minute, he lay stunned in the inside bedroom. Then he ran through the bedroom and into the office and to the door, in time to see the dark-haired man get on a big white horse. He was one of the three men. He rode away, and the boy was too frozen and too frightened to scream or do anything until the man disappeared in the night. Later, people said they saw the man and the other two riding up north. Ben Ross—though he was only thirteen at the time—had asked a lot of questions. Yes, the townspeople of Gore thought the riders they had seen must have been the same three men who had been in the sheriff's office. Yes, they had ridden to the town hotel after Jake Ross had kicked them into the gutter, and they had a couple of bottles of whiskey with them. Yes, one of them was riding a white horse, then, and later. No, nobody knew where they were headed. Nobody ever did find out their names.

... "Well," Big Max said, "well, well." He got up and walked aimlessly around the room and came back to his desk and started to say something. Then he began to walk around the room some more, and finally he said, "Look here, Ross. I'm a horse's rear end and you ought to string me up and hide me. I'm not going to try to apologize because we'd be here the rest of our lives. But I will say this. It's not because I can't stomach the notion of a man killing a sheriff. Oh, that's bad enough; killing any man is. But after the way I've acted, the only thing I can do is work with you until I drop. We'll get Gill, Ross, and we'll get the other two. I swear to that. When you're through here in Oxnard, you'll have your man. I'm only going to ask you one thing. When you do get him—and you will get him—you have to promise me you'll deliver him to me. I'll turn him back to the Texas authorities. Will you promise that?"

Ross rose up. He shouted, "No! No promises!" He pounded his right fist against Max's desk and the room shivered. "Why do you think I'm doing this? I've told you I'm no bounty dog. I'm no bloodhound. I'm a cowpoke. I never shot anybody in my life. Do you think I like doing this? No, I don't promise a thing. When we get him—when *I* get him—I'll decide. Me. Nobody else."

Big Max said softly, "And what will you do?"

Ross felt the fury pass like air from a balloon. "I don't know," he said lifelessly. "I really don't know."

The sheriff touched Ross's arm. "You'll turn him over to me. That's what you'll do. Just because you're not a man who ever shot anybody. You'll do the straight thing, the legal thing. Won't you?"

Ross raised his head and looked at the sheriff. He said flatly, "No, I'm not sure I will, Sheriff. My father wouldn't have done that. He'd—"

"Your father's dead," Big Max said. "You're alive."

"I know. That's just it. My father's dead. And the man who killed him is running around up here, free as the wind. Did you ever see a man's face after he's been shot in the eye with a heavy caliber gun from about three paces? Why, man, there's nothing left to the back of the man's head. And you want me to turn him over. For what? For some court to tell me I've got no proof?"

Big Max turned away and looked out the window. "If you've got no proof," he said, "he doesn't deserve to be held. If you've got it, the court will find against him. He'll be tried down in Texas. Do they love sheriff-killers down there? That's not what I heard about the people from your part of the country."

Ross said, "We're wasting time. I want Gill. Maybe all three of them. How do we go about it?"

The sheriff eyed Ross and seemed to wrestle with something inside. Ross heard horsemen in the street, and with every noise, he figured: that's Gill coming back, or, maybe, one of the other men leaving. The girl Laura knows and the bartender knows. Maybe they all know.

Big Max said, "Gill used to work for the Stantons. That's the Broken S spread. Gill used to ramrod it. Two months ago he disappeared. The Stantons won't talk about it, but I hear Gill was told to ride out of here and not to come back. Nobody seems to know why. The Stantons sure as hell don't say."

Ross said, "Who are the Stantons?"

The sheriff said, "Two brothers. Orville and Ed. Orville really runs the ranch, though I guess they own it between them." He stopped then and the two men looked at each other from across the desk. The sheriff said, "Wait a minute, Ross, take it easy. You're jumping. Don't do it. You don't know. Maybe the Stantons are clean."

Ross said through tight teeth, "When did they come to Oxnard?"

"About ten years ago."

"And Gill?"

The sheriff's chest heaved and the breath hissed out. He seemed a weaker man, a tired man. "Gill came a month or so later."

A muffled oath tore from Ross. "And you say take it easy! Why, it's as simple as one-two-three. My father was killed eleven years ago. The killers split up and rode around a bit, trying to cover their tracks. Finally, they settled down, ten years ago. I get a note from Gill saying the man I want is in Oxnard. How come? Gill and the Stantons have had words. Gill's been tossed out. He's sore. He takes the obvious way of getting back. He decides to spill on the man who killed my father."

The sheriff said, "But did he spill?"

Ross said, "Yes, a bit. Then he got scared. He sobered up and decided he'd said enough. He'd be implicated if anybody ever linked him with the Stantons, and the three of them with Jake Ross's death. So he took off."

The sheriff was silent. "It sounds good," he said finally. "But you don't know."

"No, I don't," Ross said. "But I will. Let's go."

The sheriff said, "Where to?"

Ross exploded. He had come up four hundred miles, thinking it was no use. And now the three men were all lumped together, the Stantons and Gill. They had just scrapped, like thieves over booty. "Sheriff, we're going to the Stanton ranch. The Broken S. At least, I'm going. If you want to stay and let me go on up there and maybe kill a man or two, that's okay with me. Lie down. Take a nap. Or go beat up another man who's out to see justice done. Forget about me. I'll handle it myself."

He started to wheel around.

Max said. "You're a very funny man, Ross. I just figured you. You're afraid, you know that. You aren't going to go on up there and kill a man or two because for some reason it would rub wrong with you to do anything like that. You talk a big gun fight, but I'd bet you've never fired at a man with that cannon you're wearing. And—by the way—where did you get that thing? I'd like one like it." The sheriff looked wistfully at the bulge in Ross's shirt. "Take it out, boy, you can wear it. I'll deputize you."

Ross dug the gun from his belt. He said dully, "I got it back in Texas. You're right, I never fired it." Max had nailed him to the wall. The sheriff wasn't letting Ross wear the gun because Ross was being deputized: he was letting him wear it because he was sure Ross wouldn't use it. Ross felt all the old terrible doubts return, crushing him. He said, "What do we do now?"

The sheriff walked to the door. He took his holster with a Frontier Model Colt .44 from a nail and strapped it on. He went back to his desk and removed a tin badge from the top drawer. He put it in his pocket. "Let's go looking for Gill," he said pleasantly. He made it sound as though Gill were down the street, buying himself a drink or waiting at the blacksmith's. "At first, I'd have sworn you didn't stand a chance, finding Gill. I figured he was out of Oxnard, and gone. But now, I'm not so sure. We might just be able to spot our boy."

"How come?"

"Gill is slick," the sheriff said. "After eleven years, he's suddenly talking about a killing down in Texas. There's got to be a reason."

"What is it?"

Big Max winked. "You'll have to go along with me. This is my play."

Ross roared, "Goddammit, Sheriff, don't make a game of it. This is my affair, not your play."

"And this is my county," Max said softly. "We do it my way here. I said I'd help you get Gill. I will. But my way, not yours. No blundering and storming around. I said there was a reason why Gill suddenly started to talk about your father's death. I think Gill is planning to take over a big hunk of this county for himself. For all anybody knows, maybe he owns a piece of the Broken S. He's acted that way in the past. Maybe he's just hanging around, pretty darn close by, just waiting to see the Stantons driven out of here. By you. By me. Down to Texas, to stand trial and to hang. Then slick boy Gill is going to be kingpin of the Broken S."

"*If* he owns part of the Broken S," Ross said.

Big Max shrugged. "The way people operate around here, you don't have to own anything to take over. So maybe he doesn't own the Broken S. With the Stantons out of the way, one or both, Gill would be in a heck of a better spot than he is right now."

The two men walked outside, and the sheriff mounted a fat dun mare. Ross thought, that horse will wheeze herself dead inside two miles. He followed the sheriff on his sorrel, and he wondered why he was feeling so let down. It was because the sheriff was in charge now. Ross thought he would have to do something about that. Gill was his man, not the sheriff's, no matter how Gill planned to slice up the county. And the Stantons, too. The people down in Texas had given him a job to do. At first it had looked hopeless, but he had decided to tackle it. Now, with the girl Laura letting him know Gill was around someplace, hiding probably, and with the sheriff letting him know he'd work with him to find Gill, it wasn't hopeless at all.

Maybe that was it. When it was hopeless, he was willing to give it a try. Because Ross knew then—inside of him—he'd never find Gill, or his father's killer. It was easy to be brave then.

But now, with a ring closing in on Gill, it wasn't so easy anymore. Maybe he'd really have to reach for the Colt Walker and draw her out, level her and squeeze. Maybe it would be his speed and skill—and courage—against another man's, a man who had already killed before. Maybe that was why he was feeling let down, why he was actually allowing the sheriff to turn him and twist him, to take the ugly chore away from him.

Then they were out of Oxnard, moving the opposite way Ross had come in; the sheriff led the way on the dun mare that was wheezing, yet showed no sign of faltering. The sheriff rode badly, lurching in the saddle, but Ross stopped forming impressions of that. The sheriff carried his fists all wrong and was an easy target, but nobody had ever beaten him.

The sun was far ahead of them, sinking quickly, and Ross felt the first day in Oxnard was going to end without a showdown. He said, "Where we going?"

The sheriff said, "I thought you'd like to see why I think Gill is hanging around. And, at the same time, I'd like to show you some of the trouble I'm up against, out in the county."

Ross said, "What trouble?"

"The usual. The fence men and the anti-fence men. Shooting off their mouths, mostly. It's the Broken S, the Stantons' ranch—and Joe Caesar's Crescent C."

Ross remembered the riders in town with the crescent moons branded on their ponies. He remembered the snarling words that passed between a Broken S man and a Crescent C.

"Who's Caesar?" Ross said.

"Caesar is the real big rancher out here. He owns maybe ten, twelve thousand acres." The sheriff waved his hand at the rolling plains that led into the foothills to the north and west. "There's open graze between Caesar's and the Stantons' spreads. The Stantons' place is much smaller, maybe one-fourth the size, but a lot of open graze. The best part of it, as a matter of fact, is on the Broken S. The Stantons want to fence their domain so their cows can eat off that choice piece of graze; Caesar says they better not. He doesn't want his cows to starve."

Ross said, "Who was here first?"

The sheriff said, "Oh, Caesar. He's been here forever."

"But he never staked his claim?"

"Not until much later. Never thought he'd have to. When the Stantons rode in—ten years back—they had a surveyor plat their land. They filed the plat with the land office and got a deed to more open graze than anybody thought was still unclaimed."

Ross was silent. The Stantons hadn't done anything illegal. Yet his sympathies were with Caesar. He had come out here first—probably during or before the Indian Wars—and he had undoubtedly borne the brunt of the early primitive days, the Comanche and Arapaho raids and the lonely winters. Now he was set up, his cows on good rich grass. There was peace on his land. Only it turned out the best part of his land wasn't his.

"What's going to happen?"

The sheriff stopped his mare and started to roll a cigarette. "Nothing, of course. Just a lot of talk. It doesn't really matter. Even if the Stantons wanted to fence their spread and even if the Crescent C had to fence its, they wouldn't be able to. Couldn't afford it."

Ross frowned. "What are they fencing with up here?"

The sheriff reached down and ran a hand along the double cinches that swept the horse's girth. Ross knew Big Max was deliberately slowing down, keeping Ross out on the grass until he was sure the angry fires had been banked. "Stone and wooden rails." Max said. "What else? Costs anywhere from three dollars to eight dollars a perimeter acre, depending on how much stone and where you have it wagoned from. The Stantons have a facing front of nearly two thousand acres. Caesar's got two or three times that. We've had drought out here and floods, both. Neither spread's in any shape to raise that sort of cash. They both carry skeleton crews, because they don't have the money to pay wages and found, and then it boomerangs against them because with undermanned help, they can barely keep the spreads in repair, much less built up."

"So what's the trouble?"

"The Stantons are planting Osage orange—mulberry hedges, you know—along one piece of the common front. Caesar says he'll burn it down if it interferes with his cows."

"Will he?"

The sheriff said, "Of course not. It takes years for Osage orange to fill in. They planted the first just last year. The cows are walking around the hedges. How dumb do you think cows are?"

"And?"

"Caesar's cows are eating away that open graze. It's making the Stantons burn a bit."

"Is that all?"

"So far."

Ross said, "Where does Gill fit in?"

The sheriff sighed. He gently nudged his mare. "You're a single-minded cuss," Max said. "I don't know for sure where Gill fits in, but it stands to reason if he's out to get back at the Stantons for discharging him, he's likely to throw in with Caesar."

Ross said, "You think Gill's hiding up at Caesar's?" Ross's voice was charged with electricity again—and down deep inside, Ross wondered what the excitement was: hope, or fear.

The sheriff looked at him closely. "I don't know, but it's worth a try."

They rode in silence then, and Ross heard a lone rider off to his right flank. He turned and saw a smallish pony with a slightly built rider, in a mild trot. He said, "Who's that?" and Big Max looked. The sheriff said, "Probably your girl friend from the saloon."

"Laura?"

"That's right."

"What's she doing out on the range?"

The sheriff said. "I dunno. She always rides out here, about this time every night. Started doing it a couple of weeks ago. Goes wide around the Crescent C and then the Broken S, just outside their spreads in a big circle and then back in again. Says she does it to keep in shape."

Ross said, "What's she do at the saloon that she's got to keep in shape?"

"Wiggles her butt," Big Max said. "Leers at the boys when she sings."

Ross shook his head. The girl disappeared in the gloom, her pony swallowed in dusk and thin woods. In front of him, Ross saw the mulberry trees, tiny, planted in the middle of green barley grass. He said, "Which side are we on?"

The sheriff said slowly, "We're crossing onto the Crescent C."

Ross's lips flattened, the feral look strong on his face again. He leaned forward, and gave the sorrel more head. The sheriff felt the pressure behind him and reluctantly jabbed the mare in the ribs. The mare wheezed and tried to look back with a sad rolling eye, but Big Max just kicked her again. She started to pick up her canter.

CHAPTER THREE

Caesar was a big man, even heavier than the sheriff, a man in his middle fifties, but the skin on his face was taut and clear, the jowl-line sharply lean. His hair was black as night. His nose was twisted and battered into a shapeless lump of cartilage.

He said, "What can I do for you, Sheriff?" There was an edge to his voice, a challenge, barely controlled.

The sheriff said, "I'm still looking for Gill. Any word?"

Caesar said, "Ask the Stantons."

Big Max said, "I have. I will. Right now I'm asking you."

Caesar made a motion with his lips as though he were going to swear. Then he turned and spat. He said angrily, "Sheriff, I told you I'd let you know. I don't run a lost-and-found here at the Crescent. You're starting to badger me, Max, and I don't like it. Stay close to Oxnard. That's where you belong. This is my land."

They stood outside Caesar's ranch house, a low sprawling white affair that was sandwiched by bunkhouses. Off behind the house stood a huge red barn. There were three corrals, one of them with open stalls for milch cows, the other two for horses. But there was a sagging disrepair to the house, to the corrals, to the barn. Rails were splintered, and a few broken clear through. Ross saw wired bales of hay on the shucked grass, some of them in neat cubes, others bursting the baling wire. The open graze itself was deserted. Ross thought Caesar's main herd was in winter quarters somewhere. Probably in the sheltering hills to the west. The hay ought to be in the barn before the fall rains hit. Caesar was plainly a man playing a huge hand with a short deck.

Max said slowly, "I'm sure sorry you're peeved, Caesar. The last thing I want to do is peeve you. But any time you feel I've gone too far, you let me know. I'll do my best to remedy it. And let me tell you something, Caesar. This may be your land, but I run this county, in Oxnard and out here. If I want to look for a man out here, I'll look. One of these days you and the rest of the big shot range bosses who think they own the whole cockeyed West are going to be in for a surprise. We've got laws out here now; one of these days we'll have lawmen and courts to enforce them."

Caesar eyed Max sidewise. He looked at Max as though the sheriff were something foreign that he didn't understand and never would. He pursed his lips and started to say something, and then he turned away and called, "Maria, Maria, you greaser bitch, come here."

Max said to Ross, "Now you'll see why Gill might be hanging around. Even if he's not in with Caesar," and Ross noticed Caesar's face darken at that. Then a door clanged inside the house, and the front door opened, and Ross saw one of the most beautiful women he'd ever seen in his life. She was raven-haired and olive-skinned, smooth as a grape. She had dark eyes, huge and sluggish, and her mouth was a warm curved gash of red. She was tiny and slim, yet round, and when she walked over to Caesar, she flowed. Ross felt his throat heat up and he thought, a man could kill another man over a woman like that.

She stood next to Caesar and said, "Yes?" She spoke without accent.

Caesar said, "Maria, you seen Gill lately?"

The girl paled a bit and shook her head. "No, I haven't." Ross thought she was telling the truth.

Caesar turned to Ross. "She used to play with Gill," and Ross wanted to smash the man's mouth.

The girl said, "Is—is there anything else?"

Caesar went on: "But now that Gill's gone, she'd even play with me. Except I don't want her. Now, isn't that something?"

Ross said, "The man who wouldn't want to be around this little lady isn't a man." He turned to Maria and said, "Excuse me, ma'am." She started to smile, a tiny smile, and then the sluggish mask dropped over her face.

Caesar stared at Ross. He said quietly, "Did you say I wasn't a man?"

Ross looked at the big rancher, measuring him. He turned to the sheriff. "Do you mind?" he said. "I didn't get started with you. The gun had me bogged down pretty bad. But I think he's more my style."

The sheriff shoved his bulk between the two men. He roared, "Darn right I mind! Save it for another time. I thought we were looking for Gill."

Ross said. "We are, but—"

"Dammit," Caesar said, "did you say I wasn't a man?"

Ross said wearily, "No. I said the man who wouldn't want to spend time with this lady isn't a man. I'm just saying you're an out-and-out liar—"

Caesar lunged at Ross. Big Max grabbed the rancher and held him off. The sheriff shouted, "No, I say, no! There'll be no brawling where I'm in charge. Cut it."

Caesar struggled to work his way around Big Max. "This is my land, Sheriff. Nobody talks to me that way on my own land."

Ross said, "Forget it." It was foolish, he knew. The tiny act of bravery, once more. Fighting a man who didn't count, who had nothing to do with the big fight, the fight to get Gill and the man who had killed Ross's father. "Forget it," he said again. "I take it back."

Max looked back at Ross, his eyes squinting. "You hear him, Caesar?"

Caesar growled. "Yes, I hear him. But he'd better watch his lip. Him and the rest of the people around here who are trying to push me around. Him and the Stantons." He glared at Ross. "Did the Stantons send you over? Are you siding them?"

That was funny, Ross thought. He was aiming probably to send one of the Stantons to his death, and Caesar wondered if he was siding the Broken S. People get involved in their own wars, until it seems there's nothing else. Either you're for or you're against. There was no middle ground. He said, "I said forget it. I'll watch my lip. I'll watch my whole mouth."

The big rancher stepped back from Max. He tugged at his belt. "You'd better," he said. "On my land nobody pushes me around. Nobody talks to me like that. Nobody fences me in." He sounded like a great wounded bear, and Ross felt sorry for the man. There was so much hollow defiance in his manner. Or maybe it was because Ross knew the dilemma of Caesar's position on the range.

Ross said suddenly, "Did you ever hear of a man named Glidden, back in Illinois?"

Caesar said, "No. What the devil does he have to do with this?"

"Everything," Ross said.

"Who's Glidden?" the sheriff said.

Ross said, "You people are a million years behind the times. Glidden is a man who's just invented something called bobwire. Those fences are going up, Caesar, whether you like it or not. And it's not going to cost a fifth what you're paying for fencing now."

The sheriff said, "Bobwire?"

"That's right. Iron wire, with barbs—stickers—attached. Barbed wire, I guess it is, but everybody calls it bobwire. They're fencing with bobwire down in Texas, and everyplace else I've been lately. Except up here. But it'll hit here soon. When it does, the Stantons will win this war after all, Max. Damn their bloody souls." He turned to the girl, Maria. "Where's Gill?" he said harshly. He thought the girl had been telling the truth before, but he didn't know for sure. He had to know for sure.

Maria said, "I—I don't know."

Ross said, "Gill doesn't love you. He loves Laura. Isn't that right, Sheriff?"

Max said, "Well, I'll be a cockeyed wonder. How much do you know anyway? You sure get around." He turned to Maria. "Of course he loves Laura. Everybody knows that."

Maria tried a little smile. She said, "You can't open me up with that game. I'm no fool. Even if I knew where Gill was, I wouldn't tell you."

Ross said, "What has this man got, that two women will protect him, lie for him? I'd like to meet this man."

Maria said, "So would I—again."

Ross said, "I don't want you to lie to me, Maria. If you're protecting Gill and a killer roams loose because of it, I won't like you at all. Neither will the sheriff. Gill knows about a killing that interests me. If you help him stay away from the law, you're an accessory. You understand all that?"

The girl snapped, "I said I wasn't a fool. Don't tell me the abc's."

Ross looked at the girl a long minute; her eyes were blazing. He said, "Maria, I'm sure sorry this is happening. If it ever turns out Caesar is right and that there are lots of men who don't want you, and you get lonely some cold winter night, please let me know. I'd just be crazy for looking after you."

Maria's face turned puzzled. She said, "You know, I think you mean all that."

"Try me sometime."

The sheriff said, "Come on, Ross, before I throw an anti-vice ordinance over this whole county."

Ross got on his horse. He said to Caesar, "Don't mess around with that girl. Sometime I'll come back here without Max and we'll see what kind of man you are."

Caesar's eyes were hot coals. He said, "Nobody talks to me like that on my land. Nobody." Then, almost as an afterthought, and with no reason other than to display his defiance further, he said, "Nobody's going to fence me in. Get that, Ross?"

Ross said, "Bobwire is. So long, Maria."

... They rode off, and for a long time Caesar stood there. Finally he dropped his eyes and saw the girl. He smiled at her and said, "Be nice to me just once, and I'll let you know where Gill is."

Maria said, "Go away. You disgust me." She wanted to leave Caesar's, and work somewhere else, but Caesar knew where Gill was, and so she stayed, hoping. Inside, she was desperate. Caesar would keep after her, and she was afraid she'd finally give in. She had to know where Gill was. Not that Caesar was a man to be trusted. Still, he knew, and if she couldn't find him herself, she might do anything. Even that.

She wished she could go to the sheriff and tell him that Caesar knew where Gill was, but then they'd be back, the sheriff and the other man, Ross, and they'd make Caesar turn Gill over to them. She didn't think it was true—she couldn't believe it—but it just might be true that Gill knew something about a killing. So she couldn't go to the sheriff. That way, she would lose Gill.

She went inside, to the kitchen, thinking foolishly: Gill will just come back. That's all. One day he'll be back, and they'd be together. It wasn't true that he loved Laura. It couldn't be true.

But she wasn't sure.

Ross said, "Do you think she's hiding Gill?"

The sheriff rubbed his jaw. They were riding in twilight, the wind was silent now, tucked back inside the deep purple hills. Ahead Ross could see the faint lights that had to be the Broken S headquarters. Big Max said, "I don't rightly know if she is. It just figures he's around Caesar's someplace. If she doesn't know, maybe Caesar does. The Stantons and Gill have had a falling out. The Stantons and Caesar are at each other's throat. If a man had a grudge against the Stantons, he could throw in with the Crescent C and make the grudge pay off. And with your damn bobwire, I'm afraid all this is going to happen, soon. Before, it was so much talk, a little grass getting nibbled away. Now, a whole parcel of land is going to be shut right in Caesar's face. I doubt he'll stand for it."

Ross said, "He didn't seem upset much over my mention of bobwire."

"No," the sheriff granted, "he didn't."

"Think he didn't believe me?"

The sheriff shook his head. "He believed you all right. Still, he should have been mad as a hornet. I don't quite get it. Not that I'm going to worry about that. If he doesn't want to start a range war, that's just dandy with me."

"A range war might smoke Gill out," Ross mused.

The sheriff turned his mare abruptly and brought her across Ross's path. Ross was shocked at the expression on Max's face. The sheriff said in a low voice, the excitement beneath, trembling in his throat, "No war's worth that, Ross. Stop thinking only of yourself. Sure you'll smoke Gill out when the range bursts wide open. And maybe a dozen people will be dead. Is it worth it?"

"It's not my war," Ross said.

"Stop acting like it is, then."

"All I want is Gill."

"You'll get him," the sheriff said sharply. "All I want is peace out here. Justice and peace."

Ross said, "All right. You've lectured me. Now let's get going. There won't be any peace with me until I do get Gill, or my old man's killer."

The sheriff grunted and pushed ahead. Then he said, almost idly, over his shoulder, "Was your dad a pretty fast man with a gun?"

Ross thought back at those days and evenings spent in the woods with the old man, practicing drawing their pistols, the old man counting, "One-two—" and if Ross didn't click the hammer shut before he said, "Two," the old man would slap his face and make him do it again. "Damn fast," Ross said. "Why?"

The sheriff said, "I dunno, for sure. But I keep wondering how come a half-drunk cowpoke, or maybe he wasn't drunk anymore but had a head on him like a bell, how come a man like that walks into your dad's office and shoots him down dead. Hadn't your father even drawn his own gun out?"

Ross fumbled with his memory of that night eleven long years ago. He thought aloud, the words coming slowly, "I was in the office less than a minute after the shot was fired. The old man lay at his desk, his head down. His hands weren't anywhere near his gun. He never had a chance."

"His desk face the front door, his chair I mean?"

"He faced square at the front door."

The sheriff said, "So he saw the man and he was a fast shot. You're sure now he was fast? You're not thinking of him as your old man now, but as a man with a gun—right?"

Ross nodded grimly. "He was the fastest I ever saw. If he had drawn, even after the other man went for his guns, he'd have killed the man, or at least got off his shot. You're hinting it was self-defense or some other rot, aren't you, Max? Forget it. He was killed in cold blood. He never had a chance."

"There's no man who can't be outdrawn," the sheriff persisted. "I'm pretty fast myself, so they tell me, yet I wouldn't bet I could beat any man to the draw. From what I hear, Gill can outdraw me. They say he's like a blur when he goes for his gun."

Ross said, "Gill's shot—a few other people?"

Max laughed and pushed his mare. "No, not so far as I know. He's a boastful man and they say he likes to show off his draw. He's fast, I guess."

Ross was silent. Gill was a boastful man, and maybe a killer. Certainly he knew of a killing and had kept his mouth shut for nearly eleven years. Ross himself wasn't a boastful man, yet he also practiced his draw. He was irritated. He didn't like to be lumped with Gill, in any way. Though maybe there was a likeness. Maybe Gill—too—was afraid. Hope spurted in Ross. Maybe it would be Gill who cracked at the end of the line.

They rode ahead and the sheriff said, "I sure would have liked to have seen that office when you did. A thirteen-year-old kid might miss something."

"Like what, Sheriff?"

The sheriff didn't answer. They dug in, the October night cutting cold on the plains. They crossed another patch of Osage orange, and Ross thought: years to make the stuff grow while bobwire would do it in three days. And the Stantons would have all that graze to themselves. He hated the Stantons, with a rising fury.

CHAPTER FOUR

Orville Stanton stood in the shadow of the big sitting room; pitch pine shavings started to crackle in the Arizona flagstone fireplace, eucalyptus logs waited to catch and throw the heat into the square, chill room. Orville Stanton was a big man, fortyish, compactly built with high square shoulders and big capable hands that were twisting themselves like eels as he stared through the sitting room window.

He had seen the riders when they crossed the thin line of Osage orange—and he damned the line of mulberry hedge that it was so thin, that it would never grow and do the job in time—and he kept watching them in the growing darkness as they neared the Broken S headquarters.

He thought the lumbering one was Big Max, but he wasn't sure. The other man looked strange, a man he thought he'd never seen before, but in the night it was hard to tell. Ives had told him that there was a manhunter in town, that a farmer had seen him this morning coming from behind an aspen thicket and stumbling down the talus slopes outside Oxnard, a carbine strapped to his pack. Ives said the manhunter had ridden into Oxnard from the southeast around noon and had had a drink. Ives said the manhunter had got into a scrap with the sheriff in the bar about carrying a gun.

Stanton kept watching, trying to see whether the man was wearing a gun. He didn't know who the man was, but he had an idea what he was doing in town. It wasn't the first time a manhunter had come to Oxnard, and each time Stanton thought the man had come in for him or for his brother Ed, or for their foreman Gill, or all three, but each time he was wrong. And each time that the manhunter left, Orville Stanton had let out his breath slowly and wondered whether he was better off, or worse.

This time—Stanton knew—if it was a manhunter, then the man was looking for him or Ed. Gill must have gone to Texas and looked up the man and sold out. Gill was the type to sell out. Stanton felt his right fist form and slap against his other palm. The devil take Gill, he thought, take him for the blackmailing bloodsucker he was. For ten years he had sucked money from the Stantons; then Orville Stanton had thrown him out. Money was scarce and Gill had been getting greedier, bolder. Stanton had given the man his riding papers. And already Gill was making him pay.

Stanton stared through the window into the darkness, trying to wipe Gill out of mind—and that night eleven years ago. He looked hard into the night, at the approaching riders. Then he felt his stomach constrict, and he turned from the window.

He had seen enough. The two men had passed the first bunkhouse and a ground lantern had thrown up a cloud of light. The first man was Big Max. The other man carried a gun in his holster. There was a carbine across the back of the horse.

He said, "Ed, Ed, come here. They're riding up."

Ed Stanton pushed open the door. He was as big as his brother, but more loosely arranged. His movements were sluggish, his hair pure gray. He was two years younger than his brother; he looked ten years older.

Ed Stanton said, "Who are they?"

His brother moved away from the window. "Take a look. Big Max and a bounty dog."

Ed Stanton pressed to the window pane. The men passed another lantern, their outlines illumined in garish yellow planes. He said in a low intense voice, "I'll get Gill for this. I swear I will. I'll kill the—"

Orville Stanton grabbed his brother. He whirled him around and shook him as hard as he could. Then he said, "Ed, I once told you I'd never hear that word in this house. You'll kill nobody, understand?"

Ed Stanton hunched his shoulders. He said, "Orv, don't ever lay a hand on me again. If I get Gill in front of me, I'll tear him apart. You won't stop me, either. Maybe you don't think I've already paid for that—other killing—but I have. I've paid for ten years, hearing Gill lord it over me, how he'd turn me in if I didn't play square with him. Every night of my life, Orv, I've gone to bed, sweating like a bull, and never knowing whether a man would tap me on the shoulder and say, 'Get up, man, you're wanted for murder.'"

Orville Stanton looked at his brother. He said, "You won't crack now?"

His brother's answer was low, misery-coated. "Now? There's nothing left to crack. Gill's sapped it all out. No, I won't crack. Don't worry about me."

"Good."

They walked away from the window and then out of the sitting room and to the back room which looked like a library, but was the Stantons' office. Orville Stanton seated himself behind a huge mahogany desk. He lit a ready-rolled cigarette and waited. Ed Stanton stared at the far wall of books. He said, "I wonder where Gill is."

Orville Stanton said, "Waiting someplace to see them take us away. Or waiting for Joe Caesar to kill us off, so he can step in and claim the land."

Ed Stanton said, "Orv, why did we ever do it?"

"Do what?" The words were a bark, or the snap of a whip.

Ed Stanton smiled thinly. "Oh, I don't mean that business in that little town in Knox County, whatever its name was. Gore, yes, that's what it was. God, what a name for a town. I don't mean that, though. I've stopped asking myself about that. That's over with. I mean, how come we let Gill have a third interest in the spread?"

Orville let his thoughts roam, back to that Texas town. Gill had been a good man, all the way up from the Plateau, dogging the steers with a sweaty persistence that Stanton admired. Orville and Ed had a percentage deal on the drive; get the herd up before a rival herd, pushing from East Texas, and an extra cut on every pound of beef was theirs. Orville and Ed had made it, with Gill prodding like ten angry men. So it hadn't seemed strange that the three had joined forces, had planned to work together in the future. The future was going to be a cattle ranch, out of the profits from the Stockton drive. The Stantons had an idea where they would buy, up in Colorado. Gill would have a job trail bossing for them, if he wanted it. Then—the shooting in town. And Gill, moving in with them after they had twisted and turned and shaken off any posse that might have sniffed at their heels.

Orville said crisply, "Did we have a choice? He had us where he wanted us. He was a leech by that time, riding in our blood. We were scared, and he knew it. I still don't know that it wasn't the right thing to do. Hell, I know *I* didn't want to turn myself over to a hanging posse."

Ed said bitterly, "Better hanged once than dangled this way for ten years."

A horse whinnied outside. Ed said, "You want me to let them in?"

Orville Stanton said, "No, I'll do it." He strode past his brother, thinking: he's going to crack, I can tell, I can tell. Dear Lord, why did he have to shoot that man, why did he do it?

Then he threw open the door and said, "Come in, Max." He looked at the other man, and his heart shrieked in his throat and then nearly stopped. The man was the dead Texas sheriff, except younger, leaner. Orville Stanton said dully, knowing suddenly that even if Ed didn't crack, it wasn't going to matter, "You're Jake Ross's son. Come in."

Ross saw the man, guilt etched across his face like a mask of another man's blood, and he wondered how he could raise himself to shoot down such a man. It was like shooting a dog that turned a piteous face up at you, wet tongue begging, because somebody had crushed its leg.

And if he couldn't shoot Stanton, it was going to get difficult again. He wondered if it would ever end, this tracking down a man, this search for courage and a canceling of debts.

He said, "Who did it, you or your brother?"

Big Max said, "Ross, I warned you. There'll be no fireworks. You reach for that cannon and I'll shoot your fist off."

Ross said angrily, "Who did it, Stanton? You or your brother?"

Orville Stanton moved away from the door. "Come in," he said again, as though certain proprieties had precedence, or maybe it was just a reflex, so numbed was the man ever since the dead man's son stood in the doorway. He had expected a bounty dog, a man working for that Texas county, working for money in exchange for a man's skin, and Orville Stanton could have faced such a man, lied if he had to, denied the knowledge of any crime, fought like a wildcat if it otherwise meant he and Ed would lose everything they had garnered these last ten years. But when the man was Ross's son, the fight leaked out of Orville Stanton. He said to young Ross, "Let's—let's get it over with. You won't have to shoot anybody, Ross. Just ask your questions. But ask them to both of us."

Max said, "Where's Ed?"

Stanton waved a hand ahead of him. "Inside. You can wrap us both up at once. Ross."

They went into the office, and Orville said quietly, "Ed, this is Ross's son, the sheriff's son." Ed Stanton paled, his hands opening spasmodically, and then he tried a crooked smile, looking at Ben Ross. He said, "That's how I should have figured it, long ago. The boy coming on up and digging us out."

The way he said it gave Ross a piece of his answer. "You did it?" he said to Ed Stanton.

"I thought everybody knew," Ed said.

"Shut up, Ed," Orville Stanton said, thinking foolishly that maybe there was still a way out, that though young Ross was here, Ed and he were both alive and perhaps there'd be a way they could stay alive.

Big Max said, "No, don't shut up, Ed. Maybe everybody knows down in Knox, and maybe you three know. But I don't. And I'm the sheriff in this county. I'm the man who'll hand any suspected killer to the Texas authorities."

Orville Stanton laughed, a thin sharp bitter noise. "Max, you're the sheriff in town. Otherwise you're nothing. We've got no sheriff this far up."

Max said stubbornly, "Maybe that's what you and Ed and Joe Caesar would like to believe, but you're wrong. You're dead wrong."

Orville Stanton said, "Try to carry your badge up here, Max, and see where it gets you."

Max removed the tin star from his pocket and pinned it to his shirt, light bouncing against Orville Stanton's face. "I just did. It got me pretty far. I carried it out to Joe Caesar's spread, and he complained like you always complain. He doesn't like me badgering him, he says, but he never does a thing about it."

Orville Stanton said, "You saw Joe Caesar today?"

Max nodded. "Just before we rode up here. Caesar sends you his respects. He says he'll bury you boys yet."

Ed Stanton said. "Come now. We can talk around corners some other time. Young Ross isn't here to hear about Caesar or the Broken S. He wants his old man's killer. That's me."

Ross recoiled. The way Stanton said it shocked him. It was unbelievable that he had just admitted it. Yet he had. All of this before was preliminary, even Ross's knowledge of a few seconds earlier that Ed Stanton was probably the man, and was going to talk. That was all a thing of latency, an explosion in potential. Now Stanton had touched off the fuse.

Ross leaped, his hands reaching for the man's throat. Ed Stanton collapsed under the weight, and Ross landed heavily on him, fingers digging into the windpipe. He felt clawing hands on his back, but he shrugged them off. Ed Stanton looked up at him, from three inches away, and tried to say something but it came out a strangled grunt. His eyes began to bulge, his face a rising brick color.

Then Orville Stanton drew his leg back and kicked Ross in the ribs. Ross groaned and fell to the side, his breath driven from his lungs. He whispered hoarsely, "I'll kill you for that, you damned coward." He got up, bent over, hands holding his side. It hurt to breathe, and he could not stand straight.

Max said, "Thanks, Orv. I was going to have to lay my pistol butt across his thick skull. Ross," he said, "you do anything like that, and, I swear, I'll throw you in the Oxnard pokey so deep you won't see fresh air for a month. I'm going to hear Ed Stanton, and so are you, and you're not going to do a thing about it. Understand?" His face was a glowering hatred, and Max knew some of his hatred was because he understood exactly why Ross had leaped on Stanton.

Ross said thickly, "No promises. I told you before, no promises. The man who did it is my meat."

Max shook his head again. "Ross, if I can't stop you from killing Ed Stanton or anybody else, I can see you go on trial for it. You put a bullet in this man, and you'll swing one day, and I'll be the man who puts you in the air."

Ed Stanton laughed thinly and rubbed his throat. "Now that everybody's had his show, let's get down to the only thing that matters. I don't care if Ross kills me or not—I don't, Ross, I mean that—or if he swings or not, or if Big Max ends up governor of Colorado Territory. I want to get this off my chest, and I'd appreciate your not killing me, Ross, until it is off. I've carried it too long not to get rid of it now."

Ross stared at the man. There was an honorable quality about Ed Stanton that confused him. He still pictured the man as swaying drunkenly in his old man's office, his breath a foul cloud and Jake Ross holding the man with one hand, slapping his face with the other, again and again and again, the sounds like pistol cracks, and then spinning him around and kicking him into the gutter.

That's how Ben Ross had seen Ed Stanton for eleven years, slack-jawed and stupid-eyed, laughing even while old man Ross slapped his face and left white claw marks on his cheek. And that's how he remembered Orville Stanton, too, a little grimmer perhaps, his eyes squinting and showing a little less vacuity, and then falling in the street, on top of his sodden stuporish brother.

The other man—he was tougher to remember. Gill. He must have been the one who had cringed and tried to pull away from Ross's father's heavy hand as it swung, open-palmed, and sent his head bobbing. He must have been the one who had sworn when old man Ross whirled him around and put his boot to the base of his spine. He must have been the one who climbed back up and stared hot hate at the sheriff, young Ross, thirteen years old, watched with his mother holding his hand, squeezing her nails into his palm, the two of them watching, and Ross's mother crying out when the one who must have been Gill went sprawling in the gutter.

Now young Ross shook his head, and the pictures all blended and tangled, and once more they were the phantoms be had seen for eleven years.

He said to Ed Stanton, "You crept back later that night and shot him at his desk. Is that right?"

Ed Stanton started to nod, and then a frown formed slowly. He cocked his head at Ross and started to say something and then stopped. He turned to Orville Stanton.

Orville said, curiosity tingling his words, "Crept back *later?* What do you mean, Ross? That's a strange way of putting it?"

Ross said, "That night. You went back to your hotel room—we traced you that far anyway—and then Ed Stanton woke up a couple of hours later and decided to get back at my father for slapping and kicking him into the street." He turned to Ed Stanton. "You went back that night. The street was deserted because my old man closed down the town early, even on Saturday, and you found him at his desk. Maybe he was dozing. Anyway, he was so surprised he never had a chance. You shot him in the right eye."

Orville Stanton said very slowly, "Ross, man, Ross. That's—that's not how we remember it. Ed got up out of the gutter and walked back inside, while Gill and I were still lying there, and he—Ed—just drew and fired his gun. Not a couple of hours later. Right then and there. That's how it happened."

And Ed Stanton said, a new note in his voice, a strange choked-up note, yet the room shivered with the note, with the impending exultancy of the note, "*Unless—unless* it never happened at all."

Ross felt his face turning into a snarl. Fury hammered at his temples. These men—so honorable looking, so straight with their words—lying through their teeth. Yet there was something else, and it was disturbing him, hindering him. Why would they lie this way? It was so easily disproved. Why would they say it didn't happen the way he, Ross, had told it? Ross said, in a low voice because he wanted to scream his rage at these men who should have been on their knees, begging forgiveness, help, anything, but instead were standing straighter now than when he first saw them five minutes earlier, he said through a tight throat, "Never happened? I wish you had seen what I saw, then. My old man's face on that desk, the blood all over. Never happened? It happened all right, the way I said it happened, and you did it."

Orville Stanton said, "Max, find Gill, Good God, man, find Gill."

The sheriff said, "How did it happen, Orville, the way young Ross says, two hours later, or right away?"

Orville Stanton said, "Get Gill. He knows. He's the one who knows. He wasn't as drunk as we were. No, not by a long shot." Stanton's lips curled with loathing, for Gill, but mostly for himself, and for his brother. "One of us had to stay half sober. It was Gill. It always was Gill in those days. He watched us, protected us. That was half his job he said. So Gill wasn't as drunk as we were. He couldn't have been. He told us later what had happened. We didn't remember. He said we had to leave Knox because— Ed had killed the sheriff. That Ed had stumbled back into that office after he'd been kicked out—funny how I remember getting slapped and kicked but I don't remember the other—and shot the sheriff. I swear, I don't remember Ed shooting the sheriff. It must have been—we always felt—that we were too drunk to remember. So we rode on out, and for ten years Gill's blackmailed us. Get Gill, Sheriff. He says Ed did it, but he says Ed did it right away. If Ross is right, then Gill's a liar. Get Gill. He remembers, all right."

Max said sharply, "That's straight now, Orv?"

"Straight as I could tell it."

The sheriff turned to Ed. "He's telling the truth? That's the way you've always thought it happened?"

"Always," Ed said. His voice was strangled, hope and despair inside.

Ross said, "There's no sense here. This is insane. Why such a lie, so wide open?"

Max said grimly, "We'll find out when we get our hands on Gill."

Ross stood in the room, a step removed from Ed Stanton.

He looked at the big, gray-haired man, and he tried to fit him to that other picture, a man on a white horse, a big, dark-haired man outside Jake Ross's office, whirling his white horse and clopping wildly down the main drag and into the black maw of Gore, a sleeping town that shed no light because Jake Ross had put his big hand over the town and said there'd be no light after dark. Ross stared at Ed Stanton and then at Orville Stanton, and he finally asked his question quietly because everything rode with this one question, and with the answer. They couldn't lie now, because if they did, they'd hang on this one answer.

He said, "What color hair did Gill have, eleven years ago?"

Ed Stanton frowned and turned to Orville, the way he always seemed to do when he was puzzled. It wasn't he didn't know the answer, Ross could see, it just was that he didn't see the significance of the question.

But Big Max did, and a taut line grew at his mouth. He barked at Ed Stanton, "Answer the man!"

Ed smiled wanly and spread his hands. "Why, Max, that's foolish. You know as well as anyone that Gill's got blond hair and always had."

The next question didn't count at all, because Ross no longer had to listen to these men. All he had to do was draw out his gun, now that the deceit was lying obscenely naked in the room. All he had to do now was shoot Ed Stanton in his lying mouth, and turn the big Colt Walker on Orville and give him the same. It would be over, and justice—of a sort, raw, cruel, but terribly equitable—would be served. Ross said lightly, "Which one of you three owned a white horse back in Gore, eleven years ago?"

Ed Stanton said, "Why, I did. Orv and Gill had brown geldings, as I recollect. I had a white mare. She was a little drawn but—"

Max leaped between Ed Stanton and Ross, his broad body in front of Ross. "All right," he panted, "all right, Ross. You win. You've proved your case. But I'm taking these men in." He stood like a heaving mountain in the room, and Ross felt his fingers twitching.

Ross said, "Take them in. Just get them out of my sight. If I have to stand here another minute, they'll be dead on the floor, and I don't care if I have to shoot them through your thick body, Max. Just get them out of here."

There was a frozen smile on Ed Stanton's mouth. He had thought the questions about the color of a man's hair and the color of another man's horse were ludicrous, last-gasp questions by Ross, who must have been nettled by the discrepancy in his—Ross's—story, and the Stantons'. But they apparently weren't ludicrous. Somehow they had pinned him, he thought grimly. He felt himself turning to Orville, to ask his help, to find out how this latest had happened, and why. But Orville's face was shock-gray. There was no help there. There was no help anywhere, Ed Stanton thought. The man hadn't waited for him to go to sleep before tapping him on the shoulder and saying, "Get up, you're wanted for murder."

Max said, "I want you boys to walk out of here slowly, your hands up and outstretched. Go over to your horses and stand there. Wait a minute. Ross, you lead the way, on your horse and straight back to town. I don't want you behind these men one foot of the way."

Ross laughed bitterly. "Don't worry, Max. I won't shoot them—or anybody—in the back."

"I won't worry," Max said drily. "You ride in front, and I won't worry at all. I'll ride behind."

The Stantons looked at each other, and Orville said, "Max, one minute. Let me talk to Ives for a minute."

Ross said, "Who's Ives?"

Max said, "Their foreman, since Gill took off."

Ross said, "All right. Make it fast, though."

Orville went to the door and opened it. Ross and Big Max watched as he stepped outside into the night. He called, "Ives. Ives. Here, man."

Two minutes later a horse galloped to the ranch house. A short stubby hand waddled in. He looked at Ross and the sheriff, blinking, and then he said, "What is it, boss?" He spoke to Orville Stanton.

The rancher said, "Ives, Ed and I are going to town with the sheriff, and Ross here. We'll be there—a short while, at least. A few days. Maybe more. Handle the spread in our absence. Here's a signed checkbook for wages. Ride into town tomorrow to the bank and get— oh, five hundred dollars. That ought to hold the place a while. I've left an order for fencing in at McQuinns. Check to see if it's arrived. If it has, get some boys to help you tote it back and start fencing the front between the hedges. Then—" He stopped short. The futility of it caught up with Orville Stanton. He said, "That's it, Ives." He turned away, making a brief motion with his hand, dismissing his foreman.

Ives stood silent for a minute. Then he said, "Right," and walked out.

Ross followed a minute later. The Stantons were behind him, shuffling, beaten men, arms up so that there was no doubt anymore to Ives— watching from the bunkhouse—where they were going. They were going to the Oxnard pokey.

They rode that way, Ross in the van, headed for the pass at the valley's end and the thin cluster of lights that marked Oxnard, the Stantons side by side, and Big Max behind them, a shambling man, lurching badly in the saddle, tired and troubled. He was not sure of what he was doing, of what he would do. There was something fishy about the whole business. It didn't ring right. His eyes burned holes in the night, boring past the Stantons to the lean broad back of Ross, up front. Max felt he could not relax a moment, not with young Ross. The sheriff knew that Ross was only a split second away from his Colt Walker; he remembered the speed of Ross's hand out there on the range, the unwavering gun barrel. Big Max thought—somehow—that fear lay behind much of Ross's actions, and a man who lived with fear, flirted with panic. Panic could whirl Ross's horse, the Colt Walker spitting orange blossoms of death.

Up front, Ross fidgeted in the saddle. He was annoyed at himself. The Stantons weren't acting like guilty men, despite their implausible stories and their confessions. Guilty men would have lied to protect themselves, not to dig a deeper hole. At times, they had told the truth. (Ed Stanton's mild words rang in Ross's ears: *He wants his father's killer. That's me.*) And when they should have told the truth, they lied. (Orville Stanton saying simply: *Ed got out of the gutter and fired his gun.*)

Ross was no longer vitally interested in Gill. He had his father's killer, his confessed killer. But Gill could clear up who was lying, and why.

On the heels of that thought came a terrible doubt, streaking across his brain like a yellow comet. It had all happened so long ago. *Maybe it was he—Ben Ross—who was lying.*

One man had no such doubts. All that day, from the time Caesar had told him that rumor had it that a manhunter was in town, he had patiently waited on the hill they called Wolfhead, dug into a hole that lay on the slope just below timber line, protected by a thicket of evergreens. He had a Winchester next to him, a Navy Colt on his hip, and he held a pair of high-powered field glasses to his eyes.

From where he squatted, all of Oxnard valley lay before him, plus the pass to town. Earlier, he had seen two riders sidle off toward the Crescent C. He recognized one as Big Max. The other had to be Ross.

He saw them ride through the twilight to the Broken S, and in darkness, lit by an obliging moon and by ground lanterns, he had seen them ride back the direction they had come, to Oxnard. But they did not ride alone. This time they had two more men with them, two men of the same approximate bulk and look as the Stantons. Maybe if he hadn't expected the men to be the Stantons, he wouldn't have known. But the man was very sure the two riders in the middle, next to each other, were the Stantons because that was the way he had planned it. The plan, he realized with a start that made him chuckle, had begun over ten years ago. He marveled at the neatness of it, the awful inevitability of it. The Stantons, going off to their doom in a town in Texas. Ross going back, avenged.

The man took the glasses away from his eyes and rubbed the furrows from his forehead. Then he ran a hand through short-cropped blond hair.

His name was Gill.

Big Max turned the key, put it in his pocket and said, "Boys, you better not need anything between now and tomorrow morning, because you won't be able to get it. Go to sleep." Then he and Ross walked out.

The jail was around the back of the sheriff's office. Big Max said to Ross, "I'll sleep on a cot in the office." Ross nodded, grimly, remembering his father. The sheriff said, "How about you? I can bed you down in there if—"

Ross said harshly, "Stop it. I'm not going to slink back there in the middle of the night and shoot down two men in a cell, in their sleep. You don't have to keep an eye on me."

Big Max grunted. He said, "Hadn't thought of that. You're full of hobgoblins. I just didn't know whether you'd arranged for a room here in town."

Ross flushed. "Sorry," he said. "No, I hadn't arranged. But I don't think I'll take you up on the cot. Is the hotel usually full up?"

Max shook his head. They stood in front of Max's office. Down the drag, there were noises and lights coming out of the saloon. In the other direction, a pale yellow glow indicated the hotel. "Always half a dozen empty rooms," he said.

Ross nodded. He started to walk to his horse and then he turned and came back to the sheriff. He said. "You can stop worrying about me. I'm pretty well satisfied you've got the right men. Ed Stanton did it. Orville must have known about it. That washes them up with me. I'll let you ship them back any way you want to."

Max said drily, "Thanks. I wish I were as satisfied as you."

"What do you mean?"

The sheriff shrugged. He was still troubled. "I'll know better when we've got Gill."

Ross said automatically, "Gill." He walked to his horse, mounted and fingered the reins. *Gill*, he thought. They still needed him, to wrap it up. He turned the sorrel away from the hotel and sauntered him to the saloon. The sheriff watched and then abruptly went inside and lay down on his cot, fully dressed, his .44 at his hip, his eyes wide open.

CHAPTER FIVE

Ross pushed the batwing doors and stepped inside the saloon. The wooden plunk of a badly tuned piano sounded above the clamor of voices. Cowhands were thick at the tables, and bellied up to the bar, most of them Crescent C help, Ross noted, drinking beer and breathing out beery breath and tobacco, to mix with the smell of whiskey and cow dung that hung in the air, a cloud over the bar and the tables.

Then Ross heard the girl's husky voice, in drawling languorous song, and through the throng he could see her in the empty floor space between the front rank tables and the bar. She was standing with her arms folded, and a hip thrust out saucily, her legs in long black net stockings that reached to tight, red, frilly shorts. She was half singing, half reciting a song about a Colorad-y miner who had found gold in Wolf Creek and then went to Denver, where he met a girl.

At noon—twelve hours earlier—Ross had thought that whiskey and an entertainer like Laura might help in opening up the mouths of those who knew where Gill might be. Now Ross didn't care. He had the Stantons. Gill would help in clearing up matters, but that was all. At first Gill had been the key to the whole business. But now the door was open, and Ross had piled through. In half a day, he had done what eleven years had failed to do.

The girl finished her song about the Colorad-y miner who finally went broke because of the Denver girl, and immediately went into another, equally naughty, equally dull. She shimmied and flounced and the men whooped it up. Then she finished, and the crowd yelled some more, and she smiled and leered and walked over to the piano where a Crescent C hand held out a drink to her and she took it.

Ross began to walk from the swinging doors through the milling noisy throng, and when they saw who he was, they fell back and made a path. Ross realized the noise had quieted some. He didn't like it. It was as though his was a different smell from the cow dung and beer smell, the smell of cow towns. His—Ross thought angrily—must have been the smell of death.

He reached the bar and said to the bartender whose name Ross remembered vaguely was Tromper, "I want a sour mash."

Tromper stared at him and down to the Colt Walker. He said, "Sorry, I'm all out of sour mash."

The bar quieted even more. Ross looked along the bar. He thought the man two places away was drinking bourbon. He said, "All right, make it beer."

Tromper said. "All out of beer."

Ross was tired. He wasn't looking for trouble. He was looking for a drink or two to ease the strain out of his bones and make sleep sweet and solid. He said mildly. "Tromper, I'm not a bounty hound."

Tromper said stiffly, a touch of pride in him because he was making this gun tough talk slow and easy, "I don't care what you're not. You're carrying a gun. There's a law—"

Ross cut in fiercely, "There's another law, too. It says Thou Shalt Not Kill. It says a man whose father's been shot down dead deserves a squarer shake than you're giving him, right now." He reached across the bar and dragged Tromper forward, the man's sweating face six inches from Ross's. Ross said. "I want a sour mash, with a beer chaser. Now. I want it now. If you're all out, get it in all of a sudden. Understand, bucko?"

Tromper tried to nod, but the hand that bunched his shirt under his throat was a huge hand, tan and muscled, unrelenting. Tromper reached with his right hand, fumbling under the counter, thinking: *I'll get me a bottle and smash it against his skull.* But all his hand did was make the bottles clink until it reached the right one, and then it dragged forth a bottle of bourbon, three-quarters full. Tromper put it on the counter, eyes begging, and Ross gave him a short angry shake, like a cat with a mouse, and Tromper's head lolled and he was free. Ross poured his own drink with a shaking hand, while silence closed in on him, fifty pairs of eyes watching him, eyes that burned hate into Ross's back.

Then he heard someone say in a hoarse whisper, "Well, maybe he's telling it straight—" and another man snarled, "What are you anyway, siding that bloodsucker?"

Ross whirled. He put his drink down and tried to spot the man with the snarl, but all he saw was a sea of faces, eyes averted now, small talk starting to rise up out of their dark mouths. Ross said, above the noise that had a vein of shame in it, and on top of the shame, a layer of defiance, "I'm not much on counting but I reckon there's at least fifty of you men in here."

The noise stilled except for a cough or two and a clearing throat. One man said, "Ah—" as though he were going to speak, but he let it drop.

Ross said, "I'm sick of apologizing to you people for my being here. If you want, pick a man and let him and me settle this thing. Let's get it over with." Nobody stirred. "I'm tired of saying I ain't no bounty hunter. Nobody's paying me for getting anybody. That's the facts, but I'm sore at myself for saying them. Now I'm going to stop saying them. You're going to stop, too. You're going to stop baiting me, or else I'll start in with the first man I can reach." He stopped, his mind adding another black mark, next to the business of drawing his gun on the range and picking a scrap with Joe Caesar. Little heroics, mock heroics. Not amounting to a tinker's dam. He said, "Maybe I am a bounty hound," and this time the man who said, "Ah," before, said it again and added, "You see?" but nobody answered.

Ross said, "So what, I'm a bounty hound? Does it matter? What the hell's the difference to you, unless you're the blackleg killer I'm looking for? It just so happens you're not. It just so happens I've found the men I want, and I'm just about through here in town."

And now the room made a gasping noise and everybody began talking, excited talk, the pressure lifted suddenly and the air coming out fast. Ross saw the girl Laura, frown and then laugh aloud, leaning against the Crescent C man she was drinking with, in relief, Ross guessed, because that meant Gill was safe. He stared at the girl's bright red laughing mouth and it made him mad. He said, "Just *about* through. Not quite," and the girl Laura frowned again, stepping back from the Crescent C hand.

Ross went on: "But suppose I hadn't finished? Suppose I were just starting, deputized to bring back somebody, and get my pay for delivering the pelt, for killing the man? Just so long as you're not the man, what difference does it make? A man does in another man, is he to be protected from bounty hounds? A man kills, does that mean you'll pressure the law until it gives up and crawls back where it came from, and the killer struts around loose? Is that what you want the law to do?" He stared at the room, moving a bit under his eyes, and the shame smeared their faces.

Then the girl said, "We've got our own law out here."

Ross snapped, "And he's riding with me."

"Yeah?" Laura said. "That's not how it looked this noon. It looked like he was riding on you," and the room laughed, knowing of the scrap in the bar.

Ross said, "Go to hell," and he turned back to the bar. He had been licked by the redhead, he knew, even though he could still say, "Sure he rode on me, until he knew the facts, and after that he sided me." But that would have been more apologizing, more excusing himself to this crowd that didn't want to hear him at all, and he was damned if he'd crawl before them again. He looked over at the piano where Laura and the Crescent C man had been standing, but Laura was walking away, shimmying elaborately, and then disappearing into a room where Ross guessed she kept her everyday clothes, a dressing room he thought they called it. He finished his drink and said savagely to Tromper, "Another one fast," and Tromper poured it himself this time eyes down.

Ross had three more drinks, none of them touching him, none of them loosening him up any or helping him forget the sordidness of the whole business, or easing him on the way to sleep. He said to Tromper, "What do I owe you?" and Tromper told him, and he paid, stamping from the room and into the chill night.

He stood at his horse's side, patting the flank of the hammerhead sorrel, and then climbing up. Then he heard quick footsteps behind him and he thought stupidly: *they're going to slug me*, but when he turned it was a woman, in heavy corduroy jacket and breeches, a kerchief over her head. Automatically, he put his hand to his hat, and then he stiffened. It was Laura. He started to grin, and Laura went to a horse on the tie line, ignoring him. He said, "Cleaned out all the suckers? No more fortunes to read?"

"Just yours," she said, turning from her neat brown pony, her face a white glow beneath the saloon's outside lanterns. "You're headed for a bullet, my friend."

He said, "Maybe I am. But I'd rather be headed for it, than turned around and taking it in the spine. There isn't a man in this town I've met so far who'd shoot me while I was headed at him."

Laura got up on her horse. "My," she said, "the manhunter is a big talker. My." She was mocking him, he knew, and if he weren't so tired he'd get down from his horse and paddle her backside until she was raw.

He cut off an oath and pushed his horse down the main drag, toward the hotel light.

She said, from behind him, "Not afraid of me? Not afraid I'll put a bullet in your spine?"

He turned his horse and said, "You asked for it." He got down heavily, feeling the ache in his legs when he hit the hard rutty road, the brand of pain across his ribs where Orville Stanton had kicked him, but not caring about either, and he was still not caring when he put his big hand over her thigh (that wasn't fat at all, he thought swiftly, but full and firm) and he reached up with his other hand to her belt and tugged her from the saddle, the girl tumbling into his arms. He turned her over while she squealed, "What are you—" and he brought his open palm against her butt. She squealed and kicked (but Ross thought dimly she was enjoying it) and he slapped just twice and let her spill to the ground.

She stood up. Her kerchief had been pulled loose and her hair streamed to her shoulders, while at the door of the saloon a half-dozen punchers watched silently, and she panted, her breasts heaving beneath the checked corduroy jacket. She said coldly in the night, her lips curling in scorn, "Is that all you can do, slap a woman? Is that what they deputized you to do, pick on a woman?"

Ross said quietly, "No, I can do more than that," and he walked over and put his arms around her and kissed her.

She was startled this time, Ross knew, more startled than when he had spanked her because somehow he was shaming her, mocking her, and when she struggled in his arms, she did so silently, all her strength against his. Then he swiftly released her, and said, "Now go on home, little girl. You've played all your games."

He mounted the sorrel and drummed quickly down the drag to the hotel, while behind him he heard muffled laughter and the girl's sharp voice, and then her pony moving along, in the same direction he had come.

Ross tugged the horse to a stop and looped the reins over the hotel hitching post without tying them, knowing the horse was as tired as he, more so probably, and not going off anywhere unless he had to. Ross went inside, and a sleepy baggy-eyed man lifted his head from the cherrywood counter and said, "Six bits for the night."

Ross said, "I want a room by the week, not by the night." It angered him. Even this sleeping man had sniffed him out and wanted little to do with him. He was the manhunter.

The hotel man grumbled and got a key and handed it to Ross. He said, "Upstairs. Third room to the left. There's bedding in the room, but if you don't like the way it looks, you can get fresh from a closet at the end of the corridor. Take what you need."

Ross said, "How much?"

The man eyed Ross, seeing the long, thin face, lines etched with weariness, the thin line of the mouth. And, more than all these, the sagging revolver at the hip in a town where guns were not allowed to be carried. The hotel man had heard that a manhunter had been slugged by Big Max for carrying a gun. This man was still carrying it. Maybe the word was wrong. Maybe Big Max—for once—had been the one who was slugged. He said, "Four dollars a week."

Ross took four silver dollars from his money belt. He said, "Bed down my horse at the stable. I don't know where it is." He left another dollar on the counter and started to walk upstairs, weary, unsure. He had been in Oxnard and the valley outside for twelve hours. Once around the clock. He wondered how many more turns it would take before it was over.

Then he heard, as he hit the upstairs landing, the hotel man say, "Good evening, Miss Laura," and Ross started to grin. Now, he thought, wasn't that cozy? He thought of the girl's bright hard challenging mouth, her firm warm thigh, the way she had felt in his arms. He undressed and lay down on the bed, thinking of the girl and of how the hard lips had felt. It was a nice feeling to take to bed with him, Ross thought.

But it didn't stay. Somewhere along the line, the girl left and Ross was back in his Texas room, behind the office where his father worked every night. And he heard the gunshot, sharply cracking through the night, riding the wind outside. A moment later he was in his father's office, the old man lying face down in his own blood.

And there was a man in the doorway, backing up, horror on his face. It was a whitewashed face, slack and stupid, the eyes smeared with drink, the lips trembling. The man had dark hair. He was a big man.

Young Ben Ross looked at the man, and the man stared down at him, foolishly, shaking his head from side to side, his hands wide open, empty. A gun hung at the man's holster. Faintly, Ross smelled gun smoke.

Then the man broke and ran, and Ross heard him scrabble onto the back of a horse. Ross had stood there another moment, petrified, and then he had torn loose and run to the door to see the big dark-haired man disappear into the dark, on his white horse.

Standing in the doorway, young Ross felt the cool night, and he shivered. He went back into the room, walking wide around the desk and behind it, and then near the window and behind the desk, he stepped on something. It was hot to his bare foot and he yelped and bent down and picked it up. It was the empty shell of the bullet that had killed his father.

He rushed to the door, screaming, and he threw it into the night, screaming, screaming....

Finally, people came and asked him questions, but it wasn't until the next morning that he could understand what they were saying.

... Ben Ross woke, in his hotel bed in Oxnard, and he thought: *I'll tell Big Max,* but he couldn't remember what he wanted to tell Big Max. He went back to sleep.

Laura was furious. She said to the hotel man, "I'll leave this flea bag. I'll find a room somewhere else."

The man said, "But he's upstairs, and you're down here. So what's the difference?"

She paced the small lobby on long nervous legs. She hated Ross. Even more than she hated what he was doing. She wished she were a man, herself. She'd shoot him down like a dog.

Then she stopped pacing suddenly. She'd take it for what it was, the turn of a lucky card. She said, "He's directly above me, you say?"

The hotel man said, "Yes, ma'am. 'Course, I can move him tomorrow to another room, but—"

"Never mind," she said. "Leave him be." It was good. She cocked her head and nodded, satisfied, and walked to her room. She listened and nodded again. She could hear him moving around, undressing probably. Good. She'd hear him come and go. Not all the time, but when she was there, below, listening. She could let Gill know. She'd have to let Gill know that Ross had said he was just about finished, but not completely. Not completely meant he still wanted Gill.

She began to tingle, just from thinking of Gill. It was awful, she knew, to feel this way, this strongly about a man who might well be implicated in a crime, in murder, maybe, if she understood Ross's veiled words back in the bar. No matter what the crime, Ross was a manhunter, and Gill one of the men he hunted.

Laura thought simply that she'd kill Ross if it ever came to that, rather than see him take Gill. Of course, it wouldn't come to that, because Gill would take care of Ross, once he knew. And she'd tell him. She'd go to Wolfhead herself, even though Gill had warned her not to show up there. Gill had made that plain enough. Check the fence, that's all. If the fence was still loose, fine. If not, if it had been repaired, then go on up to Wolfhead and let Gill know. Those were the orders.

But Gill hadn't expected anything like this, she thought. Then she frowned. Or had he? Why else was he hiding out? She didn't know whether she ought to go to Wolfhead. She wanted to see Gill. She almost wished the fence were going to be fixed by the Stantons; then she'd have reason for going up there.

She began to pace the room, as she had paced the lobby downstairs, long legs gleaming in the subdued light, the brushing of her thighs a sibilant sound in the room. She began to wonder when—or *if*—Gill would be able to take her away from Oxnard and its throttling sense of doom.

Big Max finally took the .44 from his hip and put it under his pillow. He was angry with himself. He had lost a half day because he hadn't trusted his good sense. When young Ross had said, "Bobwire," and then told Joe Caesar that bobwire was going to shut off the graze, Max knew he should have got on his dun mare and ridden straight to Denver, two hundred miles away. It would have taken him four days, with change-over of horses, stopping along Wolf Creek first under the shadow of big Wolfhead itself, and then hitting the trading posts and stables that stretched north and west to the territory capital.

But Caesar had fooled him. He had not seemed concerned by Ross's bobwire. Yet Big Max knew that Caesar believed Ross, and believed the significance of bobwire. Why, then, hadn't it bothered Caesar? It should have made him want to strap on his guns and march straight to the Broken S himself, then and there, and settle issues with the Stantons. Instead Caesar had growled as he always growled.

Big Max wiped Caesar's reaction from his mind. The simmering range feud was still simmering. Big Max knew he was going to have to have help—and fast—to keep it from boiling over to a full-sized war. Sooner or later, Caesar would strike. Caesar believed that the Stantons were choking off his own cows from grass, grass that Caesar insisted was rightfully his, no matter what the land survey said. Caesar wouldn't stand for it. Two dozen Crescent C punchers were sure as blazes going to open up on Broken S and their ten hands. Less than that, Big Max thought, with the Stantons in the pokey.

But Big Max kept falling back to the comfort of Caesar's lack of concern. He wanted to stop thinking of it because it was a pitfall. Big Max knew Caesar would have to strike, but if the man wasn't bothered by something as big as bobwire, the wire that could conceivably strangle him, then Max kept thinking, *hoping*, that the war was far off.

Then Max sat up, hard and straight. Suppose—*suppose* the Crescent C was already set to move on the Broken S? Suppose Caesar had a target date all figured out even before he knew of bobwire? Then bobwire would just confirm everything that was planned, make the attack that much more inevitable. Wasn't that what Big Max had been thinking all along: that Caesar was going to strike, no matter what? Maybe that was why Caesar hadn't stirred up at the bobwire.

The sheriff nodded, grimly, getting to his feet. War was rushing at the valley like a runaway iron horse on greased rails. Max had to have help. All he had was himself and Ross, and Ross was a man whose father had been murdered. Ross was just aching to pull out his monstrous revolver and fire it.

Max should have gone to Denver, pronto. Sure it meant he'd be gone four days each way, eight days in all. But if he waited another day, it would be nine days. Every day he waited was another day before help could arrive. And help was needed —badly.

Ed Stanton was right. A man didn't come along that night to tap him on the shoulder. Instead, Ed Stanton vaguely dreamed of a man— himself, he guessed—getting out of bed, half-stuporish, angry over something, angry with himself, and stumbling on foot through a terribly dark street, not even knowing any longer why he was in the street. Except that—in his fogged head—he wanted to explain something, to apologize to somebody. That was it. He wanted to apologize. So on he walked until he came to the doorway and he hesitated, and then walked in, while outside he heard a horse's softly muffled steps, and then the tiny unmistakable sound of a gun clearing leather.

Ed Stanton woke in a fright. He said, "Orville, I didn't do it," but when Orville rolled over, Ed knew it was useless. It didn't make sense, and it was so vague that even then, awake thirty seconds, it was sliding away. Soon it was gone, the dream. Nobody had tapped his shoulder, but he was awake anyway, and sure as hell he was getting readied to stand trial for murder.

Joe Caesar mumbled, "Bobwire," in his sleep three times. The girl, Maria, in a room off the kitchen, on a hard canvas cot that she never got used to, heard the words and didn't understand them, but they frightened her. Caesar didn't dream; he had no reason to. Before he had gone to sleep that night, Caesar had taken stock. Gill had said to hold off the big move until Ben Ross or some other Texas authority came to Oxnard, and the Stantons were hustled off to jail. Well, Ross was here, and the Stantons were in the pokey. That meant the time had arrived.

It didn't matter that Ross had told him about bobwire, and how the fences were going up. Caesar would move long before any bobwire got into Oxnard. The bobwire just gave Caesar a double-barreled reason for riding on the Broken S, burning it to the ground. For killing off the Stantons, if he had to, though he wasn't sure anymore he'd have to. Gill had said they'd be in trouble, once young Ross showed, and damned if Gill wasn't right.

So when Caesar mumbled, "Bobwire," in his sleep, he did so with contempt, as though the iron wire were just puny string. It was the contempt that Maria heard. That was why she was frightened.

Gill pulled the rough wool blanket tight around him. It would be a long night, or maybe two or three long nights, up on Wolfhead, in his protected hole dug into the slope. But it would end, and when it did he'd own the Broken S. It might be a shambles, after Caesar's boys were finished, but it would be his. There'd be some trouble claiming the ranch, Gill thought, but he had his papers, showing his one-third share. With the Stantons out of the way, the one-third would be big enough: Big Max might not like it, Gill thought, but Big Max wouldn't have to like it. If the sheriff got tough about it, Gill would handle him. If Big Max *didn't* get tough, Gill would probably still have to put him out of the way. And Gill and Caesar would rule the range. Then he'd move on Caesar. Once started, Gill thought suddenly, it didn't take much to keep the momentum going. Gill grinned, white teeth flashing in the dark. His hand slipped to his waist where the Navy Colt lay. He patted the butt fondly. The Stantons, Big Max, Caesar. He snapped his fingers. Gone like that. He'd run the range, biggest man in the whole county.

A coyote suddenly howled, its wail long and lost, throbbing to the distant stars. It didn't bother Gill a bit.

CHAPTER SIX

Joe Caesar walked out into the morning sun. It was a cold morning, cleanly cold, the air marvelously fresh, scented with piñon and sage. He washed at an outside trough, the water like ice, and then he rubbed his jaw, as though wondering whether the water was too cold for shaving. He shrugged and lathered with a harsh strong soap, and shaved without a mirror, staring straight ahead into the hills that rimmed the valley. He finished quickly and rubbed his face dry with a towel that was frosted with tiny broken crystals. Then he called, "Whitaker. On the run, Whitaker."

The heavy sound of feet hitting a wooden floor thudded in the bunkhouse. Then a huge snaggle-toothed puncher plunged through the bunkhouse doorway, buttoning a rough red flannel shirt.

"Yes, boss?" he said. He was a rawboned man, rangy and tall, and his yellow-flecked eyes were sunk beneath bony eyebrows, heavy with white scar tissue. He looked like a battling man, and he was, the best Caesar had. Caesar had found him in a bar in Kansas Territory; three men were trying to handle him. Caesar had decided the odds weren't square, so he tossed himself into the melee and got his nose broken—again—before he and Whitaker had left the other three senseless on the floor. One of the three men came pretty close to dying, Caesar heard later. He hired Whitaker on the spot. The man was loyal, and a brawler.

Now he stood before Caesar, a man only half a minute awake, yet ready to serve.

Caesar said, "Whit, tell the boys we're riding tonight."

Whitaker eyed his boss. "Riding?" he said softly.

Caesar nodded.

"Guns?"

Caesar nodded again.

"All of the men? We've got two men supposed to take off today. Day off. They ought—"

"But they won't," Caesar said. "Any problem there?"

"No-o-o," Whitaker said. "I think not. They'll ride. Oh, maybe they'll grouch a bit. But not much."

"That's good," Caesar said. He needed every man, he thought, but he knew it didn't pay to take grousing men into war. They wouldn't like it. Let them not like it, he thought angrily. Still, Caesar didn't want them talking about not liking it, where the other men would pick up the discontent. He stood there, undecided.

Whitaker broke through his thoughts. "When you want us ready, boss?"

"Right after chow tonight. Tell them when you think you ought to. But make sure they know."

"I'll tell them right now, boss, and make sure they stick around close by all day. I'll have to tell them now, what with the two men ready to take off."

"Who are they?"

"Hallahan and Stucka," Whitaker said.

Caesar was silent for a moment. He sensed that Whitaker didn't think it wise to have the two disgruntled men along. But they were good men. Hallahan especially. He said, "Whit, how would you do it?"

The foreman smiled. He appreciated Caesar's willingness to let him handle it. But he'd be damned if he'd chance a decision like that. He wished Caesar had stuck to his first stand. Caesar wasn't quite the man he used to be, Whitaker thought suddenly. When he first met him—in that bar brawl—Caesar was swift and direct. Now he lumbered. Whitaker said, "Up to you, boss."

"It's a big move we're making tonight," Caesar said tentatively, still unsure about Hallahan and Stucka.

Whitaker said, "How big?"

"We're hitting the Broken S. Full force."

Whitaker nodded, mouth pursed as though he were about to whistle his surprise, but had thought better of it. He said instead, "That's not really too big." He was giving Caesar his out. Leave the two disgruntled men out of it, Whitaker was suggesting, if you're afraid they'll carry their grudge into battle and worsen the morale of the others.

"Ten against two dozen. Even minus Hallahan and Stucka, it's better than two to one odds riding with us," Caesar said. He didn't think the Stantons would be around, either, which would make it eight men against two dozen, or against twenty-two. But he couldn't plan on the Stantons. They might somehow be out of jail by then, cleared of whatever it was Big Max had taken them away for. "Better than two to one," he said again, an edge to his voice, assertion coming back to him. But slowly, Whitaker thought, too slowly.

Caesar went on: "We'll ride in two parcels. I'll take one, you take the other. Split the men down the middle. Hallahan in one pack, Stucka in the other, so each of us can keep an eye on one of them."

Whitaker shook his head. "No." he said, not wanting to contradict the boss, but knowing he had to. The boss was taking two men along who ought not go, but once he had decided to take them, he ought to treat them the way he always did. This way they'd be rubbed wrong. They weren't men you treated like truant schoolboys. They always rode together, worked together, went to town together, got drunk together. Don't split them now. He didn't say all this, but he thought it, and Caesar nodded slowly, thinking along with him. "Don't split them," Whitaker said, and Caesar nodded firmly this time, his mind made up. But it was too late, Whitaker thought, the man isn't sure and won't be, all night. It might still be better to leave them behind, let them ride to town for their day off. The others would grouse then, but they'd see the fairness of it, the fairness of a boss who didn't deprive his men of a day off just because there was a dirty job to be done on the range.

But that's how it was left, Hallahan and Stucka to ride together.

Caesar said, "They ought to ride with you; you handle them better, you know them better, but—"

"You take them," Whitaker said shortly. He knew the boss needed them; they were two good men. Hallahan was the best man on the spread, outside of Whitaker himself, or Caesar. And Whitaker wasn't so sure just how good Caesar was. "That way you can keep an eye on them, as you said."

Caesar nodded, but the hesitation was there, the eyes veiled. Whitaker had a sudden insight. It wasn't so much the two men they were talking about. It was the whole business tonight, the raid on the Stantons' spread. Oh, sure, Caesar had talked big for the last couple of years and very big the last month or so, about ridding the range of the Stantons. But that was talk, the way big men do when they're upset. Caesar was upset by the Stantons eating away the open graze. Never—until today— had he put the words into projected ruthless action. It wasn't like the sheep man who was on the land before the Stantons. Caesar had moved hard against the sheeper, with Whitaker and a handful of the boys, burning him out and driving the stench of goat from the cow country. It wasn't like the miserable 'steaders who had squatted on the slopes of Wolfhead even before that, stealing calves until Whitaker and Caesar and Hallahan had torn down their lean-tos and shacks, and pistol-whipped them and drove them from the range.

With the Stantons, it had always been talk, tough talk. A couple of times Whitaker had brawled with Broken S men in town; once Stucka had pulled his Colt on two Broken S men who were putting up a fence on what Orville Stanton said was his land and Caesar said was *his*. The two men had looked at Stucka and then at each other, weighed the odds of going for their guns, and went back to the Broken S headquarters. The next day there was a little mulberry hedge out there, cutting across the open meadowland. Caesar had grunted when he saw it, but he didn't do anything about it. His cows walked around it. munching away.

That was all, though. Snarling bitter words in town, drunken fist fights, pulled pistols—but never a gunshot to shatter the uneasy peace.

Tonight it would change. And Whitaker saw that Caesar didn't like it. He wondered, briefly, why Caesar was doing it then. It seemed like some other man's idea. Whitaker dismissed the thought. It didn't matter, the why. Caesar was the boss. What he said, went. They'd ride tonight.

Caesar said, "Harness the dray nag to the flatbed. I'm taking hay to the winter barn. Pile the wagon pretty deep. You never know—"

Whitaker knew what he meant. The raid would probably end up as Caesar planned, what with two Crescent men to every Broken S. But if it didn't, if the Stantons rode back, their own firebrands licking the night with flame, then the Crescent C barns and grass would be in peril. Move the feed first, just in case.

Whitaker said, "I'll take it, boss. You don't have to."

Caesar said harshly, "I said harness the dray. *I'm* going."

Whitaker flushed. Then he said easily, "Sure, boss. Right away." He moved from Caesar, knowing for certain the man was on edge. The boss was doing a chore usually reserved for the lowest hand on the spread. Whitaker shook his head as he rigged the work horse to the wagon. It didn't make sense.

Caesar couldn't be that jittery. There had to be another reason.

The wagon was loaded in ten minutes. Caesar flicked a bullwhip at the dray horse. The horse had a raw-skinned abscess where the draw lines had rubbed it open. Infection had set in. That meant the horse doctor, Caesar thought, unless he could lance it himself. He'd give it a try that night, when he got back from the raid. The horse doc cost money. Everything cost money, Caesar thought angrily, whipping the dray. Rails, feed, wages, chow, mowers, cow feed. And Broken S beef eating the graze, the graze that was lifeblood to the ranch. Tonight he'd change that. He'd rule the range. Caesar had a swift uneasy afterthought: he and Gill would rule the range.

Caesar followed an old Indian foot trail that he had widened himself years back by digging firebreak discs and burning out the brush until the trail was wide enough to move the herd through, three cows abreast, to winter quarters. It had been a long hard pull, making a man's way out here, but it used to be tougher than it was right now. Every winter the Arapahos would come out of the hills, hungry, raiding and burning lean-tos, while another spearhead of braves went for supplies and feed. That was more the reason Caesar didn't mind the war coming. He'd pulled himself up too far to let go. The terrible winters were past. The sheep wars were past. The homesteaders had not proved up their claims, or when they had, Caesar had scared them off.

The Crescent C had lived through it all, scarred now, undermanned and with never quite enough cash to see its way clear to hiring men or building up its skeletal reserves, but alive and active, making its roundups on schedule, getting its herds to the railhead, growing even while it found itself more and more hemmed in by the Stantons' compact spread. That was why Caesar could go along with Gill in this one big decisive blow, to drive the Stantons from the valley, and take over, once and for all.

Caesar pushed the wagon along the trail and through a cut in the western hills and down into the sheltered winter quarters, a rich grassland sunk well into a bowl of hills; big Wolfhead to the northwest protected the land from much of the snow and wind that hit the rest of the country out here.

Caesar eyed his beef, satisfied. It was prime cattle, short-horned and thick-chested, shorter from nose to tail than beef used to be but with more meat per head than the older, rangier Longhorns Caesar used to poke down in Texas, where he'd started ranching twenty-five years ago. He directed the dray to the winter barn and unloaded the bay. Then he slipped the riglines from the horse and threw an old saddle over the heaving swayback and mounted. He looked around before he started for Wolfhead, but there was nobody near. There never was, but Caesar was a careful man.

He went up a slower, narrower trail, to where Gill would be waiting on the slope.

This was the real reason Caesar had insisted on taking the hay himself. Not that the barn needed replenishing; he had to see Gill.

Halfway up the slope, Caesar dismounted. The horse was dragging and scarcely gaining ascent. He looped a rope around a juniper and watched the horse sink to the ground, exhausted. Then he turned and looked about him once more, down at the winter valley, across the low hills to Oxnard valley and to the distant pass that marked the entrance from town. There was nobody in sight, except for a handful of punchers at each spread, near the corrals or the bunkhouses, tiny dots on the soft shimmering carpet of tawny green. Caesar didn't know that nobody was watching him, but he couldn't imagine anybody was, from the look of it. He would undoubtedly be just a similar dot on the slope, less noticeable than brush or a tree, and probably unseen because of the brush and trees.

He lumbered on up to Gill's hideout.

Gill put aside his Winchester. It amused him to hold Caesar in his sights, up the long hill, sighting down the bore at the man's chest. Now Caesar stood outside, squinting into Gill's deep cave, lined with cans of food, a stone square for fire, kindling sticks and a half-dozen logs.

Gill said, "How did it go?"

"You saw Ross come in?"

Gill tapped his power glasses. "And the Stantons go out. It was the Stantons, wasn't it?" There was a small smile on Gill's face. Caesar studied the man, the bland unconcern, the tiny smile at the mouth, blue eyes unperturbed. Gill was a big, magnificently built man, incredibly broad-shouldered and lean-waisted, lean-hipped. He was tall and handsome—Caesar granted the man this, though he did not like to; Maria was a fool over Gill, but she wouldn't come around, ever, for

Caesar. There was something else about Gill that transcended mere good looks. The guileless eyes, the cleft chin, the tanned skin, taut at the cheekbones and jaw, the rippling muscles—plus some intangible factor—made Gill the best-looking man in Oxnard Valley, a man who swaggered when he walked, yet nobody could point out where it was he swaggered, or how. Women liked Gill; men envied him.

Caesar neither liked nor envied Gill. He was wary of the man with whom he was in partnership; but he didn't trust Gill. There was, within the boyish quality, a lack, a failing somewhere. Caesar didn't know what it was, but he sensed it.

Caesar said, "Yes, it was the Stantons going out." Gill had planned it this way, Caesar knew, and though it hadn't seemed possible that it would go off so smoothly, Gill had been right. "The sheriff and Ross toted them off last night. They're in the pokey right now."

Gill nodded vigorously. "You move tonight?"

Caesar said, "Tonight." He wanted to add, *damn it*. He didn't know why, but Gill's cocksureness irritated him. The man was lying here, pulling invisible strings, and puppets bounced willingly.

Gill seemed to read his thoughts. "You want me along?"

Caesar gave a little start. "That wasn't part of the deal," he said slowly. Gill had promised to bring action against the Stantons, to have them thrown in jail and then taken away to stand trial for some crime down in Texas. Gill didn't explain much of it, but Caesar guessed Gill had been along and knew all the details. And that Gill had decided to inform on them. Caesar knew how Gill had forced the Stantons to discharge him, threatening them with exposure until they couldn't stand him around and sent him packing. Caesar wondered briefly whether men who were such gross criminals as Gill depicted the Stantons would not just shoot Gill down and be done with him. They didn't act like criminals, sending off a man like Gill who had something over their heads.

Gill said, "No, it wasn't part of the deal. But if you want me to renege on that part, I'll throw in with you." Gill tapped his Navy Colt.

Caesar shook his head. "Not necessary." He didn't want to put himself any more in Gill's debt than he had to. "We've got two dozen men ready to ride."

"How you going to go about it?" Gill asked.

Caesar said shortly, "Ride on 'em. Burn the graze they think is theirs, and the barn, too, and shoot them down. As many as we can get."

"No plan other than that?"

"What kind of plan? We're going to go in and hit hard. What else do we need?"

Gill shook his head. "Not the way I'd do it."

Caesar was silent for a minute. He didn't want to ask Gill, but Gill was teasing him, dragging him along. Finally he said, "And how the devil would you do it, wonder boy?"

Gill laughed easily. "If you ride in direct across the open graze, burning away, you'll find yourself pinched in between the two main rows of Osage orange. There's a hundred-yard slot you'll have to come through, and when you do, the Stantons could blast you to ribbons."

Caesar thought for a minute. It didn't ring right. They might blast them to ribbons, but only if they expected trouble. Again Gill rode his thoughts. "You think you're going to surprise them? Maybe you will. You probably will. But don't bet on it. With the Stantons out of the way, and the range hot as brush fire this last month, it's the ideal time to make your play. That's how they might think, too. Even with the Stantons out of it. Ives is not very bright, but he's no jughead. He might have two or three men posted along the open slot of graze, armed with shotguns. Maybe he'll lose those men, but you'll lose five times the number. And you can't afford that."

Caesar said grimly, "What would you suggest?"

Gill grinned. "Send a half dozen men, your worst men, straight for the center slot. Meanwhile have the rest of the men sweeping wide around the rear of the Crescent C. There's a stretch of fence directly behind the spread, on a line from the center slot of open graze through the ranch house and on back to the rear fence. Two weeks ago, when I got back, I loosened all the rails back there, just for tonight. You lift the rails off and come on through quiet. No fences to ax, no stone posts to be uprooted. Just lift the rails. I've got white handkerchiefs on the rails. You can't miss."

Caesar stared at the man. "Nobody's fixed the rails since then?"

"Nope."

"How do you know?"

Gill winked. "I know."

"One of those damn women of yours?"

Gill laughed. "That's right. One of them."

Caesar said, "Which one?"

Gill said, "Stop worrying. Not Maria. She's too honest. I wouldn't use her for that. She's got other uses. Know what I mean?"

Caesar flushed and his hands began to writhe. He wanted to throttle this blond man with the easy assurance. He said, instead, "You're positive now? About the fence being loose?"

Gill nodded. It was the only time Laura would ride up Wolfhead. That was the plan. When she rode every night, around the valley floor, outside the Broken S jurisdiction, on the fringe of their domain, she went by the fence, to check whether the handkerchiefs were on, and the rails loose. If they weren't, she was to ride up the slope, to report to Gill. Every night Gill had seen her riding, the evening ride before she went back to the saloon to sing and move her lithe young body. Gill thought of her body. It was the worst part of being up on Wolfhead, waiting for the battle to be fought and won. He missed Laura. He missed Maria, too, and sometimes in the night he would play a little game, thinking of the two women and comparing them, deciding which was the one he wanted most. The answer, of course, was neither. He wanted neither woman very much. Just enough to miss them now. The reason he didn't miss them very much was that they were so accessible, so easily won and then so obsequious. They were a sure thing. Gill liked a sure thing only in his plans to rule the roost out here in the valley. With women, he liked the challenge, the struggle. Once won, he wanted other struggles.

Caesar said grudgingly, "That was neat of you, working the fence angle."

Gill snorted. "I want to win," he said, "not just play. Sure, maybe the Broken S won't be ready for you tonight, and you could pour through the center slot. But maybe they will be ready." He shook his head. "A bloody slaughter, that's what it would be." He clucked, and Caesar felt the irritation wash through him again. Gill was mocking him. The clucking was contempt for Caesar's mind and how it worked.

Caesar said, "It's easy, planning up here. Down on the range I've got other things to worry about."

Gill said, "So do I, up here." A veiled amused look crossed his eyes. He thought: *I've got to worry about knocking off Big Max, because he's a sniffing bird dog, and I've got to worry about knocking you off, too, Joe Caesar, because—because you're in my way.*

CHAPTER SEVEN

Ross ambled his sorrel along the main street. The morning sun slanted in and pointed up the wagon ruts. Ahead of him, coming into town from the outside valley where the two ranches had their spreads, were three Broken S riders. Ross recognized one of them; he was the foreman Ives. Ross pulled the sorrel to the edge of the road and backed into an alleyway. The Broken S men had their horses in a tight high-stepping rack, tense men with short reins. Ross felt the compressed power of the horses as they pranced by, and he heard Ives say, "McQuinn says we can use his wagon." Ross remembered what Orville Stanton had told Ives the night before, about fencing material on order at McQuinn's, the general store. Ross knew the fencing had arrived and was waiting Ives's pickup.

He shook his head and rode on toward the sheriff's office. The Broken S was still paying heavy prices for stone and rails. He felt a little guilty that he hadn't told the Stantons about the bobwire. Then he laughed to himself, a bitter little noise. What was he doing, feeling sorry for men who had killed his father?

Behind Ross, the redheaded girl Laura rode surreptitiously, trying to stay out of sight, and failing badly. Ross had turned once and seen her, and then he made believe he was inspecting his horse's rump. But he had grinned then, and the grin hadn't quite faded. The girl was playing games, keeping an eye on him. He was glad she was. Laura wasn't interested in him, Ross knew, for her own sake. That was sure as shooting. She had made that clear in the saloon and in the street when she mocked him and he had kissed her. There was cold fury in Laura. If anything, she hated his guts. No, she wasn't trailing Ross for herself. She had to be doing it for somebody else. Ross liked that. The somebody else was Gill, he'd have wagered.

Ross dropped lightly from the sorrel, looked up and down the silent empty drag, seeing only the Broken S trio and Laura. He tied the sorrel to the sheriff's post, walked into the sheriff's office, and said, "This is getting to be a quiet town." Big Max rolled off his cot and stood blinking in the room.

The sheriff bent his head, listening. "Too quiet, if you ask me."

Ross said, "The Broken S is in town."

"Ives?"

"Ives and two hands. Going to pick up their fencing material at McQuinn's."

"Anybody else around?" Big Max asked.

Ross grinned. "Just Red."

"Laura? From the saloon?"

"That's her. Little old detective, that girl. Trailed me from the hotel. All the way up the street. Neatest job of trailing I ever saw. Spotted her only five or six times along two hundred yards of road."

Big Max said sharply, "Now what's she doing that for?"

Ross shrugged. "For Gill, I guess."

"Gill or Caesar, one or the other," the sheriff said. Then he frowned, thinking of what Ross had said when he came into the office, a minute before, "No Crescent C boys in town at all?"

"Nary a one."

Big Max shook his head. "Bad," he said softly, "very, very bad." Caesar had his boys back at the ranch, every one of them. Every day there were usually a couple or three in town, either on business or else on their own. But not today, apparently. The sheriff felt a chill cross his chest. Caesar and his boys were sharpening their knives right now, Max thought. The sheriff figured—before—that the range war was imminent, but imminent was some time soon. Not just now. Not necessarily today, or tonight. But now it looked like imminent was on top of them, fire in the hole, the fuse spitting.

He made up his mind, that minute. He said, "Ross, can I trust you, man?"

"What do you mean?"

"Just that," the sheriff barked. "Trust you not to take the law into your own hands."

Ross walked to the doorway. The girl Laura was fifty yards down the drag. She looked away suddenly and started to stare hard at a store front. He said quietly, "I'm not sure. I still feel the way I did when I rode in, that I've got to get the man who killed my old man. But I don't think I'm going to do anything about those two men in jail." He jerked his thumb toward the jailhouse.

Max said, "I can't afford that. You've got to be sure."

"All right," Ross said, turning, "I'm sure. I won't shoot them like they are."

Max peered into his face. Then he said, "I'm going up to the Territory capital."

"To Denver? You crazy, Sheriff?"

"No, sane. We need help. We need some men in here fast. This place will burn any minute now."

"So you're going to pull out? That doesn't make sense."

"Better sense than trying to stop the fire with one man."

Ross said, "But one man is better than none."

"Not a damn bit better. Two dozen men can kill a man so quick you'd never know he was ever alive. And if I get there fast and get back fast, maybe we'll be in time to stop Caesar from hitting at all. It's now or never with him. Now, before the Stantons build up their strength or before any more law comes into Oxnard. Later, it will be too late."

"So will you," Ross said. "Why, man, they might even hit tonight."

Big Max said softly, "That's the chance of it."

Ross said, "Send somebody else."

"Who? You?"

Ross still shook his head angrily. "No, not me. I'm sticking. I've got my own war."

"So who, then?"

Ross said heavily, "I don't know." The sheriff was right. Nobody else would go, nobody else would throw any weight, any authority around up in Denver. Send a man up to Denver, and he'd get sucked into Holliday Street and never come up for air until the whores had his money or the toughs his life. It had to be a man like Big Max. It had to be Big Max.

The sheriff nodded. "You see, don't you? There's nobody."

Ross said, "I see." He saw himself being thrust into a position he hadn't asked for, hadn't figured on. Himself in range war, the range war he had hoped would smoke Gill out, and instead was going to suck him in. The Broken S and its undermanned crew on one side, Joe Caesar and his hardcases on the other, the rest of the town neutral, hands off. And somehow it was his fault. Oh, not that he would have done it any different, knowing what he knew now. He still would have pressed hard against the Stantons, once he smelled out their guilt. But a man couldn't just take a little bit of the responsibility for his own acts. He had to take all the responsibility for them. Ross's presence in Oxnard had been like flint to hot rock. The two were clashing, and when the fire broke out he had to accept his role in it. He couldn't back down. And what it came to was: eight or ten Stanton men, about to be shot up or burned out by two dozen Crescent C men. He knew where he stood. He stood with the defenders, because he was the one who had put them on the defense, and when he had seen to it that the Stantons themselves went to jail, he had rendered the Broken S practically defenseless. Big Max wouldn't see it that way, because Big Max believed in the law and he would never have begun it the way Ross had, pushing hard on the Stantons. He would have sniffed and tracked, slowly, cautiously, inoffensively, until he was ready to move. Then he would have struck with an army behind him.

Well, that was Big Max, and he was going to Denver to get him his army. Ross would like to have been able to play it lone hand in the fight to clean up his old man's killing. But lone hand wouldn't do the trick. Gill was with Caesar. Caesar was going to move on Broken S. Ross wanted Gill. So he, Ben Ross, who thought the two men who owned Broken S had killed his father, or at least one of them had, would have to throw in with Broken S.

It didn't make sense, yet it did. He had brought on war. Now he had to fight in it.

Ross said again, "I see," and he heard Big Max behind him shoving clothes into a saddlebag. Ross looked down the drag, the new-old drag that had become so familiar to him, and he watched Ives and his two hands come out of the general store with stone posts and wooden rails. He saw them load them onto a wagon drawn by two swaybacks, and he watched as the girl Laura moved her horse near the wagon, her face a white frown in the early morning light. She had sidled close to Ives, and Ross could see that she was watching, and listening, too.

Ross said, "That girl's a real sneak."

Big Max walked over. "What's she up to?"

Ross shrugged. "Don't know, for sure. She's scared about something, scared bad."

The wagon was loaded, and Ives and the two men pushed toward the sheriff's office, on their way out of Oxnard. Ross said, "Max, help me here. They probably won't talk to me, but if you back me, they will."

Max looked at him curiously and said, "I'm right here," and Ross walked into the middle of the street, blocking the wagon.

Ives said, "Get out of the way, man." His mouth was thin and hard. This was the manhunter in front of him, the man who had had the Stantons thrown in jail last night.

Big Max appeared at the doorway. He said, "Ross is all right."

Ross said, "When you boys loaded the fencing back at McQuinn's, did you say much about what you were doing? You had a listener right behind you."

Ives looked confused. He said, "I don't get you. All we said was something about getting the stuff back to the ranch, to get some fences up. Or something like that. Why?"

Ross said, "I don't know exactly." He was disappointed. There was nothing wrong with some Broken S men fixing fences. Why was Laura so interested? He said, "Sorry for holding you up."

Ives said, "Is that all?" He looked at the sheriff. Big Max just stood there, big and hulking, watching Ross mostly, the man's jaws tight, a vein throbbing at his temple. The man was wrestling with something.

And Ross said then, throwing himself irrevocably in with the Broken S and hating it, "Did you ever hear of bobwire?"

Ives said, "No. What's all this got to do with anything, man? We're in a hurry—"

Ross said quickly, "Bobwire's the new idea in fencing graze. It's heavy gauge wire, with barbs—points—in it. Rolls easy and goes up fast. Costs practically nothing."

Ives said impatiently, "Why you telling me this?"

"Because I told Joe Caesar about it. He knows that with bobwire you fellows can fence off the graze he thinks he owns."

Ives stared down at Ross. He said murderously, "Who the devil you siding, anyway?"

Big Max stepped forward and put a hand on the front wagon wheel. He said, "The man's siding nobody. He's playing it square. Bobwire will solve the fencing problem for you boys, both of you. But Caesar isn't going to like it going up on what he considers open graze, or his graze. Get me?"

Ives started to nod, slowly. One of the two men in the rear of the wagon said, "Caesar won't like it, at all," and the other man said, "Wouldn't be surprised if he did something about it, and pretty quick."

Ross said, "That's what I mean." He saw the girl up close, getting another pink earful. Ross watched her, her face glowering, confused. Good, he thought, blood humming in his temples, good. Let her hear. Let her know that the Broken S is going to be ready, in case Joe Caesar decides to strike. If Laura was with Gill, and Gill with Caesar, what was being said right now in the middle of Oxnard's dry ruts might slow down the range war. Maybe Laura would tip off Gill—wherever he was—and Gill would advise Caesar: go slow for a while, the Broken S is waiting. It was a long shot, Ross knew, but it might mean no war, and that would mean he wouldn't be in the middle of a burning no man's graze with the shock of rifle fire exploding all about him.

Ives said slowly, "If we fence that graze, Caesar will move on us."

One of the other two men drawled, "Not if we're just sitting back, rifles ready for him. He's a tough boy, but he's no idiot."

Relief washed through Ross. The man had said it for him. And Laura had heard. He turned to Big Max. "All right," he said loudly, "go on up to Denver as fast as you can. I think we can hold them a while."

The sheriff said, "Someday, Ross, I think you'll make a decent citizen." He went back inside, and Ross turned to watch Laura. She was the ticket now. It was in her hands. If she were just curious for her own sake, then none of it mattered, and the range would burn, and he—Ben Ross—might be ashes within two days.

And suddenly Ross felt the old doubts gnawing at him. Why was he doing all this, why was he interested in stopping war from burning up the range? Was it because he knew the war wouldn't be a fair one, that Broken S men would be killed, mowed down by Caesar like hay before a scythe?

Or was it because he—Ben Ross—was just scared gutless? The Broken S load of fencing rolled through the street, toward the end of town. The sheriff was in his office. Ross stood in the middle of the drag, empty but for the girl.

Hate blazed in her eyes. She said, from across the stretch of dry road, "You're a meddler, Ross. You'll pay for this."

Ross laughed, a cruel sneering laugh, a slap in the face sort of laugh.

Laura had answered all the *if*'s. She was involved, all right. She whirled her pony and galloped past Ross, the horse's hooves six inches away. He watched and thought: *she's going to Gill.*

CHAPTER EIGHT

Ross unlooped the sorrel from the sheriff's hitching post. The girl was going to Gill, and he was going after her. And the red ball of flame that had lain inert inside Ross ever since the Stantons had spoken with forked tongues and gone to jail, the red rage of a man intent on seeing through an eleven-year-old vengeance, sprang alive again, bubbling hot, angry.

Still, Ross had come a long way. Maybe not far enough, he thought, but he was no longer the man with the itching finger and the sagging revolver that begged to be lifted, aimed and emptied of one snub-nosed slug. Ross frowned, his eyes intent on the girl's fleet pony clopping its way down the main drag of Oxnard, and out of town. Maybe he had never really been that man, the itching-fingered man of spite. He shook his head. He didn't know. All he knew was that the girl could take him to Gill, and Gill could clear up the mess, straighten out the gap between his story, and the Stantons'—a gap which was the chasm that kept Ross yesterday from blazing away at the two brothers, that kept Ross from the dead-sure knowledge of what was so in Gore, Texas, eleven long years ago.

Gill might do something else, Ross knew. He might kill Ross.

And so he stood, watching, listening, while the townspeople of Oxnard started to form in the street, on the plank walks, watching too, watching the manhunter who was obviously meddling in the affairs out on the range, affairs that scarcely needed meddling to turn into cattle war. Ross felt their eyes, hostile, suspicious, the eyes of people who liked to call themselves neutral because they knew no other word for indifference.

He bit off a curse, his eyes still trained on the spot where the girl had ridden out of sight. He knew he could give Laura's horse a start and still overtake her. That was why he waited, not because he was afraid his steps would lead him surely to Gill, and Gill might kill him. Laura's pony was swift, a quarter horse that would fly in short bursts, but a horse without the stamina of Ross's sorrel. Given any distance, any time at all, Ross could close the gap. He didn't want to start right away on the girl's trail for the simple reason he didn't want the girl to know he was behind her. Not that she wouldn't know soon enough, he thought bitterly, but there was no need to spell it out for her.

Big Max lumbered to the doorway of the office, grimly gray-faced. He dangled a chain of heavy keys, and then he said, "Here, Ross, take over." He flipped the chain through the air and Ross caught the keys. They were the keys to the jailhouse and the inside cells. There were others, too, keys to Big Max's files and drawers, but the important ones—to Ross and Big Max—were the two keys that locked the Stantons in the pokey.

They were more than keys. They were Big Max's trust in Ross. Ross hefted the chain, his mind troubled. It was all right to come a distance from the man who was filled with red hate, but was it all right to come this far that he was now the protector of the two men who might have been—and probably were—his father's killers?

Ross said slowly, "You're taking a chance, you know."

Big Max said, "I doubt it. Not that I have any choice, do I?"

Ross grinned thinly. "I guess not."

Big Max stared at the manhunter. "Ross," he said, "If I come back from Denver and find you've done anything to those men in there, you'll pay to me."

"Not to the law?" Ross said mockingly.

Big Max shook his head slowly. "No," he said. "To me. I'll tear you in two if you mess with those men."

The townspeople were starting to circle the pair, acting as though their own movements were unconscious of the sheriff and Ross, yet obviously they wanted to hear and see the newcomer with the revolver get his come-uppance again from the big sheriff whom they trusted and liked, even though they didn't understand his terrible concern with seeing things done in a certain manner, a law-and-order manner, so dreadfully slow and painstaking. Why, they thought, men could get killed and their killers' children could whelp more brats before Big Max, sheriff of Oxnard County, ever brought the killers to his courts of justice.

Big Max went on: "Not that you will mess with them, Ross. You're going to be a law-abiding man one of these days. I'm waiting for the day you pack away that gun."

A man in the street, fat and watery-eyed, lifted his head and forgot that he was trying to listen unobtrusively. He said, "So are we, Sheriff. Send the son-of-a-buck home."

Big Max turned, stony-faced. He said, "Abelson, why don't you sell your hardware. And you, Smits, get back to the stable. I'm going to want my horse fed in a few minutes. The rest of you, what the devil do you want? Get back to your jobs."

The Oxnard citizenry, shame-faced, started to shuffle off, and Ross thought savagely, *they're cows, every one of them.*

Ross said loudly, "You're waiting for me to pack away my gun, Max, and I'm waiting for the day I can put it to use." The shuffling in the street accelerated, and Ross knew he had done it again: scratched another notch onto the phantom gun he never fired. He was a straw hero again.

Max studied Ross and then spun around and went into his office. He knew he was doing a dangerous thing, leaving Oxnard. But Ross had slowed down Caesar and his gun toughs—if Laura was the intermediary that she just had to be.

Max lifted his saddle pack and walked outside to strap it to the dun mare. Ross still stood there, rolling a cigarette, watching the dust-spiral from Laura's pony indicate the direction the girl was traveling.

Big Max said, "That's cattle range out there. Caesar's spread or the Broken S."

Ross nodded. "That's how it figures."

The sheriff grunted and said, "Watch your trigger finger. So long, Ross."

Ross said, "Bring back your army, Max."

The sheriff mounted and rode off, slowly, for the stable.

Laura laid a hand on the quarter horse's hot neck. Blood was gushing underneath. For the past two minutes she thought she had heard a faint drumming behind her. She sensed what it would be, but she didn't want to risk a look backwards. This was different from trailing Ross in the street of Oxnard, just to keep him in sight. Sure, she knew he'd see her. But now there was Gill involved, and she wasn't going to risk Gill because she had to turn a curious head. In front of her the trail to Caesar's ranch turned and went out of view for some hundred yards; boulders obscured the arroyo that cut its way across the range and made a natural trail. Once among the boulders she could pull up the pony and peer out from behind a rock. She nodded and pricked her pony's ribs with her spurs. The game little horse stretched out. The drumming faded.

She turned the trail. Swiftly she reined the pony to a halt and tugged him to the side of the arroyo where overhanging rock provided cover. She swung the horse around and stared out at the wide open range that had been behind her and that led back to Oxnard. Then she nodded, the savage thoughts in her head returning sharply. It was Ross, all right, on his big ugly sorrel. She whirled her pony and raked his side with her spurs. The tired horse burst forward, straining to get out from under the woman who kept stabbing his sweating flesh.

Laura refused to panic. She could work it out, she knew. She and Gill had not handled it as well as they should have. She had her orders, and the orders had seemed complete enough when Gill curtly told them to her, but now she wasn't sure. Gill had said: come straight out to me when you find the fence repaired. Well, it was apparent that the fence was going to be repaired, and right away.

That was what Ives had said. "Let's get out of here and get that damn fence up." She puzzled over his words, while behind her she made sure the drumming got no closer. But it wouldn't fall back, either, and she knew that Ross's sorrel had her pony whipped whenever he wanted to catch up. So she stuck to her thoughts, worried but not giving way. She had to figure it out. She just had to. Gill was involved, and where Gill was involved, she took no chances. Nobody—neither Ross nor Big Max nor anybody—was going to lay his hands on Gill just because she had to deliver a message.

She returned to Ives's words. "Get that damn fence up." Not quite that, but something like it. She shook her head. Maybe she didn't have it right. Would a man talk about putting up a fence that was only being repaired? These were the things she didn't know. How did men talk about things like that? She'd have said, "Let's *fix* that fence."

She dismissed the thought. She couldn't take a chance. Gill had to know.

But this was daylight. Gill hadn't said what to do if she had to come out in daylight. Always—before—she had assumed it would be dark, or near dark. She always checked the fence at dusk, on her evening ride around the range. If anything had to be reported to Gill, it would be done under a cloak of darkness. She could have made good time, at night, with little fear of being discovered while she climbed the tricky side of Wolfhead. But during the day, she'd have to creep an inch at a time under cover. That is, unless she could shake Ross.

She had to. Here she was out in the open, a ferret-faced man with a gun behind her, the two of them under Colorado's immense blue sky, marred only by a dazzling sun that lit up every pot hole and draw like the fingers of a thousand million searching lanterns. She never felt more vulnerable, more naked in her life.

She had to decide. Which was more important: not leading Ross to Gill's hideout, or making sure Gill knew about the fence?

And then she laughed, a shrill high laugh that climbed from the dusty trail straight toward that blue canopy. How easy it was, playing these games with men, men like Ross, stolid, grim, stumbling men who moved so straight and simply.

She could handle both problems. She'd never lead Ross to Gill, and she'd let Gill know about the fence.

She laughed again, a joyous sound, and with it merged a husky strain that chased goose-pimples over her flesh. She knew how pleased

Gill would be with her. She knew how he'd show his pleasure. She shivered with delicious anticipation, fever staining her cheeks.

Laura turned the pony's nose straight toward Joe Caesar's Crescent C. She knew suddenly that all the time it must have been in her head, what she was going to do, for this was the way she had headed automatically, even though it wasn't the straight line to Gill's. It was the straight line to Ross's trap, though.

Ben Ross drifted from the main trail, so he wouldn't swallow dust the whole way out. He had ridden this way before, the afternoon previous with Big Max, to see first Joe Caesar and then the Stantons. He had figured the girl would go this way. He and Big Max had gone looking for Gill yesterday, and the first place Big Max had led them to was Caesar's.

Ross squinted across the dust that kept obscuring the girl. He was in no hurry to catch the girl. He didn't want to catch her. He wanted her to keep going, to Gill. He felt she had to tell Gill about what had happened in Oxnard, about the Broken S preparing its defenses against any blow from Caesar, or from Caesar *and* Gill.

Then the first gnawing worry struck Ross. What would he do about it if he found Gill hiding out at Caesar's, protected by a rangeful of Crescent C men? Ross fidgeted his shoulders and stopped thinking. He'd handle it. What he knew about bobwire and about the Broken S men lying in wait, that would be enough to slow down Caesar.

He kicked the sorrel sharply and leaned in the big saddle, easing his weight forward. The sorrel responded. The gap swiftly whittled to a few hundred yards, maybe less. Then the girl burst through Caesar's open gate, and Ross watched while she ran inside.

And a chill whipped through Ross. Oh, he was so smart, he thought. He had sneered at the girl's stupidity, when she was clumsily trailing him in town. But she had done nothing half so stupid as he was doing now.

The girl was talking excitedly, and Ross could see Caesar look up at the now slowed-down sorrel, approaching the Crescent C cluster of buildings. Caesar waved his arm and three riders came at Ross from three directions.

Ross thought wildly of turning back and making a run for town. But the sorrel was winded, and Caesar's horses were fresh. They'd collar him in two dozen loping strides.

He had been blind. All the way out, all Ross had thought was: he and Gill, he and Gill. It still was his own war, his own private war, no matter what sort of righteous thoughts he had had back in Oxnard. All he really had been thinking was how Gill was part of Ross's own war, and Gill had to be routed out. Never did he see it as all one big piece, all part of the range feud that lay all about him, that surrounded him and faced him, even now, with guns drawn, bores pointed at his belly.

Caesar said, "Well, if it isn't the sheriff's little helper. Welcome to the Crescent C, Ross." In his right hand was a .44. Ross said, dry-throated, "You're making a mistake, Caesar."

"Yeah," Caesar said with savage glee, "tell me about it. The girl says you're siding the Stantons. I told you yesterday nobody sides the Stantons out here without crossing me."

Ross laughed harshly. That was how Laura was playing it, leading him to Caesar, a Broken S ally being handed to the foes of the Broken S. It was shrewd, all right.

He said, "I'm siding nobody," yet he knew he couldn't put it over, because in a way he was a liar. He had thrown in with the Broken S just an hour earlier. He knew he was bringing war on its head, and he had to help the Broken S fight it off.

Caesar ignored Ross's words. He looked to his right and left. There were two riders, one on each of Ross's flanks, hard-looking men, surly men, big in the saddle, slouching and efficient, and with guns in their right fists. Caesar nodded to the men and they moved closer to Ross, still on his flanks. Ross knew he didn't stand a chance, drawing. He let his hands creep to his horse's neck, far from the hip where the Colt Walker bulged.

Caesar said, "If you don't side me, you're against me. That's the way it goes."

Ross said, "What you mean is, that's the way you've been told it goes." He jerked his head in the direction of the redheaded girl. "She's filled your ears with rot. All I'm doing is trying to keep peace on this range."

Caesar snorted. "Keep off the range. Go back to Oxnard. That's the way you'll keep peace. You're a troublemaker, Ross."

Ross said swiftly, "I told the Broken S about bobwire, Caesar. They know I told you, too. Bobwire will help you both in the long run."

Caesar frowned. "What's that got to do with this?"

Laura said, "The man's just a meddler, Caesar."

Caesar was silent for a half minute. If the Stanton men knew that Caesar was ready to move (that's how they'd figure the bobwire business, Caesar knew, it would mean Caesar would be riled and ready to ride before the wire went up on the common graze), then they'd be waiting. It would be as Gill had said, Broken S men waiting at the center slot with twelve-gauge shotguns. But it no longer mattered much. Gill had worked it all out. Caesar would still proceed the way Gill had suggested, throw a sharp feint with his weakest men at the center opening, and then come up from behind. Even if the Broken S were ready, they were too thin to spread out their defenses properly. It would be tougher, but it would still work out.

The girl said again, sharply, reading Caesar's hesitation as fear, "He's playing with the Stantons, Caesar. I heard him."

Caesar grunted. He didn't like the girl. She was one of Gill's women, and when he thought of Gill's women, he didn't like Gill. He said wearily, "Shut up, I heard you."

Ross watched the man, knowing his chances stood with Caesar. If Caesar weighed the odds that had suddenly grown against him, and if he weighed them sensibly, there'd be no trouble. But Caesar was a man who kept surprising Ross. He had surprised Ross yesterday when the business about bobwire hadn't come as a stunning bolt of news. Caesar didn't weigh things the way Ross figured he would. Ross felt the sweat form on his face, cold and clinging. Caesar, Ross could see, was more than just a hollow wounded bear. He was facing a showdown, and the man wasn't jittery. He just stood there, big and black-haired, his face punched out of shape from a dozen brawls, and Ross watched him weigh twenty-four guns against the Broken S's eight.

Ross said, the tension making his words shrill. "It won't work, Caesar. You'll ride into an arsenal. They're waiting for you."

Caesar stared at Ross, and Ross could see the filmy red hate in Caesar's eyes. He said, "You figure on helping 'em out, Ross?"

Ross shrugged. "I'm figuring on helping nobody. It's not my fight."

"No?" Caesar said wickedly. "Maybe I'm going to make it your fight."

"All I want is Gill," Ross said.

"I'm not Gill."

"You know where he is."

Caesar smiled. "Like hell I do."

Ross looked beyond Caesar, to the girl Maria who was standing near the edge of the ranch house, crouched and frightened. Then he looked at Laura. And he knew Maria didn't know where Gill was, but Laura did. It was written all over her face. If Laura knew, and Maria didn't, Gill wasn't here at the Crescent C.

He said to Laura, "You're helping build a war, Red. Men will die because of you."

She tried to sneer at this man, but it wouldn't come off. She was confused. She wished she and Gill had discussed it better, all the possibilities. She didn't even know now whether Caesar was in cahoots with Gill. Maybe he was, probably he was. But she didn't know for sure. She couldn't take a chance. She wanted to tell Caesar about the Broken

S fixing that fence behind their spread, but Gill had told her to tell nobody, just him. So she couldn't, even though she wasn't so sure Gill wouldn't have wanted her to tell Caesar.

She said, "You're the one who's starting the trouble. Get out of here. Go back where you came from. We don't want bounty hounds around."

Ross waited in the saddle, licked. The girl, even though she was starting to look like the scared punk she really was, still held the best cards. Caesar could hustle Ross inside, and then the girl could ride away, to Gill. And Ross would lose her, and Gill.

He started a thin grin. Hell, he thought, he stood to lose much more than that. He stood to lose his life, right here on the Crescent C range. Caesar was safe. He could say Ross burst in, gun waving, and Caesar had to shoot him down.

They'd all back him up.

Well, Ross thought, what was Caesar waiting for then? And a new hope hit Ross. Maybe—he thought, he prayed—maybe Caesar, gun toughs and all, range war and all, wasn't a cold killer. It was Ross's only hope, and he had to play it.

Caesar suddenly straightened up and waved a hand. He said, "Stucka, Hallahan—" and the two men on Ross's flanks looked to their boss.

Ross knew Caesar had made up his mind. And Ross had to shape his moves, no matter how puny they'd be. Swiftly he started his draw, the prayer in his throat as big as his fist, knowing that in a third of a second he might be full of holes. Now he had to make those thousand dummy draws, out on the empty range, pay off—now he had to test his speed not against the sighing wind, but against twenty men.

His hand flashed, under an iron control that whispered: speed, damn it, speed.

Ross had the element of surprise working on his side. All about him he heard breath being sucked in, while his hand kept streaking, drawing, clearing leather—and then dropping the big gun softly to the grass, in front of Caesar.

And nobody else had started a move.

Ross felt his chest rise and then fall heavily, his heart thumping. He had chanced it, and it had worked. If Caesar was going to kill him, he'd have to do it in cold blood, in coward's cold blood. Ross was Caesar's prisoner, but he wasn't a dead man. Not yet, not yet.

He had gone for his gun, not to use it, not to fire it, because Ross knew that suicide lay that way, firing it. He had to get rid of it, get it as far from him as possible. He had to reduce himself to a defenseless, helpless human being. That way he would—might—live. The other way he might tag Caesar with his Colt Walker and maybe one of the others, one of the two men on his flank, ten yards away, but that was the best. After that, they'd open up, the man on his flank whom Ross wouldn't have plugged, and the dozen behind Caesar, waiting with guns on the ready.

So he had rid himself of his gun. He had ceased being either a sheriff's deputy or a manhunter or an armed foe. He was just a man who didn't like them and whom they didn't like, sitting his horse on their grass, helpless, unarmed.

Caesar let a ghost of a smile wipe his mouth. He said, "Now wasn't that just dandy of you? The troublemaker's trying to tell us he's no troublemaker."

Ross swallowed the prayer that was like a fist.

Laura said shrilly, "Watch out for him, Caesar. He's probably got a hideout gun."

Caesar said, "Get off your horse, Ross. Pick up your gun."

Ross shook his head. "No," he said. "Shoot me like this. That's up to you. But I'm not touching my gun."

Caesar's face had a wicked slant to it. "Scared, Ross?"

Ross nodded, tongue licking his lips. He was playing it as well as he could, as hard as he could, but he knew inside it wasn't very difficult to play it. He was scared, no acting needed. "Sure, I'm scared."

Caesar said, "Now who's not a man, Ross?"

And Ross saw his opening. Caesar was a brawler, his face showed it.

Caesar said again, "Who's not a man, Ross? Who's a liar?" The rancher was remembering yesterday. Ross's words had raked him raw.

Ross swung lightly from his horse and stood in front of Caesar. The revolver was lying five feet away, untouched, white light bouncing from the black steel. "You're not a man," Ross said easily. "You're a liar. You're a coward, facing a man without a gun, and too afraid to put up your own fis—"

He got no further. Caesar's gun dropped from suddenly opened fingers, and then the same hand closed into a great hairy fist, and the fist smashed Ross full in the mouth. Ross felt his upper lip mash against his teeth, and then he tasted the salty blood, and he roared out his pain and his rage—and his sheer animal delight at this man in front of him who could have killed him but instead chose to fight him fair.

Caesar hooked a sweeping left hand against the side of Ross's jaw as he plunged forward, and the punch rocked Ross. Then Caesar thundered home his right fist again and Ross went to his knee, wondering foolishly how come he thought this battering was more pleasant than a single bullet in the brain. Then he got up and said through crushed lips, "You're not a man, Caesar, you're a filthy coward," and Caesar bellowed like a wounded bull. But Ross fell inside the man's rush and grabbed the rancher around the middle, working his head under Caesar's jaw and butting the man as hard as he could.

Caesar staggered away, and Ross had the breather he desperately needed. He waited a moment, and walked in to Caesar. Pumping out his long left arm, his fist found Caesar's jaw. He kept pumping out the straight left, and Caesar started to tremble like a struck ox. But Ross, overeager, lost his man, missed a wild overhand right, and Caesar grabbed the flailing right arm and wrenched down on it. Pain streaked from Ross's shoulder to the back of his right ear.

The two men stood apart, and from the crowding circle of Crescent C men, Ross heard a puncher say, "Want me to finish him, Boss?"

Ross looked at the man, a big horse-toothed cowhand, half a head taller than any other man on the ranch. Ross said, "I'll take you, too, horsey," and the man stepped forward.

Caesar said, "Leave him alone, Whitaker," and he charged Ross once more. But Ross was waiting, and the right hand wasn't overanxious this time, crashing full against Caesar's jaw and half-turning the rancher. Ross had him then, he knew. He grabbed Caesar by his shirt front and pulled the man forward, and hit him as he pulled—a short rising punch that caught Caesar under the chin and closed his mouth with a snap that clicked off a tooth. Caesar sagged limp in Ross's grasp, and then Ross dropped the man, unconscious, to the grass.

Ross stood erect, panting, in pain, and he gasped out, "All right, I'll take any one of you," but it didn't work, and he knew it wouldn't. They didn't come one at a time; they weren't such damn fools as that.

The two men from the flanks—Hallahan and Stucka, Ross remembered Caesar had called them—and the big horse-toothed man from the front—Whitaker—converged on him, and it didn't last long, though Ross fought back like a wild, terribly frightened animal. Ross started to go down, and he heard a squeal of pleasure come from the redheaded girl, Laura, and he straightened up to throw one more punch, thudding solidly into Whitaker's snaggle teeth. Then the big man raised both hands locked together and brought them crushingly down on the back of Ross's neck. He fell forward on his face, and the last thing he heard was a tiny frightened moan which he liked to think came from the girl, Maria. But it was very far off and maybe it came from his own tortured mouth. He didn't know and he didn't care. He barely felt the last dozen blows that thudded against his chest, his ribs, the sides of his head, from Whitaker's hob-nailed boots.

... Whitaker raised his leg and drew it back, and then he lowered it. He said hoarsely, "That's enough," and Hallahan and Stucka moved back, and the circle of Crescent C men started to widen and lose shape.

Whitaker said, "Truss the man up and toss him in the barn. Do a good job on it." He shook his head half-admiringly, half in anger. "He's strong as a bull."

Then he turned and saw the redheaded girl, the saloon singer who read cards. He said, "Get the hell out of here, Miss."

The man's anger pleased Laura. She walked slowly to her horse, shimmying, and she felt the men's hot eyes on her. She had done what she had set out to do, and it made her feel good. Now she could go to Gill, having done her job, with Ross out of the way. She mounted her brown pony and turned and said to Whitaker, "So long, horsey, thanks for the favor." She jabbed the pony and started the long ride to Wolfhead.

And behind her, watching, was the girl Maria. She watched Laura cantering away from the Crescent C, going further from Oxnard, and she knew where Laura was headed. Swiftly, with the grace that had made Ross's throat heat up the day before, she moved to the corral, while the Crescent C men were carrying the broken, limp body of Ross to the barn, while other men helped Caesar stagger to his feet, while other men drifted in small clusters, talking about the terrible fight they had just seen. Unnoticed by any of them, Maria mounted a swift cream-colored horse and, with a wariness she scarcely was conscious of, followed Laura, staying out of sight along the thin woods that marked the edge of Joe Caesar's domain, searching out and finding cover in the short noonday shadows at the foot of the slope that rose up from the meadowland.

CHAPTER NINE

Gill wiped his mouth with his sleeve, and then he frowned and set down the tin cup, half-filled with coffee. He had seen, without understanding, the two riders enter the Crescent C, and he had seen the cluster of dots on the grass, the swiftly active dots that probably meant a fight of some sort. It didn't mean much to Gill. Joe Caesar was a rough-grained man; so were his hands. It didn't matter if two of them suddenly had decided to beat each other's brains in. Just so long as they didn't do so much damage they wouldn't be able to ride with the other Crescent C cowhands against the Broken S tonight. That was the only concern of Gill's. He grunted and wiped his mouth again, the frown still heavy on his otherwise smooth, handsome face.

There was something else.

He stood up in the small cave, crouched a bit, and splashed the remaining coffee into his tiny fire and covered his mouth with a kerchief as white smoke boiled up and filled his hideout. Then he moved to the edge of the cave to look out. He had heard—or thought he had heard—while eating his late morning meal of cold biscuits and coffee, another sound, closer to the cave than the activity of the Crescent C. It was the cantering clop-clop of a horse, far distant but getting closer.

And when Gill raised his field glasses and stared down at the shimmering, yellow-green field before him, noon heat convulsing the valley so that the land seemed alive, laboring under the sun, rising and falling, he saw the girl.

When the field glasses came away from his eyes, his face was smooth, unlined, imperturbable. Only the tiniest tic at the side of his left temple betrayed the sudden seething turmoil that rose up in Gill.

For days he had prepared himself for the unexpected.

Ross, the manhunter, suddenly riding up the slope. Or Big Max, perhaps. Or anybody. The Stantons, even, finding out somehow where Gill was and seeking out their smoking vengeance on him.

But when days had passed by, each one alike, except for what he saw happening on the Crescent C or the Broken S—and even that activity had a routine sameness about it—Gill began to relax in his cave. The unexpected just wasn't going to happen. He had seen Laura make her little ride on the outside of the Broken S, near its fence, every evening. He had expected her to. He had seen Ross ride up with Big Max. Gill nodded. Even this, with its roots sunk back in Texas, eleven years ago, was to be expected. He had seen the Stantons shuffle off to their horses, obviously prisoners of Big Max and the manhunting Ross, who probably carried a deputization from his home county. This, too, had been expected, welcomed.

So the vigilance of a man who had come prepared to fight or flee, to do what was required, began to fade. He hadn't known it was fading, but the twitch at his left temple told him all he had to know. He hadn't expected anybody to ride up here, even though he thought he was prepared, and when somebody—even the girl, Laura, who was his ally, one of his closest allies, actually, in this whole affair—rode up in midday, the suddenness was nearly like physical shock.

Gill stepped back into the shadows and quickly broke open his Navy Colt. He nodded grimly and returned it to his holster. He studied his rifle and then propped it against the back wall of the cave. Then he pressed the back of his hand against his temple, where the vein leaped like a spastic worm. Finally, long seconds later, the vein quieted. Gill grinned. It hadn't been so bad. He was himself, again.

When he returned to the cave front, the girl was halfway up Wolfhead. He cursed once, mildly. She was coming full up the slope, not caring a damn about covering herself with the strand of timber. Well, he would have to straighten her out about that. She'd sure as hell not go back down the same way. She'd crawl down on her horse's belly, an inch at a time.

Gill ducked back in and waited for her, wondering. At first he was angry with Laura, but then he felt something inflate inside him, a pleased feeling of vanity. She just had to see him, Gill thought. She shouldn't be doing it, but it made him feel good, just to know that this long-legged, velvet-thighed girl, who made men want her every night in Tromper's saloon, wanted only him.

A second thought struck Gill. Maybe it wasn't that. Maybe the girl had some news to tell him, about Caesar, about the fence, about the whole business on the range, about the fight he had just seen at Caesar's, about Ross, Big Max. *Jesus*, Gill thought, there was so much he *didn't* know about what was going on. And the worm crawled back to life under the skin of his temple.

The girl swiftly steered her pony near Gill's own horse, behind the cave, tying him tight to a thin evergreen in the center of a thicket of such evergreens, where he could not possibly be seen. Then she walked into the cave and looked at Gill.

A smile crossed the girl's face, and then it broke into a giggle, high-pitched.

Gill said, "What's so damn funny? And what the hell are you doing up here at this time of day? I thought I told you—"

The girl stared at his face and pointed. She said, "I didn't know you had a twitch."

Gill frowned and said, "What's the difference?" His voice was harsh, openly antagonistic, and the girl suddenly stopped giggling. "What are you doing here? That's what I want to know."

Laura moved deep into the cave and sat herself on a log. She said quietly, "They're fixing your fence."

Gill's frown deepened. "What the hell are you talking about?"

"The fence. The fence behind the Broken S, with the loose rails. They're fixing it."

"How the devil do you know? You rode the perimeter last night and didn't come up. You haven't ridden there since."

She said in the same quiet tone, wondering a bit at her own calm and at his harsh suspicion, "I saw Ives in town this morning, with two other Stanton men. They had purchased some fencing from McQuinn's."

Gill fell silent, staring at the dead fire. *Damn*, he thought, Caesar had to know about it. He would be sending his men to that fence, ready to pour through in silence, and they'd hit a stone wall instead. They'd have to hack their way through, every night noise like a clap of thunder. He sucked whistling breath through his teeth. "Tell me about it," he said.

The girl nodded. She told him about trailing Ross in town—and Gill sneered at her—and she told him about overhearing Ives say, "Let's get that damn fence up," and Gill fell back into deep silent thought, and she told about Ross telling Ives about bobwire and how Caesar knew about it, and how if Caesar was mad enough he'd make a big move and the Stanton men had to be ready. Gill heard it all, and his mind picked over it, concentrating only on what the girl was saying and what he had to do to counter it all, hearing nothing else, knowing nothing else. The girl went on, quietly, dutifully, taking Gill's alternating sneers and praise, his frowns and quick smiles, knowing that when it was over, he'd appreciate what she had done. He had to.

... When Laura had finished, she leaned back and waited. Gill turned toward her and said, "You figured that out all yourself? How to lead Ross to Caesar's, so they'd hold him off while you rode on up here?"

She nodded.

"Good girl," he said, and then he lapsed back into silence.

She flared with anger. "Thanks," she snapped, "Throw me a bone or a pitcher of milk while you're at it."

He grinned softly. "I mean it. You're a good girl. You've done a helluva job." She had. Ross was trussed up on Caesar's land, a prisoner until it was all over. There was only one flaw in their plans. The fence was being fixed. Then he let his grin open wide. The girl. All she had to do was retrace her steps back to Caesar, and let him know about the fence.

He said, "Laura, get back on your horse and tell Caesar about the fence."

The girl nodded. She had thought Caesar ought to know.

"But take your time," he said. "None of this racing up the slope business."

She cut in. "I had left Ross behind me. I couldn't see the sense in letting too much time go by."

He shook his head. "Ross isn't the only one. Don't hurry. We've got lots of time. Caesar isn't making his move until nightfall. Creep down the damn hill. Understand? I can't take, a chance of your being seen."

The girl nodded again. It didn't matter to her. She'd do as Gill said. Even if she didn't understand all the caution. She'd just do it.

"Tell Caesar the Broken S is going to repair that fence, maybe it's already repaired. Tell him to go back to his first plan. Just ride in through the center slot. Every man in the pack. Right down the middle," He nodded. That was the only ticket. No frills, no foolishness. Just a straight ride, burning, killing. It would sap Caesar a bit more this way, but it couldn't be helped. He had twenty-four men. The Stantons had ten, maybe eight.

He said, "The Stantons? They in jail?"

"That's what I hear."

"You didn't see them released this morning? Big Max didn't let them out?"

She shook her head. "Big Max won't be letting them out at all, for a while. He's on his way to Denver."

Gill exploded. "What?" he shouted. "What the hell are you saying?"

The girl was flustered. What did it matter? "I'm sorry," she said. "I meant to tell you. He was getting ready to leave when I rode out of Oxnard."

Gill bit his lip. The sheriff had a long trip. He wouldn't be moving too fast. "Did he plan to ride his dun?"

"Saddle pack and all."

Gill nodded. "That's better." The girl had whipped across the range to Caesar's on her quarter horse. The fight hadn't lasted more than five minutes in all. Then she had raced like a crazy fool to the foot of Wolfhead, and up the slope. Big Max had to go the long way round to Wolf Creek. The dun mare was a shambling creature. The saddle pack had to slow her up even more. Big Max had to feed her first. Gill still had time.

He said harshly, "All right, get going. But take your time."

Laura stood up, in the rear of the hollowed-out cave, a pale glow in the gray dimness. She moved slowly up to him. "You're not even going—to kiss—"

She swayed up close to him, and Gill thought grimly, *what a fool she is, to think I have to give in to her, just like that.* He started to say, "Don't be a kid—" when her hand brushed his chest, and the days and nights of longing for a woman's body turned Gill to heat and liquid. He swept the girl into his arms, his mouth searching and hungry. They stood locked in the dark cave, mouths bruising each other, bodies pressed close, and Gill was thinking, my God, my God, how could I have gone so long—

It was fierce and intense, and the cries that emanated from that cave were like the cries of animals in pain. But the pain—if it was pain—was like nothing compared to the pain of the girl, Maria, crouched outside, listening.

... Finally she stumbled back down the slope to her horse, and without much thought, without knowing why she was doing what she was doing, Maria took the horse to the foot of Wolfhead and around the back to the shaded side of the hill, and there she sat, eyes blinded, heart cleft. She couldn't go back to Caesar's, no, not after what she had seen there.

Caesar was a mad animal, a man planning to kill, this very night. She had stayed on at Caesar's because Caesar knew where Gill was. Well, so did she, so did she.

She sat, crushed, humiliated, wondering why. Why? Why had he done it? Couldn't he have waited, for her? Couldn't Gill have waited until it was over, this whole terrible bloody business on the range, and then come forward for her? She'd have waited. She'd have waited through a hundred such plans and plots and raids-to-be. Why had he done it? She didn't know. She had to know. The thought of his cheating was a dagger in Maria's heart. She had to know why he had done it. She crawled into deeper cover, waiting to hear the sound of the other woman's horse going back to Caesar, with news of destruction.

Gill said, "All right, honey, you'd better go now."

She nodded, brushing dust and dirt and dried leaves from her clothes. She didn't mind going. She could go, triumphant. She had done what she had set out to do, and she had received her reward. She could go easily, and wait easily, for the next time.

"Tell Caesar to ride straight through. You got it?"

She nodded again, unthinking.

"And you'll take your time?"

"I'll crawl," she said. She dismissed the message. It meant little to her. That was, once more, man's way of doing things. Men had their special provinces, painful provinces, where men shot each other or built fences so other men could tear them down. It was no business of hers. She had her man, and he wanted her to do him a favor. What the favor signified was none of her business; she'd have passed on any message Gill wanted: no matter whose death it entailed. She'd have crawled for the man, no matter what the reason.

She turned for a brief kiss, a light brushing of Gill's lips against hers, and then she went out of the cave, a slender, straight-shouldered woman who walked with unconscious, unashamed pride into the early afternoon sunlight.

Gill watched her as she mounted and moved painfully slowly—as he had ordered—and he smiled. Then, as she must have known he would, Gill passed immediately into one of those provinces Laura termed as man's. He looked out to his right flank, eyes searching the thin trail that crawled along Wolf Creek, headed north and west toward Denver, two hundred miles away. This was the way Max would come—unless, Gill thought, a chill striking to the marrow, unless he had come already, while he and Laura were satisfying themselves.

It didn't seem likely. Time was against it. Gill clicked off the minutes in his head. Big Max shouldn't be this far, yet. But even if he were, even if he had passed by, Gill knew it didn't matter. He'd wait another half hour, and then if Big Max didn't show, he'd go down the trail. He'd find track of Big Max's dun mare, if the sheriff had come by. If he had, Gill would follow swiftly. The overtaking of Big Max would be simple. If Big Max hadn't come by, Gill would wait, in ambush.

Gill nodded, eyes glued to the trail, and the half hour wasn't half gone when he saw his quarry lumbering up the trail—the heavy, graceless man and the heavy, graceless horse. Gill let the sheriff ride out ahead, and then he eyed the terrain below him: the twisting creek bed, the cottonwoods, dried out from the summer sun, spraying the banks with dead gold leaves and providing cover for any man who sought to use innocent trees for that purpose. Gill moved out of his cave, to his own horse in the thicket of evergreens, the smell of pine and fir a clean, cool smell. Gill clucked quietly to his horse and the animal, a big bay, moved down the slope, a well-rested, well-fed, obedient horse. The two melted swiftly into the cover of the slope; Gill's eyes were intent on Big Max and on the trail. He struck across the slope, headed down and angled ahead of Max, so that he would reach his ambush in plenty of time. The sniffing bird dog of a sheriff was riding simply, directly to his death.

Gill's sudden plunge down the slope had come as a surprise to Maria. She had waited at the foot of the shaded slope, asking herself the single question: why had Gill deceived her? And now that he was moving past her, a few hundred yards distant, she raised her head to call out. But she couldn't. It was as though the question couldn't bear asking. The answers to the question, as she thought them out, were all too painful to hear from Gill's lips. "I kissed Laura because I wanted to. I did it because I love her. I wanted her, damn it. Don't you understand?" There were others, all alike. None of them said, "I did it because I couldn't bear waiting any longer for you," which wouldn't have been good enough, but which would have been far better than the others. So Maria crouched, trembling, tiny, crushed, and let Gill move out ahead of her, and then, with the obsequiousness that killed desire in Gill, followed the man she still loved (and slightly hated). If she didn't follow, she'd never be able to ask the question. That was logical, Maria thought. Of course, even if she did follow, she doubted she would ask. She doubted she'd be able to say anything. But maybe he'd see her and understand. She followed, quietly, staying far behind, and hoping in her secret, fearful heart that Gill wouldn't see her at all. For—she realized—

seeing her was the same as her asking the question. He might smirk or sneer at her, laugh at her, mock her (for what, dear Lord, for loving him? for loving him that much she'd follow him even out of the arms of another woman?). Would he do anything else? Would he smile gravely at her, kiss her, fondle her, talk gently to her? She shook her head, tears staining her huge magnificent eyes. No, he wouldn't. It wasn't like Gill.

There was no purpose, then, in following him. She followed.

Big Max looked at his large, heavy watch. It was not quite two. He would have seven more riding hours, maybe eight if it didn't get too cold. He kept the dun mare at a controlled canter, not holding her too much in check, because that would strain the animal, but not allowing her free head, because that would reduce her to a pained trot in a few hours' time. They would ride this way, Big Max thought, an hour at a time, with five minutes for a blow, a drink, and a quick bite for the nag.

Occasionally Big Max heard a horseman crashing through the brush of Wolfhead, but he paid it no heed. A Crescent C man riding the extreme northwest boundary, he thought. It was a good sound, the sound of nearby human beings in what stretched out ahead as desolate wildness. And Big Max liked the noise for another reason. Joe Caesar had his men—for that was who it had to be, Max thought—performing the everyday chores of cattle ranching. Good. A man who checked fences wasn't a man likely to burn down his neighbor that same day. Not that Big Max figured Caesar to be a decent, law-abiding citizen. Not by a hundred and one miles. All Big Max wanted out of Joe Caesar was time. Fix your fences, Big Max thought. Tote your damn hay to your barns and to the winter quarters. Look for stray calves. Keep every hand working. Anything. Just so long as they didn't get on their horses to ride the Stantons down.

Then the sound was suddenly very close, just around the turn ahead of the sheriff. And when Gill said clearly, calmly, his bland face untroubled, "End of the line, Sheriff," Big Max knew that in a way he had been the wrong man for the job all along.

A man doesn't go into a grizzly's cave with a smile and a prayer. He goes in with a heavy caliber rifle, if he's damn fool enough to go in at all.

That was what Big Max thought, either then or maybe a little later. But he knew it didn't matter what he thought; all that mattered was that he had tried to win on hope and time, when what he needed all along was a brace of guns and the courage of a rustler.

He said, trying to keep alive because that was the only way he could lick these people, "Why don't you give yourself up, Gill?"

The big, blond man grinned and stepped out into the trail, the Navy Colt firm in his right fist. "That's very funny, Max. Get off your horse."

Max studied Gill. Gill was supposed to be the fastest man getting a gun out of a holster in the whole county. Max would never know.

Gill wasn't even taking that chance. The gun was already out, level and primed.

Big Max knew the odds. His own revolver lay at his right hip; a rifle was strapped behind him. It was as if both weapons were back in Oxnard, for all the good they'd do him. He could go for his hip while dismounting, but it would be all tangle and sluggishness, moving from that position. The only advantage he had would be the horse, getting behind her head and neck and trying to live through the first two shots Gill would pull off. By then, maybe, he'd have his own gun out and firing. Of course, the horse would be dead. Big Max shook his head. Right now the unfairest thing he could think of was that the only way he—Big Max—might live through the gun duel would be by letting the old dun mare get killed. It made Big Max very angry.

He got off the horse, hands away from his hip so Gill wouldn't shoot and maybe kill the horse. A man doesn't get much chance to do a decent thing in his lifetime, Max thought, and maybe nobody would ever think this was decent, but he didn't want the mare to be killed. It had suddenly become very important that the mare not be killed.

Max knew here was his inherent weakness. His softness. He liked other living beings, he liked them very much, and he respected them. He was a sheriff in a lawless Colorado county, and his philosophy of life—he thought with a certain amount of anger and a little pride—was live and let live. Wasn't that funny? Fury whiplashed him.

He said to Gill, who surely was going to kill him anyway, "How did you do it, back in Texas?"

Gill grinned again. "I cash in on other people's weaknesses, Max. That's all."

Max thought: a man lives a certain number of years. There was no way you could avoid the end. All you could do was postpone it. Instead of fifty years, it might be sixty. How important was that? He tried to tell himself it wasn't very important, but he knew he was lying. He said, "Tell me about it," knowing that he was trying to stretch out that period of living, even if by another few minutes.

Yet there was more than that.

Big Max had become involved, through young Ross, in a killing, and the search for justice. It was Big Max's job to keep pushing that search, for as long as he was alive. On a practical level, it didn't matter, because Max knew—now that Gill had done the killing, and this knowledge was wasted, out here on Wolf Creek trail, all alone. But on another level, an intangible level that Big Max could not explain because he did not quite understand it, it mattered greatly that he continue the search.

Gill shrugged. He said, "Go and take your left hand, Max, and reach over and remove your gun from your holster. Make sure the barrel faces straight down. If it moves up, even by accident, I'll kill you. Then toss the gun over here."

The sheriff looked down at his hip and then watched, with detached interest, as his left hand crept to the holster and with thumb and index finger removed the .44, swung it back and then looped it underhanded toward Gill. Gill kept his eyes on Max, and with his right foot kicked the gun into the brush.

The man seemed to relax then, and Big Max thought angrily that a sheriff ought to carry a hideout gun, a one-shot derringer, anything at all. But it just wasn't like him. Guns were useless. That was very funny, too, he thought furiously.

Gill said, "Ed Stanton got out of bed in that hotel room back in Texas, and he was mumbling a lot of gibberish. But I've always listened to people when they talked. The gibberish amounted to his being sorry for insulting that woman in the street. He said he wanted to apologize. He was very, very drunk, of course. So I led him outside and gave him a little push and told him to apologize to the sheriff, to Old Man Ross, he'd take care of passing it on. Meanwhile I swapped guns with him, and got on Ed's horse and took off just behind him, telling him every so often what he was doing. He staggered along—it was two blocks in all, and he must have fallen on his face a half-dozen times in the dark—and finally he got to the sheriff's door. All the time, of course, I knew what I was going to do. It was a cinch."

Big Max thought of Jake Ross, the bullet wound in his eye and the back of his head, and how young Ross had led him to believe the bullet entered the eye first. But it hadn't. He said, "You went around to the side window?"

Gill nodded, enjoying himself. "It was in the cards, I guess. Ever since the ride up from Stockton, I'd hated the Stantons. They weren't a damn bit better than me, maybe not as good. But they had cooked up a deal with the boss, a dirty little money-making deal on every cow they got up to Gore, if they got them up by a certain day. The money was going to buy a cattle ranch. So I attached myself to them. I worked like a dog, I tell you, Max, I worked like a dog. Nobody worked harder. Nobody could have."

The sheriff said drily, "Nobody had the idea you had, either."

Gill flushed. He was quiet for a minute. Then he said, "You know,

Sheriff, that's exactly right. I had the idea ever since I can remember. Cashing in. And even in the beginning, when there wasn't anything in it for me but maybe a job with the Stantons, I kept pushing it, knowing somehow it would lead to big things. It did, all right." He chuckled. "Ed Stanton wandered into the sheriff's office, and I fired the revolver I was carrying—his, of course. Then I pushed his white horse toward him and told him to get on the damn beast and ride on back to the hotel. He did, and we did, and then I routed out Orville, and we rode the hell out of there."

The sheriff frowned, staring at the ground. "How come," he asked, "you told them it happened right after you boys got slapped around?"

Gill laughed. "I was dealing with drunken frightened men, Sheriff. I figured that if I was going to tell them a story—as I had to—I'd better make sure I stayed away from the truth, just in case it reminded them of what really had happened. I didn't figure they'd ever really know— that's how far gone they were, especially Ed—but I didn't want to talk about going on back to the hotel and stir up their memories too much."

"That's why?"

Gill mused for a minute. Then he said, "You're a shrewd man, Max. No, that wasn't the only reason." He spread his legs, making himself a little more comfortable. They were two men on the trail, talking to pass the time. That's how Gill made it look. He said, "I figured I could tell Ed Stanton he'd been slapped and kicked, and he didn't like it, so he marched himself around and shot down the man who'd just kicked him. That's pretty bad, but maybe a man could carry that around, killing a man a minute after the man's busted him up a little. But if I ever told Ed Stanton he'd gone back to the hotel and had a drink or six or seven, and two hours after he'd been insulted, he got out of bed and quietly walked to the sheriff's office and killed the sheriff, well, that wouldn't have set right. That would be cold, premeditated murder, wouldn't it, Max?" Gill didn't wait for the sheriff to nod. He said, "Ed Stanton wouldn't have been able to carry such a story. It would have bitten at him too much. He'd have had to investigate such a story. And I couldn't afford him investigating. So I handed him the other—a whopping lie, all the way—and he bought it."

"You took a helluva chance, you know."

Gill shrugged. His body was elastic, power flowing beneath the big frame. "That's the way I used to play it."

"You're a liar." Big Max said, surprised at his own words.

Gill smiled thinly. "That's right, Sheriff. Talk big. You won't ever have another chance."

"You are a liar, you know," Big Max said quietly. "You didn't take a chance at all. Nobody would see you in that town. The gun wasn't yours. The man wasn't you. All you'd ever have to say was you didn't do it— and it would be pretty easy proving you didn't. You'd say you ran out after Ed trying to stop him, but you were too late. That is, if anybody caught you in the street."

Gill said evenly, "And if they caught us running out of town? You think a posse would have waited for explanations?" He snorted. "The hell they would. They'd have hanged the three of us."

Max knew Gill was right. He had hoped to rile up the man, for what foolish reason he had no idea. He tried it the other way. He said, "You were a braver man then than you are today, Gill." And that was the truth. The boy Gill had planned to cash in on the Stantons' weaknesses, but it took guts to run it through. There was a crawling loathing in Big Max for such courage, for the uses of such courage, but he had to admit it was courage. Now Gill lay in hiding, waiting for the Stantons to go to jail. Now he waited in ambush, to shoot down a thick-witted sheriff.

Gill said, "Of course I was. I was also a stupider man. I know better today. Today I don't take those chances. I don't have to." He drew a deep breath, a man expanding on his fortunes. "When the Stantons go to Texas, I take over the Broken S." Gill wanted to go on and tell Max about how Caesar was to make him full partner in the Crescent C, and how Caesar, therefore, had to go, too. But that wouldn't prove anything. The sheriff would be dead when Gill made good those boasts. That was too bad, Gill thought. He'd have liked to tell somebody, so somebody would know what he planned to do and then watched enviously while he did it.

Max said, "You've forgotten one thing."

"What's that?" Gill said, surprise at his eyebrows.

"Ross."

Gill laughed.

"Ross," Max insisted. "Ross will kill you. Ross will find out about the business in Texas. He'll kill you for sure."

Gill laughed harder. "Ross," he said, "is lying in Joe Caesar's barn, all tied up nice as you please like a cow for branding. Ross, if he tries to cause any trouble tonight, will be dead as—as you're going to be, Sheriff."

Big Max stared at the man. He knew that Gill was telling the truth. If Gill said Ross was in Joe Caesar's barn, trussed up, then it was so. It didn't seem likely that Gill could know this, but he obviously did. The sheriff said, "You'd better check on Ross, Gill. I still think he'll kill you."

Gill said, "What makes you think so, Sheriff?" He was pleased by the conversation. Prolonging it in this manner added to the joy of killing Big

Max.

Max said, "He's the fastest man with a gun I ever saw."

Instantly Gill's face darkened. It was as if the sheriff had touched the tenderest nerve in Gill's body. The man looked like a thundercloud. The sheriff was amazed. Gill was vanity, pure hundred per cent vanity. No man could draw a gun quicker. He wouldn't stand for it.

Max said quickly. "Helluva man with the ladies, too."

Gill frowned more deeply. He said, "You know, Max, you're a smart devil. I wish I were as smart as you. Why, with your brains, I'd go a long way." He raised his Navy Colt. "You dirty bastard," he said, viciously, and he shot the sheriff through the head.

Maria looked up at the sun, nearly directly overhead, canted slightly to the west. She thought, automatically, it must be two o'clock. The men at the ranch will be wondering about their chow. She kept staring at the sun, her eyes blinded by it, and even when she finally lowered and closed them, a dozen black-rimmed yellow balls burned through her eyelids and danced before her.

Then she swung her cream-colored horse—one of Caesar's horses actually, she knew—back onto the trail along Wolf Creek. She laid a trembling hand on the horse's mane, and she listened very hard. Gill's horse had gone. She cocked her head and brushed the soft dark hair from her ears so that she might hear better. There was no sound. Gill had returned up the slope to his hideout cave on Wolfhead. He had passed her minutes earlier, while her horse had been standing stock-still above the bank and above the trail, in the cover of trees, Maria's hand pressed to her mouth, her teeth dug into the flesh, and no sound tearing from her throat. She had thought dully: all I wanted to do was see him, so that he might see me and love me again. That's all, dear God, I didn't want anything else.

But she had seen much more. She had seen Gill kill Big Max and cover the sheriff's body with dead brown limbs and leaves, and then Gill had ridden by.

She shivered. His face. He had ridden past her, tall and erect in the saddle, broad-shouldered and graceful, his long, lean legs hugging the horse's ribs, his bronze hands lying limply on the saddle horn, a purposeful man who had just done the most terrible thing one man could do to another. But his face! *Gill had been smiling.* The image chilled her heart. Not the sneering nasty look you might expect on the face of a killer. Not the crafty, tight, thin-lipped smile of a man who had been determined to do this job no matter how terrible it might be, and who had done it, the thin grin belying the fat chalk-white fear within.

No, it was nothing like that. You could understand that, even if you couldn't understand the killing itself.

He had been smiling softly, gently. The way he smiled when he kissed her or when they lay together, when he stroked her cheek or fondled her breasts. The same smile, not a whit different.

Maria rode back along the Wolf Creek trail that led into the valley and across the meadowland. It led many ways, to the Broken S, to the Crescent C, across the open middle-ground that lay between them, split by hedges and fences, and to Oxnard, beyond. She could go any of these ways, once she burst out of the cottonwood cover. None of them was any good anymore. She could go many ways and many miles, but what was the use? Her hand drifted uncertainly, to her blouse, to the gracefully modeled Frontier Colt that the sheriff had tossed to Gill, and Gill had kicked into the brush. Maria had got down from her horse and retrieved the gun after Gill had gone by. She smiled gently. Not to use on Gill, though the thought had crossed her mind. She didn't think she could ever do violence to Gill, because—and this was one of the most awful parts of the whole day that was filling with awful parts—Maria still loved Gill.

But she was a frightened woman, alone, out on a trail far from where she ought to have been, on a stolen horse, headed nowhere. The gun had reassured her, then, lying there quietly in the brush, half-covered, the sheriff's gun that the sheriff had not used, that the sheriff probably never liked to use. The sheriff had been a decent man, Maria knew suddenly. Never before had she thought of him one way or the other. When he had come to Caesar's, looking for Gill, yesterday, she had resented and feared him. But now she saw him only as he had been, a man doing a duty that others felt strange, repugnant, and that even he probably felt alien, but which he followed faithfully—to his death.

She had his gun, a decent man's gun, and this, too, was reassuring. She touched it again, lightly, inside her loose blouse.

Maria wandered her horse away from Wolfhead, in the direction of the Broken S. She knew that if she wanted to cross the range, she would have to steer away from Joe Caesar's spread. So she kept the horse moving, and soon she was at the rear fence, behind the Broken S, not sure of what she was doing or why, but merely doing it. She saw a fence with white rags wrapped about it, and swiftly she surmised that the fence had been marked by one of the Stanton men to be repaired. She rode up to it and saw the loose rails. She got down from her horse and lowered two rails to the ground and got back on her horse and stepped the horse through. Then, because she was a neat woman, moving automatically, she got back down again, replaced the rails as they had been, and mounted once more. She rode at a tired trot across the Broken S.

It was Ives, the stubby foreman, who saw her first. He had been riding the range all that day, studying the terrain, seeing it really for the first time, so that he might place his men to do the Crescent C hardcases the worst damage.

He spotted this lone rider, on a horse he didn't recognize, and he drew his .44 and yelled, "Hey, you."

Maria saw Ives, saw his hostility, his drawn weapon, and she shrank back into the saddle. She thought: someday I shall erase this entire day from my mind. All of it.

She halted her cream-colored horse and said weakly, "It's—all right. I'm not—" She didn't say anything else, because she didn't know what to say. It was a day when men rode and fought each other with fists and boots, and when men cheated their loved ones, and when men killed and smiled afterwards. It was not a day for soft, weak people. She thought of Ross, suddenly, and somehow he fitted into that latter category. He was lying, now, in Caesar's barn, helpless. Like herself.

Ives rode up and said, "What are you doing out here?" His eyes flashed anger and suspicion, and she half-expected him to swear at her or strike her.

She said, "I don't know," and she tried to smile, but it broke in the middle and came out in a tiny sob.

He frowned then, a confused man, knowing he had terribly important and difficult details to work out now, and later, but unable to rid himself of an uneasy thought that this girl's obvious unhappiness had an importance of its own that could not be ignored.

He said, "Why aren't you back at the Crescent C?" The very words *Crescent C* brought iron back to Ives' voice.

The girl trembled and said, "I can't."

Ives said, "Look here. You belong on Caesar's side. Get back there. Did he send you over?"

She shook her head, wordlessly, her huge eyes staring at Ives and wondering when the lightning would strike.

Ives looked around, but there were no riders nearby. He shrugged his shoulders, wishing Orville Stanton were here, or even Ed. He said, "Come along, Miss," and he started riding for the headquarters, the girl tagging behind. It would take time but it had to be settled, he could see. The girl lay somewhere near hysteria, she was so frightened. It was the wrong day, but there was nothing he could do about it....

He pushed open the door to the office, and she followed him quietly. He said, "Tell me what's eating you."

She shook her head again, not at what he had said, but only at what she knew. There were certain things, dark and terrible, that she could not tell him, even though—in his words—they were eating her. She said, "Ross—is hurt."

Ives looked at her queerly, "What's that to me?"

She shook her head and said, "I don't know. I thought—"

"What's wrong with him?"

"Caesar's men beat him up."

Instantly Ives was alert. "When?"

When? she thought. Long, long ago, before she had lost Gill and Gill had killed Big Max.

"Around noon, I think."

Ives stared through the window, toward the Crescent C spread. It was early afternoon, now. "What happened?"

... She told him, finally. About Ross, and Laura, riding up, and how Laura had egged on Caesar—she didn't know why—and how they had talked about bobwire and how Ross must be siding you people—

"Then they fought?"

"Yes."

"Who?"

Who? All of them, she thought. "First it was Ross and Caesar. Then it was Ross and Stucka and Hallahan, and then finally it was Ross and Whitaker. Maybe they're others, too. I don't know."

"Ross hurt bad?"

She said, "I don't know. He was—lying very still. They carried him into the barn. Whitaker told somebody to tie him up because Ross was strong as a bull, Whitaker said."

Ives nodded slowly. The man wouldn't likely have been hurt too bad. Knocked cold, no doubt. Ives tried to dismiss the thought. It didn't matter, he told himself. What the hell was Ross to him? But it wasn't dismissing very easily.

"Why are you telling me all this?" he asked harshly.

The girl shrank back again, fear in her eyes. "I—don't know," she said. "Caesar said Ross was siding you."

"Well, he wasn't," Ives snapped. The damned manhunter was buying himself trouble, all over the range. "He and Big Max took the Stantons away. That's how much Ross was siding us."

The girl gasped out then, a torn animal cry, and Ives looked at her queerly once more. There was something wrong with the girl. Her eyes were like a slaughtered cow's eyes, the whites straining to burst out of their sockets. He said, "Wait here," and he stepped outside and called, "Adams, Jensen, come here. On the quick."

He went back to the terror-struck girl. She was twisting her mouth into words, but all Ives caught was, "Big Max—"

He said, "What about Big Max?"

The girl fainted.

The three men stood around the sofa where the girl lay, her eyes open once again, some of the strain gone from the edges of her mouth, but undoubtedly still a terribly frightened girl.

Ives said, "What do you want us to do? Get a doctor?"

Maria shook her head. There was nothing anybody could do.

Adams, a tall skinny man with a shock of red hair and wide cuplike ears, said, "Miss, we'll ride you into town, but not until tomorrow. We can't today."

Jensen, even shorter than Ives, and very thin, an elf of a man, with a deep gravelly voice, said, "She can share a room with the cook's wife. It'll be all right."

Ives said, again, "What do you want us to do?" The thought of Ross was rubbing at him. She didn't really expect them to ride on the Crescent C, over Ross.

"Just let me stay here," the girl whispered.

"No," Ives said, "you can't." The girl would be in the way, just when Caesar would be striking. It wouldn't be fair to her, or to them. "This place won't be safe." He looked at the girl. "Is Joe Caesar hitting us tonight?"

She said, "I—don't know. I think he may." She tried to remember what she had heard. Nothing, actually. Just whispers from the men as they moved about the ranch, and a restless uneasy spirit that hovered over everything. "Ross seemed to think he was. He said something about you people having an arsenal waiting."

Ives smiled thinly. Ross was playing it the best he could, for the Stantons. "Sure," he said, "a whole army."

Maria said, "None of the men took off today. That was unusual."

Ives whistled. He turned to Jensen. "I told you, Jenny, I didn't smell the usual Crescent stink in Oxnard this morning."

Then Maria remembered the fence, how Gill and Laura had talked about a fence. She said, "The fence you're fixing, is it the one behind the spread?" She waved a hand. "With the handkerchiefs on it?"

Ives stared at her. "What are you talking about? What fence with handkerchiefs?"

She said, "The one directly behind the building, straight back. With the loose rails."

Ives frowned, and then he walked to the far wall. He wished Orville Stanton were here. Ives didn't know of such a fence. He said, "Adams, ride back there and check the fences. Make it plenty quick. Then come on back here." Adams moved swiftly, in angles and lines, a loose-jointed man. But his hand was near his hip, Maria noted, where a gun—another terrible gun—lay, butt up.

Ives said to Jensen, then, "Do you think we can ride over there?"

"Where?"

"To Caesar's."

Jensen stared at his foreman. He said, "I've been wrestling with the same thing myself, Boss."

Ives said shortly, "Who won?"

Jensen smiled, a humorless movement of his lips. "I sure as hell didn't."

Ives said, "You're willing to ride over there with me?"

Jensen said, "Seems like that's what a decent man ought to do."

"Even today, with what may happen tonight?"

Jensen said, "Seems like that's exactly why. Anybody could ride over there if he's going to get smiled at when he arrives."

Ives said, "We're a pair of crazy buggers, aren't we?"

Jensen said, "We sure are."

Ives said, "What do we do about the girl?"

Maria stared at the two men.

Jensen said, "How about sending her in with one of the men? Getting her set up at the hotel in town, say?"

Ives nodded. They would be short another man, for a few hours. Yet it had to be a good man, a man who would know what to do if he ran into trouble. Ives said, "Think Adams would mind?"

Jensen grinned. "Mind escorting this here gal around? Hell's fire, I'd do it myself if I didn't have a more interesting chore."

Ives went to the window. Adams was drumming his way back. Adams was a good man, without an ounce of fire, but straight and steady.

Adams walked through the doorway and into the front sitting room and through it into the office. He looked down at the girl. She was resting quietly, her eyes staring at the ceiling, but without that terrible bursting strain about them, quiet eyes now, deep-set, but lusterless.

He said, "The girl's right. There's a fence needing repair pretty bad. Marked neat as you please with two white handkerchiefs."

Ives grunted. It must have been one of the men riding range who had noticed it and marked it, and then forgot about reporting it. Or one of the Stantons, intending to deal with it later. He gave his head a short, sharp shake, not quite sure he had added it all up correctly.

Jensen said, "What's wrong with the fence?"

"Two rails sawed through, then loosely wired together."

"*Sawed?*" Ives said. "*Sawed?*"

"Reckon so. You can see the grain all dusted down. It didn't break by itself, I'll tell you."

Ives breathed, "Gill," and the other two men nodded, grimly, understanding.

"Gill, by God," the foreman said, and even the girl stirred. Sawed out the rails for Caesar to use. Must have done it a couple of weeks back. Why, nobody ever rides those fences. We can see them from here. Naturally we'd know if a fence was in bad repair. But not if a man secretly sawed it loose and then replaced it somehow."

Jensen said, "Still want to make that trip that afternoon?"

Ives said, "Damn right I do. Damn right," and Adams said, "What trip?"

They told Adams, and they sent him back toward town with the girl, and told him to settle her and ride on back. Adams grumbled, because he was embarrassed with his task, and because he felt the other two were cutting him out of a tougher, more interesting task. None of the three men liked Ross, none of them trusted the man, but Ross had stuck his head into a bind, and he had done it apparently for them.

They probably wouldn't get very far, riding across the open middle land, but they had to try it. There was no war as yet, maybe there wouldn't be any. Maybe it wouldn't be dangerous at all.

Adams left then, with the girl, still palely quiet, frightened, but the jagged edge of hysteria smoothed off. She spoke to neither Ives nor Jensen, but she made a tiny smile at them, and then her hand crept to her blouse front where—inside—the sheriff's gun lay, unknown to any but herself. She let Adams lead her to the cream-colored horse, and toward Oxnard.

CHAPTER TEN

The smell of fresh-mowed hay tickled Ross's nostrils, and he opened his eyes. Dull pain was in his head and other parts of his body, but the darkness of the barn was soothing. He understood where he was, and why. He flexed the muscles of his wrists, not even sure where they were, and he felt wire eat into the skin. His fingers opened and shut, to circulate the blood, and then he realized his hands were lashed behind his back. He tried to flex his ankles but he could barely move them, so tight were they bound. He let his mind direct nerve-ends down his body, searching for other facts of his imprisonment, but there were no other facts. It was only his wrists and ankles that were bound. Nothing else. He grinned behind closed lips. What else mattered? He was trussed up and would remain trussed up for quite some time.

Then a voice nearby said, "What's so funny, Ross?"

Ross moved his head, and the dull pain tightened its grip at the back of his neck where Whitaker had clubbed him with his hammer-head fists. Ross said, "You. You're funny. You and the rest of Caesar's men."

The man stood over Ross. He was one of the men who had come from Ross's flank, a bullet-headed man, big and square-shouldered, heavy-chested. Ross said, "You're Hallahan or Stucka?"

The man nodded. "Hallahan," he said. He looked down at the battered manhunter. He grinned thinly. "You take an awful whipping."

"Thanks," Ross said shortly. "How many of you was it, after Caesar went out?"

"Three," Hallahan said wickedly. "And if you'd handled us—though God knows how you could have—there were twelve more just waiting for their licks."

Ross lay quiet. He was flat on his back, on thin straw, with bales of hay piled all around him. His wrists were tied behind him, under him. His ankles were wired together, his legs straight. He could move his legs, bend them and unbend them at the knees if he so chose. A man with a gun stood over him. His own Colt Walker lay out on the grass somewhere, or else had been picked up, turned over admiringly by some Crescent C hand, and quickly sheathed. He was a man completely helpless. He saw no way to remedy this, certainly not in the immediate future. And the immediate future was the only time he had left to do any good in the brewing war. Either he could get up and could help, or else Caesar would hit the Stantons' spread and mop it up tonight. He wondered what time it was.

He said, "Build me a smoke, Hallahan."

Hallahan stared at the man, flat on his back. He grunted and reached to his back pocket for the makings. Ross watched carefully. The man turned his left side toward Ross when he did this, his right hip carefully pulled back so that his gun was farthest removed from Ross. Ross shook his head briefly. They had put a good man on him. There was no doubt about it. He wondered whether Caesar had anything but good men.

Hallahan scratched a horny thumbnail against a match and lit the tight cigarette. Then he shoved it into Ross's face with his left hand, his right hand at his hip.

And Ross saw what he wanted to see. Excitement kicked up through his chest.

He sucked on the cigarette and said through muffled lips, "Thanks. That's it, I guess."

Hallahan removed the barely smoked cigarette and ground it out on his heel. Then he flicked it through the open door. Outside, Ross looked at the square of shimmering sunlight. It was still early afternoon. There would be five or six hours before Caesar would give his men the order to ride.

Hallahan watched Ross. Then he said, "I don't think you're going to need any more cigarettes." He moved away from Ross, to the doorway, and he sat there, across the doorway where he could see what was going outside, and still keep an eye on Ross. Also, he had removed himself from Ross's reach. The man was a caution, Ross admitted. He had to have Hallahan back, within reach. Otherwise he was licked.

He wondered what it would mean, being licked, not being able to free himself. What would happen to him after Caesar made his raid and burned out the Broken S cowhands?

He said to Hallahan, in the doorway, "What do you reckon Caesar's going to do with me?"

The puncher turned his bullet head slowly. He looked at Ross with indolent eyes, yellow-flecked and lazy. He said, "I wouldn't know."

"Think he'll kill me?"

The man started to shake his head and then thought better of it. "I wouldn't know," he said again. There was an edge to his voice.

Ross said, "Why wouldn't he?"

The cowpuncher got up and moved one step inside the barn and said mildly, "Why don't you stow it?"

Ross said, "Seems to me if Caesar was going to kill me, he'd have done it already. How does that strike you?"

Hallahan stared down at Ross. He said, malice in his words, "Maybe he will, when he comes to."

Ross laughed bitterly. He hadn't thought of that. He had knocked Caesar cold. Maybe the man was just pulling out of it now, angry clear to the bone. Still, he'd have to be the kind of man who could take such an anger and hold it long enough to dig his gun out, and walk from wherever he was to where Ross was, and then shoot down a defenseless man. Once more, it meant giving Caesar a tag, a label that did not seem to fit the man.

Ross said, "I don't think your boss is a killer. What do you think?"

Hallahan said, "I don't think."

"Oh, come now," Ross said, "sure you do."

Hallahan turned back to the doorway. He said over his left shoulder, "Shut up, Ross." He sounded like a tired man, a man with a slow-burning grievance. Good, Ross thought, he was starting to irritate the man. He had to bring Hallahan back to him.

Ross said, "Let's say he doesn't kill me. What then?"

The muscles in Hallahan's solid square back twitched beneath his checkered shirt. Then he turned, and Ross knew the man had decided it was easier to talk than to be needled this way. He said indifferently, "Let you ride, probably."

Yes, Ross thought. That was exactly what would happen. It was reason, he knew, laced through with hope, but not just crazy hope. It made sense. Caesar would let him go, finally. Why not? The deed would be done.

He said, thinking aloud, "He'll let me ride because I've really been witness to nothing."

"Something like that," Hallahan said.

"Caesar will say the Broken S men started the whole shebang and he just had to fight them off and burn them out. Like they were wolves."

"They are," Hallahan said.

"Big Max won't buy that story," Ross said.

"So what?" the cowhand said, shrugging. "Big Max ain't so big out here."

Ross fell silent, to absorb it all. Big Max was important. Hallahan was whistling in a graveyard there. Big Max would dig it all out, the tracks of Caesar's men riding across to the Broken S, not the other way around. Big Max would have it all figured out. It might take some time, but if he came back with his army from Denver, he'd be able to take his time without much fear of anybody stopping him.

And then Ross would be where he started, he realized suddenly. He'd have the Stantons; he'd still need Gill to clear up the stories. Ross shook his head. It wasn't that easy, returning to his own private war. Caesar was riding him out of the big fight. By the time Ross would be ready to pitch in again, it would be over. The idea of Caesar's men stampeding across no-man's graze and onto the Broken S, guns chattering, kept nibbling away at Ross.

He said to Hallahan, "How come you men are so goddam greedy?"

Hallahan looked at him, surprised. "Who's greedy?"

"Caesar, for one. Isn't this place big enough? What's he want the Stantons' spread, too?"

"Caesar was here first."

Ross said angrily, "The hell he was. The Comanches were here first. Or maybe the Cheyennes or the Arapahos. Caesar stole the land from them to begin with."

Hallahan snorted, "Indian lover."

"He's a greedy bastard, that's all he is," Ross said. "What the hell does he need another five thousand acres for?"

"I wouldn't know," Hallahan said evenly. "That's Caesar's business."

And Ross said wickedly, "Your blood, though."

Hallahan snarled, "Shut up!"

Ross knew he had reached the man. "Yours and the rest of the poor cruds who sweat so Caesar can steal some more land."

Hallahan walked over. "I told you to shut up," he said, his mouth tight as a hawk's.

"Sure," Ross said, "you don't want to hear it. You want to be working for your found and getting a day off"—(*now what the hell*, Ross wondered, *why did that make him jump so?*)—"and get drunk or laid or a pile of money set aside so you can buy yourself a couple of sections someplace. That's what you want. But you're not going to get it. You're going to get a six-foot plot, and a hole in your head, that's what you're going to get. You and three or four or a dozen more men. You're a damn fool, Hallahan."

Hallahan leaned over and slapped Ross, and Ross drew his tied legs back, bent at the knees, and shot them forward, as hard as he could, catching Hallahan around the ankles and toppling the man upon him. Ross rolled over and ground his shoulder into Hallahan's eye, and then he flipped himself so he lay on Hallahan, Ross's back against the Crescent C man's chest, Ross's bound hands, fingers clawing, at Hallahan's pistol belt. But not at the right side, where the .44 was sheathed in oil-slick leather. At the left side.

And then his fingers touched the cold metal, while Hallahan pushed big hands against Ross's back, and Ross floundered forward, landing on his hip and then rolling onto his back again, his hands beneath him.

Between his clawing fingers, however, were Hallahan's wire cutters.

The Crescent C man cursed and panted, standing over Ross, his .44 in white-fingered grip, hammer back. Ross stared at the open bore of the gun, and he knew death was as far away as Hallahan's temper was from murderous fury. Maybe a hair. No farther.

Hallahan said, "You want me to use it? I will, you know." His left eye was red and swelling shut, his chest heaving like a mad bull's. "Just give me a chance," he said, "and I'll use it. I'd just love to use it on you."

Ross said, quietly, "Save it for the Stanton boys." He had to keep talking, move the man's mind away from what had happened, what Ross had planned on happening ever since Hallahan lit him that cigarette and shoved his left hip toward Ross, and his right away from him. One hip held the dangerous gun. The other held a cowman's usual kit: knife and wire cutters, for handling baled hay or any shucked wired grain. Most cowmen carried such kits, barely noticed on their hips, neat and light, tilted up and out because of the sagging weight on the other hip where a man usually carried his revolver. Ross had seen the kit and he had known then, that this was the hope and the out. It also could have meant—and it still might have meant—Ross's death.

So he said again, "Forget it, Hallahan. It was a damn fool trick. Save your gun for the Broken S. You'll need it."

Hallahan said, "Aw, the hell with it," and Ross sensed a desperation in the man's voice. Hallahan walked back to the doorway, wanting to be away from this fighting fool who tried crazy things like wrestling a man who had a gun, even though his own wrists and legs were bound. Then Hallahan turned, suspicion making his eyes crafty. Maybe Ross's wrists weren't bound that tight. The man had been flexing them before, straining at the wire. He said to Ross, "Roll over," and Ross knew panic like a sledge in his chest. He pushed his hands into the thin straw, pushed and prayed again, hoping he could bury the cutters.

Hallahan walked close, but not that close. He snapped impatiently, "Roll over, I said." And he reached out his foot gingerly, and prodded Ross in the ribs.

Ross thought: here goes, and he flipped himself, over and as far from where he had been as possible.

Hallahan stared at the rolling squirming figure. He shook his head. Ross was helpless, all right. He bent down, watching Ross's legs to make sure the man didn't lash out again. Then he put a hand on the wire and tugged. It was tight as a drum head. The flesh at the wrists was puffy and purple. Only the fingers waved free, but they were swelling, too, blue-tinged. Ross could bring his fingers together and separate them, but that was absolutely all he could do. From shoulder to finger tip, his arms were locked hopelessly together, just by the wire that cut in above the knobby wrist bones.

Hallahan grunted, and walked back to the doorway. He said, "Don't ever try a stunt like that again." He felt a grudging admiration for the manhunter. He had fought three men—no, four, he had first licked Caesar—and looked then as though he'd have fought four more or forty. Now he had tried to tackle a man with a gun, even though he was trussed up. Hallahan shook his head. He was a man to ride with, this crazy manhunter. For a brief fleeting moment, Hallahan wanted to be out of the whole mess. Then his mouth clipped shut again, the hawk's mouth that Ross had seen before, and he stared out at the range.

And suddenly be cocked his head forward, his body bent at the waist, tensed, coiled, like a striking beast. Ross heard a horse gallop past, and words rolled into the open air.

"Broken S men. Raiding. Raiding."

Hallahan plunged through the barn door, and then stopped. He came back and looked at Ross, a confused man now, not knowing where his immediate duty lay.

He rushed over to Ross and he kicked him savagely in the ribs, the air whooshing out of Ross's lungs and making him gasp hungrily for breath. "No tricks," Hallahan said fiercely, "no tricks now, you foxy bastard. You move from here, and I swear I'll kill you." Then he ran out, his hand at his pistol butt.

Ross heard Hallahan yell, "Where are they?" and another man said, "Straight up the middle," and Hallahan said, voice fading as the horse raced from the barn, "How many did you say?"

Then there was quiet around the barn, only a faint steady drumming as horses beat the earth, driving toward the center graze where mulberry hedges stood erect and wispy but where no man dared move in certain directions. Men had so dared. Broken S men. Ross could not believe it. It was foolhardy, stupid. It was more than that. It was the signal for war, war that had lain so close to the surface anything might have blown it, but until now nothing had.

It was worse than that, too. It would wipe Big Max out of the picture. Now the sheriff could no longer ride back and start digging up facts. The facts he'd find would not be the ones he or any sensible man would have expected. Instead of showing Caesar's men driving on the Broken S, he'd piece together the unmistakable tracks of Stanton men cutting across from their own spread toward Caesar's. Without a doubt, the initiative, the aggression lay with the Broken S.

Still, Ross thought, he was damn glad the poor fools had tried it. It gave him the breather he needed, time to try to grapple with his wire with no Crescent C man on top of him, gun cocked.

Ross rolled back to where he had been before Hallahan made him turn over. His fingers dug under the straw and clumsily held the cutters. He drew his legs up behind him, bent back at the knees, heels raised as high as Ross could force them. He lay on his side, his back to the rear so nobody would see what he was doing if anybody chanced a quick look-in. Ross would be there, lying uncomfortably on his side, but still a captive.

Ross's fingers opened the cutters. Then he put pressure on them, forcing the jaws against the heels of his shoes and working up until the wire was snagged. He closed the cutters with his bloodless fingers.

Nothing.

Sweat started to form under the wire on Ross's wrists. He felt a fury inside that made his fingers tremble weakly. He tried again to work up enough strength to close the cutters on the wire and cut through. He couldn't do it. He just didn't have the power in his fingers. Now the sweat dripped into Ross's eyes, scalding him. He took a deep breath, dropped the cutters and manipulated his fingers. The wire cut cruelly even while blood spurted hungrily to the finger tips. The more still Ross kept his hands, the less blood flowed through, and the weaker his fingers got. But the more active he was, the more blood he forced through, the more painful was the cutting of the wire around his wrists. The pain had a liquefying quality to it, a watery weakening that infuriated Ross and made him feel like a child. He stopped moving his fingers for thirty long seconds (*while outside*, he thought, *Broken S men were riding to their doom*), and then he placed one of the iron handles of the cutters against his right palm. He pressed himself to his right side and then over onto his back with his left hand directly beneath his buttocks and his legs drawn up. The weight of Ross's own body, lying against his hands, closed the cutters.

The wire sang gently, and then it parted.

Ross stood up on wobbly legs. He set the cutters on the floor and bent down and fitted the wire of his wrists inside the cutting jaws. Then with his foot, he pressed down on the cutters. Once more, the wire sang. Once more the pressure eased. Wire fell quietly to the straw floor.

Ross was freed.

Ives had sat his dappled gray at the extreme edge of the Stantons' spread. He had built himself a cigarette and said, between slow-drawn puffs, "All right, Jenny, here we are. What next?"

Jensen stared across the hedge rows. In front of them was the Crescent C. There wasn't a rider in sight. A mile and a half away were the Crescent C buildings: bunkhouses, headquarters, barn, sheds, corrals. But nothing at all between the hedge rows and those buildings. No men, no cows.

Jensen said, "He's finally shifted his hay to winter quarters."

Ives nodded. "You read it the way I read it?"

"Sure as hell means business tonight," Jensen said. The men knew that Caesar didn't want to leave his precious hay out on the range or any place nearby, where the fight might reach out and fire it.

Ives said, "We'll spot a couple of men here, ready to blast out if they hear anything at all. Then the rest of us, most of us, will be at the rear fence, waiting." He let his cigarette burn out and fall to the grass. "We'll cut them to ribbons," he said quietly.

Jensen said, "That is, if you and me are alive that long." He nodded his head to the open graze in front of them.

Ives said, "Let's go."

"Which way? Straight through?"

Ives pondered. There were rises and falls between the center slot and the Crescent C barn that could hide a dozen men. They'd be damn fools to go straight across. Still, it had to be done quickly, if at all. See about Ross, see if anything could be done to help the man, and get the hell back, so they could still have time to get ready for tonight. The empty meadowland beckoned in front of Ives. He knew he shouldn't go this way, but it was so tempting. "None of it makes sense," Ives said, and Jensen said, "That's the truest thing you ever said."

Ives touched his horse and gave him his head. He headed straight across the open graze, through the center slot which was Stanton land, and then to the chewed-up, chomped-up, hooved-down middle grass which was probably Stanton land, too, but which Caesar swore was his and would never be fenced to keep his beef out.

They pressed across, and in the center, fear prickled along Ives's back. For Ross, he thought savagely, for a man who's tossed the Stantons in the pokey. What the hell was he thinking of, doing a trick like this?

But he moved his horse at a controlled canter, down the middle, Jensen at his left flank, and in Ives's head was the memory of Ross telling him, in the middle of Oxnard's main drag, about Caesar and bobwire, and the impending raid. If anybody had done anything to save his—Ives's—life, it was Ross, right then and there. Ives had known there was trouble a-plenty, but he had never smelled it so raw and close as when Ross, the stranger, told him what Caesar was planning to do. They moved, he and Jensen, angry hotheaded men, stupid and brave, and when they got a half-mile across the meadow-land, cut by arroyos and dried-up draws, a grass front that was losing its green as sure and steady as a man losing his hair—when they got that far, Ives's horse started to wave his head and nicker nervously. Ives patted the horse's gray mane and the horse tried to turn his head and bite his rider. Ives frowned and pulled the animal to a stop, and Jensen on his flank halted, too.

Jensen said, "What's wrong, Ivy?"

Ives shook his head, worried. The horse sensed danger, that was sure. It could have been the tricky up-and-down footing, or an abandoned gopher hole, housing a sleeping rattler.

It was neither. It was Caesar's horses.

They came suddenly, swooping from left and right front, four riders in pairs, and Ives heard a man howl, "Broken S, Broken S."

Ives cried sharply, "Beat it, Jenny," and he gave his horse its head. The dappled gray turned, with the Crescent C riders three hundred yards off, and the Broken S men plunged back in the direction they had come.

Ives rode with his head low to the horse's neck, knowing he was out of range of a pistol shot, but inside a well-aimed rifle, expecting the shrill whine of a bullet, the soft thud of a slug against flesh. But there were no shots, and all Ives could think was how he had bungled it.

He and Jensen raced for the center slot, together, a fat target, but unable to do anything about it. It was the only way through to their own land, and their safety. They would have been less easily picked off had they shot off in two directions, not one, but there was no other place to go. So they rode bunched up, hemmed in, fear in their throats, and Ives muttering to himself, "You stupid halfwit, you stupid, block-headed, midget-brain."

They hit the center slot, and still no shots had been fired, and then they were inside and still drumming, and the sound of hooves behind them ceased.

Ives reined his gray and turned. The Crescent C riders were at the edge of their spread, shaking fists and waving guns, but not a one of them was venturing across. Then they turned, and started back.

Ives shook his head. He said to Jensen, "Now when they strike tonight, we've given them perfect reason."

He turned his horse back toward the Broken S headquarters. He was in charge, he thought. He was in charge of sending men to slaughter and not even being able to own their names afterwards. He and Jensen had crossed that uncrossed line; they had carried the feud to Caesar. Now when Caesar stormed back, he'd be merely retaliating for the aborted raid Ives and Jensen—the Broken S, in other words—had directed at the Crescent C.

Jensen said, "But why didn't they follow us and get it over with?"

Ives said, "Four men?" He snorted. "How far would four men get?" He felt a dismal, unshakeable grayness steal over him. It was a sealed-in fate. He turned his face toward Wolfhead, big and overpowering and immutable, spiked with pine cone and wild grass, crowding down on the range beneath it.

Wolfhead gave the range a stifling quality, pressing in on the valley, big as fate itself. Wolfhead, at moments such as these, hypnotized Ives, held him, frightened him, awed him.

And so he stared at the big hill that choked off the valley to the northwest and bottled it up, stared at the hill that somehow Ives associated with that dismal, gray feeling, that sealed-in inevitability.

He saw the girl.

She was leading her horse, walking slowly and carefully, almost like a person barefoot on brambles, picking her way down so slowly she hardly seemed to move at all. Ives studied the girl—Laura, the redhead, he knew instinctively, though she was too far to identify except as a slender, graceful woman—and he let his eyes move ahead of her horse, to where she'd probably hit the bottom of the hill as it eased into the meadow.

He said in a tight voice, "Do you think I could stop her, Jenny?"

Jensen said, "What the hell are you raving about?" He followed Ives's eyes, and he saw the girl.

Ives said, "That girl's up to no good, hasn't been all day. Do you think I could intercept her, Jenny, before she hits the Crescent C?"

Jensen looked, squint-eyed, and he said quietly, "By God, I think you could. She's going to come down on our land sure as buckshot."

Ives said, "Go on back, Jenny, and line up the boys for tonight. Two at the slot here. The rest back near the fence. Hell may pop any minute. I'm going to get me that nosy redhead." He kicked his gray and took off, the mane streaming in his face, keening like the wailing wind.

CHAPTER ELEVEN

The twitch would not stop.

Gill thought he had licked it when he sent Laura off, and when he had handled Big Max—God, that was easy—but now it was worse than ever. He slapped his palm against his temple, a stinging shot, and he pressed his palm against the writhing vein until it stilled, but as soon as he pulled his hand away it continued to crawl.

Gill used to think nerves were clean, straight things, like wires, sort of, neat and in place. Now he knew they were a tangled, jumbled net, dormant until you stuck them with the wrong thought, the wrong word, the wrong act. Then they lashed back. They were lashing Gill, now.

Wrong thought? He grinned thinly. Christ, yes. Wrong everything. Wrong day, mostly. Eleven long years, and it had come plunging down to this day, and it was the wrong day. Everything. God, everything was wrong.

He didn't know where she came from, but he had seen her. Maria. Going through that marked fence, into the Broken S. What the hell did it mean? He didn't know. He used to know everything that happened around him, especially when it was a woman who did it, one of his own women. But he didn't know this. That was wrong.

Then two men coming out of the Crescent C barn. Two men. He didn't know who the first was. He had no idea. But it had to be a Crescent C man. So he didn't matter. But the other. He was getting to know him pretty well, now. It was Ross, walking out of that barn, flapping his arms like a live scarecrow, walking over to a lone horse that stood nearby, and getting on, and riding the hell out of Caesar's place, nobody even watching. That was bad. That was wrong.

And everybody, then and before and after, riding hell for leather for the center slot. That was when Gill saw the two Broken S men, and the four Crescent C men after them. It was all wrong. Caesar was screaming his plans, painting them in the sky. Why didn't they just let those two Broken S slobs ride across; what harm would two men have done? Instead it was all lunge and parry, smash and block, a miniature war, a war in rehearsal, but with the enemy looking on from around the corner.

That was wrong.

And now Laura, taking forever and a week, making sure she moved the way Gill had told her, all right, so slowly nobody saw her, nobody heard her, and then walking right into the Broken S horseman. She should have taken her time, all right, but not that much. She should have been down the slope an hour earlier. But no, she had to inch it (and inside, Gill knew he had told her to take her time, to inch it), exuding such care she never noticed she wasn't hitting the Crescent C, but the Broken S. Gill cursed her wildly. She was going to Caesar with the news of the fence under repair, but she had been so careful not to hurry, she wasn't ever going to get there. A Broken S horseman—Ives, Gill thought—had her in tow, a gun at her back, and she rode, slumped on her horse, straight towards the Stantons' ranch house and headquarters.

Wrong, wrong, wrong.

So there it was. Caesar was going to hit the wrong spot. Ross was riding to town, free as air. Maria had been at the Broken S, spilling God knows what stories about him, about the Crescent C, what plans of Caesar she had overheard. Laura was headed the same way, unable to tell Caesar the one thing Caesar had to know if the man wanted to live. If Gill wanted to rule the range.

But worst of all, much much worse than anything else, were the last words Big Max had hurled at Gill, before Gill had shot him dead. "Ross will kill you.... Ross is the fastest man with a gun I ever saw."

It just couldn't be. Nobody was faster.

That was what had started the whole fool business, the twitch that he had stopped earlier when he realized it was only Laura coming up to see him.

Nobody was faster.

Gill's gorge rose. The day he had planned on, eleven years back, all snarled up like a tenderfoot's bridle. Crashing, crashing about his ears.

Ross couldn't be faster. No man could. It was written that way, that's all. His hand went to his Navy Colt. He gripped it, trying to win back that old feeling, that insurmountable feeling. He tried to think of other moments, other times when he had squeezed sweet juice out of life, when he had tasted nothing but victory. He made his mind center on such thoughts, blended and whirling, until one stood out above the others.

Gill thought of how he had shot down Old Man Ross.

It was a good thought, to Gill. It was the first real climax of his life, the first sure sign that he had a road picked out, down which he would charge, sweeping everything before him. For when Gill killed Jake Ross, he owned the Stantons. And owning the Stantons meant—eventually—owning the Broken S. And owning the Broken S meant owning the Crescent C, the whole of Oxnard Valley. It was a road with no turning, straight as a rifle barrel, just as sure.

But now, the barrel had curled.

Gill wouldn't let it stay curled. The thought of killing Old Man Ross remained poised in his head, and he remained poised with it. The gun lay in his palm, now. He stared, unseeing, into the valley, and slowly the twitching slowed, flared, slowed, ceased. Gill continued to stare down into the valley—*his valley*—gun in hand, and the barrel started to straighten out, the road that had gone smash began to take on its old true shape. Gill nodded, slowly, three or four times, the pictures becoming bright. At nightfall, no matter what Caesar did, Gill would own the range. Nothing could stop him. Nobody.

Nobody was faster.

CHAPTER TWELVE

The sun was at Ross's back. He slapped the sorrel, whispering hoarsely into the pricked ears, and the horse stretched out, its vein-etched, dark red coat covered with the sheen of sweat. They moved past the first frame buildings, onto Oxnard's main drag, and reluctantly Ross slowed the animal.

The town seemed to be holding its breath. People moved along the plank walks with an exaggerated slowness, people treading on eggshells. Ross saw the stableman—Smits—pause at the open pillared doorway, a horseshoe in hand, and Smits frowned at Ross and then, almost like a puppet, moved his head up and down, the tiniest nod of greeting Ross had ever received.

But tiny or not, grudging or not, Smits had acknowledged Ross, had greeted him.

Ross went past the saloon, and Tromper pushed open the batwing doors, an apron around his middle, a pail of water in his hand to tamp down the dust in front of the saloon entrance. He tossed the water and said as Ross went by, "What's new out there?" and Ross merely shrugged. But the impact of Tromper's words were not lost on Ross. Suddenly—or was it so sudden? Ross wondered—Oxnard was concerned with what was happening out on the range.

Ross went up to the sheriff's office, dismounted and quick-looped the sorrel. He went through the dirt alleyway to the rear of the office where Big Max had turned an over-age public outhouse into a town jail. Ross sorted out the keys in his hand and fitted one to the old wooden door and pushed on through, and then he walked over to the Stantons' cell.

Behind the bars, they looked like two ordinary men, grimier perhaps, unshaven, lined by poor sleeping and worse food. Ross stared at them grimly, and Ed Stanton turned slightly to his brother. But Orv stared back, hard-eyed, unrelenting, a man who wasn't giving Ross an inch. Some of the hatred twisted inside Ross, but not much, and he said, "Need anything, boys?"

Orville Stanton shook his head and kept his eyes on Ross, but Ed Stanton turned and walked to the tiny rear window with two widely spaced bars across its face. He stared through the eye-high window at the dust-caked backside of Oxnard. "Yes," Ed Stanton said, "I need some food. Where's Big Max?"

Ross said, "Max has gone to Denver."

Orville Stanton drew his shaggy eyebrows together. "Denver? What for?"

"To get some help, in case Caesar hits your ranch."

Ed Stanton walked back to the cell front. "Is he going to?"

Ross said, "I don't know. I think so, yes."

Orville Stanton gripped the cell bars, knuckles white. He whispered to Ross, "You're making a mistake, Ross."

"How so?" Ross snapped.

"We've got to get out of here," Orville said. "We've got to protect those men."

"You should have thought of that when you shot down my old man."

Ed looked at Ross. He said, "Ross, I've been doing a lot of thinking these past hours, and I would like to talk to you about what happened down there."

Ross stared at the man. "Save it for the authorities in Texas," he rasped. But he kept looking at the man, and Ed Stanton took a deep breath and went on: "Ross, I never shot your father."

"I saw you," Ross said. *But did I?* he thought.

Ed Stanton shook his head. "No, you couldn't have. You've confused some part of it."

"You were drunk," Ross said. "You're the one who confused it." A pain started nagging Ross's temples, and he wondered whether it was from one of Caesar's boys' fists, or just from the knowledge that the afternoon kept slipping away, the shadows lengthening, and Caesar was crawling to the edge of his boundary, ready to leap across, twenty-four murderous guns slicing the night to bloody shreds.

"I was drunk," Ed Stanton said hoarsely, "sure I was. But that doesn't make me a killer."

"No," Ross said. "It doesn't. But you were in my old man's office a minute after the shot was fired. You went back out of there, then, and got on your horse—a big white horse, I saw that, too, and *I* wasn't drunk or confused—and you took off."

Ed kept shaking his head. "Everything you say may be true. But I didn't shoot your father. I couldn't have. It just doesn't make sense."

Ross jeered the man. "Make sense? Sure it makes sense. He had slapped you around, and you hadn't liked it."

Ed turned then and walked back to the rear window. He said through a tight muffled voice, "Have you found Gill?"

"No," Ross said.

Orville Stanton said, "Look, Ross, let us out. We'll find him. We'll turn him over to you and you can dig out the truth. Just let us out."

The man was desperate, Ross knew. Orville Stanton had no intention of finding Gill or turning him over to Ross. He just wanted out, to save his ranch, and his men.

But that was reason enough. Wouldn't any man want out for that reason? Ross frowned. No, that wasn't so. A man in jail for murder or for abetting murder wanted out because he wanted to get away. The Stantons didn't want to get away; there was nothing of the fugitive about their manner. And the fears were back at Ross; was he making a mistake?

He said shortly, "Can't be done. Max threw you in here. Here you'll stay."

Ed Stanton turned and nodded. "That's right, Ross. I wouldn't want you to let us out on what Orv just said. It may be true for him that he'd turn Gill over to you if he found him, but it's not true for me. I'd—"

"Shut up, Ed," Orville said sharply.

"I'd kill the man," Ed went on evenly. "That's all I'm waiting for. Just to get my hands around Gill." He walked up to the cell door and put his hands around the bars.

Ross studied the man. How far would he go? He saw criminal hands, wrapped around the iron bars. He was surprised at what he saw. Orville's hands were big and bony, white-knuckled and powerful, holding the bars. But they weren't nearly the size of Ed's. Ross hadn't noticed it before. Ed was the man you didn't notice, the quieter man, the more peaceful man, the man less likely to strike out at anyone, yet his hands

They were big and dark and hairy, the fingers squared off at the tips and the knuckles like small blocks of dulled-down granite. The muscle between the thumb and index finger was another knot of granite, but with the stirring life of muscle beneath. They were the hands of a man who could easily have killed, with a gun or without.

Ross said, "Thanks for telling me, Ed. That cinches it. You'll just stay here. I'm looking for Gill, but I want him alive."

Ross knew he was traveling the road Big Max had pointed out to him. A day earlier Ross wanted Gill in front of his gun so he could kill the man.

Ed Stanton said, "All right. Don't let me out, then. He's a man I think I'd be able to smell now. I think I'd dig him out of wherever he is. So don't let me out, because if you need Gill to clear up your doubts—you do have doubts, Ross, I can see you do—you'll never have him alive once I find him. And I think I'd find him."

Ross didn't answer the man. It didn't seem as though Ed expected response. He said, to Orville, "I'll rustle you up some chow. Is there anything else?"

Orville said, "Ross, if you're making a mistake, and my men are killed tonight, I'll hold you responsible."

Ross squinted at the man. He said quietly, "I don't like you to threaten me, Stanton. Big Max put you here, not me. I'd just as soon hand you a gun and let you take a chance, drawing against me. So don't threaten me, Stanton. You should have thought of that, too, eleven years ago." He spun and walked out and locked the front door.

He stepped across the street, and a couple of riders went past, but nobody spat this time. Then Ross looked down and he realized why the town had changed. He wasn't wearing his gun. He didn't have a gun.

Ross pushed through the saloon doors and into the cool darkness of the big room. He half-expected to see Laura's mocking face glowing at him from a nearby table, but all he saw were five or six near the bar, Tromper behind it, and a couple more at tables. A game of cards went on at a rear table: five men playing a small-chip poker hand.

Ross wondered about Laura. She had gone on to Gill, wherever that was, but that was now over three hours back. Where was she now? Still with Gill? It didn't seem likely, not if Gill was interested in the raid tonight—if there was to be a raid. Gill wouldn't jeopardize himself by spending too much time with Laura, not if he was part of Caesar's preparations. Then Ross dismissed the girl. She wasn't around. That was good. He'd leave it that way.

He stood at the bar, and men made room for him, but not the obvious cold-cutting way they had shown the day before. He said to Tromper, "Whip up some chow for those two men in the pokey when you get a free minute." He put a silver dollar down on the counter, and Tromper looked at it and pushed it back at Ross.

"Don't need to pay me," Tromper said stiffly.

Ross stared at the man. "What's that mean?"

Tromper looked down at Ross's hip and smiled, just a trifle. "You've put up your gun."

Ross paused. He could let it go and accept the man's clumsy way of squaring matters. But it wasn't fair. He was taking advantage of Tromper. He said, "You've got me wrong, Tromper. I didn't put it up."

Tromper shrugged. "No matter. You're not wearing it. I'm not one to pry." But he kept looking at Ross, half-waiting for the man to go on.

Ross said, "Joe Caesar took it away from me."

Tromper said, "Oh," and walked away. There was a deflated quality about the man. He said to the cluster of patrons, off to the side of Ross, "Gentlemen?"

Ross knew he had been snubbed. He puzzled it out. He said, "Tromper come here a minute."

Tromper walked back slowly. "Yes?"

Ross said, "I licked Joe Caesar, first." He said it quietly so it wouldn't be bragging.

Tromper waited.

"Then three of his boys jumped me. I was on my own, and I'm no match for three men." He didn't say any more because he didn't want to brag, and he didn't want to beg.

It was getting very important, this whole business here with Tromper. For some reason, Tromper was interested in Ross's battle.

Tromper said, "Three of them?"

Ross nodded.

Tromper grinned, slowly. "That's the way I would have figured on it. You don't look like a man Joe Caesar could lick."

Ross said, "Tromper—" Then he stopped. He didn't know how to go about it. But it had to be done. He said, "Tromper, Caesar's got twenty-four men. The Broken S has eight." He stopped again and waited.

Tromper said, "That's big odds."

"Dirty odds," Ross said hotly.

Tromper looked down the bar. He seemed to be weighing his next words. "Yes," he said finally, "dirty, I'd call it."

Ross studied the man. How far would he go? He said, "Caesar will kill them. Probably kill them all."

"Probably," Tromper said.

"He'll take over the Broken S."

Tromper nodded. "Can't see how he can be stopped."

"Can't you?" Ross said. "Can't you, Tromper?"

The look of interest started to fade in Tromper's eyes. He said, "I'll have to hustle up that chow. Your prisoners ain't going to like it—"

Ross snapped, "Don't worry about the goddam chow, Tromper. Can't you see how Caesar can be stopped?"

Tromper busied himself with slabs of cold meat. He took out a knife and sliced up half a loaf of bread. He said, looking down, "It's not my business, stopping Caesar."

Ross took a deep breath and moved back from the bar. He didn't know how he could do it, and he didn't know if it would matter even if he did do it, but he had to keep trying. The shadows outside were longer, darker. He said, "You know those men on the Broken S?"

"Course I do," Tromper said, looking up at Ross, and Ross thought he saw pain streak the man's eyes.

"Most of them?"

"I know all of them," Tromper said. Once more Ross detected pride in Tromper's voice. "I know everybody in the valley."

"They married men, the Broken S hands?"

"Some of them."

"Kids?"

"Some of them."

Responsibility, that's what it got down to. What Orville Stanton was saying in the pokey, a few minutes back. You do something, almost anything, and you become responsible for the consequences. But did it work the other way? Suppose you did nothing, were you then responsible for the consequences?

Ross didn't know. He said, "Those men will be dead in three or four hours, Tromper. Their wives will be widows. Their kids will be a helluva load on those women. That's what's going to happen tonight."

Tromper said, "That's not my business," but his face was white.

"You know those people and you can say that?" Ross eyed the man coldly, thinking he was playing a big lie here, saying things he wasn't sure of, asking men to do things he himself might not do. But that's the way it was, some men can and some men can't. All Ross could do was try. "Tromper, you're going to stand here all night and wipe glasses and peddle your suds and corn? That's what you're going to do?"

Tromper said quietly, "Ross, what do you want? I'm one man. I never fired a gun in my life. What do you want? Leave me alone." The man's mouth was white and thin, his eyes pleading. Ross was raking him, putting pictures in his head he couldn't stand seeing.

Ross said, "We won't need guns, Tromper." He put his hand to his holster and tilted it, to remind Tromper. "No guns, Tromper. I don't have one, and I wouldn't know where to go to get one."

Tromper laughed, a short barking sound. "You're crazy, Ross. You can't go out there and stop Caesar without guns."

"How do you know we can't?"

"I know."

"Try it, Tromper. Just give it a try."

"Look," Tromper said. "Just me and you? Am I crazy? I won't do it."

Ross said, "Why does it have to be just me and you?" He looked down the bar, to the six men drinking slowly, watching and listening. He thought he recognized one of them.

Ross said, "You're Abelson, aren't you?"

A bald-headed man with fat lips put his glass down. "Yes," he said.

"You're the hardware man?"

Abelson nodded. He was a flabby man, in his middle forties, with watery eyes and heavy lips, a bald man with white hands.

Ross said desperately, "Ride with us, Abelson."

"What for?" the fat man said.

"To stop Caesar."

"It can't be done."

That's what Tromper had said. They both were probably right. What was he trying to do, involve innocent men in further bloodshed, probably their own? He said, "It has to be done."

One of the other men said, "What's it to you, Ross?" They all knew him, by now, by the gun he once carried, by the fight he had with Big Max, by his nasty, bitter mock heroics of the night before, when he had challenged the whole lot of them. Now he was pleading with them. Ross was disgusted. No wonder. They ought to throw him out. He said, turning away, "Forget it. You're right. It can't be done. Hustle that chow, will you, Tromper?" He walked through the saloon, and one of the poker players, green visor over his eyes, his cards tossed face down on the table, said, "Afternoon, Ross," and Ross said, "Afternoon, friend," and walked out.

It was different now. They were talking to him, they respected him. Just because he didn't wear a gun. They were glad he didn't carry a gun, because he wouldn't cause any trouble that way. They respected him for taking on a fight that wasn't his, but they were mostly glad he was in town without his gun. He walked to the sheriff's office, and he sat at Big Max's desk.

There was nothing to do.

The four-hundred-mile trek was half over. Now he'd go back. He couldn't stop Caesar from hitting the Broken S, not without help. Big Max would get back to Oxnard in time to help put the pieces together. The sheriff would contact the Knox County authorities, to effect the extradition of the Stantons to Texas, to make them stand trial. Ross had nothing more to do with them. He'd have Tromper bring their meals; he even thought he could leave the keys with the saloonkeeper. Then? Big Max would be back, and the Stantons would go down to Texas, and that was all Ben Ross had hoped to accomplish.

Then why was the empty feeling jabbing at his guts? Why did he feel that nothing—really—had been accomplished? He shook his head, sitting there, knowing that by night he'd be riding once more, away from this town where men lived out their days behind green visors and doors. He'd ride away from this valley where law still was mocked, ignored.

He had tried his best. The people of Oxnard hadn't wanted him, and his best.

Ross was tired and angry, beneath the emptiness. Not angry at them—the Trompers and Abelsons and the rest. Oh, he was angry at them, too, but that wasn't the real thing. Ross knew he was still standing in the middle of nowhere, drawing a toy gun and shooting down his enemies. He was still a tin soldier. Now they could talk in Oxnard how Ben Ross tried to get an unarmed posse together to stop Caesar. Those who wouldn't laugh would think it was a brave act.

Except when Ross fired his toy gun, nobody died. When he tried to round up a posse, nobody volunteered. How brave was a man who didn't accomplish anything?

For that was the truth. Even with the Stantons jailed and waiting extradition, Ben Ross knew—inside—he had accomplished nothing.

His fingers drummed Big Max's desk—old, chipped pine, thumb-marked and splintering. But a big desk. For a big man. Empty, now, even with Ross sitting behind it. Ross thought of Big Max lumbering along the trail, headed for Denver through desolate darkness. To get him an army to help stop range war, or, if it was too late to be stopped, to pick up the pieces and start again.

Even if he failed, Big Max would do something.

So would he. He'd be riding. Back.

Ross heard the footsteps outside the office, and he stiffened. They were a woman's steps, and he felt his hand clawing. The redhead, he thought, she's back.

A small shadow fell across the doorway, and Maria walked into the room, two steps. Ross frowned, his throat catching again, staring at this sinuous girl, her skin pale, drawn, marred by recent tears, and something else.

He said, "What are you doing here?"

She said, "I saw you from the hotel when you rode past. I—I am staying at the hotel now."

Ross stared at the girl. "So?" he said.

"I—I can't go back to Caesar's. I took a horse and—"

The girl was standing in the doorway, her fingers strangling themselves. There was something wrong, terribly wrong.

Ross said, "You saw the fight, didn't you?"

She nodded, her face pained.

"You saw the redhead ride up?"

Again the brief pained nod.

"You heard what she said to Caesar? You know what's going on, don't you?"

"Yes," she said. "I know."

Some of the emptiness, the sense of failure left Ross. The girl was their hope, after all. Even though two Broken S riders had gone across no-man's center ground, even though Caesar could say he had struck back only in retaliation, and then the affair had got out of hand—there'd always be the girl, Maria, to tell the other side of it. How Caesar had primed his men all that day, how they had beaten Ross. She must have overheard some of the conferences that had to have gone on all that day. She had to know. She was witness to Caesar's guilt. With Big Max to lead her on, she'd turn the key. Ross could go now, in peace.

He said, "You'll remember it all, later? You'll be able to tell Big Max when he gets back?" The fight would be over, and the Broken S would lie in ruins, a charred smudge in the broad, soft meadowland, but Caesar wouldn't get away with it.

The girl said quietly, "Big Max is dead."

It was the natural end, Ross thought. It had to be. Now he could truly leave.

He said, "How do you know?"

"I saw it happen," Maria said in a terrible voice.

"Tell me," Ross said quietly. Big Max had gone out for his army, but he wasn't coming back.

She told him.

... Ross got up from the desk—Big Max's desk—and walked around the office; the girl Maria was crying softly. But even though two people now stood in the room, nobody was there. It was Big Max's office, his alone, and nobody else could fill it the way the sheriff had.

The sheriff.

Ross thought of Big Max, and he thought of another sheriff, back in Texas, in Knox County, eleven years ago, Jake Ross, a man he still thought of as the sheriff, not as his father. He thought of Jake Ross, while outside the sun sank through the west, and shadows blotted out great areas of the town and of the western hills. Ben Ross remembered many things he had forgotten. That was funny, he thought. A man forgets things, but he doesn't. They're there, all along.

The girl Maria had told Ross how Gill had boasted of killing Jake Ross, of firing his gun through that rear side window. Ben Ross nodded, in the growing gloom of Big Max's office. Yes, that was right, that was how it had to have happened. He remembered now. The hot empty cartridge shell, just inside the room, below the window, behind the desk. Gill had shoved his arm through the window and fired the gun.

That was why Jake Ross had slumped forward, his head on his desk. That was why the man in the room—Ed Stanton, of course—had no gun in his hand, why he kept shaking his stuporish face from side to side. Ed hadn't done it, and Ben Ross remembered all these things, now.

But it was Big Max, four hundred miles away and eleven years later, who had cleared up the killing of Jake Ross.

Big Max had smelled it wrong all the time. He had never felt sure and easy about the Stantons and their obvious guilt. He had seen the tiny signs, given by Ross's faltering memory, and he had read them right.

It hadn't been Big Max's job to straighten out Jake Ross's murder. He had done it anyway, even though it was surely the last thing in the world he'd ever do, even though Big Max thought the words he was pinching out of Gill would never reach another pair of ears. A man in front of a killer's gun ought to think of himself, how he might fight or beg his way out of it, even though common reason said he couldn't. But that wasn't Big Max. Against the gun, he had worked on Gill, and cleared up Jake Ross's killing. And he had done more—if the girl Maria was telling it straight, and Ross was sure she was. There was a mechanical, automatic way about the girl, the way she told the story that ruled out anything other than that this was the exact truth, as she heard it.

Big Max had riled Gill, at the very last, throwing Ross at him, telling Gill that Ross would kill him, that Ross was faster. It meant of course that Gill would fire his gun more quickly at Max, to shut him up forever, but it also meant that Gill had been shaken. Ross did not know Gill, but he sensed the man's ways. Gill was a man who thought he was a giant. When he found himself only a man again, he wasn't even that. Big Max dragged Gill down to his proper size.

Ben Ross shook his head. The man was a marvel. Another man would just have dived for his gun and died, or crawled to Gill's boots.

And yet Big Max probably never even thought of what he was doing. It was the way he acted. It was his job to deal in justice, to balance accusation with fact. The killing of Jake Ross had not balanced on Big Max's scales, so he kept trying, right to his death. There must have been satisfaction in what he had found out.

And hellish dissatisfaction, too.

Big Max had died, knowing Gill was a killer, but thinking the Stantons would pay.

Ben Ross stiffened, near the doorway. He had been ready to run. Now he knew he couldn't. Big Max's ghost wouldn't stand for it. Ross had to stay and fight. He had to get Gill. But more than that, he had to take up Big Max's load out there on the range, the range that slopped spit and ridicule all over law and order. Ben Ross knew nothing about law and order, but he had to do the job.

More, even more. Big Max had thrown Ross at Gill. Now Ross had to measure up. Not just the fastest man with a gun. That meant nothing. Ross had to be the antithesis of Gill out here in Colorado, where Gill and Caesar made war and others watched, and nobody fought back. He, Ben Ross, dummy hero, mock soldier, a toy pistol notched a thousand times with victims that never existed—he had to fight back, one man against a range.

... He said to Maria, "Wait here," and he walked out of the office, back to Tromper's saloon.

He shoved the batwing doors, and they clattered against the inside wall. He strode through the saloon, to the bar, and he said, "Tromper, Big Max is dead," and the room stilled as though Ross had thrown a heavy cloak over it.

Tromper said, "Who did it?"

Ross said, "Gill."

The two men stared at each other, and Ross knew he wouldn't have to say it to Tromper, about how Ross had come in that first day looking for Gill, and how Tromper had tried to warn Ross off, to tell him to go back to Texas, or else he might leave Oxnard dead. Tromper remembered, and shame began to streak the man's plain, homely, honest face.

Ross didn't know how else to do it. Before, he had nothing to tell Tromper, to get him from behind the bar and out on the range. Now, he

had a dead man. He didn't want to take advantage of Big Max, but he
didn't know how else to do it. And Big Max wouldn't have minded. Hell,
no. It was what he would have wanted, being used, even dead, to
reduce chaos to order, lawlessness to law.

Tromper took off his apron. He wiped his hands and nodded at Ross.
And Ross felt the breath come out slowly. He had not even been aware
he had been holding it while they had stared across the damp mahogany
bar.

Then from Ross's left, Abelson said, "Count me in, Ross." Ross looked
at the man, bald and flabby, heavy-lipped and watery-eyed, the last man
in Oxnard you'd want on your side in a scrap.

Which was exactly why it made Ross's heart sing inside.

It wasn't going to be a scrap. It was going to be a one-sided massacre,
except not a gun would be fired. Hell, not a gun would be carried.

"You're game, Abelson?"

The fat man snapped, "I said so, didn't I?" There was a decisiveness
about the man, the heavy lips looking not so pulpy, but just heavy, the
watery eyes squinting a bit, taking on a harder light. Abelson turned
to his drinking companions, men whose names Ross didn't know and
whose names he doubted he'd ever know, though he wanted to know
them. Abelson said, "You coming, gents?"

One of them said, "Coming where?"

Abelson said, "How the hell should I know? Wherever Ross wants.
They've killed Big Max. I won't let them do it. You coming?"

And the man, tall, austere, a man in his sixties and looking more like
a banker than anything else, said, "Why, sure I'm coming." He looked
at Ross and smiled. "Friend, just lead the way."

Ross said to Tromper, "Bring that food over to the office. Leave it with
Maria. She'll take care of the Stantons." He stopped and thought for a
moment. The Stantons were in jail, but they were innocent men. Ross
shook his head. He wasn't that much of a lawman, yet. Ed Stanton had
blood in his eye. Blood wouldn't do it, tonight. The Stantons had to stay
put.

Ross turned to the men at the poker table, five men looking at Ross,
and before Ross could say anything, one of them drawled, "Deal me into
your crazy hand, Ross," and the others got up, leaving their cards and
their chips where they lay.

They were thirteen then, Ross and Tromper, Abelson and his five
drinking companions, and the five poker players. He could round up
some more, Ross thought, but that would take time, and time was the
only real enemy. He said to Abelson, "Can you fix up some flares?"

Abelson said, "Sure can. McQuinn here"— pointing to the tall white-haired man—"can whip some up, too."

"Good," Ross said. "A flare for each of us." He looked at his men. There wasn't a cowman in the group. He said, doubt in his voice, "You men can ride?"

Abelson laughed. "Hell," he said. "I punched cows for fifteen years. I broke horses out on that range nobody ever thought could be broke. There ain't a man here who can't ride. McQuinn once rode to Oregon with old bigmouth Fremont."

Ross stared at his crew, and suddenly he knew once again how wrong he was, sizing the way he always had, a quick look, a quicker judgment. A man wasn't always what he seemed.

He said, "In ten minutes, then, every man on a horse, ready to ride. And," he added "I want every man to carry a white shirt, a white rag, anything at all big and white and flapping."

"Why white shirts?" Abelson said.

"That's our weapon," Ross said grimly. "A flag of truce."

The men broke from the room, swift and sure men, going along with Ross not because he was Ross, but because Big Max had died. Ross knew he himself was a failure, but there were men who could do things on their own, and others who had to suck strength from another. The leaders and the apes.

He strode out into the street, and he got on his sorrel, his lightweight white cotton shirt draped over the pommel. The Crescent C—Broken S battleground was over an hour away on fast horses. With flares burning, thirteen men like these men would take two hours. Would it be soon enough?

It had to be, Ross swore.

CHAPTER THIRTEEN

Caesar looked across the range toward the Broken S. It lay in coral sunshine. Beyond it was Wolfhead, big and dark violet now. When the sun hit Wolfhead's peak and sank behind it, the whole range would darken. Then night would swoop in, and the coral colors on Broken S grass would turn dark. Caesar nodded, thin-lipped, tasting the crusted blood in his mouth where Ross had mauled him with his big fists.

Caesar's mouth curled. Ross didn't matter a fig. The man had whipped him. So had other men, a few. Ross was still just a useless figure. Caesar thought of how Ross had worked his way out of the barn and back to Oxnard. It was the only part of it that bothered Caesar. Not that Ross had got away. Caesar was glad about that. It took the problem out of his hands. Caesar didn't know what to do with the man. Holding him for a while to let the girl get up to Gill—that was all right. But afterwards, he didn't know what to do.

It was how Ross had accomplished his escape that riled Caesar. Caesar had left Hallahan in there. Then Ives and Jensen had tried their fool raid. And when Hallahan got back to the barn, there was the wire, cut neat as you please where Ross had been lying.

Hallahan was an honest man. He had told Caesar about the tussle he'd had with Ross, and how Ross must have taken his wire cutters.

It worried Caesar. It was a bad sign. Hallahan was a good man, but he shouldn't be fighting today. He should be getting drunk in Oxnard, on his day off. Hallahan would take his orders and do his job, but he wouldn't have any heart, any instinct for it.

Caesar said, "Whitaker, come here."

The snaggle-toothed foreman rode up swiftly. Then Caesar nodded his head, and Whitaker followed; they went up front toward the middleground.

"Whit," Caesar said, "make sure the men rendezvous off the flanks of the middle slot."

Whitaker nodded. The two men studied the ground, where Ives and Jensen had left their hoof-marks on Crescent C land. Caesar didn't want twenty-four men messing up the tracks that would implicate the Broken S and point it out as the aggressor in this battle. It was the best break of the day, wiping away some of the stigma of guilt from Caesar.

"You've got the six men lined up for the feint at the center?"

Whitaker nodded again. Six men who might be blasted to shreds in that first direct assault. He had taken the six worst men and given them the job. It was a dirty job.

Caesar said heavily, "Let's go back to the bunkhouse, Whit."

Whitaker said, "Right, Boss," but he was thinking the man was just wasting time this way. First Caesar had wanted him to ride, to see the tracks made by the Broken S—Whit had seen them a half-dozen times that afternoon—and now Caesar was going back to the bunkhouse.

At the bunkhouse, Caesar said, "Get all the men in here, Whit," and Whit bit off a curse and went riding over the range, yelling men's names. Nobody had strayed far off, because they knew that any minute after dark Caesar would want them ready to ride, and the sun was over the lip of Wolfhead already.

In five minutes the men were in the bunkhouse, a shuffling assortment of men, tan-necked and big, mostly, twenty-four counting Caesar and his foreman.

Caesar said, "You men know what's in store for you tonight?" He stopped. It was the wrong way. He didn't want them thinking ahead. Men would die, some of these twenty-four right here. That was what was in store.

A man spoke up from the rear rank, "How come we're splitting up, Boss?"

Caesar turned to Whitaker. He thought the foreman had gone over that with them. He probably had. The men were nervous, wanting reassurance.

Caesar said, "The main strike will be at the rear fence that's down and passable. Whit and I will lead that group, Hallahan and Stucka riding the left flank, close to the Broken S fence. We'll have to travel in a long file because the trees outside the Broken S will pinch us in. That's a break, of course. There's less likelihood of losing contact."

A man said, "What happens if we do lose contact?"

Caesar stared at the man. Damn, he thought. He had brought up trouble again. Christ, the men were jittery, ready to pounce on the slightest wrong word.

Whitaker spoke for Caesar. "You won't," he said drily.

The man was silenced.

Then a man stepped forward, a thin wispy man with legs so bowed they looked rickety. He said, "How come we're not all hitting the rear fence?"

Caesar studied the bowlegged puncher. It was the same question, again. The splitting up of the force was worrying the men. Caesar said angrily, "Because that's the way we've got it planned."

The man started to grumble, and Whitaker said, "Speak up, O'Hara, that's what we're here for." But Caesar had squelched the man.

Whitaker said, "Boss?" and Caesar nodded. "Men," the foreman said, "this ain't the first time most of you have ridden in with guns. Maybe a couple of you ain't ever got into a gun scrap, but the rest of us have." Caesar nodded. Most of the men were the type common to Colorado ranching, semi-transients, men who worked a spread for a year or two and then moved on. Most of them had been in range wars. It was difficult for them not to have been.

One man said, "But not with Caesar. The Crescent C's never done anything like that."

Whitaker said smoothly, "There's never been reason before, Thewen. Your boss won't make any man fight unless there's good reason. The Stantons are pinching us in. They're going to throw bobwire around our necks and strangle us with the stuff." The men had heard about bobwire from Whitaker, and because it was new, it had them properly scared, and Whitaker knew it.

The foreman went on: "So tonight Caesar wants to clear up this mess, once and for all, to make sure the Broken S doesn't take over our spread any more than they have already. Why, you saw what happened today." Men began to nod with Whitaker, agreeing, faces hardening. "Ives and Jensen—just two men—rode on up and got halfway across our land before we made them skedaddle. In a year's time, they'll have ten men doing that every day. Do you want the Broken S to raid you, to kill you in your sleep one night, to burn down this place? That's what it amounts to."

But O'Hara, the man who had asked about the split-up of duties—his courage renewed by Whitaker—spoke up again. "All I want to know," he said, half-whine, half-defy, "is why us six men have to hit that middle spot while the rest of you go around the rear. That's all I want to know."

Whitaker said, "Because sometimes you ride fence, O'Hara, and sometimes Thewen cleans bunkhouses, and sometimes it's the other way around. It's just a chore. I pass them out. Maybe next time—if there's a next time—you'll go one way and Thewen and five other men will go the other. That's all."

O'Hara said quickly, "Tell me, Whitaker. Is it going to be more dangerous hitting the front?"

Whitaker studied the man. This was all Caesar's job, he knew, but the boss was fumbling badly. He said quietly, "Yes, it probably will be. I tell you what, O'Hara, I'll swap jobs with you. How's that?"

The man began to flush, and then he got hot-eyed. He spun around and walked to the rear of the bunkhouse and a few men began to snicker. Whitaker took a deep breath. He had them on the run now. He said, "I'll go further. If there's any man who doesn't want to ride tonight"—his eyes caught Hallahan's and Stucka's, and he pinned the men—"he just has to step forward right now and say so. He can sit right here on his lardy butt until the rest of us get back. Just say the word, and he stays behind. Come on now, step up." Whitaker kept his eyes on the two men as long as he dared, and then when he saw they weren't moving, he swept the room, and the men flinched under his gaze. Not a man stirred.

Whitaker said to Caesar, "Is there anything else, Boss?" and Caesar smiled faintly at his foreman. "No," he said, "I think that's all."

Whitaker turned back to the men. "You've heard the boss. That's all. Be ready when we need you. I'd advise you men to stick close to the bunkhouse. We'll ride in an hour or so." Then he and Caesar stepped swiftly from the room.

Caesar said, "Thanks, Whit."

The foreman snorted. "What for? For telling them what you told me?

You've got it planned perfect, Boss."

Caesar shook his head, his eyes on Wolfhead—where Gill hunkered in a hole. It was Gill who had planned it perfect. If it had been up to Caesar—the rancher thought suddenly—it probably wouldn't have been planned at all. The Crescent C had staggered along all right in the past without picking a fight on its neighbors—if you forgot about the Indians, the steaders and the sheep man. Hell, they didn't count. Nobody counted them. And even there, it hadn't really been a war; it was just driving the stink of goat off the cattle graze or else ridding the range of Indians or cow thieves or filthy squatters. This, though, was war. And it was war brought on by the Crescent C, even if all the right was on its side.

Caesar started to move away. Whitaker said, "You want me, Boss?" and Caesar turned around, startled. Then he said, "No, Whit. I—just want to ride off by myself for a spell. I'll be back when it's time to give the word." He looked at the twilight all about them, and then he tugged a heavy watch from his pocket. "An hour, like you said, Whit. I'll be back."

He rode away, to the front first, across the thinning grass, some of it burned yellow-brown by the summer sun, all of it needing rain. Well, when the winter came, it would get rain, and snow both. It would green up, tiny and tender in the spring, and then full and sweet by May, the barley and oats starting to show little honey-tan granules that the horses liked to munch. Caesar studied his grass. Too thin, no matter how good the winter rains and snows. Every year the land seemed to lose some of its fine edge, its thick ripeness that had so overwhelmed Caesar when he first saw it, virgin and wild, twenty-five years ago.

And with the Stantons' hedges and fences, it had to get worse. His eyes turned black with fury. Damn them, he thought. Gill was right. They were wolves. They had to be driven off. He'd do it, tonight.

Caesar swung to the northwest, following the general known line of his spread, as the surveyor had pointed it out. Caesar didn't need a fence to see his boundaries; he knew them too well. What a fool he was, not laying claim to all this land when he entered Oxnard Valley, back in the '40s. He edged to the west. Facing Wolfhead now, too dark up there to see any movement from the trees, where Gill had his horse. Caesar worked his way along the west flank of his domain. Beyond Wolfhead was his winter graze, the only real hope for cattle in the valley. Even the Stantons, with all that choice center grass, would suffer before long. You can't send a herd of cattle across that grass and hope to keep it replenished year after year. Some years there were no rains, no really heavy snows to rush down Wolfhead and soak the meadowland, rejuvenate the grass seed. The winter graze, huge and barely touched, was Caesar's trump. Without it, he'd have been licked years earlier. Without it, the Stantons couldn't make a real go of it.

Caesar cursed, facing south now, riding back the direction he had come. Then why rout out the Stantons, why burn down the Broken S? Just because of some hedges and a fence or two? Even if this bobwire did rope in the whole graze, what good would it do the Stantons in the long run?

So why the war?

He didn't know.

Caesar rode back along the south flank and then he swung east, facing the entrance of the valley, where the ridges flattened and the town of Oxnard lay. It was dark there, though lighter than any part of the valley, because the sun was directly west, its rays still filtering through the bulk of Wolfhead, through the ridge behind which it had dropped a half hour earlier, and bouncing a frail light off the eastern extremity of Oxnard Valley.

Caesar hit the east border of the Crescent C, and he knew his hour would be up unless he nudged his horse and made tracks for home. The men would not like waiting, even though they did not like riding. He himself did not like the waiting. He almost wished they had followed Ives and Jensen across the center slot and onto Broken S grass earlier today; by now it would be over, one way or the other. But he and Whit had known that was foolish; maybe Ives and Jensen were just taunting him, maybe the Broken S, undermanned, was trying to force a showdown before the Crescent C was ready. So Caesar had stilled his riders. Now he was sorry.

He started to turn his horse, when he heard—or maybe he didn't hear, but just sensed—the riders in the valley.

He whirled his horse, knowing he was alone, but Caesar was in no sense a coward, and he knew that if he had to he could always make it back to the ranch before any rider reached him.

He squinted into the night, and then he saw the bouncing light. It looked like a small fire, a grass fire probably, but then there was a second fire just behind it, and a third on its flank. He thought for a flashing second, real panic hitting him, that somehow the Broken S had flanked the Crescent C and was putting the grass to the torch. But the fires, all of them, were bouncing and moving crazily, not cutting in one direction as they would if they were grass fires pushed by whatever freak wind howled at the southeast mouth of the canyon.

Caesar stayed a minute longer, hesitating, wanting to draw out his gun and fire it to alert his men, yet not sure what it was he was seeing, and wondering how it was that the fires kept growing. He counted ten and then twelve and finally, far in the rear, he counted a thirteenth. He waited another minute, but that was all, and by this time the first fire was less than a mile off.

And Caesar knew what it was.

It was a flaming torch, a flare, a burning brand of some sort, carried by a man on a horse. They were too numerous to be the Broken S. Then who were they? Caesar didn't know, and not knowing, his courage broke, and he whirled around, racing for the ranch.

Ross turned to Tromper; the man's face was garish and dramatic in the flames that held off the quickening night. He said, "All right, now we have to move. Follow me." Tromper nodded and waved his arm over his head, and the rest of the men swung their horses to the left front, headed for the in-between land that marked the boundary between the Stantons and Caesar.

The men drummed the earth, not in full careening gallop, but moving swiftly for thirteen men riding one-handed and trying desperately to keep fire from spilling to the dry grass below their feet.

Abelson had suggested a man ride behind, with a horse blanket, to fight off any spitting fires. Ross had looked for such a man, and then Abelson said, "I'll do it."

Ross said, "And keep up?"

Abelson snorted. "Hell, boy, I'll pass you coming and going. I'll ride bobtails around you, boy. Don't sell me short." He had stayed a hundred yards behind, a sloppy fat man who made his horse dance like a show animal, cutting back and forth as Abelson one-handed the reins, and the blanket dragged across the little fires that kept jumping up from spilled sparks. Abelson had strapped his torch to his left thigh, canted out a trifle, and every so often he'd whirl his horse and beat down his own fires. Then he'd jab the animal in its belly and the horse would leap forward and cut down the distance between him and the other men. Never did he fall more than his hundred yards behind.

Now the men cut for the center ground. Here, Ross knew, if the war had not been fought, it would be. This was the open slot that fed into each spread. Here Crescent C riders would stream through; here Broken S men would lie in wait, to fire back. Here the battle for supremacy of the range would be waged.

Unless Ross and his men were able to thwart the whole business.

They drove forward, onto thinner grass now, with less chance of fire starting, and Abelson edged even closer, and then they were at the beginning of the center ground, the faint dark shadows of the Stantons' mulberry hedges indeterminate blobs in the night. While ahead of them, to their right front and moving even farther ahead and away, one rider pounded the ground.

"We've been spotted," Ross yelled, knowing that they would before too long, and Tromper, just behind him said, "It figures."

Now was the ugly waiting period. A Crescent C man had seen them and was off for his headquarters. Now the Crescent C would come forward. But there would be some time yet, just a little, but some.

Ross said, "I'm crossing over to the Broken S," and Tromper said, "They won't know who you are. They'll shoot your head off."

Ross shook his head. He had to get to the Broken S and let the men know; otherwise Ives would have them opening up. Ross said, "I don't care. It's got to be done. Run our men across in a single file, covering the whole hundred yards of slot. That means—"

Tromper said drily, "Beat it. I can divide."

Ross went trotting across the center slot, waiting for the shot-gun blast that would drive him from his horse and open the night to bloodshed. But no sound came. Then he yelled, "Hey, Broken S. It's me, Ross."

A voice answered from pitch darkness, "Come along, friend, and show yourself. Drop your gun along the way."

Ross said shrilly, "I've got no gun," and he split the slot and was onto Broken S land. He saw no one. Then, from a dozen yards away, a man loomed up out of a hole dug in the ground. The man said, "Get off your horse, Ross."

Ross said, "I can't," and a hammer clicked. He said, "I can't, man, I've got no time."

A man said, "Let him talk. He ain't going to hurt us. Ives says the man's siding us."

Ross had to say the truth then. "I'm siding nobody. That's what this is all about. There's thirteen of us, out there, spread out over the slot. Nobody's going past us without shooting us down, first. And I don't think Caesar's going to do that."

There was silence for a minute, and then a man—the second man, Ross thought, who had slowed down the other said, "You're taking a helluva chance."

"It's that," Ross said, "or nothing. Either Caesar doesn't fight or you're licked."

"We can hold 'em," the first man said sharply, but Ross felt the man was talking big, not sense.

Ross said, "Give us a chance, that's all we ask. If Caesar blasts us out of the way, you're no worse off than before. But don't open up until you hear the Crescent C firing. Is that a deal?"

A Broken S man said, "Mister, it's your funeral," and the second man said, "Sure it's a deal. We won't fire unless we're sure it's Caesar coming through." Then he muttered, "Ross, you're a decent man for a bounty hound."

Ross turned then, back to the center slot, where the twelve men stood, facing the Crescent C, flares high, white shirts aloft.

Caesar reached the bunkhouse, his throat constricted, fear leaping in his belly. Thirteen men with torches, headed for the center slot, to hold him off. He didn't know what it meant.

Whitaker stood at the bunkhouse door, watching the boss come in. He knew the man was in a turmoil, the way his horse had been moving.

Caesar hit the ground on the run. He said, "Whit, here man!"

The two men ducked behind the bunkhouse, and Caesar said, "There's thirteen men riding for the center slot."

Whitaker whistled. "Broken S men?"

Caesar shook his head, trying to grab his breath. "No. Can't be. Too many. And they came from town."

"What are they up to?"

Caesar said, "I don't know. They've got me—buffaloed, Whit." He wanted to say *scared*, but he knew it wasn't fair to throw his panic all over the other man. But Whitaker sensed Caesar's meaning. He walked to the front of the bunkhouse, staring out at the open range. He saw the twisting flares, headed for the middleground.

"Think they intend to fire the grass?"

Caesar said helplessly, "I don't know."

Whitaker studied the flares and held up his hand, rotating it slowly. He made a pinching motion with his fingers, as though he were caressing the night air. He said, "Wind's all wrong for that. They'd blow the fire right in their faces, straight back at the Broken S."

Caesar said, "What else then?"

Whitaker said slowly, "I don't know, Boss, but I think we ought to look into it."

"Us?"

Whitaker nodded grimly. "You and me, Boss, and maybe a few others. Just a handful."

Caesar said, "You're right. Who'll we take?"

Whitaker said, "Hallahan, Stucka, you, me, Thewen. That ought to do it."

Caesar stared bleakly at his foreman. Five men, against thirteen. Suddenly the night was turned topsy-turvy. What had been, a triple-knotted cinch was now a shot in the dark, five good men going out against thirteen unknowns. He nodded at Whitaker and jerked his thumb at the bunkhouse. "Tell 'em," he said shortly. "And tell the rest to sit tight, unless they hear gunfire. Then they should ride straight up. One of us will meet 'em and tell 'em what we want."

Whitaker said, "Right, Boss," and strode inside.

Three minutes later, the five men started for the slot, riding in a loose diamond, Caesar and Whitaker together at the lead point, Hallahan and Stucka at each flank, slightly behind, and Thewen, a rangy man with yellow hair and worried eyes, bringing up the rear point.

They rode at a trot, rifles slung across their left shoulders, the reins in their left hands. Their right hands stayed close to their hips.

Whitaker said, "I don't figure it, Boss."

They were a quarter-mile away, and they could see the riders, sitting their horses quietly, brands burning halos around them. Caesar said, "It's a trap, that's what it is."

"Funny kind of trap," Whitaker said. He stared into the night, his eyes biting through until he had settled the one nagging point. It didn't make sense. But he was pretty sure—from where he sat—that those men, twelve now, with another man coming up from behind to make it thirteen, were completely unarmed. Certainly they had no rifles. It didn't look like they had pistols, either.

He said to Caesar, "Nothing to worry about, Boss."

"What do you mean?" Caesar said sharply.

Whitaker pointed at the riders, three hundred yards ahead. "Not a gun among them. Queerest damn posse I ever saw."

Caesar leaned forward. "By God, you're right. The crazy fools."

He kicked his horse and put him to a canter. He moved up on the riders and then he saw that the man in front was Tromper. Next to him was Abelson, the hardware man. Three men away was McQuinn, the general store man. Next to McQuinn was—Jessup, the town schoolteacher! Caesar started to laugh, quietly, a giggling high-pitched noise in his throat. They were going to stop him with a crew of store-keepers and bartenders and schoolmarms.

He said, "Tromper, get the hell out of here."

Tromper said quietly, "You get out of here, Joe Caesar." The words were cool and clean in the night, ice-pick sharp.

Caesar said shrilly, "I mean it, Tromper. You men are going to get hurt." Then Caesar saw the other rider, and the whole situation took on a new shape. The other rider, coming up from Broken S graze, was Ross.

He said, "Well, the troublemaker is back."

Ross came up past Tromper and stopped his sorrel in front of Caesar. He said, "Take your men back, Caesar. There'll be no trouble tonight."

Caesar gnawed at his lip. He eyed the tall lean Texan. He said, "Ross,

I'm going to give you men two minutes to ride off my land. After that I won't be responsible for what happens."

Ross said, "Yes, you will." That was exactly it. Once more it got down to responsibility. Caesar was making this war; Caesar would carry the burden. He'd make him.

Caesar said, "The Broken S sent two men across before. They've started this thing."

And Ross smiled wickedly and said, "Prove it." He watched Caesar's face as the impact hit him. Caesar had come out of the shadows of his own bunkhouse with four Crescent C men a few minutes back, frightened, uncertain men. And they had marched straight across the middle path taken earlier, in the opposite direction, by Ives and Jensen. "Prove it," Ross said again. "You've messed up, Caesar. You've covered the tracks."

Caesar said, "To hell with that, Ross. I meant what I said. Get your men off."

Whitaker came close to his boss and said, "I'll take care of him," knowing that Caesar couldn't handle Ross, and knowing that if Ross could be handled, the other twelve men would go on back, beaten. He said, "Boss, I'll send him packing."

Ross licked his lips. The night was cold and crisp, but his mouth was dry. He had to make a stand. No heroics this time. Just steady strength. From behind him he heard a man—Abelson, he thought—say, "Don't fight him, Ross," and Ross was surprised at the tension in Abelson's voice. Well, he thought, in a way it made sense. The man was not a fighter. He had done more than Ross ever expected, tonight, but he had run his race. Now he was nearly through. If Ross didn't cave in, Abelson could keep going. But if Ross went down, then Abelson would go down, too. They were like a house of cards, atop Ross. He thought bitterly, the ape has to lead. It wasn't right. He wasn't fit to do it.

Ross said to the big foreman, the man who had helped kick and punch him unconscious, "Whitaker, just say the word."

Whitaker was suddenly the key man. If Whitaker could be checked, then Caesar had lost his right arm. And Caesar, Ross suddenly sensed, was a man who didn't really want to fight, who had no stomach for this war that was shaping up right here at his feet. That part was certain. Caesar didn't want to fight a killing war; there had to be somebody else pushing Caesar all along.

And Ross knew who it was, who it had to be. Gill, from some hidden hole, was directing the whole affair. It was like Big Max had suggested. Gill had the most to gain; Gill was going to take over the shambles of the Broken S; Gill probably would try to rule the Crescent C roost, too.

Caesar was just the means to Gill's end.

But right now, if Ross could swing Whitaker, he'd swing Caesar too, and that would mean Gill would have to come out of his hole, to fight his own war.

Whitaker started to climb down from his horse, his rifle still slung, his holster still bulging with death.

Ross climbed down, too, a man with a flaming torch in his hand, but nothing else. Where his Colt Walker had lain was a gaping holster now. His rifle was back in Big Max's office, where Maria sat guard.

He thought fiercely: merchants, frightened girls and a deputized coward. That was what they were. But inside he knew it wasn't exactly that; it was more.

He said, "Put down your rifle, Whitaker."

The big foreman said, "Sure, Ross," and he started to unsling it from his shoulder. Then suddenly he straightened up, lunging, the rifle barrel held in his fists and the stock smashing Ross' left arm, striking Ross above the elbow and sending a white sliver of agony to the brain. The flare tumbled from his numbed hand, the fingers opening and twitching. He gasped out, "Ah-h," and then he groped on the ground for the flare, but Whitaker's rifle came crashing down again, and Ross rolled away, but not before the butt struck his shoulder.

Ross heard a man say, "Quit it, you yellow dog," shock and horror in the words, but nobody was moving up to help, nobody was doing anything.

Ross kept rolling and then he got to his feet, three yards away from big Whitaker, cast in gloom. Ross said thinly, "Tromper, keep some light on him, man. Damn it, show him to me." And Whitaker stopped and stared at Ross, wondering for a second why the man didn't pass out, his shoulder was broken and maybe his elbow as well. Then he stopped thinking and moved forward, into the light of Tromper's flare, and Ross said, "Come on, Whitaker."

Whitaker cursed viciously and swung the rifle in a sweeping arc with his right arm, but Ross leaped forward and with his good right hand punched Whitaker as hard as he could, on the heavy biceps of the man's club arm. Whitaker's arm leaped up and the rifle popped into the air, and Ross swung his useless left arm, hitting the rifle and sending it bouncing to the dirt and grass, twelve feet away. A man picked it up and flung it behind him, into the night.

And Whitaker, eyes glittering in the strange planes of light that made his face look like slabs of colored marble, drew his pistol from his holster and aimed its mouth at Ross's belly.

It should have stopped Ross. It would have, too, on another day, at another time. But Ross was suddenly a man who had nothing to lose. His left arm was useless, from elbow to shoulder. He had no weapon. Whitaker was big and strong as an ox. He had a .44.

Whitaker must have expected Ross to falter, to stand still. Then the big foreman would have stepped in and swung his pistol, whipping Ross to the ground. The other men would shuffle off. The night would belong to the Crescent C, and the graze, too.

But Ross guessed that Whitaker never meant to squeeze the trigger of his .44. He guessed that Whitaker had gauged the stolid waiting strength of the twelve men behind Ross; if he killed Ross, he might as well continue and shoot down the rest. For they surely would have to be killed. Beat Ross, smash him to the ground, yes, that would discourage them. But murder would only put the steel back inside them. So Whitaker must have known he'd have to kill thirteen men, if he killed one.

Whitaker couldn't. No man could, unless that was his job.

And Ross jumped Whitaker's gun hand.

He came leaping at the Crescent C trail boss, and Whitaker had to pull up the .44 and jab it forward, with the barrel aimed for Ross's face. Ross threw up his bad arm—once more, he knew he had nothing to lose: Whitaker had crippled that arm so badly it would be useless for weeks, so he might as well make it months—and the .44 dug cruelly into the battered elbow. Ross's legs went watery, but even as he stumbled and went nearly to his knees, his right arm lunged forward like a battering ram, digging deep into Whitaker's guts, as low down as Ross dared hit the man.

There was a popping noise, and Ross staggered away, his hand over his head to ward off any pistol whipping. But nothing happened, and Ross righted himself and looked at Whittaker.

The foreman was standing on wide-spread legs, his hands to his belly, as though he were preventing his entrails from spilling to the ground. His eyes were straining from their sockets, bulging like perfectly round small white rocks. And all the pain in the world was at Whitaker's mouth, a twisting mouth that tried to form words but made only gibberish sounds.

Then Whitaker threw his arms up like a preacher and collapsed.

He lay like a broken rag doll, a convulsing figure on the grass, shriveled and moaning.

Ross said quietly. "All right, Caesar, take him away. You're through for the night."

Caesar stared down at his foreman, at the man who had lent him strength all day—at his right arm, as Ross had guessed—and he started to nod, started to turn his horse and get down, so he could help toss Whitaker on the man's own horse, so they could ride back, slowly— shambling defeated men.

And gunshot shattered the night. A man screamed. In the distance came the wild pounding of horses' hooves, as men rode up from the Crescent C.

Gill had come sliding down the slope of Wolfhead, a sobbing, panicky man, his face alive with wormy nerves. He had seen the new riders, grim night riders carrying flares, turning the odds suddenly against Joe Caesar. Thirteen men, plus eight Stanton men—and it had become an even fight. But worse, Joe Caesar was sending five men toward that open center slot.

That meant he still didn't know about the repaired fence. That meant—to Gill—Joe Caesar was still planning a feint at the middle, shooting his main striking force off to the rear of the Broken S and through that passable fence that was by now as solid as stone. The men would hit the fence, pile up there in the night, frightened men, confused, thinking they'd been tricked. The Stanton men would wait back there, near the fence, and when the night would split by the noises of Caesar's men all pinned at the fence with nowhere to go, a milling bewildered crew of men, the Broken S would open up. It would be slaughter, pure, simple slaughter.

Gill had to let Caesar know about the fence; he had to divert the man's force.

He moved down the slope, his horse stumbling and clawing. Gill had his Navy Colt in his hand. He pushed the animal and tried to hold its head up high and back, and he tried to keep his own seat way back in the saddle, deep down, so the horse would be less likely to fall, but mostly he just rushed the horse, because it had to be fast now.

If Caesar was whipped tonight by the Broken S, he'd never give Gill that half-share of the Crescent C. All Gill would win would be the piece of the Broken S that was his anyway, and if the Broken S men ever smelled out his complicity, his life wouldn't be worth a pistol slug. Gill had to help Caesar; he had to reduce the Broken S to burned ruins.

He pushed through the thin line of trees and burst onto the fringe of the meadowland. In front of him, thirteen—no, twelve—men stood in a line. Four Crescent C men were facing them in a bunch, while in between the two groups, two men fought. Suddenly Gill saw it was Ross and Whitaker, and Ross had hit Whitaker a sickening blow to the belly, way below Whitaker's pistol belt, and the Crescent C ramrod was down.

Gill raised his Navy Colt.

He saw it all now. Those thirteen men weren't armed. They had come with white shirts and torches to stand on the middleground where no man could stand, to let it be known to Joe Caesar that there'd be no trouble tonight.

And with Ross whipping Whitaker, it looked as though the thirteen unarmed men were right. They were winning their fight. There'd be no gun fire. Gill knew that all the range needed was gun fire. Gun fire would be spark to dried straw.

Gill saw Caesar get down from his horse, and he knew the man meant to pack Whitaker back on his animal and ride off.

Gill felt the fury in his mouth; his temple was alive with twitching nerves. He had to stop Caesar. Caesar was deceiving him. Caesar was quitting. Gill had to throw the two forces at each other.

Only with war could Gill win. Only if the two ranches cut each other to shreds. Then he'd move in, owner of the Broken S, half-owner of the Crescent C, strongest man in a battered, bloodied valley of sapped men.

He squeezed the trigger of the Navy Colt, and even as the red blossom of flame merged with the night, even as the sound of the revolver cracked out over the dark range, Gill opened his mouth and screamed, "The fence is up, Caesar, the fence is up." Then he paused and fired his gun again and screamed again. "Hit the middle, Caesar. The fence is up. Hit them in the middle."

Gill waited then, a confident man who had a picture of glory in his head and didn't believe any man could rub it out. He waited for Caesar to wave on the rest of his men, while the remainder of the striking force—driving now, Gill could hear, from the Crescent C—would join in the concerted attack on the center slot. Gill waited for all this to happen, and for the Broken S to fight back, and for the thirteen men to go down, riddled by bullets, thirteen foolish intruders.

Ross heard Gill. He said between the two pistol shots, "Don't move, Caesar," and Caesar looked across the flickering yellow shafts of light and said wanly, "I'm not going anywhere, Ross."

Caesar knew it was Gill, too. He knew that Gill had come down to direct this war that had been without reason for Caesar, except when Gill pointed it out. Gill wanted the war; nobody else. All right, Caesar thought wearily, let him have it.

Behind him, Caesar heard the riders coming up, full force. Enough to turn the tide, even now. Nineteen men pounding towards the center slot, four others standing here. Caesar shook his head. It didn't matter. It was Gill's war.

He said, "Thewen, ride back and stop those men. Stucka, Hallahan, get Whit on his horse. We're going home."

Ross said to Tromper, "Stand still, man, I'm moving back."

Tromper said, "Where to?"

"The Broken S."

Tromper shoved a flare in Ross's hand. He said, "You'll need more than this, friend. You'll need luck."

Ross turned his horse. He had to hurry because Gill would see what was up, and the man would melt back into that hill from which he had come, and Ross would have lost him.

He rode two hundred yards into Broken S territory, to where he thought the other men had been waiting before. He said, "It's Ross," and a man whispered. "Let 'em come, Ross. Let 'em come. We're waiting."

Ross felt shock ride through him. The man was in a murderous mood. He said, "Nobody's coming."

The Broken S man said, "Send 'em through here. By God, we'll show 'em."

Then another man said, "That was Gill, wasn't it?"

Ross said, "Yes."

The first man said, "That's who I want. Send him through here."

Ross smiled thinly. "You won't see Gill. He's not the type."

The man swore. "I want Gill. Just let him come through."

Ross said, "Nobody gets Gill. He belongs to the law."

The man snorted, "You want him."

And the words came from Ross simply, naturally. He said, "Right now, I am the law."

"You want him for your old man's murder," the man said, "You're the same as the rest of us."

Ross shook his head stubbornly. He had to cool off these two men, because two men could still upset the balance. Two Broken S men could get on their horses, smoking guns in their hands, searching out Gill. And Joe Caesar might read it wrong; he might see it as a direct threat to his spread. Anybody would read it that way. The war, stilled for the moment, would break out its ghastly chattering.

Ross said, "While we're talking Gill is getting away. Nobody's catching him, this way."

"I know it," the man snarled. "Let me at him."

Ross grinned thinly. He wasn't stopping the man, yet somehow the man felt he was. That was good. He said, "No, I won't. Stay here. No, better still, ride back to Ives and tell him there's not going to be war tonight."

The man made muttering noises, but Ross heard him rise and move back. Then he heard a horse nicker softly, and the man said, "Adams, you wait here. Blast the buggers if they come through."

"Don't worry," Adams said. "I ain't moving. Nobody's coming past."

Ross turned and headed back to the center slot. He had the men under a mild control, but it wasn't good enough. Caesar could be trusted now, Ross felt, but it was the Broken S, hounded, frightened, that could cause the trouble. And Ross suddenly knew the answer. The Broken S was leaderless.

He went over to Tromper, standing in the center of his twelve men, while Caesar's horses melted into the night, toward the Crescent C. Ross said, "Can you boys hold the line?"

Tromper eyed him suspiciously. "Where you off to now?"

Ross said, "Back to Oxnard. I've got a job to do."

Tromper didn't say anything. He just nodded, trying to pierce the gloom and see Ross's face. The night still hung on a delicate scale. Gill was out there somewhere, untouched. Yet Ross was taking off for town.

Ross said, "I'm going to let the Stantons out of the pokey," and Tromper breathed easy. That was all right. The man was all right. He was making sure the scale stayed just that way. The Broken S needed the Stantons right now, even more than they would have needed them in a war. The Stantons could keep the night under tight check. Then, with morning, everybody could pitch in, just to hold the line another day, another night. Nobody was betting on peace. Just on no war, each day.

Ross turned the sorrel. Gill was out on the range, but he couldn't bother with Gill. He nudged the sorrel, tired from the trek up from Oxnard, back toward the town. They moved slowly.

CHAPTER FOURTEEN

The night rushed past Gill; his big bay was still fresh, unwinded. They swept the range, wide around the Crescent C, the long way round, but he knew he'd win his race.

They'd licked him out on the range, but it was back in Oxnard that his final hopes lay. That's where the Stantons were buried in a jail cell. Gill knew they couldn't be well guarded. Big Max was dead. Ross was shuffling back and forth at that damned center slot. The respectable citizens of Oxnard, most of them anyway, were out here on the range, playing out their strutting new roles.

Gill pounded the dry night earth, his horse flying. He had to rid himself of the Stantons. The Texas authorities would do it, eventually, but that might be too late. Now that Caesar had quit him cold, there would be no war. The Stantons and Joe Caesar might just see through the whole business, and know that Gill had been dragging them closer together all along, until their heads clashed. And when it got out that the Stantons had once sold him a third interest in the Broken S, and Joe Caesar had promised him a half share in the Crescent C, the whole range would make Gill its target. Gill had to see to it that the Stantons and Joe Caesar never got together to swap information. He couldn't get to Caesar; he was crawling back to his Crescent C, surrounded by his own men. But the Stantons were sitting ducks.

Gill didn't bother planning the rest of it too carefully. He knew it would follow. First the Stantons. Then, when he had his chance, Joe Caesar. With Big Max dead, nobody would have the guts to press charges they couldn't prove against a man who would be by then the biggest, most powerful man in the valley. Certainly not Ross. Maybe Ross could draw a gun pretty fast. He sure as hell didn't want to. Ross was a chicken-hearted man, with a soft spot inside. He was a frightened man, who wouldn't even wear a gun if he could help it. Gill smiled in the dark night. Ross was easy pickings.

Gill hit the low, sandy draw at the southeast end of the valley and drummed into Oxnard.

Gill slowed his horse and led him to the alley that ran behind the main drag. He had to be quiet, and he had to be careful. Oxnard was getting ready to sleep, what remained of it, but there'd be a few men up and around, a handful of men at the saloon, tended by Tromper's wife. It was the kind of night men stayed close to home; Gill knew the temper of Oxnard when trouble brewed. They drew their roofs over their heads and stayed put.

But he took no chances. He got off the horse and tied him in darkness behind the abandoned office of the mine assayer, a man who had left Oxnard when the false rumors of gold strike were proved just that. Gill nodded, satisfied. He could move directly to the jailhouse, inching along the alley slowly and in comparative silence. He strapped his rifle to his saddlebag, drew his Navy Colt from his holster, and started walking.

It was, he thought, so easy. Like the time in Texas, when he shot down Jake Ross. Then, he had worked on Ed Stanton that night, filling him with rotgut, getting the man so drunk he didn't know what he was doing, and telling him that Gill would take care of everything, that all Ed Stanton had to do was listen to Gill, that Gill would see to it everything was straightened out, with the sheriff, with everybody.

And Ed had believed him. That was the joker. Gill knew why he always succeeded; he had always worked with honest men. Honest men were such fools, such dupes. Honest men thought other people were honest, too. It made it so easy. Finally Ed had begun to jabber about apologizing, and Gill had prodded him to the sheriff's office, swapping guns first, Ed on foot, Gill on Ed's big white horse. And Gill had stood by the window, watching Ed stare helplessly at the Texas sheriff, Old Man Ross, wondering foolishly what he was doing in the man's office.

A thin line of sweat crawled down Gill's chest. In a way, this was so much easier. He had been lucky then. After he had shot Old Man Ross, Gill had expected an alarm to sound through the town. But nothing had happened.

This time nothing *could* happen. There was nobody to sound any alarm.

Gill kept walking, slowly, past dark frame houses, pillared and propped by lumber that had been twisted into folderol by the turning lathes that knew only how to make good, clean, straight timber into something round and foolish. The boy, Ben Ross, had been the biggest break of Gill's life. It had been a big gamble, then, and the kid could have ruined it. But the boy didn't scream, and Gore, Texas, just figured the gunshot was nothing, a prank maybe, a stumbling drunk falling down and discharging his pistol, anything at all that wouldn't mean anything serious, just so Gore, Texas, could sleep. Gill had got away.

Now the boy, Ben Ross, was back, but he still was Gill's big break. He wasn't a fighter, this Ross. Maybe with his fists, yes. But that didn't mean a damn. Only a fool fought that way. That kind of fighting was only a beginning. Gill jabbed the gun he held in his hand against his thigh. This, Gill thought solemnly, was the finish. It wrapped matters up. He nodded, in the darkness, and his feet crunched gravel as he came up to the side of the jailhouse.

Ben Ross, manhunter, put his spurs to his sorrel. He had risked too much time already. There was a rider in front of him, not too far off, but paying no attention. Ross knew it had to be Gill.

He saw Gill and his horse hit the edge of Oxnard, and Ross pushed the hammer-head until the gap was a few hundred yards. Then he stopped the animal and dropped the reins and got down. The rest he'd do on foot.

Ross moved swiftly, watching Gill's shadow before him, inching into the alley, and Ross knew what the man was up to.

He thought, once, *they repeat themselves, these people*. First, Gill had shot down Jake Ross this way. Now he was moving—sure as hellfire—straight to the jailhouse, to do the same to the Stantons. Ben Ross walked behind the man, walking toward the spot where everything came together, his search for his father's killer, the ending of the war on the range, his own discovery of his strength. Ross walked on, not caring whether Gill heard him, ready to face his man, and settle it all. He walked, tall and broad-shouldered, the burning torch in his numbed left hand, his heavy right hand drawn back a little, near his holster. The pain in Ross's shoulder and elbow had dulled down, and Ross disregarded the remnants. There'd be time enough for healing, later.

He moved swiftly, twenty yards behind Gill, and he watched Gill bend and strike a match against his spurs. He also saw Gill's gun, and when Ross saw the gun, he thought to himself: *NOW.*

It was not the way he wanted it to end, shooting the other man in the back, though Gill was going to do the same thing to the Stantons. But Ross had no choice. He had come up from Texas to do this job, and other men's lives depended on it. It had to be done, and if people thought he was a coward for doing it this way, Ross couldn't help it.

Ross couldn't help lots of things. He had a knowledge now that he never had before. It had to do with fears and doubts. They were part of his life, he knew, and he had been wrong trying to wipe them out. They were part of everybody's life, unless man was animal only. It was part of civilization. It was what had kept Ross from shooting down the Stantons earlier. Doubt. The honest-to-God doubt that was back of all justice, and without which law didn't exist, but only necktie posses.

Well, Ross thought, in the one flashing second that existed from the scratching of Gill's match until Gill had thrust it into the jail cell and raised his gun and started to poke it between the bars, well, doubt had its place but other things had theirs. Now was the time for Ben Ross to grow into the role he had tried to create for himself: manhunter, doer of justice, avenger of his father's death.

He reached, with sure grace and skill, with unconscious speed, for his gun.

And clawed air.

He had no gun. He had turned into a peacemaker, to save the range, and now he was going to lose it.

He thought one last thought before he acted. He thought of the boy Ben Ross hearing the shot that killed his father, standing rooted for a moment, finally entering the office and still not doing anything, just aimlessly wandering around, automatically reacting, but not really doing anything.

And eleven years slid by.

... Ross screamed.

He screamed the scream he should have screamed eleven years ago, but hadn't. He splintered the night with the scream, long and tortured and directed almost like a blow itself at the broad, faintly illuminated back of Gill, a man crouched a bit, leaning forward, arms thrust forward through the bars, but absolutely motionless, caught up in the sound of that scream—the scream that should have doomed him eleven years ago. For the scream had grasped Gill like nothing else before, like icy tentacles of white fear, holding him rigid, paralyzed.

But not for long.

With a scrabbling frenzy, an oath at his lips, Gill whirled, disentangled his arms, spun around to stare at Ross—for he knew it had to be Ross—and the two men were face to face at last.

Gill's arm started to come up, the arm with the Navy Colt clenched in his hand, and at the same time, Ross's right hand went diving toward his holster.

And Gill staggered back. He saw Ross's holster, he knew it was empty, he knew Ross had no gun, he knew Ross couldn't hurt him, he knew all these things, but it didn't matter.

Because Ross was faster.

Gill had started with the gun in his hand, and Ross had gone to his empty holster, swooped and aimed his empty fist before Gill had leveled his Navy Colt. It was as if Ross had shot him in the chest.

Gill hit the window bars with his back, and the feeling of the cold iron behind him helped. It helped Gill remember that an empty fist couldn't kill anybody, and that Ross was too far away to stop him.

Gill righted himself. He shook off that terrible scream and he tried to shake off that even more terrible knowledge—*Ross was faster*—and he aimed the Navy Colt through the bars, where the Stantons had been lying. No need for a match now because he had seen them and that was enough, and his finger clutched at the trigger.

And once more he was in a terrible grip.

Not the grip of fear—oh, that was there, he'd always feel that, Gill knew, so long as he lived—but the grip of real fingers, not icy, ghostlike ones. Real fingers, a man's two hands, grabbing him by the neck, pulling him slowly forward until his forehead hit the cool iron bars, until his shoulders pressed tight against the narrow frame of the window, and even then the fingers pulled and squeezed, and Gill saw in front of him the face of Ed Stanton.

They were three inches apart, on opposing sides of a jail window, and Gill knew it was he who was really inside, and Ed Stanton outside. One man was free, the other trapped. Gill felt the crushing pressure against his throat, the airy lightness puff to his brain. A message tried to filter through that lightness, tried to penetrate consciousness and save Gill's life. It was a simple message, directed from the reeling agonized suffocating brain to the right arm and down to the right hand, where five trembling fingers held a gun.

The message got through.

Gill started the long struggle back. He closed his fingers around the butt of the Navy Colt. He began to raise the hand. He concentrated on the hand, cocking it up on the hinge that was his wrist, and when he felt the bore of the pistol rest against human flesh—Ed Stanton's ribs—Gill turned his attention to the next part of the message. He forced himself to think about his right index finger, and slowly the finger curled around the trigger. Then he thought the final message, even as a yellow light entered behind his eyeballs, and the feeling around his throat started to fade far, far off. The final message told Gill to press that index finger as hard as he was able.

A shot rang out in the night.

Gill's gun fell from nerveless fingers, clattering to the wooden floor of the cell. Ed Stanton gave the man a final shake, a mastiff shaking a rat, and Gill's head lolled on his lifeless neck. Orville Stanton, next to Ed, picked up Gill's gun and turned it over slowly. Then he looked at Ed Stanton, wondering how he had misjudged his own brother all these years.

... Outside the girl Maria crept close to Ross, who involuntarily put his right arm around her and drew her near. She held out the gun to Ross— Big Max's gun—smoke still pouring from the .44, the smell of powder acrid in the night, and Ross took the gun.

Gill dropped to the ground, dead, the bullet from Big Max's gun deep in his spine.

Ross and Maria walked forward. Men rushed through the main drag of Oxnard, into the alley. Somebody snatched the torch from Ross's left hand and held it over Gill.

A man put his foot under Gill's body and turned him over on his back.

"God," somebody said, "look at him."

Gill's face was black and swollen. His mouth was twisted nearly vertical, so hard had the man struggled for air. His eyes, stiffly open, stared out with unseeing horror. The whole face was disfigured, agonized.

"He sure ain't so pretty anymore," somebody said quietly.

But Maria remembered the other face, the gentle smiling face, the face of a man who loved her, the same face that had ridden by after Gill had killed Big Max. This, down here on the ground, was far, far the better face.

CHAPTER FIFTEEN

Ross rode the sorrel southward, the Colorado wind a sigh behind him. His hand crept to his pocket where the curl-edged warrant still remained, saying that Ben Ross was deputized at such-and-such a place and such-and-such a time to bring to justice his father's killer, or else to kill him.

The manhunter shook his head slowly. He had failed. Big Max had seen it all through, and it had taken an accused innocent man and a poor frightened girl—together—to bring Gill down. All Ross had done was to scream and draw his phantom gun.

The night had not ended with Gill's death. There were so many things to do, to explain about Gill and Jake Ross—as Maria had told Ross, and as Gill had told Big Max, and Big Max had unwittingly told Maria. Ross had released the Stantons, and then at midnight the three men had ridden out to the Crescent C, to see Joe Caesar.

And there in the Crescent C ranch house, the Stantons and Joe Caesar—not liking each other, maybe still hating each other, but knowing no good would ever come from war, from war they never wanted and that was being waged by and for Gill alone—the three ranchers had decided to settle their differences.

Ross grinned now, in the high noon warmth as the hammerhead sorrel moved slowly through the Raton pass into New Mexico. It had been so easy, squaring the trouble. Ross had watched and listened while a Crescent C rider fetched a doctor, and the doctor worked on Ross's shoulder and elbow, and the ranchers talked over their squabble. It never needed gunfire. Joe Caesar had turned the winter quarters open to the Broken S; the Broken S the next morning would begin to rip away the Osage orange. The center graze was available to both ranches. So was the winter grass. A war ended before it was fought; both spreads would profit. So would the whole valley, dependent on the cattle in the meadowland.

That night, before Ross rode from the Crescent C, Joe Caesar said, "Here, Ross," and handed him the Colt Walker.

Ross took it and sheathed it, wondering what he was going to do with it.

The next day, when the Broken S began tearing out the mulberry, Ross went out the Wolf Creek trail with Maria and a group of men from Oxnard—Tromper, McQuinn, Abelson, Smits the stableman—Whitaker from the Crescent C, Ives from the Broken S, a few others, to bring back the body of Big Max, and to lead the patient dun mare back to Smits' stable.

Big Max was buried that afternoon, at the exact center of the middle ground between the Broken S and the Crescent C, and when the first dirt fell over the sheriff's casket, Ross knew what to do with the Colt Walker. He walked over to the open grave and tossed the gun inside. The dirt fell over it, burying it. It lay, forever now, with a man who didn't believe in the firing of guns.

No longer was the center slot no-man's land. Now it belonged to Big Max.

The man had died in his quest for law and order. In a way, Ross knew it didn't matter. Men like that don't matter, almost, as human beings, but only as symbols. Big Max still lived, as a symbol. If anything, he was more alive than ever. He straddled that hoof-churned center slot, a ghost of a man more powerful than all the guns in the valley. His quest had been successful.

Only Ross had failed. He had come out to do a job, but it had been done for him.

Yet he could not feel bad about it. He had wanted to ride down his father's killer and shoot the man dead. He had accomplished something else instead.

He didn't know what it was, exactly, but it was there. Tromper had said it for him. He had said, "Ross, you'll come back here after you've reported all this?"

Ross looked at the man, in surprise at first, and then with a warming glow. He said, "Why, yes, I guess I will."

"It's not over yet," Tromper said. "This place still needs lawmen."

Ross frowned. He had never thought of himself as a lawman. Yet that was what he had become.

A few days later, his left arm in a sling, he rode through town, and out. Just before he swung south, a Concord stage rumbled by, and when Ross looked through the cloud of dust, he saw the redheaded girl, Laura, inside, headed back for North Platte. He had just had a brief second to view her face, behind dust and dimmed by the dull light within the coach. It was a face gentled by pain, the hard thin mouth softened. Ross raised his hand to wave to the girl, and then she was gone.

Now he pressed through the lonely green hollows of New Mexico, his horse's hooves striking echoes from the great canyon walls. He was suddenly a lonely man. Yes, he would be back. He felt it very likely that Maria would need him. She might even want him.

Behind him, the Colorado winds whispered. The sun was blotted out.

Rain rode through the air, carried from the north. Ross began to sing softly:

> *Weep, all ye little rains,*
> *Wail, winds, wail,*
> *All along along along*
> *The Colorad-y trail.*

THE END

Arnold Hano Bibliography
(1922 –)

Novels

Fiction
The Big Out (1951)
The Executive (1964)
Marriage Italian Style (movie tie-in; 1965)
Bandolero (movie tie-in; 1967)
Running Wild (movie tie-in; 1973)

Sports
A Day in the Bleachers (1955; reprinted in new editions in 1982, 2004 with new forward by Ray Robinson & new afterword by the author, and 2006)
Sandy Koufax: Strikeout King (1964)
Willie Mays: The Say-Hey Kid (1966)
The Greatest Giants of Them All (1967)
Roberto Clemente: Batting King (1968)
Willie Mays: Mr. Baseball Himself (1970)
Kareem! Basketball Great (1975)
Muhammad Ali, the Champion (1977)

As Gil Dodge
Flint (1957)

As Matthew Gant
Valley of Angry Men (1953)
The Manhunter (1957)
The Last Notch (1958)
The Raven and the Sword (1960)
Queen Street (1963)

As Ad Gordon
The Flesh Painter (1955)
Slade (1956)

As Mike Heller
So I'm a Heel (1957)

As Ghostwriter
Why Me? An Autobiography by William Gargan (1969)

Short Stories

As Arnold Hano
The Crusher (*Esquire*, Nov 1950)
Little Punk (*Mystery Tales*, June 1959)
Nobody Pushes Me Around (*Argosy*, Apr 1956)
O'Rourke (*Argosy*, Dec 1954)
The Umpire Was a Rookie (*The Saturday Evening Post*, Apr 28 1956)

As Matthew Gant
The Crate at Outpost 1 (*Ellery Queen's Mystery Magazine*, May 1954)
The Hungry Look (*Ellery Queen's Mystery Magazine*, Jan 1958)
The Testament of Dummy Slott (*Mystery Tales*, Apr 1959)
The Uses of Intelligence (1952; *Sleuth Mystery Magazine*, Oct 1958)
Wetback (*Mystery Tales*, Oct 1959)

As Ad Gordon
Justice Is Blind (*Justice*, May 1955)
Two Little Bullets (*Justice*, July 1955)

Editor

Western Roundup (1948)
Western Triggers (1948)

Made in the USA
Middletown, DE
14 June 2021